A GILDED LADY

Books by Elizabeth Camden

HOPE AND GLORY SERIES

The Spice King
A Gilded Lady

The Lady of Bolton Hill
The Rose of Winslow Street
Against the Tide
Into the Whirlwind
With Every Breath
Beyond All Dreams
Toward the Sunrise: An Until the Dawn *Novella*
Until the Dawn
Summer of Dreams: A From This Moment *Novella*
From This Moment
To the Farthest Shores
A Dangerous Legacy
A Daring Venture
A Desperate Hope

HOPE *AND* GLORY

BOOK TWO

ELIZABETH CAMDEN

BETHANYHOUSE

a division of Baker Publishing Group
Minneapolis, Minnesota

Published by Bethany House Publishers
11400 Hampshire Avenue South
Bloomington, Minnesota 55438
www.bethanyhouse.com

Bethany House Publishers is a division of
Baker Publishing Group, Grand Rapids, Michigan

Printed in the United States of America

Library of Congress Cataloging-in-Publication Data
Names: Camden, Elizabeth, 1965– author.
Title: A gilded lady / Elizabeth Camden.
Description: Bloomington, Minnesota : Bethany House Publishers, [2020] | Series:
    Hope and glory; 2
Identifiers: LCCN 2019054300 | ISBN 9780764232121 (trade paperback) |
    ISBN 9780764236297 (cloth) | ISBN 9781493425105 (ebook)
Subjects: GSAFD: Romantic suspense fiction.
Classification: LCC PS3553.A429 G55 2020 | DDC 813/.54—dc23
LC record available at https://lccn.loc.gov/2019054300

Scripture quotations are from the King James Version of the Bible.

This is a work of historical reconstruction; the appearances of certain historical figures are therefore inevitable. All other characters, however, are products of the author's imagination, and any resemblance to actual persons, living or dead, is coincidental.

Cover design by Jennifer Parker
Cover photography by Mike Habermann Photography, LLC

Author is represented by the Steve Laube Agency.

20 21 22 23 24 25 26   7 6 5 4 3 2 1

This novel is dedicated to my mother,
Jane, the inspiration for Caroline.
Like Caroline, my mom is smart, classy,
and a lot tougher than she looks.
That's always been a lot for me to live up to,
but I am forever grateful.
Thanks for everything, Mom!

One

JULY 30, 1900

There was no such thing as a typical day at the White House, but Caroline Delacroix's morning took a particularly difficult turn the moment she walked into her crowded office.

"The king of Italy was assassinated last night," George said from his desk. George Cortelyou was President McKinley's personal secretary, while Caroline served in the same capacity for the first lady.

"What happened?" she asked in stunned disbelief.

George relayed the appalling details in his typically efficient manner. After awarding medals at a sporting event near the Italian city of Milan, King Umberto had boarded an open carriage. An anarchist rushed the carriage and fired four shots directly at the king, who died on the spot.

"He was the target of assassins for years, but they finally got him," George said, his expression grim. With his graying hair, trim mustache, and flawless suit, George projected implacable confidence, but it was obvious the morning's news had rattled him.

"I'll arrange for the first lady to make a condolence call to the Italian embassy this morning," Caroline said.

George sent her a grateful nod, for few people liked dealing with Mrs. McKinley. Ida McKinley was short-tempered, judgmental, and blunt to the point of rudeness. It was Caroline's job to soften the first lady's reputation. It hadn't been easy, but Caroline was good at it. Her day began before breakfast and ended only after Mrs. McKinley turned in for the night. She worked seven days a week alongside George to coordinate schedules and manage the official business of the White House. The work was exhausting, but it was also an honor and a privilege.

Today her main task would be to orchestrate the condolence call to the Italian ambassador's wife, the Baroness Vittozzi. Caroline would help Mrs. McKinley navigate the minutiae of diplomatic protocol with grace, for any misstep would reflect badly on both the president and the United States. Unfortunately, Mrs. McKinley was prone to veering off on ill-advised tangents, so Caroline needed to be on guard.

Two hours later, she boarded a carriage with Mrs. McKinley and set off for the Italian embassy.

"The baroness is addressed as Lady Vittozzi," Caroline advised Mrs. McKinley. "She doesn't speak English, so I will translate for you. Given the number of people calling on her today, our visit should last no longer than ten minutes."

"Excellent," the first lady said with a brief nod of her regal head. Mrs. McKinley's steel-gray hair was woven like a coronet around her head. She'd once been a beautiful woman, but illness had marred her face into a permanently sour look.

Carriages lined the street for blocks near the ornate Italian embassy, where every window was already covered in black mourning crepe. A dozen visitors filled the lavish drawing room, all waiting their turn to offer their condolences to the baroness in her private receiving room. Caroline guided Mrs. McKinley to a padded sofa to await their turn. It wouldn't be long, for protocol would move the first lady to the front of the line.

The gilt-encrusted door at the far end of the drawing room opened, and the archbishop of Washington left the baroness's parlor, his audience concluded. He walked slowly, his black and scarlet robes swaying majestically as he moved through the crowd of mourners. The usher nodded to Caroline, and she leaned over to help Mrs. McKinley rise. Ida McKinley was only fifty-three, but her prematurely gray hair and the cane she used to compensate for a nerve-damaged leg made her seem older.

The baroness was dressed in full mourning, her black silk gown spread artfully across a bench and her face covered with a transparent black veil. She nodded in greeting.

"*Avete le nostre più sentite condoglianze,*" Caroline said with a deep curtsy as she entered.

The baroness murmured a response, and Caroline provided the translation for Mrs. McKinley.

"Lady Vittozzi appreciates your sympathy. All the people of the city have been so kind since the terrible news arrived last night."

Mrs. McKinley nodded and took a seat. "Tell her that if there is anything our nation can do to assist during Italy's time of need, she need only ask."

Caroline translated as the first lady continued to offer perfectly appropriate generalities about the mysteries of God's ways and praise for the fallen King Umberto. All was proceeding smoothly, something that could never be taken for granted with Mrs. McKinley.

Then the first lady began recounting the one time she had visited Italy during a grand tour of Europe several years earlier. "We enjoyed Rome, especially the ancient ruins and the opera house. Sicily, on the other hand, was terrible. No electricity, leaky roofs, and the only plumbing dated all the way back to the Renaissance. It was mind-boggling."

Caroline froze, praying the baroness truly didn't understand English, for the ambassador's family came from Sicily. Behind her veil, the baroness swiveled to look at Caroline, her face perfectly blank as she awaited the translation. Caroline couldn't tell an outright lie, but neither could she translate what Mrs. McKinley had just said. Both women looked at her with expectation, and Caroline chose her words carefully.

"Mrs. McKinley admired the architecture of Italy," she said in Italian. "How clever the Italians are to have had modern conveniences like plumbing all the way back to the Renaissance. It was truly astounding."

The baroness smiled and nodded, and the remaining few minutes proceeded without incident. Beneath her skirts, Caroline gently tapped Mrs. McKinley's foot, signaling it was time to rise and end the call.

"That went quite well, didn't it?" Mrs. McKinley pronounced once they were aboard the carriage and heading back to the White House. She didn't wait for a reply before continuing her monologue. "Terrible tragedy about the king. Simply terrible. Nothing like that would ever happen to the Major, of course."

Mrs. McKinley always referred to her husband as the Major, for they had met shortly after the Civil War, when Major William McKinley was still in uniform. Over the years he'd served as a congressman, a governor, and now the president, but his wife still called him the Major. Caroline thought it rather charming.

"The Major is too popular to ever arouse that sort of ire," Mrs. McKinley continued. "Everyone likes him."

"While it's true that everyone likes him, that doesn't mean they will vote for him," Caroline said. She was veering into dangerous waters, but it had to be done. The presidential election was in four months, and despite William McKinley's popularity, nothing could be taken for granted. He had been too busy with the duties of his office to campaign, and his wife never offered to help. She was the least popular first lady in history, and Caroline had been hired to help correct that image.

Working for Mrs. McKinley was like walking a tightrope. At any moment it could snap, but so far, Caroline had been able to support the infamously difficult first lady without allowing Ida to trample her. When in public, Caroline was the epitome of deferential respect, but in private their relationship shifted. They bickered, gossiped, laughed, and fought. The first lady even insisted Caroline call her Ida in private.

"I want to wear your sapphire earrings tonight," Ida said.

"Why?" Caroline challenged. She and Ida regularly borrowed each other's accessories, for they were both shamelessly vain when it came to fashion. Still, if Ida wanted a favor, she ought to ask nicely.

"Because the last time I wore them, the Major said they lit up my eyes."

"Then buy your own sapphire earrings."

Ida let out a bark of laughter. "You have no respect for your elders."

"Why should I?" Caroline tossed out. "I'm the one with the sapphire earrings you want so badly."

If she gave Ida an inch, the woman would take fifty miles. Still, Caroline had a grudging respect for the first lady because she saw a side of her few people did. Ida's health was brutalized by epileptic seizures, a crippled leg, migraine headaches, and periodic spells of melancholy that robbed her of the ability to rise from bed. Mrs. McKinley was in danger of becoming a recluse due to her infirmities and often stayed locked in her bedroom, where she obsessively knitted baby booties.

Both the president and Mrs. McKinley's doctor recommended more interaction with the world, so Caroline had begun arranging regular tea parties with charitable groups and the wives of government officials. If loaning Ida a pair of sparkly earrings made her feel better, Caroline would happily do so.

Especially after the kindness both McKinleys had shown her. Last month Caroline's brother had been arrested for treason in

Cuba. Caroline had immediately offered her resignation, but the president refused to take it. Luke hadn't been found guilty yet, and the military was keeping the scandal quiet until his fate could be decided.

Luke had always been a reckless daredevil who tempted fate and got into one scrape after another. But a traitor? Caroline couldn't believe it of him. Somehow Luke had stepped into a dangerous mystery down in Cuba, and she would do her best to unravel it.

But if that failed, she needed to nurture her connections in the White House in the hope of someday winning a presidential pardon for Luke. Treason was a hanging offense, and if Luke was found guilty, her connection to the McKinleys might be her only chance to save her brother's life.

Two

Nathaniel Trask was a lucky man. Returning to Washington, DC, fresh off a major triumph and the assurance of a promotion, he vaulted up the steps of the Treasury Department. Exhilaration from his victory in Boston still pulsed in his veins, for he loved nothing better than solving complicated criminal schemes.

It was seven o'clock on a Thursday evening, but it went without saying that his boss would still be in his office, for Nathaniel and Wilkie were like-minded people. They shared a friendship that dated back to their Chicago days, when John Wilkie was a crusading journalist and Nathaniel a hard-boiled detective on the city's south side. When John Wilkie became the unconventional choice to lead the US Secret Service, he brought Nathaniel along with him, and ever since they had worked side by side to restore the agency's tattered reputation into one of faultless professionalism.

Nathaniel's footsteps echoed in the empty corridors as he made his way toward the wing housing the Secret Service administrative offices, where Wilkie welcomed him with a broad grin. At forty, Wilkie was only two years older than Nathaniel and the youngest chief in the history of the Secret Service. He dressed in completely ordinary clothes and had nondescript hair. Only a reckless flash in his brown eyes hinted at his adventurous streak.

"There's the man of the hour," Wilkie said, giving Nathaniel a hearty handshake.

Nathaniel returned both the handshake and the grin, the tension from the five-month Boston assignment beginning to ease. Now that he was home, it was time to file the paperwork documenting how a gang of forgers had pulled off a million-dollar fraud by making counterfeit postage stamps. It had been a clever scheme. Fake paper money was under constant scrutiny, but who ever thought to look for fake postage stamps? The gang had made a healthy living off those counterfeit stamps for years before Nathaniel managed to track them down in Boston.

"News of the arrests has already made the local papers. Have a look at that," Wilkie said as he tossed Nathaniel a newspaper folded open to the feature article.

Government Agent Foils Band of Scoundrels and Their Postal Depredations

"'Postal depredations'?" Nathaniel asked. "Who writes this dreck?"

The slow smile that spread across his boss's face was all the answer Nathaniel needed, for Wilkie had made a name for himself in the Wild West of yellow journalism in Chicago and knew how to spin the press. "I suggested a few colorful phrases to the reporter. I'm glad he took them. You're a hero."

"So long as they didn't mention my name," Nathaniel cautioned. The Secret Service was the wrong line of work for anyone craving fame or riches. While he loved the challenge of hunting down criminals and hauling them into a court of law, he'd never cared for attention.

"No names," Wilkie assured him. "Still, it was brilliant

work, and you've saved the government a mint. Literally. We should go out for a drink."

"We should, except I don't drink, and you never go out carousing this early in the evening."

Wilkie snapped his fingers in mock dismay. "That's right. Foiled again."

Nathaniel and Wilkie were complete opposites, but it never hampered their friendship. Nathaniel was obsessively tidy, sober, and a rule-follower, while John Wilkie was freewheeling and hard-drinking, but they respected each other.

"Now," Wilkie said as he returned to his desk, "about that promotion I mentioned."

"Yes, about that." It was hard to guess what Wilkie had in mind, for Nathaniel already occupied the top position in the counterfeit division.

"I know you hate the prospect of a management position," Wilkie said.

Nathaniel stiffened. "Yes."

"Which is why I have something completely different in mind. You'll like it. A new challenge. You'll meet interesting people and have loads of responsibility."

Then why was Wilkie suddenly so eager to sell the position to him? Nathaniel had never balked at an assignment before. He'd sweltered in copper mines in New Mexico, ridden payroll trains through the desolate flatlands of the West, and once he'd lived for six months above a fish cannery to spy on international exports.

"What's the job?" he asked softly.

"It's the most important one in the agency. Pays well. Good housing."

"What's the job?"

"Guarding the president."

Nathaniel bolted out of his chair. "Absolutely not. I'll never work as a bodyguard. You know that."

Wilkie held his hands out in a placating manner. "Calm down. President McKinley doesn't want a bodyguard either. He thinks it smacks of European royalty and wants nothing to do with it."

"Then why are we having this discussion?"

"Because I need a detective in the White House. One who never misses details, even if he's been on duty around the clock. You don't need to be plastered to the president's side. He doesn't want that any more than you do. But I need someone to monitor who has access to him. King Umberto of Italy was assassinated last night, and the man who shot him was a known anarchist. A system should have been in place to keep an eye on troublemakers like him. I need you to design such a plan for the White House."

"Get someone else to do it."

Wilkie shook his head. "You're the best we have, and the problems are getting worse. In the past ten years, more heads of state have been assassinated than at any other time in history."

Nathaniel stalked to the window, clenching his fists as he stared at the White House directly across the street. He didn't want to be a bodyguard. He *couldn't* be a bodyguard. The last time he'd been entrusted to protect someone, she ended up dead, and it still haunted him. The nightmares had finally eased, but the thought of being responsible for another life made his stomach clench.

"I track down counterfeit. I am trained as an engraver and got a degree in art history, all so that I could spot forgeries. I'm not going to be a bodyguard. Why don't you assign Sullivan to the job?"

"Sullivan doesn't have your eye, and you're not going to be a bodyguard."

As Wilkie outlined what the position would entail, Nathaniel had to admit that it didn't sound like a bodyguard so much as a detective on the lookout for security flaws inside the White House, just as Wilkie claimed.

"I wouldn't ask if I didn't know you were the best man for the job," Wilkie said. "McKinley will be an easy man to work for. Everyone likes him. Spend the next four months observing activities in the White House and designing an improved security plan. After the election in November, I'll find you an assignment more to your liking."

"Only four months?"

"Four months," Wilkie confirmed. "Design a new security plan, then you're free."

Nathaniel paced, thinking. Four months wouldn't be too horrible, and it was true that presidential security was appalling. It was also true that he was the best man for the job, and it was impossible for him to turn his back on duty.

He would do it. The job meant living in a shared dormitory on the top floor of the White House. It meant almost constant vigilance during his waking hours, seven days a week, until the November elections. It would be a challenge, but perhaps it could also be a way to prove himself worthy and absolve himself of the failures in his past.

⁓𝒢⁓

That night the old dream came back. Nathaniel picked up Molly's body, sopping wet and broken by the rushing current, her eyes staring blankly at nothing.

"Please, Molly," he sobbed, but she was already gone and her flesh was cold. He carried her home, riding the streetcar through downtown Chicago with a dead child draped across his lap. People stared, but he didn't care. His soul was vacant.

Nathaniel snapped awake, the sheets soaked in sweat. It had been years since this nightmare tormented him, but it had come roaring back as vivid as ever. To this day he remembered the feel of Molly's sodden gown dampening his shirt.

He shouldn't have agreed to the White House assignment.

With all his heart, he wished he could turn away from it, but he'd given his word.

He began the next morning on his knees at the chapel near his boardinghouse. It had been twenty years since Molly died, but her ghost haunted him still. The mistake he'd made at eighteen was a scar that would never fully heal, but he couldn't let it cripple him for the rest of his life. It was time to let it go. He leaned his forehead against the pew in front of him.

"Oh, Molly, I'm so sorry," he whispered. "I should have protected you better. I will honor your memory by carrying out this assignment with complete diligence, with no stone left unturned."

For the thousandth time, he wondered why God had taken an innocent child. To punish him for putting his love of art above his duty to family? After two decades of wondering, he still had no satisfactory answer.

Jesus, I know there is a reason for this, but I don't understand it. Can it be so that I won't let my guard falter this time? Every day I will do my best to serve my country and honor Molly's memory. I am praying for guidance. If you send me a sign, I will follow.

He listened, hoping for a sign that would let him escape the assignment, but he heard nothing.

And that was his sign. He had his marching orders, and it was time to go to work.

Three

Privacy was nonexistent for staff who lived at the White House. Caroline had never shared a bedroom before accepting this position, but now she slept in a dormitory alongside nine other women. Two cooks, two telephone operators, three maids, a seamstress, and a laundress all slept in this long, narrow room on the top floor of the building, with beds lined up like sardines in a tin.

It was two o'clock in the afternoon, so most of the women were downstairs, but Caroline had a rare moment of privacy with Ludmila Vuković, a young woman from Croatia who worked in the laundry. Ludmila was smart, ambitious, and only twenty-six. She wanted more from life than washing and ironing other people's sheets, and Caroline wanted to help.

"The school is going to open in two months," Caroline said, sitting on the end of her bed as Ludmila returned freshly laundered undergarments. There wasn't even enough room for proper wardrobes or closets in the dormitory, only a long bank of open shelves for each woman to store basic belongings. Ludmila said nothing as she went about putting the clothes away, so Caroline kept talking. "We expect the school to fill up right away, but I can save a spot for you. There will be classes in typing and bookkeeping and translation work. You can have your choice."

"I don't have the time," Ludmila said, reaching for another stack of laundry.

"The classes will be at night, and there's no reason you can't take a streetcar to the school three nights a week. It will be a challenge, but over time those three nights a week will change your entire world."

How different Caroline's own education had been. Fancy boarding schools in Boston, and then a year in Paris and a year in Rome for finishing school. She came back to Virginia when she was eighteen, but that hadn't worked out so well. She and Luke had gotten into such trouble together, which prompted her father to send her to Switzerland, far enough away that her rebellious behavior couldn't permanently tarnish her reputation in America. She resented the banishment at the time, but her father had been right. The two years in Switzerland tamed most of her wild streak, allowing her to step back into respectability in Virginia.

Ludmila finished shelving the laundry, and Caroline joined her alongside the clothing shelves.

"An education will buy you freedom," she said, covering Ludmila's chapped, work-roughened hand with her own. She looked away, embarrassed at the difference in their skin. Ludmila was two years younger than Caroline, and yet the laundress's hands looked like an old woman's.

"You can become anything you want," Caroline continued. "A typist. A translator. I know the two extra hours each night will be hard, but it will be worth it."

"Man on the floor!"

The loud voice echoing down the hallway was a rude interruption. Caroline sighed as a brisk knock on the door was followed by a senior White House usher tipping his head inside.

"Meeting downstairs in the assembly room." A scowl of

disapproval darkened the usher's face. "There's a new man in charge of security, and all staff are required to be there."

Even Ludmila noticed the resentment in his tone. "What's wrong with him?"

"He's new," the usher said, then closed the door behind him.

That said it all. Most of the staff at the White House had been there for decades, and outsiders were looked at with suspicion. The only reason Caroline had been welcomed was because she was an effective buffer between the staff and the difficult first lady.

"We'd better go," Ludmila said as she reached for the hamper, but Caroline laid a hand on her arm.

"Please think about the school," she said. "It will never be easier than now. You don't yet have a husband or children demanding your time. I know it will be hard, but it's the hard things in life that make us most proud. Use those classes to fight for your future. You won't ever regret it."

"I'm already so tired," Ludmila said as she balanced the hamper on her hip. "School will only make it worse."

But Caroline caught the flash of hope on the laundress's face. No matter what it took, Caroline would help clear the path for Ludmila to nurture that spark of hope into a flame.

⁓

By the time Caroline arrived in the assembly room, the other forty-five people who worked in the residence had already gathered. They were cooks, ushers, cleaning crew, telephone and wireless operators, and mailroom clerks. Even the gardeners had come in for the meeting. Rows of chairs filled the room, all facing the podium and blackboard at the front.

Caroline scanned the crowd, looking for George, who sat near the back. "What's this I hear about new security rules?" she asked as she took the empty seat beside him.

"Long overdue, if you ask me." George's modest title as the

president's secretary drastically understated his importance in the administration. From the moment she met George, he had seemed like Atlas as he carried the immense burden of the White House on his shoulders. He masterfully navigated the tricky Washington maze of politics and backroom dealing. It was George who had recommended Caroline for this position and helped her survive a baptism of fire working with Mrs. McKinley.

Caroline glanced at the dozen White House ushers lining the back wall. The term *usher* was deceptive. The men wore suits and ties, but they were actually building security. They carried side arms beneath their suits and walked the halls at all hours of the day and night to protect the White House.

"You think we need more security?" she asked, for she'd never been able to move around the building without seeing plenty of ushers on their rounds.

"I think the *president* needs more security," George clarified. "He can't stand having people hovering nearby and always travels alone when outside the residence. That needs to stop."

A new man entered the room. Tall, slim, and dark-haired, he seemed *chiseled* to Caroline's eye. He wore an ordinary suit, but there was nothing ordinary about the way his eyes studied the audience. He paced across the front of the room, constantly on the move as he absorbed every detail about the people in the chairs before him. His hands were in his pockets, his face revealing nothing, but each time someone moved, whether it was to change seats or simply to whisper to their neighbor, his gaze flicked in their direction. He was calm and measured, as though nothing could unsettle him, and Caroline liked that in a man. She lifted her chin to send him a warm smile of welcome, but he ignored it as he walked to the podium. Behind him gathered six brawny ushers.

"Good afternoon," he said in a measured voice. "My name is Nathaniel Trask, and I will henceforth oversee all aspects of security in the White House."

What kind of man used a word like *henceforth*? She hid a smile, rather liking his buttoned-down formality.

"Tourist hours for visiting the White House will be drastically curtailed, and sightseers will no longer be permitted to see the president."

"Good luck with that," George whispered in her ear. President McKinley was famous for his willingness to glad-hand with tourists and his unannounced jaunts downstairs to mingle with sightseers. He also liked to take the carriage out for impulsive moonlit rides with his wife. He would never tolerate such restrictions on his freedom, but the new man continued speaking.

"If any of you have business with outside vendors, I will need to see a list of their names forty-eight hours in advance. They will not be granted access to the White House without my authorization. I will screen all visitors who have business with the president or first lady." He looked directly at Caroline and George as he spoke, as they had complete control over access to the first couple.

George stood. "Mr. Trask, may I simply submit a list of every member of Congress, the Senate, the Cabinet, and officers in the US military? The president meets with dozens of them every day, and I would not want to overwhelm your office."

"I already have that list, Mr. Cortelyou. I also have the list of all the department officers, every ambassador and foreign legation, and members of the judiciary. Anyone else will need to be cleared with me."

One of the cooks raised his hand. "I've been teaching my nephew how to bake. Does he need to be cleared?"

"He does. Personal visits to the residence will be curtailed, and no visitor may bring parcels into the building. Visitors meeting the president will be required to keep their hands out of their pockets and will have their belongings inspected before proceeding inside."

Caroline's mind whirled. This man was unreal. He wouldn't last ten minutes with Ida McKinley before she kicked him out of the building. As he continued outlining the exhaustive new security procedures, she shifted in her seat. She'd give anything for a cigarette right now. She'd been trying to quit, but this job was stressful, and on days like this she longed for the momentary rush of calm that only a cigarette could deliver. She'd managed six days in a row without a single slip and fiddled with her beaded bracelet to soothe the fidgets.

When the meeting finally came to an end, she headed into the hallway alongside George.

"Do you think this new man has a prayer of success here?" she asked, for these rules seemed ridiculous. Instead of agreeing, George surprised her.

"I hope so," he said. "Better security is long overdue, but the president's popularity is based on his reputation as a man of the people. Walking behind a phalanx of bodyguards or inspecting people's pockets will go against his grain, but it's time. If Mrs. McKinley complains, you need to rein her in. I know she believes the entire world adores her husband and wishes only to strew rose petals in his path, but it's not true. Do your best to support the new rules."

She already had her hands full supporting Ida. Still, George's instincts were good, and she would trust him, even if the thought of catering to these new security measures gave her a headache.

"I'll meet you back in our office in twenty minutes to go over next week's schedule," she said, because as hard as she'd been trying, she really needed a cigarette right now.

＊

Nathaniel gathered his notes following his presentation, but he glanced at the two secretaries as they left the room. The manner in which Mr. Cortelyou and Miss Delacroix embraced the new policies would set the example the rest of the staff would follow. As the people with the closest access to the president and first lady, he needed to recruit them to his side.

He stuffed his notes into his bag and hustled after them. By the time he got out into the staff hallway, Miss Delacroix was already gone, but the clicking of her heels could still be heard echoing up the eastside stairwell. There wasn't much up there, but he filed it away for future reference as he chased down the president's secretary.

"I hope I can count on your cooperation, Mr. Cortelyou."

"Call me George," the president's secretary said, offering a handshake. "Whatever you need, don't hesitate to ask. We're glad to have you aboard."

The strength of the handshake, the steady gaze, the slight lean forward—all of it added up to a man who was telling the truth.

"I've been charged with creating a comprehensive plan for White House security," Nathaniel said. "I'd like to meet with you to discuss the president's typical schedule and the nature of his activities outside the White House."

"Let's set up an appointment," George replied agreeably.

Nathaniel followed him back to a cramped office, set up an appointment for later in the day, then wasted no time heading up the east wing stairwell in search of Miss Delacroix. The stairs led to an unused corridor and the roof, so it was hard to imagine why she'd gone up there. His nose prickled at the dust in the corridor, which seemed to have become a dumping ground for leftover construction materials and coils of electrical wire. The White House had been under almost constant renovation as electrical wiring and telephone lines were haphazardly installed over the years.

He was still staring at the abandoned materials when the door from the roof opened and Miss Delacroix stepped inside, spritzing herself with cologne. She startled at seeing him, clutching her reticule as a blush stained her cheeks. By heaven, she was even more dazzling up close, with golden blond hair and the bluest eyes he'd ever seen. He'd never been the sort to fall for a pretty face, but it was hard not to stare. She looked like she'd just stepped out of a Gainsborough portrait . . . except for the guilty flush.

She wiggled the bottle of cologne back into her bag. "What are you doing up here?"

She'd just smoked a cigarette. He was certain of it by the flustered way she clutched her reticule and the tiny peppermint candy he could smell on her breath. Surprising for a woman of her class to indulge in such a vice, but he wouldn't embarrass her by calling attention to it.

"I was looking for you. When would be the best time for us to discuss security for the first lady?"

"Mrs. McKinley rarely leaves the White House, and we are safe as sardines here. Why must she submit to all these intrusive rules?"

"Because she hosts hundreds of visitors per month. I need you to begin turning in a list of her social engagements and who is attending them. I need at least two days' notice, preferably more."

A silk-encased foot began tapping on the concrete floor. Miss Delacroix appeared to resent the rules.

"Mrs. McKinley's only visitor today is her niece, who is visiting from Ohio. Can we safely assume Miss Barber is not an assassin? The first lady has doted on her since she was born."

He nodded. "Her family members are fine, but I saw a meeting with women from Iowa and another with local military wives later in the week. Those are the types of people I want submitted for screening."

She folded her arms across her chest, prepared to do battle, but the movement caused a little packet to drop from her skirt pocket and splat on the ground. Cigarette rolling papers. Her eyes widened, and she froze. She looked so horrified, he immediately rushed to set her at ease.

"Don't worry, your secret is safe with me," he whispered, trying to block the amusement from his voice.

"It's a terrible habit," she admitted. "I almost made it an entire week until just now." The frustration in her voice echoed off the bare concrete stairwell. It hadn't escaped his notice that she'd dashed for the roof the moment his meeting came to an end.

"Please don't tell me I caused your fall from grace."

"No, no, I take complete responsibility," she admitted. "When my older brother first caught me smoking, he warned me about the dangers of tobacco. I ignored him, as I so often did. And now here I am, sneaking out onto the roof, a slave to this horrid vice."

"So your brother was right."

"Gray is *always* right. Tedious and boring, but right. Don't overindulge in sweets. Don't neglect your prayers. Don't go for moonlit swims in public fountains."

His eyes widened. "And did you mind his instructions?"

If possible, the blue in her eyes got even deeper as she smiled. "Two out of three isn't bad."

He bent down and collected the wrapping papers. "Here. Please call me Nathaniel. The rules won't be too hideous."

She took the papers and shoved them in her reticule, then offered a handshake. "I'm Caroline, and I hate rules."

"Why is that?" he asked, genuinely curious. She seemed so poised and successful, as though the world had dropped into the palm of her hand like a ripe plum. Why would a woman of such privilege be so determined to throw it all away?

She shrugged. "Rules are meant to be broken. Everyone knows that."

"Anyone who genuinely believes that is either dead or stupid. You are neither."

"All right, then you explain my atrocious history with rules. My brother Gray would pay a small fortune if you can provide an explanation."

Since she'd extended the invitation to be dissected, he obliged, studying her golden hair, upswept but for a few artfully loose tendrils. It was intended to imply disarray but actually required careful arranging. A cursory look at her qualifications revealed she spoke at least three languages, and she had the complete trust of George Cortelyou, one of the savviest men in Washington.

"You are a beautiful woman who is used to getting her own way. You are smart, accomplished, and successful, and as such, secretly believe the rules don't apply to you."

Instead of being insulted, her eyes brightened. "How very perceptive," she admitted. "Please continue."

"You don't mind when people underestimate you, for it allows you to run rings around them behind their back." He must be right, for she looked delightfully smug. "You work in the White House, so you aren't afraid of a challenge. You work for Ida McKinley, a woman whose reputation sends a chill through Washington society. It is a thankless task . . . for Mrs. McKinley never does thank you, does she?"

"I'm far too discreet to answer that," she said with a knowing smile.

"A woman like you could have any man in the city, but instead of settling down in a comfortable marriage, you are here. I wonder why that is?"

He caught a quick flash of pain before she tightened the strings on her reticule. "When you think you know, please tell me," she said in an artificially bright voice, then leaned in shockingly close to whisper in his ear. "And on that count, you will surely be wrong."

She left him standing in the hallway while he extinguished the involuntary thrill of attraction that raced through him at that intimate whisper.

Caroline Delacroix might have the trust of George Cortelyou and the first lady, but she was trouble.

Four

It was the dead of night, and Caroline wore only a robe hastily pulled over her nightgown as she raced in bare feet to the White House basement, where a telephone operator was on duty at all hours. It was two o'clock in the morning, and there wasn't time to pull on a proper set of clothes, not when the first lady needed a doctor.

The telephone operator was asleep, her mouth slack as she leaned against the pillar beside the switchboard. No matter. Caroline was perfectly capable of placing a telephone call.

She lifted the receiver and mouthpiece. "White House calling for Dr. Tisdale, please."

"Yes, ma'am." The operator on the other end was instantly alert and didn't need to ask for the extension, for Dr. Tisdale was regularly called to the White House. He lived only a block away, which was a blessing on nights like this.

The extension was patched through, and the doctor's bleary voice answered the call a few moments later. "Tisdale here."

"It's Mrs. McKinley," Caroline said. "She's having a seizure. A bad one." The word *epilepsy* was never uttered. The president protected his wife's privacy with unfailing devotion, even from most of the staff, to whom her vague illnesses remained a mystery.

"I'll be there in ten minutes," the doctor said and hung up.

Caroline replaced the receiver without waking the telephone operator, then hurried back to the main floor to find the usher who patrolled the hallways overnight. He perked up the moment he saw her hurrying toward him.

"Dr. Tisdale is expected at the north entrance. Please have someone ready to lead him up to the president's bedroom."

"Yes, ma'am," he said.

She nodded in gratitude, then raced up the staircase to the presidential bedroom. Unlike most of the previous occupants of the White House, the president and his wife shared a bedroom. Caroline knocked on the door, pressing her ear against the cool paneling to hear the answer.

"Come in," the president said softly.

The first lady lay curled on the bed, moaning gently as the president sat on the mattress near her head, rubbing her temples. These overnight episodes were an almost weekly event, and being on hand was part of Caroline's duties.

"Dr. Tisdale will be here in a few minutes. Is there anything I can do to help?"

"Perhaps you could fetch your mandolin," the president said. "Ida so enjoys hearing you play."

She nodded. "Of course. I'll be back in a moment."

She scurried up to the dormitory to fetch the small stringed instrument stored beneath her bed. No matter how quietly she crept, the floorboards creaked, and one of the maids awakened, lifting her head.

Caroline put her fingers to her lips but made no sound. The maid nodded and laid her head back on the pillow. These dead-of-night forays were familiar events to the women in this dormitory.

By the time Caroline arrived back in the bedroom, Dr. Tisdale was in attendance, holding Mrs. McKinley's hand and speaking in soothing tones while he took her pulse, his calming voice as good as any tonic. Caroline took a seat on the far side of the bedroom and looked to Mr. McKinley for instruction.

"Mrs. McKinley enjoys Paganini," he said, and Caroline began playing the most mellow tune she knew by the famous composer. Her gaze strayed to a spot in the corner, anywhere but the invalid on the bed being tended by her husband. It seemed such a shocking invasion of their privacy to be in this room, but Ida desperately needed attention when these spells overtook her. First the seizures, then the savage headaches that made her weep for hours on end. It was going to be a long night.

She didn't mind. She wanted to become indispensable to the McKinleys, for a presidential pardon might save her brother from a hangman's noose. The more the president depended on her, the more likely that pardon might someday be granted.

Whatever it took, Caroline would serve both McKinleys with unfailing care until it was time to ask for the ultimate favor.

⁓✒⁓

Nathaniel needed to read Caroline Delacroix the riot act. He had been explicit in his requirement to see a list of names of all visitors to the first lady. It had been a week, and she had ignored both his verbal and written requests.

Each time he reminded her to submit the lists, she sent him one of those half-teasing, half-dazzling smiles. Women that beautiful were probably accustomed to being able to wrap men around their finger, but he was immune. A dozen visitors were expected this afternoon to chat with Mrs. McKinley in the family's private living room on the second floor. They would be within yards of the president, and he had no idea who they were, all because Caroline Delacroix didn't think the rules should apply to her.

The problem was he couldn't find her. Mrs. McKinley was

playing a hand of solitaire in her private study, and George said Caroline hadn't been in the office all morning.

But Caroline had to eat, so he headed to the kitchen to see if the staff knew her whereabouts. White enamel tile lined the floors and walls, and a cook kneaded dough on an oversized marble-topped table while others chopped mounds of brightly colored vegetables. Pots and pans dangled from overhead hooks, and heat poured from ovens lining the walls. The aroma was mouth-watering. Was there a more tempting scent on earth than warm cinnamon rolls? He'd only had two cups of black coffee for breakfast, and his stomach growled.

"You can help yourself," Mrs. Fitzpatrick said with a nod toward a towel-covered bread basket. "I always make enough for the staff."

"No, thank you," he said. "I'm looking for Miss Delacroix. Do you know where she is?"

The housekeeper shook her head, but the woman kneading dough looked up. "She's in the women's dormitory on the third floor. She's sleeping."

At eleven o'clock in the morning? It was appalling, but he blocked his displeasure before it could show on his face. He'd mastered the impassive expression decades ago.

"Thank you," he said simply, then turned and headed toward the staff staircase. It didn't take long to vault up the two flights to the women's dormitory. The door was closed, and he knocked but heard no answer.

"Man on the floor," he announced, then knocked again and waited for a sign of life on the other side of the door. He didn't want to frighten someone who might be in a state of undress, so he knocked louder, repeated his warning, and waited. When he got no response, he cracked the door open and stepped inside the dim room.

Caroline Delacroix was tucked beneath the covers, so deeply asleep that she didn't even stir as he stepped farther inside. He pulled the switch to turn on the overhead light, then banged open the shutters to let the sunlight inside. She remained sound asleep, even when he plunked a straight-backed chair down at the foot of her bed and took a seat.

When she still didn't stir, he kicked the foot of the bed. "Wake up."

She scrambled upright, tugging the sheet up to her chin. "What's going on? Am I needed?"

The panic in her eyes awakened a hint of sympathy. "No emergency, but I need the names of the people visiting the first lady this afternoon. You're late. You should have turned it in days ago."

The tension drained from her as she scrubbed a hand across her tired eyes. Although why a woman who slept in until eleven o'clock in the morning should look sleep-deprived was a mystery.

"The women are from the Iowa Baptist Relief Society," she said. "They're here to knit baby booties with the first lady. They're harmless."

"You don't know that."

A hint of amusement lightened her features. "Do you think they might be anarchists in disguise?"

Her humor rubbed him the wrong way. He folded his arms across his chest and glared at her. "You don't think it's a bit odd that a group of women would travel a thousand miles to join a complete stranger for an hour of knitting?"

Caroline rolled her eyes in an overly dramatic show of pique. "Oh, for pity's sake," she muttered as she punched her pillow and dropped back onto the mattress, turning her back to him. "Cover the windows on your way out."

He stretched his leg out to kick the bedpost again. "Women can be just as lethal as men. Charlotte Corday was a noblewoman who assassinated Jean-Paul Marat while he took a bath. No one suspected her either, until she stabbed him through the heart. Six months ago, a madwoman tried to kill Kaiser Wilhelm with an axe."

She pierced him with a bleary eye over the edge of the bed-sheet. "Do you memorize these little tidbits for fun?"

"Trust me, it isn't fun," he said tightly. "I want those women's names. I have a list of suspected anarchists and need to cross-check them. And before you ask, yes, there are plenty of female anarchists."

The way Caroline's honey-blond hair spilled over her shoulder was worthy of a Botticelli painting. She looked warm and alluring, but her tongue was pure vinegar.

"The president left for Boston this morning, and the first lady is low-hanging fruit. Any self-respecting assassin would go to Boston, not Ida McKinley's knitting circle. I didn't sleep last night and intend to finish my nap." She burrowed deeper into the mattress, presenting him with that tempting shoulder again.

She had a point, but he'd die before admitting it. He leaned back in his chair, wishing he didn't find her so attractive. Women like her were trouble. She probably spent more on a single outfit than he earned in a year.

But she wasn't lazy, and he'd made a mistake in thinking she was a lie-abed. "Why didn't you sleep last night?"

She lifted her head to crack a glance at him over the covers. "Didn't you inspect the overnight logs and notice Dr. Tisdale's arrival at two o'clock?"

"Yes, and he left an hour later."

"Leaving me with the first lady until six o'clock. Then I went downstairs to cancel her morning appointments. Then I visited her pharmacy for more medication and her seamstress to pick up the gown she is to wear for tonight's dinner, and then I mailed invitations for next week's memorial breakfast. Half an hour ago I came up here for a nap before the ladies from Iowa arrive. Thank you for waking me up and suggesting they might be harboring homicidal tendencies. What a soothing thought to lull me back to sleep."

He leaned forward, bracing his elbows on his knees. "I'm sorry about waking you up. In the future, I really do need those lists, even if the president is out of town."

Nothing could be taken for granted. The security here was looser than a typical bank, and his first step in tightening it was to change the lackadaisical attitude of the staff.

Caroline rolled upright and reached for a glass of water on the bedside table. She drank it all, then plunked the glass down with resolve. She paused. Beside the glass was a slim cigarette case, and she was staring straight at it.

"You don't need them," he said gently.

"But I want them."

"There's a difference between—"

"Between needs and wants, I know." She pulled back from the table and folded her arms across her chest, her hands fidgeting and squeezing. "Do you have any vices?"

"None."

"How did I know you were going to say that?" she quipped.

He simply shrugged. "Our world is made of rule-breakers and rule-followers. I think we both know our designated roles."

She grabbed the cigarette case and emptied the contents into her palm. Then she leaned forward and plunked the pre-rolled cigarettes onto the mattress at the foot of the bed, a hint of challenge in her eyes. "Take those with you. As you can see, I don't need them."

He slipped them into his suit pocket and stood to leave.

"Don't let me catch you smoking them," Caroline called after him. "My good opinion of you will be shattered if you let me down."

He battled a smile the entire walk back to his office.

After that day, Caroline began submitting official visitor lists to Nathaniel's office. The lists were an extra burden on her overfilled day, but it wasn't a completely unreasonable request.

What *was* unreasonable was the way Nathaniel began haunting the East Room each day during visitors' hours. The grandiose room looked like something straight out of Versailles. It featured lavish artwork and huge chandeliers that twinkled with thousands of crystals. It was a favorite among the tourists, who gaped at the coffered ceilings, velvet drapes, and gilded mirrors.

Nathaniel Trask perched on a chair in the corner, scrutinizing the visitors like a cat waiting to pounce. He did it for an hour every day. The only time he tore his gaze off the visitors was to scribble in a little notebook. Caroline itched to know what he wrote, for his concentration was fascinating. Something about a man completely absorbed in his professional duties was inexplicably attractive.

One morning she simply couldn't stand it another moment. He watched an elderly woman waddle past with a cane, huffing and out of breath as she admired a pair of marble lions flanking the fireplace. Nathaniel was almost holding his breath as he watched her, his stare disconcerting.

She slid up beside his chair and leaned down to whisper, "What do you think, arsonist or assassin?"

A smile fought to emerge, but he killed it quickly. "Sorry to disappoint. I think she's an ordinary tourist. One who hails from the Midwest, if her accent is any indication." He closed his notebook and slipped it inside his suit jacket. "I've got what I need for today. Let's go outside."

She followed him out to the southern portico, the semicircular balcony framed by the iconic white columns. She snapped open her fan, for the August heat was sweltering. "No one will think poorly of you if you shed that suit jacket."

His lips curved into one of those slow, closed-mouth smiles.

"Somehow it doesn't seem right to be on White House grounds without a suit jacket."

He always wore a somber three-piece suit that looked oppressively hot. The only hint of decoration he wore was a silver tie clip with a little bird clinging to a slim branch. It was so heavily stylized that she must have seen it half a dozen times before she spotted the bird in the intricate silverwork.

"Tell me about the tie clip," she said. "It's surprisingly whimsical for such a serious, sober man."

He touched the tie clip, flushing a little. "It's a memento of my greatest professional failure."

"Oh?"

"The Kestrel Gang. A dangerously clever group of counterfeiters. I've been hunting them for a decade. Once I spent almost a year in St. Louis on their trail, but it came to nothing."

"Why are they called the Kestrel Gang?"

"Kestrels are the smallest breed of falcon. They are smart, tricky, and migrate all over the nation, which is how this gang of counterfeiters operates. Somehow they figured out that the Secret Service code name for them was *kestrel*, and they sent me this tie clip after I gave up in St. Louis."

She smothered an appalled laugh. "And you choose to wear it?"

Amusement danced in his eyes. "It's a daily reminder for me. I'll catch them someday."

Oddly, learning of his professional failing and his sense of humor about the tie clip made him even more attractive. She liked his old-school formality, especially now that they were outdoors and he had dropped the stalking cat demeanor.

"Why do you scrutinize the tourists so intently? There are plenty of ushers keeping watch."

"I'm educating myself." At her quirked brow, he continued. "When looking for counterfeit bills, you don't study fake currency, you study the real thing. Thousands and thousands of authentic bills of different denominations, age, and wear. Only by being intimately familiar with what the real thing looks like can I spot the fakes."

"And the tourists?"

"Same principle. None of them look alike, but I'm studying how they behave. Some are excited to be here, others look hot and tired. Some are distracted by fussy children. Some gawk at the ostentation while others are moved by patriotic emotion. All these things are normal. I need to observe thousands of examples to get it engraved in my mind so that when someone who isn't really a tourist shows up, I'll spot him."

He went on to explain that the notes he compiled would be provided to the rest of the security guards. Most of the guards had worked here for decades but probably had no formal training other than some fighting and shooting experience. Nathaniel was going about things much more methodically.

"Who is the guest you've asked to visit the White House next Monday?" he asked.

As requested, Caroline had submitted a short list of personal guests along with the lengthy list of official visitors. This was the first time he'd asked about her personal guests.

"Petra Stepanovic is a close friend," she said carefully. Petra had always been the most daring of her friends, a turban-wearing fifty-year-old widow of a Serbian diplomat who'd traveled the world, had affairs with Russian aristocrats, and perfected the art of holding a slender cigarette holder as she smoked. "Petra and I will be appealing to the first lady for her help supporting a school for immigrant women and girls."

"She's from Serbia," he said. "Why didn't she return home after her husband died?"

Because Petra's free-thinking ways were not a good fit for Serbia, but that probably wasn't what Nathaniel was driving at. Serbia was known as a hotbed for anarchists, and it might be enough to set off his alarm bells.

"She likes the cafés in Washington," Caroline replied, trying to sound nonchalant. "If you'd like to know if she associates with anarchists, why don't you just ask?"

"I'm sorry if this line of questioning makes you uncomfortable, but I wouldn't be doing my job if I ignored this."

Her jaw tightened as she moved away to stare out at the lawn. She wasn't angry on Petra's behalf so much as fearful for her brother. What would Nathaniel say if he knew her twin brother was currently being held in a Cuban prison, suspected of plotting treason against the United States?

Luke's arrest had been a stunning shock. As always, thinking about him caused a crushing weight of sadness to settle on her chest. This time last summer, she and Luke had been indulging in outdoor picnics and long afternoons sailing on the Potomac. She had been teaching him to play lawn tennis, while he'd been tutoring her in Spanish. How long ago those memories seemed now.

"Petra is seeking funding for a girl's school," she said, trying to mask the defensiveness in her voice. "You have nothing to fear from her."

She retreated into the coolness of the house, unable to bear Nathaniel's scrutiny any longer. At all costs, she must ensure that he didn't learn of Luke's dilemma, or he would boot her from the White House without ceremony.

Five

Caroline was still worried about her tiff with Nathaniel as she headed to afternoon tea with Petra the next day. Despite her Bohemian ways, it was Petra who first suggested the idea of establishing a school as a means of lifting immigrant girls out of grinding poverty and into a respectable profession.

Caroline's hope was that Ida might help raise funds for the school. Last month the first lady had visited a factory of female lace makers in Baltimore, and the associated publicity had garnered hefty donations from as far away as San Francisco to improve the working conditions. Caroline hoped for similar success with Petra's school.

Tea had already been set up in the back garden of Petra's townhouse when Caroline arrived.

"Darling," Petra drawled, although in her thick Serbian accent it sounded more like "daaahlink." They embraced and kissed on both cheeks as the Europeans did, and then Petra gestured to the table set beneath cherry trees. "Come try this new tea. It's imported from the Himalayas."

Petra poured tea and sliced an almond cake with the elegance of the diplomat's wife she once had been. Caroline gamely took a sip of the Himalayan tea and winced.

"It's not very good, is it?" Petra asked.

"You taught me better than to answer a question like that." Caroline had learned much from Petra, everything from how to flatter a disgruntled bureaucrat to carefully navigating a minefield of politically charged conversations.

After finishing their almond cake, Petra launched into the reason for their meeting today. She had already leased a building close to a streetcar stop so students could get to it without difficulty. Rooms would be designated for English language instruction, typing, and switchboard skills.

"I also want the school to help the students find jobs," Petra said.

Caroline nodded. "I can help there. I know plenty of people who own businesses in Washington, and my brother knows even more." Her brother Gray employed hundreds in his spice business and had connections all over the East Coast.

Petra opened a petite jade box filled with loose tobacco and began rolling a cigarette. Caroline looked away, focusing on a squirrel gathering acorns for the coming winter. Anything to distract her from the craving for a cigarette. It had been twelve days since she'd given in to temptation.

The strike of a match startled the squirrel, and a moment later Petra released a long sigh as she drew on the cigarette. "Are you sure you don't want one?"

"I'm sure."

Nathaniel wouldn't like a woman who smoked. Not that she would ever change to suit Nathaniel Trask. It was merely that he knew how hard she was trying to quit, and she refused to be a failure in his eyes. She wanted his respect.

"There is a new head of security in the White House," she said, hoping the topic would divert her from the tense, tingly desire for a cigarette. She stood and paced in the small garden. "He's completely irrational. He won't even permit men to have their hands in their pockets if the president is nearby."

Petra shrugged. "What sort of person would act so casual when the president is in the room? That sounds like good manners to me."

"It's paranoia. He's afraid any given person might have a gun or a knife in his pocket. It's embarrassing."

Petra gave a world-weary sigh. "My friend, I'm afraid you are sadly naive. We live in a dangerous world with hostile people who would force change at the end of a gun. It's far easier to eliminate the head of your enemy than to take on his army. That is why the assassins are so dangerous these days. Let your new security agent enforce his rules, even if you think them silly. Someday you may be grateful for that."

It was a worrisome thought. Caroline's entire life had been spent among wealthy, high-society intellectuals who fought with words, not guns. It was hard to imagine the world Petra described, but maybe she was right.

─────※─────

Nathaniel strolled the White House grounds to inspect the new security fence along the perimeter. Cormac Sullivan stood guard at the main entrance, broiling beneath the hot August sun. He was a newly promoted field agent and the son of Irish immigrants from Boston's south side. Next week a guardhouse would be installed to provide shelter for the men on guard duty, but for now Sullivan stood in the open, the beginning of a sunburn on his pale Irish face.

Nathaniel moved in close to speak in a low voice. "I overheard a tourist from Maryland say she thinks you look like Prince Charming."

Sullivan blanched. "Really?"

"Don't let it go to your head."

Nathaniel continued patrolling the grounds. A pair of electricians worked to install new lampposts every twenty yards along the perimeter, a desperately needed addition to their nighttime security. The new fencing, the lamps, the guardhouse, and the nightly patrols had already greatly improved security outside the house.

The problems *inside* the White House were atrocious. The building was only partially electrified because Mrs. McKinley refused to tolerate construction racket. She had scuttled the west wing addition for the same reason. The house lacked proper office space and staff quarters, resulting in cramped and inadequate facilities. A west wing would have doubled the size of the mansion, but it wouldn't be built until a new administration took office. For now, the western lawn was filled with a series of greenhouses to supply fresh flowers, fruits, and vegetables.

He strolled toward them, scanning for problems. This afternoon Mrs. McKinley would be posing for some official photographs in the greenhouse, and he needed to be sure the space was secure. The greenhouses covered almost two acres and were made of glass. Glass! Any radical anarchist could smash through that glass and be inside before a guard could even draw a gun. It made Nathaniel's blood run cold.

A flash of amethyst silk inside the greenhouse caught his eye. Too much foliage blocked his view to identify the woman, but only one lady working at the White House was likely to wear that brilliant shade. He wandered closer, spotting Caroline as she glided among the aisles of potted herbs in the fruit and vegetable conservatory. She was with another woman, but he couldn't tell who it was other than it was not the first lady.

Why was Caroline wandering in the conservatory at three o'clock in the afternoon? Given the casual way she strolled among the plants with the other woman, it seemed to be a social visit.

He slid toward the greenhouse door and held his hand over the mechanism to muffle the sound as he cracked it open and slipped inside. The air was warm and heavy with a green, peaty fragrance. He slipped behind a bushy screen of tomato plants to observe.

The woman was the young laundress from Croatia. Ludmila had a habit of giggling whenever his guards came into view. Most of the people who worked in the White House were single because there were no living quarters for married staff. The giggling Ludmila didn't seem the sort of person Caroline would normally socialize with, so he slid closer to eavesdrop.

"I like apple on my oatmeal," Ludmila said.

"Apples," Caroline corrected. "Try again."

"I like apples on my oatmeal," the maid amended.

"Correct. If you like oatmeal and I like steak, that's like comparing apples and oranges. What do I mean when I say that?"

"I know! It means they are two very different things."

It seemed Caroline was testing the younger woman on the confusing idioms of the English language. They turned down a new aisle, and Nathaniel darted toward a trellis of squash plants to continue eavesdropping.

"If I say someone is a bad apple, what does that mean?"

"That means he is no good," Ludmila said.

"And if someone is the apple of your eye?"

There was a long pause. Nathaniel leaned in, hoping the laundress would get it right, but this was a strange turn of phrase, and the maid struggled.

"Give me a hint," Ludmila said.

"I was the apple of my father's eye. He thought I was the perfect child. He blamed anything that went wrong on my twin brother, because Luke could be quite naughty, but Father adored me. I was the apple of his eye. What does that mean?"

"It means he liked you very much."

"Correct!" Caroline said enthusiastically. She continued coaching Ludmila on quirks in the English language, using the plants surrounding them. Cool as a cucumber; low-hanging fruit; spill the beans; sour grapes.

Time and again Caroline put the idiom in context to help Ludmila guess its meaning. Most of the examples involved Caroline's brother. *Luke and I are like two peas in a pod. Luke upset the apple cart. Luke got into big trouble and is in quite a pickle.* At one point Caroline stopped altogether to tell a story about Luke. They stood before a series of sprawling artichoke plants.

"Luke and I are twins, and he always gave me artichokes on our birthday. It was a private joke between us. He'd give one artichoke for every year. As I got older, it was a challenge to find that many artichokes in October." Her voice was achingly sad as she reached out to touch a heavy artichoke bud. "Toward the end, he needed to deliver them in a great big basket."

"Toward the end?" Ludmila asked. "He no longer does this?"

Caroline wandered toward another aisle. "That's enough about Luke. What does it mean to be a shrinking violet? I'll give you a clue. Mrs. McKinley is no shrinking violet."

"It means she is a scary woman?"

"Shh!" Caroline laughed. "It means she is a strong woman who isn't afraid to voice her opinions. And now I need to go ensure the first lady is ready for her photograph."

The pair wandered toward the herb garden and out of Nathaniel's range of hearing, but he'd learned a good deal from his surreptitious spying. Contrary to all appearances, Caroline Delacroix had a deep well of kindness beneath the glamour. She adored her twin brother, but he seemed to cause her a mysterious sadness, and Nathaniel wondered why.

Six

Nathaniel stood before the oversized map of the city tacked to the wall of his office. He had completed an initial draft of a plan to secure the White House, but the bigger challenge was to secure the president's safety as he traveled. His gaze tracked the route from the White House to the Capitol, the War Department, and the Treasury, all of which the president visited on a weekly basis. All the routes to and from the buildings needed security plans. Then he needed plans for carriage travel, train travel, and when the president preferred to walk or ride his own horse, both of which he enjoyed.

Nathaniel pointed out a route to Sullivan. "I want you to meet with the head of groundskeeping and tell him to trim all the shrubbery along the route between the White House and the Capitol. That's almost a mile of road that can hide anarchists and bomb threats."

"Yes, sir." Sullivan's inflexible respect for the rules made him exactly the sort of man Nathaniel wanted as his second-in-command.

"Next week the first lady is hosting a luncheon at the Corcoran museum," he continued. "I'll inspect the museum to design a security plan, but please be sure the bushes and shrubs are cut back on that route as well."

Sullivan's freckled face bunched in confusion. "We are to protect the first lady too?"

"Why wouldn't we?"

"It doesn't seem right when she's not in the building. If she wants to leave the White House, the people shouldn't have to pay for security."

Sullivan's adherence to the rules was usually welcome, but it could be a stumbling block too. Congress hadn't authorized security for the president's family, but it was a gaping flaw that needed to be filled.

"Two years ago, the empress of Austria was assassinated while shopping," he told Sullivan. "She was accompanied only by a single friend and was an obvious target. Now her husband is cracking down on the radicals, which is exacerbating the situation in Europe. I don't want that here. We will protect the first lady, no matter what Congress says."

"Then Congress ought to change the law."

"Yes, they ought to, but we can't let the congressional budget interfere with our mission to protect the president and his family. We cannot expect them to be prisoners in the White House. That means that when the first lady leaves the house, she will be protected."

Sullivan's light blue eyes were troubled, but he nodded. "Yes, sir. I just don't like breaking the rules."

Nathaniel didn't either, but he liked the thought of an assassin's bullet even less. And that meant he'd break the rules if it meant protecting Mrs. McKinley.

———

The Corcoran Gallery of Art was only blocks away from the White House, but any time the first family left the residence, Nathaniel was on edge. He had less control in public buildings, with their myriad entrances, exits, and unfamiliar staff.

At least he'd had plenty of notice about the upcoming reception for senators' wives to be hosted by Mrs. McKinley at the Corcoran. The museum had been chosen for its charm rather than safety. It was going to be a security challenge, which was why he spent the afternoon inspecting the museum with Caroline as she outlined her vision for the luncheon.

"The formal portion will be in the upstairs exhibition gallery," she said as they headed down the marble-lined corridor to inspect the only elevator in the building. "Mrs. McKinley has difficulty with stairs, and some of the other ladies may need to use the elevator as well. Senator Himmelfarb's wife is eighty-six."

"Mrs. McKinley will ride the elevator alone except for you and two members of my staff," Nathaniel said. "I can't allow her to be trapped in an elevator with people I don't know." He was pleased at how readily Caroline agreed. After a bumpy start, the two of them had been cooperating quite well over the past few weeks. Overall, working with Caroline was a joy.

No, that wasn't quite right. It was better to think of her as a colleague for whom he had professional regard and nothing more. The other feelings that sometimes tugged at the edges of his awareness needed to be ignored.

Which was challenging today. Caroline stood only two feet away from him as they waited for the elevator, and her up-swept hair exposed the curve of her neck, making it difficult to concentrate. The elevator arrived, and he stepped inside with Caroline.

"Going up?" the uniformed attendant asked. Nathaniel nodded, making a note to check the credentials of the elevator attendant who would be on duty the day of the event.

The luncheon would be held in the exhibition hall, a cavernous room with a domed ceiling. Their footsteps echoed as they entered the huge chamber.

"Each of the senators' wives will have a special keepsake from Mrs. McKinley placed at her seat," Caroline said. "I'll make arrangements for the gifts to be delivered the morning of the event."

She continued outlining how the tables would be arranged, the timing for the event, and how the servers would deliver and clear the meal, but Nathaniel's attention kept drifting to the art on the walls, a collection of Renaissance engravings on loan to the museum for the rest of the year.

Renaissance engravings were his Achilles' heel. His love of engraving dated back to his art school days in Chicago, when he used every dollar he could save to be trained in the creation of steel-faced copper plates used for making prints. Engraving merged artistic skill with attention to detail, and he loved it. It required hours of exacting concentration to make the plates that could produce designs on a grand scale.

He wandered over to admire Albrecht Dürer's woodcut of *The Prodigal Son*. Dürer had perfectly captured the desperation in the young man's clasped hands as he prayed for redemption. Nathaniel had always longed to be capable of portraying human emotion with such mastery. He was a good artist, but he'd long been reconciled to the fact that he would never compete on this level. Now he simply stared in silent admiration at the work of a long-dead genius.

Caroline came up alongside him. "That man looks like he's seen better days," she quipped with a nod to the prodigal son.

"Dürer changed my life," Nathaniel said quietly.

What had made him say that? Caroline had no need to know of his long-ago visit to the Chicago museum where Dürer's work set his adolescent imagination on fire.

"How so?" she asked.

He backed away from the truth and used a safer answer. "His engravings use similar techniques to those for printing currency. I went to art school and studied the process."

"You can do art like this?" she asked, gaping at the exquisite woodcut before them.

To his mortification, a blush started to heat his cheeks. "No," he rushed to say. "Albrecht Dürer is the holy grail of engravers. I'm only an amateur."

"But it was your engraving skills that got you hired to sniff out counterfeit?"

He nodded. "Engraving is the foundation for creating the most lucrative counterfeits. Currency is the most popular, but stock certificates, land deeds, and even postage stamps can all be faked. It's actually not that hard for me to spot anomalies in engravings."

The Kestrel Gang he had sought for so long had mastered dozens of types of engraved forgeries, and his hand instinctively trailed to the kestrel clip holding his tie in place. Caroline noticed.

"Any luck tracking them down?" she asked.

He shook his head. "I'll find them someday. It's only a matter of time. What's frustrating is that forgers disappear quickly, but their work slips into circulation and can go years without anyone noticing. In fact, there's one in this very building. Do you want me to show you?"

Her eyes widened. "Absolutely!"

He'd spotted the Vermeer painting two years ago and was almost certain it was a fake. His footsteps echoed on the marble staircase as he headed down to the room of seventeenth-century European masters. He strode past the old-world paintings of grim-faced Dutch merchants and epic battle scenes to stand before the barefoot peasant girl with a rabbit on her lap. She sat on an overturned barrel in a rustic barnyard so perfectly rendered that he could almost smell the hay and dust.

The painting was enchanting, with the girl's fingers splayed to clutch the rabbit poised to jump from her lap. An open window in the farmhouse behind the girl showed cooling loaves of bread on the windowsill.

"It's charming," Caroline said.

"Yes."

"I love how it looks like the girl is holding her breath, as though she knows that rabbit is about to make a leap for freedom."

He smiled, for that was exactly the expression on the girl's face. "Yes. Sadly, I think it's a forgery."

"How can you tell?"

There were only around forty known paintings by Vermeer, so it was hard to establish a pattern. Most of Vermeer's paintings were of domestic scenes inside well-appointed homes, but not all. Most of his subjects were people of means, but not all. That made this painting atypical on two fronts, but the other details, like the mastery of light and shadow, were classic Vermeer.

"I can't be certain," he said. "I notified the museum director of my suspicion and asked to study the back of the canvas, to look for clues of its age and construction, but he denied the request. So there it hangs."

"What does it matter?" Caroline asked. "It's a charming addition and just as good as any of the other paintings here."

He strolled to a real Vermeer several paces away. *The Woman in Green* wasn't particularly interesting, showing a plain-faced woman reading a letter in a lackluster room. But it was real, and that vaulted it far above the girl with the rabbit.

"A painting is more than the arrangement of pigment on canvas," he said. "A real Vermeer is centuries of history and a chance to step into an earlier time and place. It's a chance to be in the Dutch master's studio, look over his shoulder, and glimpse what had him so entranced. He *knew* that woman reading the letter. Who was she? Why did he choose to memorialize her for all time? Does the letter contain good news or bad? A fake will never capture that aura of mystery and authenticity. It's flawed from the start."

Caroline glanced back at the girl with the rabbit, skepticism on her face. "I hear what you're saying, but I disagree. If I could have one of these paintings on the wall of my home, the rabbit wins every time. The woman with the letter is hopelessly dull and frumpy."

He was torn between laughing and tearing his hair out in frustration. The rabbit painting was a fraud, and he knew it in his bones but couldn't prove it without the museum's cooperation. And why would they? The privately owned museum had probably paid a fortune for that fake Vermeer, and the government had no jurisdiction over them.

"Somewhere out there, a con artist is wallowing in ill-gotten riches from that painting."

"And that bothers you?"

It drove him insane. "I don't like cheaters. The artist is to be commended for his talent, but why did he have to cheat?"

This was probably the point at which she was going to call him a Puritan and a killjoy. But she surprised him.

"He cheated because he understood the value of Vermeer's style and knew he could never create one to surpass it. You should pity him."

And just like that, she forced him to consider the rabbit painting and its artist in a new light. "The rabbit painting has more charm," he conceded. "But the woman reading the letter has more heft."

"And you like heft?" she teased.

"I like heft."

"And I like laughing girls and impish rabbits. Does that make me hopelessly frivolous in your eyes?"

As she spoke, she slid next to the counterfeit painting to look back at him, her countenance alive with laughter and charm. She was breathtaking, and he'd be a fraud if he pretended otherwise. He'd been attracted to women before, but this felt different. Beyond her obvious beauty was a luminous spirit that drew him like a lodestone. She had intelligence and humor, and he longed for more time to bask in this magnetic attraction.

He couldn't. He *couldn't*. He had a job to do, and Caroline was a distraction.

"We should return to the White House," he said.

"Must we?"

He had a duty, and so did she. "I'm afraid we must."

"Why did I suspect that was exactly what you'd say?"

Without changing his expression, he cocked an elbow toward her, and she immediately curled her palm around it and smiled.

The oddest thing was that she didn't seem disappointed. Quite the opposite. It was almost as though she'd been hoping he would adhere to his staid, pedantic routines.

And that made him want her even more.

Seven

Caroline sought out the best criminal attorney in the city to help her file the paperwork for a presidential pardon. Jeremiah Alphonse was also the only attorney to have won a pardon from President McKinley. Every window in his law office was open, and a ceiling fan slowly rotated overhead. Mr. Alphonse had a massive salt-and-pepper mustache but kindly dark eyes as he let her know what she was up against.

"McKinley has granted only one pardon after almost four years in office. Ever since I successfully petitioned for it, my office has been swamped with people hoping to repeat the miracle. Presidential pardons are as rare as hummingbirds in the Arctic. They take years and have only a minuscule chance of success. Who do you want pardoned?"

"I'm only asking hypothetical questions. No one in particular." News of Luke's arrest hadn't yet been widely circulated, and she intended to guard his privacy.

"*Hypothetically*, then," Mr. Alphonse said with a knowing tip of his head. "It all depends on the severity of the offense. How bad was the hypothetical crime?"

"Pretty bad," she admitted. That was an understatement. Short of murder, treason was the worst crime imaginable.

"That's a problem," the lawyer replied. "Presidents are willing to extend a second chance for crimes of youth, cowardice, or perhaps trifling financial indiscretions. The man I won the pardon for had been found guilty of blasphemy. Still, even such minor offenses are hopeless this close to an election."

She blanched. She couldn't bear the thought of Luke sweltering in jail until after the election in November. Even worse, if President McKinley lost the election, she would have no hope whatsoever. Her shoulders sagged, and it felt like she'd just aged fifty years.

"Miss Delacroix, you just plunked down a fortune to purchase my services and complete confidentiality. I can't render effective counsel unless I know the details of the offense and the identity of the perpetrator."

How could she keep her chin up and admit that her twin brother had confessed to treason against the United States? Luke was only six minutes older than her, but he'd always been her hero. He was utterly and completely fearless. Not like Caroline. When she was a child, she was afraid of everything. Of the dark, noises in the attic, unfamiliar foods, even caterpillars.

Luke never made fun of her. He simply gathered up a bunch of caterpillars and let them crawl all over his arms, his neck, the top of his head. Then he spoke calming words as he carefully lowered one onto the back of her hand so she could see that it would be okay.

On their fifth birthday, her father arranged a treat by shipping in artichokes from California. She'd been leery of the odd-looking vegetable, mistrusting its scent and tough outer layers. Coaxing from her father and Gray did no good. It wasn't until Luke gamely ripped off an artichoke petal and pretended to relish the mushy, strange-tasting food that she dared try it.

Every year after that, Luke presented her with a perfect artichoke in memory of her newfound courage. It didn't matter that sometimes he was away at college and once traveling in

Spain. On her birthday, Luke made sure she received a basket of artichokes, one for each year they'd been alive.

His example taught her to outgrow childish fears, and soon she was tromping alongside him as they searched the countryside for Indian arrowheads and buried treasure. They snuck out of the house after dark to watch the flurry of bats careen wildly about the trees in their backyard.

The problem was that as they got older, she continued to embrace Luke's daring outlook on life. Together they set Washington society on fire. There was never a party they didn't attend, never a race they didn't run. Once when her father was overseas, she and Luke arranged a wild birthday party for themselves aboard a barge in the Potomac. They lit off fireworks and drank champagne straight from the bottle. Caroline borrowed a sword from a naval officer to cut the birthday cake. It was the sort of daring caper that made them the most celebrated people in town. She'd always thought it was harmless, but Luke eventually started crossing the line into real trouble.

She would have to confess everything to Mr. Alphonse if he was going to help her.

"My brother was arrested for espionage and treason in Cuba," she admitted quietly. "He was consorting with Cuban revolutionaries who are trying to force an end to the American occupation of the island."

Mr. Alphonse let out a low whistle of incredulity.

"He's not guilty," she rushed to say. "He confessed, but I think maybe he was tortured or wasn't in his right mind. This doesn't sound like my brother. Luke was always a little wild, but he was never evil. He doesn't have any interest in politics! I have no explanation for how he could have gotten mixed up in this."

"Miss Delacroix, no man guilty of treason will ever be pardoned by a sitting US president. Is Mr. McKinley aware of the pending charges?"

"He knows. I told him the day I learned of it and offered my resignation. He wouldn't take it."

"I think it would be best if I return your retainer," Mr. Alphonse said. "I see no possibility of winning a pardon for your brother."

"I won't take it. I'm going to get that pardon."

"Not before the election. Even if McKinley wins a second term, I don't see him endangering his reputation until his very last week in office. You are in for a long wait."

Caroline swallowed hard at the news. She couldn't risk Luke's freedom on the outcome of an election. If Mr. Alphonse wouldn't help her get a presidential pardon, she would pursue one on her own.

~~✦~~

The only person Caroline completely trusted to help with Luke's situation was her older brother, Gray Delacroix. He was in charge of their family's spice company, which had given him the freedom to go to Cuba several times over the three months since Luke's arrest. He had returned from his latest visit only a few days ago, but duties kept Caroline trapped in the White House until Sunday afternoon, when she hired a carriage to take her to their family's townhouse in nearby Alexandria.

"How's Luke?" she asked the moment she took a seat across from Gray's desk. With his dark coloring and serious face, he was practically a replica of their father. At forty, Gray was twelve years older than Caroline and Luke and the natural leader in their family.

"He's being difficult," Gray said bluntly. "He fired the attorney I hired for him and insists on maintaining his guilty plea. He also rejected my attempts to get him transferred to the American prison."

Luke had been arrested for siding with Cuban rebels to oust the American presence that had been on the island since the conclusion of the Spanish-American War two years earlier. The island had been ravaged during the war, but the American government had flooded Cuba with money, supplies, and soldiers to rebuild the infrastructure. Most Cubans welcomed it, but a rebellious minority distrusted the American occupation and wanted them to leave. By siding with the Cuban rebels, Luke had made enemies of the local population who wanted the reconstruction of their island. He had been arrested alongside a group of rebels and had been sweltering in a Cuban jail ever since.

"I want him out of that jail," Gray said tightly. "I toured the American military prison in Havana, and the conditions are better. Luke would be better off there, but he refuses to permit a transfer."

"Can we pay the attorney to keep working on the transfer, even if Luke won't cooperate?" she asked.

A brief smile flashed across Gray's face. "I've already paid him to start the paperwork. There's a hospital at the American jail, and decent medical care too."

She sucked in quick breath. "Has Luke been ill?"

There was a long pause as Gray's face darkened and he glanced away. "He got beat up by a couple of the guards the other day. I didn't want to tell you, but we can't keep secrets from each other. He looks bad. He's lost weight."

She flinched. The feeling of helplessness was strangling, but she couldn't give up. "If the Cubans hate him, why won't he ask for a transfer to an American prison?"

Gray had no answer, and it was just one of the many questions that swirled in her mind ever since hearing of Luke's arrest.

"How are his spirits?" she asked.

Gray shrugged. "You know how he is. He always puts a bright face on everything."

Caroline made no comment. From the time Luke was in long

pants, his behavior had been outrageous. He indulged in endless pranks, broken curfews, overspending, and pushing the limits. He loved flirting with disaster and running risks. No matter how wild his behavior, he seemed to know exactly how far he could bend the rules before the hammer would crash down, and he usually managed to scramble back to respectability just ahead of the law, the debt collector, or the outraged father.

And the one time he hadn't, Caroline was the only person he let know how deeply he'd been wounded. It was when he'd been expelled from the Naval Academy. His grades had been exceptional, but his demerits left him teetering on the edge of expulsion for three solid years.

His balancing act came crumbling down a month before graduation when he was sent home in disgrace. All they knew was that his final offense involved an admiral's daughter, but Luke remained tight-lipped about the details. That night was burned into her mind. She'd huddled outside this very study while her father raged at Luke. Gray was overseas, managing their East Indian holdings, but she doubted he would have had any more luck in prying the story from Luke.

But he told Caroline everything.

It was after midnight when he tapped on her bedroom door. The two of them headed toward the harbor only a few blocks away so they could speak privately. They leaned against the railing and gazed at the moonlight glinting on the water. Luke had dropped his typical lackadaisical air and stared moodily out over the sea.

"Sally is a nice girl," he said. "Her father ignores her, and she was desperate for a little attention. I was happy to give it."

"Luke," she said in an aching voice, dreading where this conversation seemed headed.

"He forgot her birthday," Luke said dismissively. "It isn't the first time that's happened, and he swore he wouldn't forget this year. I found her bawling behind the library and just wanted to cheer her up. I rounded up a few midshipmen, and that night we all stood beneath her bedroom window to give her a rousing serenade. She leaned out the window, and I've never seen anyone so elated. Her father woke up and started tearing into her. I could hear everything from outside. All the other guys ran, but like an idiot, I stayed to make sure she'd be okay. Anyway, I got left holding the bag for it."

"That's all? You hadn't taken any other liberties with her?"

He shrugged. "A peck on the cheek, but I guess when her father questioned her, she confessed to carrying a torch for me. I didn't know, I just wanted to cheer her up. My hand to God, I never touched her aside from that one kiss on the cheek. Her father went to the academy's superintendent, and that was the end for me."

"Do you think she might intercede for you? If her father blew this out of proportion, maybe there's still hope."

Luke shook his head. "If I was squeaky clean, I might have been able to survive it, but I guess I've been walking along the edge for too long."

To her horror, tears welled up in his eyes. He swiped them away with an impatient hand, but he couldn't block them from his tone.

"It's probably just as well," he said in a shattered voice. "I never wanted to be a naval officer. I just wanted to make Dad proud, you know?"

That was the only time she'd ever seen Luke cry. He clung to her as he wept, each of his wrenching sobs cutting her to the bone. Luke was irreverent and reckless, but he wasn't a traitor. She couldn't believe it of him.

"I still don't think he's guilty," she asserted as she stared at Gray across his desk.

He sighed. "Caroline, he looked me straight in the eyes and confessed. Why would he lie if he's innocent?"

It was a mystery. Luke had been locked up for three months

with no communication to the outside world except an occasional visit from Gray. He wasn't allowed to send them letters. He refused to see the lawyer they had hired and maintained his right to silence when questioned by military personnel.

"I spoke with an attorney about filing paperwork for a presidential pardon," she told Gray. "Mr. Alphonse refused to take my money. He says it's hopeless until after the election."

Gray straightened in his chair. "But McKinley might not win. I know everyone in Washington loves him, but William Jennings Bryan owns the west. We can't take anything for granted."

The hint of panic in his tone was worrisome. "I know," she said. "I think it's time for me to appeal straight to the president. No intermediary. No lawyers or paperwork."

It was time for her to act.

Eight

Although Caroline lived in the same house as the president, she wasn't free to wander in for a chat like people in a normal household. George reluctantly squeezed her in for a brief appointment before the president's afternoon meeting with the Treasury Secretary.

A few minutes before two o'clock, she paced in the waiting room outside the president's office, where the Secretary of the Treasury also cooled his heels. She'd been too nervous to eat breakfast or lunch, only drinking several fortifying cups of strong black coffee. Now she trembled in a combination of fear, hunger, and caffeine as she rehearsed how best to frame her request. Luke had already pled guilty, so trying to convince the president of his innocence was pointless. All she could do was beg for mercy.

She was shown into the president's office promptly at two. She'd only been in this room a few times, but it never failed to surprise her. It was an imposing room, but two thick electrical cords dangled from the ceiling directly over the president's desk. One serviced the lamp and the other a telephone.

"Any plans to improve the wiring?" she asked, already knowing the answer, but the question was a subtle reminder of the challenges Ida brought to his life.

The president gave a congenial laugh as he took his seat. As always, he was formally dressed in a suitcoat, vest, and tie, his face haggard from three years in office. "Not unless Mrs. McKinley has a change of heart about construction noise. Now. Tell me what I can do for you."

This was it. Her mouth went dry, and her heart threatened to leap from her chest.

"You are aware of my brother's unfortunate situation in Cuba," she began. "I fear he is losing weight and has been mistreated in prison."

"I'm truly sorry to hear that," the president said gently.

"I don't know how much longer he can last. Luke may not deserve your mercy, but you have the power to offer it."

President McKinley could not have been more sympathetic as he looked at her with kindly eyes, but his voice was resolute. "Miss Delacroix, I sincerely hope you're not about to ask me to intervene on his behalf."

She swallowed hard. "You are the most powerful man in the nation. You could help."

"It may appear that way, but I am answerable to the people for every move I make." He gestured to a tall set of drawers in the corner. "That bureau is filled with desperate requests from all over the country. They are pleas to spare someone from bankruptcy, or a farm from being seized, or a husband from the hangman's noose. I can't grant even a tiny fraction of them."

Worry lines fanned from the corners of his eyes, and he had more silver in his hair than when she began working for him less than a year ago. She didn't doubt this job had taken its toll, but she had to save Luke.

"Would I have more luck if I submitted a formal request through an attorney?"

His smile was sad. "I would put it in the bottom drawer of

that bureau with all the others I've received. At this point in my term, I cannot spend political capital on a man charged with treason, no matter how highly I value his sister's services to my wife. I'm sorry, Miss Delacroix. I can't consider a presidential pardon at this point. Perhaps if I win a second term, I can consider it in a few years, but not now."

It was as her attorney had warned her, but she couldn't give up. Not yet. "What would you do if you were in my place?"

The question took him by surprise. He swiveled in his chair to gaze out the window for a moment. He seemed baffled by the request, but only for a moment.

"I would get the War Department on my side," he said. "Those old boys have a byzantine set of rules, but if you win them over, they may be willing to delay things to give your brother a fighting chance. Keep him alive, that's the main thing. In four years, if he's still in need of a presidential pardon and I'm still in this office, I'll put his case in the top drawer of that bureau."

He stood and crossed the room to consult a directory near the telephone stand. "In the meantime, get in touch with Captain Michael Holland. He's a miracle worker over in the War Department. He's a navy lawyer, and he knows everyone. Does everything. Handles the budget, pushes contracts through, can dance around legal issues to get things done. He's the man to see."

Caroline had met Captain Holland on several occasions. During a White House reception for military officers, she'd exchanged pleasantries with him and his wife. More importantly, she'd spoken with him at a regatta last summer, where he had plied Gray with all manner of questions about the business of cargo ships. At the time she thought it was mere professional curiosity, but she later learned he was looking for ways to help his son find a foothold in the business.

Captain Holland was no stranger to the anguish of having

a black sheep in his family, for his son had been dishonorably discharged from the navy because of drunkenness. That had been three years ago, and rumor claimed the son had been sober ever since. It was obvious that Captain Holland had been subtly suggesting that Gray might find a position for his son on their family's merchant vessel, but Gray let the overture go unanswered.

Perhaps a man like Captain Holland would sympathize with Luke's tarnished past. At this point, he might be her only hope.

—⁓—

Caroline couldn't let herself be discouraged by the president's refusal to help. She would go see Captain Holland on her next free afternoon, but in the meantime, she needed to ensure McKinley would be reelected. For today, that meant working with Sven de Haas, the chairman of McKinley's re-election committee.

Sven had resented Caroline from the day the president invited her to attend the campaign meetings. Rail-thin but with the leathery skin of a man who spent most of his life in smoke-filled rooms, Sven didn't believe women belonged at this particular table. After all, women didn't have the vote, so why was Caroline even here?

She ignored Sven's sullen frown as she glided into the chair next to George for the weekly update on the campaign, prepared to coordinate the first lady's schedule for campaign appearances. The only topic on which she and Sven agreed was that President McKinley needed to get out of the White House and begin actively campaigning or he was in danger of losing.

"The people don't like thinking you take their loyalty for granted," Sven said to the president. "Everyone understands you can't spend months on the trail the way Bryan can, but even a few public speeches will send a signal to the people that you appreciate their support."

Caroline held her breath, hoping Sven could sway his opinion, but the president impatiently gestured to a stack of postcards. "I thought that's why you spent thousands of dollars printing up campaign literature. That will get my message out."

The postcards would be inserted into newspapers across the land, but who read campaign literature? Caroline skimmed the postcard. It dutifully recounted the president's accomplishments but didn't warm up his image. President McKinley was a solidly built man with a barrel chest and deep-set eyes, and his face was naturally inclined to a scowl. While he had once been a handsome man, the stress of the presidency and care for an ailing wife had prematurely aged him. He looked like a tough, scowling bulldog.

It was an illusion. Caroline saw the president's compassionate side almost every day, but the voters didn't. William Jennings Bryan was young and spoke with a fervent idealism they couldn't afford to ignore.

"Perhaps we could stage a photograph of you taking tea with Mrs. McKinley, or a casual stroll with her on the lawn," she said impulsively. "People love candid photographs like that."

Sven rolled his eyes. "*Women* love photographs like that, but women don't have the vote. The vote is reserved for men whose labor and property gives them a legitimate stake in who runs the government."

Caroline bristled. "I own one-third of a global spice company that employs hundreds of people. Why shouldn't I be entitled to vote?"

"Read the Constitution, Miss Delacroix," Sven said, and it was like a bur wriggling beneath her skin.

She fought to speak cordially. "I know your Viking ancestors might be appalled at the notion of women having their own opinions, but the typical American woman is actually a major contributor to her household's labor. Why shouldn't we be allowed to vote?"

"Miss Delacroix makes a good point," President McKinley said. "My wife certainly thinks women ought to have the vote. Perhaps we should work on changing things."

Sven vaulted off his chair. "Don't say that! At least not in public. You're not so popular that you can go out on a limb on a position like that."

"Time is growing short," George said. "We need to get you out on the stump with coverage in the newspapers."

"Absolutely not," the president said. "I will be judged by my diligence in office, not by how many babies I kiss."

A discreet knock on the door interrupted the discussion, and a White House usher entered and crossed the room to Caroline. "Mr. Trask has requested your presence in his office," he said in a low voice.

She turned in surprise. "Did he say why?"

"No, ma'am. Just that you are to come at once."

It was frustrating to be pulled out of this meeting, but everyone was under orders to obey Nathaniel without question.

She sent an apologetic glance at the others. "Forgive me. Hopefully this will be quick."

Nathaniel had one of the newer offices. This was the first time Caroline had seen it, and she stood in the open doorway to admire the new paneling, the electric fan on his desk, and the pretty view out the single window. But those weren't the biggest surprise. Her eyes widened as she spotted an unexpected luxury.

"How come you get your own telephone?" There were only four in the entire building: the president's office, George's desk, the switchboard in the basement, and now here.

"Because I need one," he said blandly.

"You also got the only new office with a window."

"Security."

The hint of amusement in his gaze and the way he kept his answers as terse as possible made her think he was flirting with her. An odd flirtation, but maybe that was how Puritans flirted. His suit was plain, but the way he sat behind the desk as though it were a command post gave him an aura of authority that stirred her reluctant attraction. She needed to squash it.

"Come inside, we have business to discuss," he said.

And downstairs, decisions were being made about the presidency. "I was in the middle of an important meeting and would prefer to get back to it."

"Come inside and close the door." He flipped open a file on his desk.

"I'd rather leave it open."

"Even if it means any passing usher can overhear your explanation of why you were meeting with a criminal attorney last week?"

She closed the door, carefully keeping her face expressionless. "Were you spying on me?"

"Part of the job, Miss Delacroix. Why the criminal attorney?"

"I don't think that's any of your business." Her palms began to sweat. If he learned about Luke, he would try to fire her, and she couldn't afford to lose access to the president.

"If your visit to Mr. Alphonse was a social call, I have no concern. If you were there for his professional services, I need to know. Someone with pending criminal legal issues is a potential blackmail target. Why were you there?"

She needed to divert this conversation. She was good at talking men in circles and would funnel this line of questioning away from Luke. Men could be easily manipulated through the right mix of flattery and teasing.

"While I admire your sober and respectable comportment, it doesn't pair well with the scary tone you're using. The overall effect is terribly dour. You could pass for one of those grim Puritans, like Jonathan Edwards, threatening sinners in the hands of an angry God."

"Thank you," he said mildly. "I wrote a paper on Edwards in school. I've always admired his way with words."

"That does not surprise me. Tragically. The black suit and lack of color is perfectly in keeping with puritanical fussiness."

His gaze flicked to her gown, a white brocade with a blue portrait collar. "While I think the oyster-white shade of your gown is overly conventional, the cerulean blue trim is a classic symbol of piety and loyalty. It's one of my favorite colors."

She leaned forward in the chair, intrigued by his effortless assessment. "Really? I chose it because of its association with the freshness of spring."

"In August?"

"I believe in putting a good face on things, even in the sweltering heat of summer."

Nathaniel tilted the electric fan her way. "Miss Delacroix, you always have a good face."

"You must think I'm arrogant," she said.

"No, I think you're confident. There's a difference."

She loved that he understood the distinction. Maybe she shouldn't be surprised, for he seemed to be a master of interpreting human behavior. He hid it behind that calm, somber exterior, but somehow that made it even more exciting.

"How come you seem determined to make people dislike you?" she asked. "All these rules and fussiness and no-hands-in-pockets nonsense."

"My job isn't to be liked, it's to keep the president safe. How come you met with a criminal attorney?"

"Mr. Alphonse is a very nice man," Caroline said. "Of course, he smiles a lot more than you. With actual teeth showing. When you smile, it's always a closed-mouth smile, like you're being stingy with it."

One corner of his mouth curved into a reluctant smile, making a dimple appear in his cheek. The half-smile reached all the way up to his eyes, which warmed and sparkled. But still no teeth showed.

"See?" she challenged. "There it is. As if you can't bear to deliver a real smile."

Before he could answer, a tap on the door interrupted her, and an usher opened it. "Mr. LaFontaine is here to see you, sir."

"Tell him to wait," Nathaniel said, but she used the opportunity to divert the conversation.

"Do you think our head chef is an assassin? Or consorting with anarchists? I can assure you that Mr. LaFontaine has worked at the White House for thirty years. There were other presidents far more worthy of assassination, if he was so inclined."

"Yet he accepts shipments of food every day from unknown sources, and that needs to stop."

"Agreed. You should see to it immediately." She rose and opened the door to beckon Mr. LaFontaine inside. "Mr. Trask will see you now," she said while gliding away, knowing Nathaniel was too discreet to haul her back in front of witnesses.

She'd won a reprieve, but he would surely come after her again.

Nine

Nathaniel had learned long ago that sometimes prayers worked, but sometimes they seemed to go unanswered. Ever since accepting the White House job, he'd been praying for his nightmares about Molly to fade, and they had—but only to be replaced by a dull, grinding unease that was always present.

Heat and sun pounded down on him as he crossed Fifteenth Street to the Treasury Building, anxious to get this meeting with John Wilkie over with and get back on duty.

His pathetically small budget meant he had to clear all additional expenditures through Wilkie. Anything involving the president required public scrutiny. Penny pinchers questioned everything spent on the president, from the price of wine served at state dinners to the guards who protected him. During the last administration, President Cleveland's wife had created a scandal when she requested guards during a summer trip to their New York home. It didn't matter that the president's young children had been the target of kidnapping rumors. When the Cleveland family was on vacation, Congress decreed the public should not pay for security.

Those days were mercifully over, but Nathaniel still had to account for every penny, and today's request was odd.

"I want Caroline Delacroix to be tailed," he said the moment he sat across from Wilkie's desk. Everyone else working in the White House had spotless reputations, but Caroline made him uneasy. He didn't like the idea of spying on her, but it had to be done.

Wilkie didn't bat an eyelash. "Why?"

"She's met with a criminal attorney and refuses to tell me why. I can find no blemish on her reputation, but her refusal to be forthcoming is troublesome. The first lady has become unusually dependent on her, and it worries me."

"Consider it done," Wilkie said. "I'll arrange for surveillance and report anything I find to you."

"Thank you." Now for the more difficult request. Everything about being responsible for the safety of the president reawakened the grief over Nathaniel's deepest failing. He'd agreed to the presidential assignment on a short-term basis, and the time was up.

"I've done as you asked and designed a solid security plan for the White House, but you need to find someone else to lead this team."

Wilkie reached for an unlit cigar, slowly tapping and rotating it on the desk. "I wouldn't have appointed you if I didn't think you were the best man for the job."

"I haven't had a decent night's sleep since the day I accepted. Assign me somewhere else. The Treasury or the State Department."

"To investigate tax fraud?" Wilkie's voice dripped with disbelief.

"Tax forms don't die in front of you because you fell asleep on the job." It was his deepest shame, for he'd literally fallen asleep while he was supposed to be watching Molly.

Wilkie dropped the cigar and leaned across his desk. "You've got to get over what happened to your sister. It was twenty years ago."

"You never get over the death of someone you were supposed to protect."

And he had been Molly's only protector. After their father died, it was just him and Molly, for their mother had run off with a traveling salesman years earlier. He was fourteen and Molly only six when their father died. He didn't like leaving a child as young as Molly on her own, but he had to earn a living and couldn't afford to hire someone to look after her. He dropped out of school to work the overnight shift at the *Chicago Tribune*. Feeding huge spools of paper into noisy printing machinery wasn't the ambition of any young man, but it paid the bills. Over time, his eye for detail got him promoted to the photoengraving department, where he learned the techniques that made the reproduction of photographs commercially viable for newspapers.

Every night he worried about Molly. When he returned home each morning, he breathed a sigh of relief as he jostled her awake, got her dressed, and walked her to school. Then he collapsed into bed and slept into the afternoon.

But he'd yearned for more. As the years passed, he grew accustomed to his overnight shift, but he wanted more out of life than black-and-white newsprint. He wanted color and art and beauty. By the time he was eighteen, he'd saved enough money to take art classes while Molly was in school, but it played havoc with his ability to sleep. He grabbed a few hours here and there, but it seemed he never had enough.

And in the end, Molly paid the price.

"Find someone else for the job," Nathaniel stressed. "I'll never be a bodyguard."

"You're not a bodyguard, you're a detective. You've already spotted a potential security flaw with the first lady's secretary, but we'll need to keep the investigation quiet. The Delacroixs are a powerful family."

"What can you tell me about them?" Nathaniel had limited experience with high society, but Wilkie mingled with ease.

"They are one of the first families in Virginia society. Old money and old roots. Her elder brother is the leader of the family. Gray Delacroix lives like a monk, but the younger brother is a scoundrel. I think he and Caroline are twins. The pair of them used to be the toast of the town. They lived fast and dangerous. She mostly outgrew it, but he never did. Luke Delacroix is the sort who eventually gets kicked to the curb, blackballed, or wears out his welcome."

Possibly the sort who would need a criminal attorney, but no self-respecting man would use his sister to handle his legal problems. "Where can I find him?"

"If he has a job, I've never heard of it," Wilkie said.

That meant Nathaniel now had two people to spy on. Caroline and her brother Luke . . . if he could be found.

~⁓~

There wasn't much room to get dressed in the dormitory, and Caroline needed help from Ludmila to get into her formal gown of peacock blue draped with black lace. She'd had it sent from her family's townhouse for this evening's state dinner. She only had room for a few gowns in the women's dormitory, but she kept others at home, and Ida even let her store a few in her generous closets, because Caroline needed a huge range of clothing for her various duties. She would only attend tonight's dinner if the first lady fell ill at the last moment, but Caroline always dressed in case she was needed.

The small tabletop mirror in the dormitory wasn't adequate, but Ida had a full-length mirror in her dressing room, and it was time to go attend to her.

Caroline gasped when she saw the first lady dressed in a splendid gown of mauve satin and a diamond choker. Ida looked spectacular, but her hair ornament was a problem.

"Let's see what else might work better with that gown," Caroline said diplomatically.

"I love egret feathers," Ida said, adjusting the spray of snowy white feathers in her hair. The problem was that the egret had been driven nearly to extinction by ladies who craved the latest fashion. Only three months ago, the Lacey Act had been passed to stop the sale of endangered bird feathers across state lines. It would be a diplomatic disaster for Ida to wear them at a state dinner.

"Your husband signed the bill," Caroline pointed out. "It might reflect badly on him if you wore the feathers."

Ida immediately lifted the headdress from her tightly styled hair. "Quick! Help me find something else."

This was the best part of the job. Ida McKinley had a wardrobe that would make Marie Antoinette envious, and Caroline loved helping coordinate the outfits. She opened the silk-lined armoire where the formal headdresses were kept. There were jeweled combs and floral scarves, but Caroline's favorite was the delicate snood encrusted with crystals.

"This is the most beautiful thing I've ever seen," she said. "It's subtle, but no one can miss it."

The corners of Mrs. McKinley's mouth turned down. "A little plain. I want some height."

"The tiara?"

An eager look flitted across the older woman's face. "Do I dare?"

"Do you remember what the Spanish ambassador's wife wore at the last state dinner?" It had been a diamond choker so wide she could barely lower her head to eat. "If Doña Maria can wear a king's ransom on her throat, you can wear one on your head."

Ida sat on the bench in front of the vanity while Caroline set the tiara in place, carefully hiding the pins and arranging Mrs. McKinley's hair to its best advantage.

"Perfect." She reached for the crystal snood to return it to the armoire, but Ida stopped her.

"You wear the snood," she said, and Caroline quickly traded places on the dressing bench so Ida could drape the fragile silk cords over her hair. It was the prettiest, most feminine thing she'd ever seen.

"My sister and I once traveled in Europe," Mrs. McKinley reminisced. "I bought this in a fit of youthful exuberance after seeing *Romeo & Juliet*, because the actress wore something just like this. There you are, my dear."

Downstairs, the Marine band began to play, which meant guests would be arriving soon. Aperitifs and informal conversation would take place in the East Room for an hour, then the guests would progress to the state dining room for the dinner.

"Quick, let me powder your nose," Caroline said. She would also add a bit of color to Ida's cheeks, for Mrs. McKinley's naturally gaunt face could use some warmth. Caroline and Ida both indulged in the semi-scandalous practice of using cosmetics, but the trick for getting away with it was to use a subtle hand.

"Ready?" she asked as she handed Ida the cane.

"Ready," Ida replied firmly.

Caroline tried to memorize every detail of the glamourous evening as she accompanied Ida downstairs. This job was hard and might never result in a pardon for Luke, but she must still count the blessings of being able to participate in grand events such as these.

～⚬～

Nathaniel took a spot on the staff staircase, his notebook at the ready. From this angle, he could see through a narrow interior window to the guests gathering in the East Room below. It was an elegant display of old-world royalty, new-world money, and spectacle on the grandest scale. The waiters wore formal suits, and earlier he'd seen towering floral arrangements so large they needed to be wheeled into place.

A rustle of silk sounded behind him. He twisted around to see who was coming and nearly choked. Caroline Delacroix looked like a fairy princess straight out of a picture book.

"Are you attending this fancy dinner?" he asked, drinking in the sight of her layers of silk and lace. Diamonds glittered in her ears, and she carried long white gloves in one hand.

"Hopefully not. I sometimes step in to facilitate if the first lady falls ill, but she seems in good health tonight. I doubt I'll be needed."

"Who are those men with all the medals?"

The scent of lemony perfume surrounded him as she leaned closer to peer through the slim window. "The German diplomatic corps. They love their epaulets and awards."

"And the man with the scarlet sash?"

"That's the papal nuncio. He's the official envoy from the Vatican." She glanced down at his notebook, both surprised and appalled. "Are you spying on them?"

"Of course. I know what to expect from ordinary tourists now, but this is a different crowd. I need to learn what's normal at an event like this." Would she make fun of his exactitude like she usually did?

"Scoot over and let me interpret for you." To his amazement, she settled in beside him, sitting on the same step while her skirts billowed around them, and he wondered if her hair was as soft as it looked. They had to lean over to peek through the narrow window into the room below.

"The footmen are serving Riesling wines from Bavaria in honor of the visiting German dignitaries. We always serve something in tribute to the highest-ranking guests."

He nodded toward a cluster of American military officers. "It looks like only the navy is represented here tonight. Why?"

Maybe it was his imagination, but it seemed Caroline stiffened when she spotted the trio of officers. "That's Captain Holland," she said. "He's very high up in the navy. I'm not sure about the others. There has been an effort to improve relations between the American and German navies."

She continued answering all his questions, and he loved the way she was so confident but not the least bit condescending as she huddled beside him on the step. She probably took part in this sort of pageantry often. It underscored the huge gulf between them, and yet he'd always felt comfortable with her.

No, *comfortable* wasn't the right word. The tug of attraction, the unwelcome desire . . . none of it was comfortable, but he savored it all the same.

In the room below, the president entered with Mrs. McKinley on his arm, both looking hale and stately.

"They're breaking protocol," Caroline whispered. "Normally the president should escort the wife of the highest-ranking diplomat, but he always sticks close to Mrs. McKinley. She will sit beside him at the dinner table too."

"Because of her epilepsy?"

She nodded. "He's very attuned to the signs, and if she is going to be indisposed, he makes sure she has privacy. The spells usually don't last long, but if it's a bad one, he gets her out."

Nathaniel gazed down at the gilded world below as the guests socialized. Over time, it was almost like a dance. Couples slowly rotated though the room as they jockeyed for position near the president. Mrs. McKinley rarely spoke, usually just watching her husband and nodding at whatever he said. Waiters in formal attire offered tiny delicacies on silver platters.

"Do those hors d'oeuvres taste as good as they smell?" he asked.

"Wait here," Caroline whispered, then gathered her skirts and scurried down the staircase before he could call her back. Long after she disappeared, the clicking of her heels echoed in the stairwell as she descended to the basement.

Five minutes later she was back with a fully loaded platter.

"Apparently they don't like the stuffed mushrooms," she said as she rejoined him on the step. "There were plenty left, and they're all ours."

"They just gave them to you?" he asked, helping himself to a mushroom cap brimming with spinach, herbs, and a hint of sherry.

"The kitchen staff likes me," she said. "Maybe because I never pretend I'm not staff too."

He couldn't afford to warm up to anyone. Even this clandestine huddle on the stairs probably wasn't a good idea, but sometimes the need for simple human contact got the better of him. She was the most beautiful woman he'd ever seen, and his weakness for pretty things went all the way back to his early years when he saved every dime to attend art school. Whether it was a flower in full bloom, a spectacular sunrise, or a gorgeous woman huddled on the staircase beside him, he liked beauty.

His gaze kept trailing to her. "I like that thing in your hair."

"A snood," she said.

"What an awful word for such a delicate thing," he replied. Tiny golden strands were held together by crystals, a piece of art in and of itself. "It makes you look like a princess. Like Juliet or Guinevere." He wished he could sketch her at this exact moment. He memorized her features. He would draw her later tonight so he could remember this stolen interlude forever.

The reception lasted an hour, during which he and Caroline never stopped talking. Her insight was surprisingly helpful. He wasn't well-versed in the subtle language of protocol, but she explained how the order of the people engaging with the president was determined by rank, and how the flowers in the arrangements were selected to celebrate the nations of tonight's guests.

When the mushrooms were gone, Caroline set the empty plate on a higher step and slid a few inches closer to him in the dimly lit stairwell. "I don't think I'll ever be able to eat another mushroom and not remember this night," she whispered.

Her face was inches from his, and he couldn't look away. There was a quiet magnetism humming between them. It was exhilarating and perfectly comfortable at the same time. He leaned forward a fraction of an inch, and she closed the distance between them.

Never had a kiss felt so easy and natural. She smiled against his lips, and he deepened the kiss.

"I hope I'm not breaking some sort of Secret Service rules," she said as she pulled back a little, excitement glinting in her eyes.

"I never break the rules."

"Never?"

"I'm tedious that way. So no, we aren't breaking the rules."

"Good. Then kiss me again."

He did, and it felt like the most perfect thing in the world. In his entire life he'd only courted two women. One was the daughter of his minister, which involved nothing more than some awkward holding of hands, and the relationship ended quickly when she fell in love with an accountant. His other relationship was more heartfelt, but the dressmaker from Chicago threw him over because she found him too serious.

Caroline felt different. Their attraction felt both natural and exhilarating. All except that one, niggling detail.

He pulled back, and the question popped out. "Why were you meeting with a criminal attorney?"

Her face chilled, and her chin rose a fraction of an inch. "Back to that, are we?"

"You clearly have the trust of the president," he said. "I'm not looking to expose any personal embarrassments, but I need to know of potential security flaws."

She looked exasperated. "I'm not a security threat. I have a reputation for enjoying a party and a fine wardrobe, but I'm actually quite tame in the rest of my conduct. You already know my one and only vice."

The cigarettes. "How's the abstinence going?"

"Sixteen days," she said proudly.

"Good for you."

"I almost gave in to temptation once, but do you see that man with the muttonchops talking to the papal nuncio? He's the postmaster general, and every time he visits, the stink of tobacco is so bad that I can smell it from yards away. All I had to do was summon his image to kill the urge."

She continued pointing out stories about the various people mingling in the room below, but it didn't escape his attention that she had smoothly diverted the conversation from her attorney. Again.

He let her but moved a few inches away from her on the step. Kissing her had probably been a mistake. She was smart and attractive, but he couldn't trust her. Wilkie had promised the results of the investigation into Caroline by the end of the week, and then he'd nail down what it was she was trying to hide.

Ten

It took over a week before Caroline succeeded in getting an appointment with the navy officer President McKinley had suggested could help with Luke's case. Captain Holland had a top-floor office in the War Department with a commanding view of the White House across the street. He was a fine-looking man, with neatly groomed black hair and flawless military bearing. He rose as she entered his office.

"Miss Delacroix," he said, curiosity rampant on his face. "I trust you are recovered from organizing the state dinner last week?"

"It was an honor." She lowered herself into a chair opposite his desk. "It was a splendid evening I will never forget."

He gave a polite laugh. "My wife certainly won't! She danced such a lively jig at the ball afterward that she twisted her ankle. She had to leave early. A terrible disappointment."

"Oh dear, I didn't realize."

"Not to worry. I rang for my son, who came straightaway to escort her home. All is well! She's up and walking again."

"Thank heaven for your son. They are both doing well?" she carefully inquired.

"Yes, both well. Now, how can I help you?"

He clearly wasn't open to discussing his son, but alluding to him had still been helpful. Even the most successful families had prodigals who sometimes went astray.

"President McKinley said you might provide guidance on how best to navigate a tricky legal quagmire," she began, for it never hurt to reference her connections. "I expect you are aware that my brother has landed himself in a bit of a scrape down in Cuba."

Captain Holland's expression hardened. "I'm aware of it."

"I'm concerned about the conditions of his confinement. He is a civilian. It doesn't seem right for a civilian to be held in a military—"

"He committed treason in an occupied territory. That makes it our business."

"He is *accused* of committing treason in occupied territory."

"He pled guilty."

This wasn't going well. Her goal wasn't to prove Luke's innocence, but to get him transferred to a jail in the United States. She needed the ability to see him regularly and try to talk sense into him. If she could get him out of the hands of the military, she could hire lawyers to slow the proceedings. Otherwise Luke could find himself in a hangman's noose before the end of the year.

"I confess my brother's case looks dire, but as a citizen, he is entitled to a presumption of innocence, and I want him to be transferred to the United States for trial. I want him to have decent living conditions and the benefit of a sound attorney."

"He'll get a fair trial in Havana, which is the proper place for it."

Captain Holland's voice was implacable. She looked away, scanning his office for clues about how best to make her case. The windowsill was covered with diplomas, awards, and framed photographs of Captain Holland with prominent citizens. He was obviously a man who took pride in his position. It hadn't escaped her notice that he'd had his son escort his wife home from the state dinner rather than leave early and forgo mingling with the cream of Washington society. Perhaps she should lean on that weakness.

"President McKinley suggested you are a man who might be able to help me. He touted your knowledge of byzantine military laws. Surely he wasn't wrong about that. . . ." She let the sentence dangle.

Captain Holland's spine stiffened. "I am the navy's top legal advisor, and as such, I won't have my credentials questioned by a woman with no understanding of these affairs."

"I confess to having no military experience, but I understand plenty about politics. I know that a quick trial overseas will be the easiest way to sweep this scandal under the carpet and pretend there is no ongoing rebellion against the glorious American occupation. I want my brother transferred to the mainland, where I can be certain his rights are protected."

Captain Holland's face looked like it was carved from stone. "He stays in Cuba. End of story."

"Then I want him to be given permission to send letters to his family and an attorney on the mainland," she countered. "You are holding him incommunicado, and since he hasn't been found guilty yet, I want to be able to exchange letters with him."

Captain Holland's gaze strayed out the window as he considered the request. "You are aware that all communication with a prisoner of his status will be read by the authorities before it leaves the island."

She would expect no less, but she was surprised he admitted it. "I understand."

He gave a brusque nod. "I will issue the command today. Have a good day, Miss Delacroix."

The conversation was over. Allowing Luke to send letters to them was a tiny concession, but at least she wasn't leaving empty-handed.

The following day, Caroline attended another meeting to discuss the reelection campaign, but it was repeatedly interrupted by the first lady. Ida had forgotten to take her nerve tonic the previous evening, so she awoke in a ferocious mood. That led to a migraine, which meant only her husband could calm her down. The president had been called out of the meeting to attend his wife, and Sven de Haas simmered in resentment as they sat in the reception room outside the president's office, awaiting his return. On a day like this, it was hard to guess if that would be in ten minutes or two hours.

"Why can't she be like a normal woman and support her husband?" Sven grumbled as he paced a circle around the cluster of chairs. "Why can't she be a helpmeet instead of a constant, incessant, irritating, and annoying drag on him?"

Caroline bit her tongue, fighting back the urge to ask why Mr. McKinley had run for the highest office in the land when he knew his wife wasn't up to it. She didn't like Ida's tantrums any more than Sven, but the first lady had been dealt a brutal round of blows in her life and was more fragile than most women. It was the way God had made her, but trying to reason with a man like Sven was pointless, so Caroline cut straight to the point.

"Ida McKinley is the First Lady of the United States. If you can't show her a modicum of respect, you may be in the wrong job."

Sven heard the veiled threat and whirled to point a finger in her face. "I am an essential member of the president's team. You're only here to help his wife manage tea parties."

"Oh, sit down and shut up, Sven," she groused. "You sound like a hummingbird with whooping cough."

He threw himself into a chair in the corner and glowered at her. Before he could make any other nasty remarks, the door banged open, and Nathaniel strode inside. He looked out of breath and furious, and she instinctively stood.

"What's wrong?" she asked.

"I just met with the chief of the Secret Service. Mr. Wilkie had interesting things to relay about why you've been meeting with a criminal attorney."

She blanched, glancing over at Sven, whose eyes had widened in shock. The last thing she wanted was the only enemy she had on the president's staff to know about this. Her mouth went dry, and her hands were clammy.

"Let's step outside where we can speak privately," she said, managing to keep a calm tone.

Nathaniel looked taken aback by Sven's presence, for he sat in a shadowy corner, his face awash in cool, calculating fascination.

"Get out," Nathaniel bluntly ordered.

"Actually, I'm enjoying the fireworks," Sven said.

"This is a matter of national security. You can leave of your own accord, or I can have you removed," Nathaniel said. "Your call."

Sven's face tightened in displeasure, but he collected his stack of papers and left, closing the door softly behind him.

Caroline forced herself to breathe smoothly. Nathaniel's boorish behavior would not ruffle her. She was a proud daughter of Virginia and would not act guilty or ashamed, for Luke's freedom rested on her ability to keep this job.

"Is this how they teach gentlemen to behave in Chicago?" she asked the moment the door clicked shut behind Sven.

Nathaniel's eyes narrowed. "I don't know the rules for how to behave when you find someone you trusted withheld information."

She raised a single brow. "I was under no obligation to disclose my family history to you."

"You didn't think it was relevant for me to know that your

twin brother is currently imprisoned and confessed to treason against the United States?"

"He's not guilty," she defended. "I don't know why he confessed, but maybe he was tortured. That's the only explanation I can think of. I know Luke is loyal to this country, but frankly, his legal situation is none of your business."

"That's a lie and you know it. You and your family may be the biggest security risk in the entire White House. I intend to tell President McKinley everything."

"He already knows," she snapped. "I told him the moment I learned of it, and he refused to take my resignation."

Nathaniel's jaw dropped in disbelief. "Why would he want you here?"

It hurt. Ida had become almost like a mother to her, which was ridiculous but true. Her own mother had died when Caroline was four, and Ida lost her only two daughters when they were children. Maybe that was why she and Ida had bonded so easily. Their relationship was unconventional, but it was nobody else's business.

Caroline pointed to the embroidered silk vest she wore. "Do you see this vest?" she challenged. "It's Mrs. McKinley's. She asked me to wear it because she thinks the blue complements my eyes. And look at the shawl she's wearing today. It's mine! We trade clothes. We plan meals and parties and floral arrangements. When she falls ill, I play the mandolin for her, sometimes all night long. We bicker and fight, but in the end, I always deliver exactly what the president needs. He needs someone his wife can't trample but who can still calm her down, steer her in the right direction, and make her happy. I *can't* be fired."

She prayed that was true, for Nathaniel looked ready to combust. She'd never seen him angry before, and she instinctively took a step back as he drew closer to her.

"I'll be watching you," he said in a cold voice. "If you place one foot wrong, I'll find out about it and see you escorted out of here."

She remained frozen in place, unable to draw a breath as he strode toward the exit. When he finally left, her knees felt like water, but she would not collapse. She would take this in stride and never falter, even if this journey took years.

"Oh, Luke, hang on," she whispered, fearing his position was more precarious than ever.

Eleven

Nathaniel seethed. It was the day after his blowup with Caroline, and she was the last person he wanted to see, but there was no escaping her. He was providing security for the first lady today, which meant he was required to be trapped only inches from Caroline in the close confines of a carriage. As they rolled along Eleventh Street, Caroline sat on the bench opposite him, glancing through a fashion magazine as though she didn't have a care in the world.

They were traveling to the Naval Hospital, where Mrs. McKinley would unveil a plaque commemorating sailors injured during the recent war. It would be an indoor ceremony, so Nathaniel was the only guard, but they'd brought along a photographer to memorialize the event. His name was James Remberton, but everyone called him Rembrandt in deference to his artistic bent.

The normally spacious carriage felt cramped from all the photographer's equipment along with the two huge bouquets Caroline had brought to deliver to the sickrooms. Nathaniel wanted to tell her she shouldn't have bothered—injured soldiers didn't care a fig about flowers—but she insisted they be placed inside the carriage to ensure they were protected from the breeze. The cloying scent of tuberose made his head ache.

"Look!" Caroline said as she paged through the magazine. "The Countess of Windover wore scarlet opera gloves to a performance in Rome. Shall we order you a pair?"

Mrs. McKinley looked intrigued. "Do you think I could get away with something so daring?"

"You're the first lady. You can dare whatever you wish." Caroline laughed.

Nathaniel fought to keep his expression blank, but this was the sort of nonchalant disregard for the rules that always irked him. Caroline and Ida McKinley could flout decorum while their minions were bound by rules and ordered to serve.

But it wasn't flowers or opera gloves that really angered him, it was the fact that he'd ignored so many warning signs about Caroline Delacroix. She had flat out told him she had no respect for rules the first day they met. She had a criminal attorney. She flouted one rule after another inside the White House, and yet he'd overlooked those clues because she was charming and flirted with him.

He'd spoken to George Cortelyou about terminating Caroline's access to the White House, but George claimed the first lady depended on Caroline. Nathaniel privately thought it was all the more reason to remove a woman with undue influence, but he'd made no progress in plugging the security breach.

And here she sat, side by side with the first lady, gossiping about fashion.

"Scarlet is increasingly worn in high society," Rembrandt said. "It doesn't photograph well, but if the correct shade is selected, it can look both daring and stately."

Mrs. McKinley did not welcome commentary from an underling like the photographer. She pursed her lips while frowning at Rembrandt's vest. "Couldn't you have found clothing that fit? You are representing the White House today, and that vest looks like it belongs to a man half your size."

It was true that Rembrandt's vest was too small, but didn't Mrs. McKinley realize how little a photographer earned? Rembrandt flushed but made no comment. Nathaniel glanced at Caroline, wondering if she would intervene, but she kept perusing the fashion magazine.

"It says here that Madam Zane's shop in Richmond is now selling scarlet gloves."

Mrs. McKinley sniffed. "I wonder if Madam Zane can tailor a gentleman's vest to make it fit."

Rembrandt wilted even further, and Nathaniel had to bite his tongue. It didn't matter how much he disliked Mrs. McKinley, it was his job to protect her.

"We're here," he said tersely as the carriage came to a halt outside a three-story brick building. A small crowd had gathered, for it had been announced that the president would be dedicating the plaque, but he'd been called away by a crisis with the budget, and Mrs. McKinley had taken his place.

Nathaniel hopped down from the carriage and greeted the officer who'd been waiting for them in the hospital yard. Captain Dorset was the hospital's administrator and the man who'd organized the ceremony today.

"I'll need some help getting Mrs. McKinley's wheelchair unstrapped from the rear boot," Nathaniel said to Captain Dorset. "The first lady also brought some bouquets that need to be unloaded."

Captain Dorset ordered a pair of soldiers to help with the tasks while Nathaniel scanned the grounds. The yard was small, bordered by a hip-high brick wall and shaded by towering oaks. There were no clear lines of sight. A small Marine band of a dozen soldiers were in formation with their instruments at the ready. A few civilians gathered outside the wall began clapping as Mrs. McKinley descended from the carriage. The two

Marine guards maintained a stoic expression as they carried the towering bouquets of daffodils and tuberoses that were so tall, they completely obscured their faces.

"Let's get inside quickly," Nathaniel said to Captain Dorset. He didn't want to wait for the band to play. All that could be handled indoors.

"Actually, we've moved the ceremony outside," the captain said. "The weather is cooperating, and the hospital cafeteria is a dreary venue for an unveiling."

Nathaniel straightened. "But the cafeteria is a protected location. I didn't bring enough security for an outdoor ceremony."

"Let's move the bouquets to either side of the podium," Captain Dorset directed the two Marines. A podium and ring of seating had already been set up. The band moved into position, and the small crowd began to clap.

"We're moving the ceremony inside," Nathaniel insisted. Captain Dorset had no authority over this event. As the agent in charge of the first lady's security, Nathaniel had the ultimate say on anything regarding the first family's safety.

"Are you sure?" Caroline asked. "It's so much prettier outside."

"I'm sure," he said, striding toward Mrs. McKinley, who was already seated in her wheelchair.

Captain Dorset reluctantly agreed and gestured for the Marines with the bouquets to head inside. The band members stood, and Caroline turned the first lady's wheelchair, heading toward the front door.

Someone in the crowd began shouting. Something about the war and blood on McKinley's hands. Sunlight glinted off the barrel of a shotgun among the civilians.

People screamed, and Nathaniel scooped Mrs. McKinley into his arms, lurching with her toward the open door of the carriage. He grunted as he hoisted her inside. Two loud blasts shattered the air. Flower petals scattered everywhere. People yelled. A pair of civilians vaulted over the low brick wall, heading straight at him, one shouldering a shotgun. Nathaniel dumped Mrs. McKinley onto the carriage floor, then threw his body over her and pulled the door shut.

"Go!" he shouted at the driver. "Go!"

Mrs. McKinley lay sprawled beneath him, but he jerked upright, looking out the window at the yard. Caroline was screaming and huddled behind the wheelchair, and flower petals drifted in the air like snow. Marine guards tackled the men, but one of them hurled red paint at the door of the hospital.

The carriage reached the street, and the horses gained speed, the yard disappearing into the distance.

"Are you all right, ma'am?" he asked.

She looked up at him in a combination of fear and horror. "I'm all right. Are you?"

Something warm trickled down his neck, and he touched it, his fingers coming away bloody. He'd been hit. Strange, he hadn't felt the pain until now. A few pellets of birdshot rolled off his suit jacket. He pulled away so the blood wouldn't drip on her.

"I'm fine," he said. He grasped Mrs. McKinley's arms to heft her up onto the bench. The roar of blood in his ears pounded like a drum, and perspiration covered his body.

He started to shake, finding it hard to breathe. He'd done his job. The first lady was safe. He looked out the window, but the hospital was no longer in view. He'd abandoned Caroline and the others, but he'd done his job.

~⁂~

It took less than ten minutes to get back to the White House, the carriage careening through the streets at breakneck speed. Someone must have telephoned ahead, for members of the staff and Dr. Tisdale awaited their arrival. Mrs. McKinley was unharmed but given a sedative nevertheless.

Sullivan immediately briefed Nathaniel on what happened in the hospital yard. The two protestors were tackled by members of the Marine band. Both men rambled about war atrocities and the blood on President McKinley's hands. They'd obviously hoped for a shot at the president, but when it was clear he wouldn't be there, they settled for a shot at his wife. The president had cut short his trip to the Treasury and was already back home, comforting his wife, whose nerves were still tightly wound despite the sedative. Caroline and Rembrandt arrived home minutes later, both shaken but unharmed.

Not so Nathaniel. He'd been hit with a spray of birdshot. It hadn't been able to rip through his wool suitcoat but caused a mass of wounds on his exposed neck and left hand. Dr. Tisdale cleaned the wounds and spread a bandage over the side of his neck. The skin on his hand was torn and swollen. The doctor insisted on putting his arm in a sling to keep the hand elevated and close to his chest.

Nathaniel stayed in his office late that night, nervous energy making it impossible to relax. Besides, he needed to write a new rule forbidding any alterations to a meeting with the president without written approval from the Secret Service. It shouldn't even require stating, but a high-ranking man like Captain Dorset had made the blunder, so it needed to be formalized in writing. The sling was on his left hand, but it still slowed down his writing.

It was after nine o'clock when someone tapped on his office door. All day he had been visited by members of the staff to congratulate him, though he didn't feel like a hero. His lack of vigilance had put Mrs. McKinley in an unsafe situation.

"Come in," he said.

It was Caroline. The fact that she was still circulating with complete freedom in the White House was another security flaw, but he'd already tried and failed to have her removed. She was dressed casually, but a spray of lilies of the valley was pinned in her hair. The lilies reminded him of those ridiculously huge bouquets of flowers he'd been forced to bring in the carriage. They'd ended up being a distraction and a security breach. He would add a ban on security agents assisting with carrying frivolous items to his list of new rules.

"I came to see how you are," she said, glancing at his sling and swollen hand.

"Fancy opera gloves won't fit," he said tersely.

"You don't need to be rude," she replied, still standing in the open doorway.

"And you could have stood up for Rembrandt when Mrs. McKinley attacked him over his vest."

She lifted her chin. "I choose my battles carefully."

"As do I."

And he wanted out of this particular battle. He was in over his head. The first lady had been within yards of a potential assassin, and her secretary consorted with traitors. Even thinking about it made his ulcer ache.

"Caroline, I'm very busy, and unless you're here to tell me that you are leaving White House employment, I'm not interested in anything you have to say."

A range of emotions flashed across her face before it finally settled into an expression of wounded anger.

"I came to see if you were all right after the stress of the day," she said. "I can see that you have enough spit and vinegar to keep you fueled for decades. Good night, Nathaniel."

Her voice radiated anger, but she closed the door with a soft click.

~ ~ ~

Caroline found it impossible to sleep that night. Every time she began drifting off, something caused her to jolt awake, the sound of shotguns echoing in her mind. She'd never been so terrified in her life as when she dove behind Ida's wheelchair, hiding like a coward. She had inanely covered her ears and squeezed her eyes shut, as though that would help her hide. She'd also screamed like a banshee, because that was what cowards did.

While she'd collapsed into mindless screaming, Nathaniel scooped Ida up like she weighed no more than a feather. He'd been so brave, but his abandonment hurt.

Logic said that Nathaniel had done exactly what he was supposed to do: protect the first lady at all costs. But the way he left her behind still stung. It was the Marine band's clarinet player who came to her rescue, darting to her side and ushering her to safety.

Thank heaven for clarinet players, or she might still be cowering in the dirt behind that wheelchair.

Back at the White House, the staff were eager to hear her side of the dramatic events. She'd sat in the basement dining area while Mrs. Fitzpatrick made her a cup of chamomile tea. When Ludmila noticed Caroline trembling, the laundress gave her a warm hug. Later, the housekeeper turned down her bedsheets and offered to bring her a cool compress.

Everyone was so kind, but nervous agitation made the thought of sleep impossible. Caroline had gone to Nathaniel's office to seek a bit of comfort from someone who had been there and might understand. Ida was being comforted by the president, and Rembrandt didn't live at the White House, so that left Nathaniel, but he was as cold and nasty as he'd been since he learned about Luke.

Despite the trauma, life went on. Gray had said some of their care packages were now getting through to Luke, and Caroline intended to send him an extra-nice one, since their shared birthday was next week.

The first thing she did the next morning was carry the box to the basement and pay the clerk a small fee to include the care package in the outgoing mail shipment. Then she went to the kitchen for breakfast.

She hadn't even taken her first bite of oatmeal before Nathaniel came barging in. His arm was still in the sling, and his neck was bandaged. She started to inquire after his health, but he didn't let her get a word out.

"What's in the package?" he demanded.

She winced, kicking herself for not taking the time to deliver it directly to a post office. Somehow Nathaniel had been informed of a package destined for Cuba, and it aroused his fear-mongering ways.

She glanced around the kitchen to see who else might overhear. Two cooks, two ushers, and Ludmila. None of them knew of Luke's plight, and she wanted to keep it that way.

"I'm sending a care package to the imprisoned," she said defensively. "I hope you don't have a problem with that."

"What's in it?"

"Peppermint sticks, some beef jerky, and a Mark Twain novel. Too wicked for you? Maybe I should swap out the Twain for a book of sermons."

His face darkened, and he scanned her attire. He obviously disapproved as he looked at her frothy lace jabot and old-fashioned cameo. "It looks like you were pilfering the first lady's wardrobe again this morning."

She hadn't pilfered! Yesterday had been unsettling, and the conservative attire made her feel composed. Yes, she'd gone to Ida's closet, for Ida generously let Caroline store some of her clothes upstairs.

"I only have eighteen inches of wardrobe space in the ladies' dorm," she defended.

"I can hear the angels weep."

Ludmila stifled a laugh, but Caroline was beginning to seethe. He *still* hadn't bothered to ask how she fared after yesterday. All he'd done was fling insults at her.

"I survived yesterday's shooting very well thanks to a brave clarinetist. Thank you for asking. Your concern means the world to me. Incidentally, I have invited my friend from Serbia to have tea with the first lady today. Should Petra come armed with a grenade or other anarchist weapons, perhaps there will be a brave clarinetist or a trombone player on hand to come to my rescue." She was being a snotty brat but couldn't help it. He still wore that expressionless mask, and she needed to crack it. She turned to Ludmila. "We all know that knights in shining armor have a limited number of damsels they are willing to save."

"I was doing my job," Nathaniel defended.

She shot to her feet. "You could have acted like you cared! I have no experience with how to behave when someone shoots at me, so I cowered in the dirt and screamed like a nitwit. It was horrible and embarrassing and frightening."

She must have gotten through to him, for he looked away and spoke under his breath. "Caroline, I'm sorry."

It was an infinitesimal budge, but it was enough. He'd done exactly the right thing yesterday. It was childish to wish he had deviated from the rules for her, but the fact that he admitted regret was enough.

"Thank you," she said, and returned to her breakfast.

Nathaniel left the kitchen without a backward glance. The war would probably be back on the next time she saw him, but at least there was still a scintilla of human warmth in him.

―――⸲⸲――――

The day went from bad to worse, for Ida was in a roaring mood. She awakened with a headache, her leg hurt, and breakfast did not agree with her. She focused her ire on the starch from the president's newly laundered shirts.

"They smell," she groused. "I won't subject the Major to foul-smelling shirts while he is sacrificing himself for the good of this country. They must all be washed and pressed again, and this time, tell that girl to do it right."

98

Ida dumped the shirts on the floor, ensuring they would need to be laundered again. That meant Ludmila would endure hours of additional work, all because Ida was in a crabby mood. Caroline swallowed back a retort.

"It will be done," she said, calmly picking up the shirts. It was the same starch that had been used for years, but Ida was still tense after yesterday's events at the Naval Hospital, and the starch was an easy target for her anxiety. She flatly refused to meet Petra to discuss funding for the girls' school, so Caroline spent the day planning dinner menus for the following week.

In the evening, she retreated to the roof of the White House to watch the setting sun and quietly pray.

Dear Lord, I want to build a school, she silently implored. *It's the only truly selfless thing I've ever done in my life. Please grant me the wisdom and the patience to see this through.*

The worries and tensions of the day began to unknot, and peace settled around her. She couldn't know if Petra's school would succeed or if Luke would ever enjoy another day of freedom, but there was dignity to be found in fighting for a cause.

She gazed at the streaks of gold from the setting sun and closed her prayer.

"Thank you," she whispered.

Twelve

Sharing a dormitory with nine other women made sleep a challenge for Caroline, especially since everyone had different work schedules. The kitchen staff were always first to rise. Caroline snapped awake as soon as Betsy, the kitchen maid whose bed was closest to hers, rose from her mattress.

It was only five o'clock and still pitch dark as Betsy and the other kitchen staff quietly dressed, then tiptoed from the dormitory. Caroline burrowed deeper into her mattress in hope of finding a little more rest.

It was not to be. A few minutes later, the patter of light footsteps sounded in the hallway, and the door squeaked open. Betsy tiptoed to Caroline's bedside and tapped her shoulder. "Caroline, wake up," she whispered. "Happy birthday."

Ludmila was still sound asleep, so Caroline kept her voice low as she rolled over to peer at the maid. "How did you know it was my birthday?"

In truth, she had completely forgotten about it, but as of five hours ago, she was twenty-nine years old.

"A gift was delivered for you last night," Betsy whispered. "Come down to the kitchen and see."

It must be from Gray. He was the only person likely to remember her birthday, and a tiny niggle of delight stirred inside. She loved presents, even if they were only from her brother.

She quickly pulled on her plainest gown and followed Betsy down the servants' staircase. The kitchen smelled good, for coffee was already percolating and Mrs. Fitzpatrick was making cinnamon rolls. The counters were filled with food for the day: crates of vegetables, stacks of bread, chickens soon to be plucked, and a bowl of eggs.

"Something arrived for me?" she asked Mrs. Fitzpatrick.

The cook nodded to the far side of the kitchen where a basket overflowing with artichokes sat on the staff dining table. Caroline stood in dazed amazement, then walked over to it, still not believing her eyes.

A card rested atop the mound of artichokes, reading simply, *Happy Birthday, Caroline.*

Luke was the only person who ever gave her artichokes, and her fingers trembled as she picked up the card. There was no signature or return address. The message was typed, so she couldn't even study the handwriting.

"You adorable fool," she whispered.

"Who sent it?" Mrs. Fitzpatrick asked.

Luke. He was the only person she could imagine doing such a thing, but she could hardly say so.

"I have no idea," she finally responded. It seemed impossible, but every instinct told her that Luke had somehow pulled this off. Maybe he had worked through Gray, who knew about Luke's tradition of giving her artichokes on their shared birthday. But if Gray was responsible for this, he would have signed the card.

She turned it over, and to her surprise, there was another typed message. *Look for a better gift on November 15.*

That was odd. November 15th didn't have any special significance for her, and it was almost a month away. Could she expect another midnight delivery?

"It's a little worrisome, Miss Delacroix," Mrs. Fitzpatrick said. "That basket wasn't here when I closed the kitchen last night, but there it sat when I unlocked things this morning. I asked the overnight guard about it, and he swore he didn't put them here."

She couldn't imagine how Luke had gotten these to her, but she needed to quit underestimating him. Over the past few years he'd been running rings around all of them. A few months ago, he even helped Gray orchestrate a prank against their family's archrival, all from his jail cell in Cuba. If anyone could figure out how to smuggle a basket of artichokes into the White House, it was Luke.

"The house is locked up tight as a drum overnight," Betsy said. "Even the door at the end of the hall leading into the kitchen gets locked to stop anyone from getting into the wine cellar when no one is looking."

That hallway had the only door into the kitchen, but slim windows high on the wall could open, letting a little natural light into the basement. Caroline ran her fingers along the windowsill and came away with plenty of dust. No one had come in through that window last night.

How could someone break into the kitchen? It was an appalling lapse in security, but she affected a casual tone.

"It must be someone on the staff," she said, picking up the basket with a bright smile. "Don't give it another thought."

But Caroline thought about it for hours. All through the morning as she answered Mrs. McKinley's mail, her thoughts constantly strayed to the basket of artichokes. It was impossible to stop the helpless smile that tugged on her mouth. It was so classically Luke. He loved pranks, and this was a good one. It had his signature all over it, even if she couldn't begin to imagine how he'd done it or what he could possibly have planned for November.

At ten o'clock she headed down to the White House mail

room, where a telephone was on hand for staff use. She had
to wait in line for it, but this call wouldn't take long. All she
wanted was to ask Gray if he was responsible for the artichokes,
but the butler at their townhouse said Gray wasn't available.

"He's headed to the War Department to meet with that Lieutenant Ransom fellow."

Philip Ransom was Luke's best friend. They'd been room-
mates at the Naval Academy, even though they seemed ridiculously mismatched. In contrast to Luke's roguish charm, Philip
was so bashfully shy that she'd teasingly dubbed him Philip the
Meek. It was a kinder nickname than what his fellow midshipmen at the Naval Academy called him, which was Twinkle Toes.

Philip now had the world's dullest job cataloging maps in
the basement of the War Department. Luke had never gotten
over being expelled from the academy, but she secretly thought
he was probably a lot happier for it in the long run. Otherwise
he could have ended up like Philip, who graduated first in his
class but was little more than a clerical drudge.

She hung up the telephone and raced off to intercept Gray at
Philip's office. Between the two of them, they might have insight
into how those artichokes had magically appeared overnight in
a locked and secured room.

⁓

The basement of the War Department was a bleak maze of
dimly lit corridors with the same dank smell that permeated
most basements. Caroline's heels echoed in the concrete halls
until she arrived at the map room, its door firmly closed.

She knocked. A moment later Philip Ransom opened it, looking as thin and pale as ever. He was a handsome man, with a
lanky frame and blond hair clipped to military precision, but he
suffered from the pallor of being trapped in a basement all day.

"Caroline," he said in surprise. "Come in. Your brother is
here."

Gray rose from behind the worktable as she entered the room, but a crate of rolled maps clogged the space between them. Philip dragged the crate aside to clear a path, accidentally bumping into a coat tree. It wobbled, but he managed to catch it before it crashed to the ground. In the past few months, this cramped map library had become their war room as the three of them strategized ways to mitigate Luke's dilemma. She didn't know how Philip could stand working in this overstuffed, windowless room, but for now she appreciated its privacy.

"Happy birthday." Gray smiled as he stepped around a floor globe to kiss her cheek.

"Thank you," she replied. Gray held a chair for her at the single table. "Did you perhaps remember it with a particularly unique gift?"

He quirked a brow. "That's a little forward, even for you. Of course you're getting a gift, but it isn't wrapped yet."

"I'm speaking about the twenty-nine artichokes that mysteriously appeared in the White House kitchen this morning."

Gray's jaw dropped. It took a lot to render him speechless, but the artichokes did the trick. After a moment, he found his voice. "How did he pull *that* one off?"

"So it wasn't you?"

"It wasn't me." Gray met Philip's eyes across the table. "Philip? Do you know anything about this?"

"I have no idea what you're talking about."

Philip was so squeaky clean, he wouldn't know how to lie if given a script and acting lessons. Besides, artichokes smuggled into the White House in the dead of night was a classic Luke stunt, not something from Philip the Meek.

She told Philip how Luke began gifting her with artichokes from the time they were children, and he confessed to being equally baffled as to how the artichokes could have appeared in a locked White House room.

She showed Gray the back of the note. "Does November 15th mean anything to you?"

He thought for a moment but shook his head.

"It's a Tuesday," Philip offered. "And it's my parents' anniversary. Aside from that, I can't think of anything special."

She would simply have to wait until next month to discover the surprise, even though every nerve ending in her body tingled with curiosity. But more importantly, she wanted an update on Luke.

She turned to Gray. "Did Luke really fire the attorney you hired for him? Again?"

"He really did," he said, the frustration palpable in his voice.

"Hire him back."

Gray shook his head. "Luke swears he's turned over a new leaf and wants to accept his punishment with no excuses and no defense."

That didn't sound like Luke, and she swiveled her gaze to Philip. "You must know people in high places. Who is the best person to start negotiating a plea deal with?"

Philip shrugged. "If Luke doesn't want to cooperate, we aren't going to get anywhere."

How could her daredevil brother become such fierce friends with the timid, rule-following Philip Ransom? She fought to keep her voice serene. "Philip, please understand that I am prepared to unknot that tie around your throat and use it to strangle you unless *you* cooperate."

Philip flinched. "I don't know anything!" he squeaked. "I report to the officer in charge of navigation, and he's got even fewer connections than I do."

"What connections do you have?" Gray asked, leaning forward.

"I know *her*," he said, pointing at Caroline. "I think knowing the first lady's secretary is pretty highfalutin." He accidentally knocked a slide rule to the floor, and he grimaced when the tiny screw securing the cursor rolled off. "Drat, this is my favorite slide rule," he muttered, trying to fit it back into place. It was hopeless. He was all thumbs.

"Give it to me," she sighed. If Philip's head wasn't attached by flesh and bone, he'd probably lose it too.

"You're both invited to my house for dinner tonight," Gray said. "I've got a new variety of paprika I'd like your opinion on."

Caroline wasn't free to escape the White House, and Philip didn't seem any more eager.

"I've got a dance class tonight," he said, which surprised them both. Philip seemed too timid to venture into something so engaging. "Mrs. Barclay's finishing school always needs men to partner with her students. I earn a little extra income."

"Are you in need of funds?" Gray asked.

"The money is welcome," Philip replied, not meeting anyone's eyes.

Gray leaned forward, his face even more serious than usual. "Philip, if you need money, come to me. I can help with investments that will be easier than taking second jobs at night."

"Stop it, Gray. You're embarrassing him." She returned Philip's slide rule with the cursor back in place, and he sent her a grateful smile but sobered quickly as he rotated the slide rule in his hands. It suddenly seemed as if a world of sadness overcame him.

"Actually, the dance classes help get my mind off Luke," Philip finally said. "I feel so helpless. Sometimes I just need to forget."

Her heart turned over and she felt rotten about teasing him, because Luke's arrest had hit Philip hard too. The three of them had become extraordinarily close over the past few months, and they were learning together how to cope with this new and terrible feeling of despair.

And if the president didn't win the election in November, they would be more helpless than ever.

As election day drew near, it consumed all of Nathaniel's waking hours. In two weeks, the president would be casting his vote in his hometown of Canton, Ohio. That meant guarding the entire presidential party on the train to Ohio and then during the four-day visit.

Nathaniel had never been to Canton and would be forced to lean on the local police for help. Security on election day would be a nightmare, with thousands of people swarming around the president, and potential assassins surely salivated at the chance to strike during a high-profile event. Planning for the upcoming train ride and the festivities in Canton required all his attention, and yet here he sat, silently fuming over the latest outrage from Caroline Delacroix.

This morning's kitchen break-in should have been reported immediately. He could forgive her for waiting until the household was awake. He could even overlook the delay while she conducted her regular morning check-in with the first lady.

But first she'd paid calls around town, then had lunch with the household staff, then consulted with the cook about some menus. In the afternoon she hosted a tea alongside the first lady and a group of local suffragettes.

Unbelievably, she then took a leisurely stroll in the conservatory for almost an hour. An hour! He fumed, giving her all the rope she needed to hang herself. But instead of taking two minutes to write him a note about the unauthorized access someone in her circle had orchestrated to deliver a basket of artichokes, she headed upstairs to change for dinner. Like many rich people, she indulged in the affectation of dressing for dinner. Dinner was a small affair tonight, with only the president's chaplain and a few of his old army friends in attendance. In light of Caroline's birthday, she had been invited as well.

Nathaniel waited in the staff stairwell to catch her before

she could sashay into dinner as though she hadn't a care in the world. She looked typically spectacular as she glided down the staircase. He blocked her path.

"Happy birthday," he said without smiling.

"Thank you. Such heartfelt good wishes mean so much to me."

She tried to angle around him, but he shifted and blocked her again. "When did you intend to report the break-in last night?"

"Have we determined it was a break-in? That must be distressing for you."

"Who gave you the artichokes?" He knew about her brother's tradition of giving her artichokes from the day he'd eavesdropped on her and Ludmila in the greenhouse. He wanted to see if she'd volunteer the information, but as usual, she evaded him.

"I have no idea," she said casually.

"How did they get into the locked kitchen?"

She sent him an abashed smile and shrugged. That probably worked on her parents, but never him. Everyone in this house had a duty to report potential lapses in security. This was a big one, and she hadn't raised the alarm. He only learned of it because the cook thought to warn him—*after* Caroline suggested to the entire kitchen staff to pay it no mind.

That smug expression annoyed him, but he wouldn't let it show. By firing a steady stream of probing questions from different angles, he'd shake her composure eventually, and she'd let something slip.

"Why artichokes? The Greeks used them as a symbol of hope. What are you hoping for?"

She rolled her eyes.

"Who is the 'adorable fool'? Mrs. Fitzpatrick heard you say it."

"Don't you think giving a huge basket of artichokes is a little on the foolish side?" she asked.

"No. I think it's something a felon and a traitor might do. Something you have some experience with."

The humor evaporated from her face. "You can leave my brother out of this. He's safely locked up and not prowling around White House grounds."

"A relief to all loyal Americans. What's going to happen on the fifteenth of November?"

"I have no idea."

"It was on the note, and I think you do know. What other birthday traditions do you have?"

She lifted her chin with a lady-of-the-manor expression. "People are nice to me. We treat each other with respect and good cheer. There are no insults to my family and no slurs on my character. Those would be the main things."

"That's what happens on your birthday. What sort of November 15th traditions do you have?"

He was getting to her. The veneer was starting to crack. "We yank off our clothes, drink whiskey, and dance around a bonfire. Don't blame me if you have lousy security. No one knows how those artichokes got into the kitchen, but that's a poor reflection on you, not me."

The comment set him back on his heels, mostly because she was correct. He drew a steadying breath. Everything he knew about human nature indicated that Caroline was loyal to the McKinleys and that she believed her brother to be innocent. In all likelihood she was wrong about her brother, but that meant she deserved pity, not anger. He needed to do better.

"We are in for a challenging few weeks," he said. "In terms of security, it will be the most dangerous since I joined the White House. I would appreciate your cooperation in helping me protect the first family."

"Of course," she said tightly.

He owed her more than a begrudging offer to bury the hatchet. Maybe he wasn't born to the manner, but he was an honorable man who treated women with respect. Caroline could get on his last nerve, but that was his shortcoming, not hers.

"And I'm sorry for acting like a wet blanket," he said. "Please forgive my lapse in temper."

She assumed a mask of polite serenity, the one she wore when Mrs. McKinley was at her worst. "All is forgiven," she said as she lightly waltzed past him.

He didn't believe her and felt only shame for his loss of control whenever she was near.

Thirteen

Nathaniel arrived at the train station well ahead of their departure for a final inspection of the private railcars that would carry the president and his team to Ohio. He spotted the first problem from a hundred yards away. Annoyance simmered as he strode toward the eight-car caravan where Caroline was directing workers to hang patriotic bunting on the outside of the train.

"Unacceptable, Miss Delacroix," Nathaniel said as he tugged on the fabric nailed to the window of the presidential sleeper car. "You might as well hang a bull's-eye and invite people to shoot through the window. These cars need to look as nondescript as possible."

"Not everyone hates pomp and circumstance as much as you," Caroline said.

He asked a station attendant to bring him a claw hammer so he could pull the nails holding the bunting in place. Once it was down, he began inspecting the interior of the cars designated for the presidential party. There was a dining car, a passenger car, a lounge car, two sleeper cars for the staff, and a private sleeper for the McKinleys. It would be a thirty-six-hour journey that would deliver them to Canton a full day ahead of the election.

The good news was that Wilkie had promised to transfer Nathaniel as soon as the election was over. The plan for securing the White House was completed and submitted. New guards had been trained. It was time for him to leave.

Caroline would become someone else's problem. He could no longer be rational about her. It had been nice to have a friend and a confidant inside the White House, but he shouldn't have let her get to him.

Even though she annoyed and frustrated him, he already missed her.

Caroline felt like a wide-eyed innocent as she helped Mrs. McKinley move into the private sleeping car, for it looked like someplace royalty would live. The sitting area had walls of polished cherrywood, embellished with sumptuous brass fittings and velvet upholstery on the furniture. A partition created a sleeping room complete with a king-sized bed and a private marble-tiled bath.

"This bed is almost as comfortable as the one at home," Ida said while testing the mattress.

After hanging Ida's gowns in the wardrobe, Caroline unpacked other personal articles. She propped an anniversary photograph of the McKinleys on the bedside table along with a bowl of Ida's favorite mint candies and a box of the president's cigars.

Caroline had forgotten to bring a box of matches for the president. He never smoked in public, but he enjoyed a nightly cigar after dinner. Rummaging through her purse, she found her own match case and set it beside the president's cigars. It had been six weeks since she'd indulged in a cigarette, but she'd brought a few in case the craving became unbearable during the trip.

Ida caught a glimpse of them in her purse. "Don't tell me you're still smoking."

"I won't be this week," Caroline said. "I just donated my entire supply of matches for the good of the nation."

Mrs. McKinley gave an approving nod. "You must abstain for more than a week. This battle must be a lifelong commitment. Men don't like a woman who smells like an ashtray."

"I don't smell like an ashtray." After all, she brushed her hair, spritzed on rose water, and took a mint each time she indulged in a cigarette.

"I can always tell when you've been smoking."

"No, you can't."

"Oh yes, I can. It's not ladylike, Caroline." Ida limped toward the sitting area and lowered herself onto a chair, gesturing for Caroline to join her. She reached into her bag of knitting and began to work on a baby bootie. "It isn't natural for a woman your age to still be single. You need to stop smoking, and please, don't speak so directly to men. You'll scare them off."

"*You* always speak to men in a direct manner."

"But I'm already married, so there's no need for me to worry about it! You don't want to be an old maid," Ida cautioned. "Are there no men in Washington who appeal to you?"

Nathaniel immediately sprang to mind. He had a famously reserved and puritanical comportment, but there was a passionate side quietly smoldering just beneath the surface. As much as he pretended indifference, she sensed it every time his eyes tracked her with carefully restrained intensity.

"I'm not interested in any man while I have commitments in the White House."

Ida smiled. It was the right thing to say, for Ida expected Caroline's full attention until the last hour of the last day of the McKinley administration.

Sleeping quarters on the train for the staff were only curtain-covered berths, but Caroline was thrilled with the dining accommodations because everyone would dine alongside the McKinleys. Two long tables filled the center of the dining car, with another for the buffet at the end.

By morning, the train had crossed into Ohio, but they were all treated to a full breakfast in the dining car. Caroline filled a plate for Ida while everyone else served themselves and ate together without regard to wealth or status. The president sat next to the White House clerks, and Ida sat beside junior guards. The delicious scent of bacon and scrambled eggs filled the traveling caravan, silverware clattered, and laughter was plentiful. In a few hours they would arrive in Canton, and the air hummed with excitement as the train sped through the rainy countryside. This was their last opportunity to relax before the whirlwind of election day tomorrow.

Caroline circulated to chat and refill everyone's coffee cups while Rembrandt took impromptu photographs of people as they mugged for the camera.

The only gloomy one in the group was Nathaniel, whose grim expression sucked all the energy from his corner of the railcar. Rather than join the others at the table, he had curled up in the sitting area on the far end of the car. The corners of his mouth turned down as he scribbled in his notebook.

"Why don't you join the rest of us at the table?" Mrs. McKinley asked him. "You can't protect my husband if you're fainting from hunger."

Nathaniel glanced up. "I ate before everyone else was up. I'm fine."

He didn't look fine. He looked tense and moody, and he was making Mrs. McKinley nervous. If possible, his mood darkened even further as the train arrived in Canton. He was always edgy when guarding the president outside the White House, but Caroline wasn't going to let him spoil her day.

Canton was charming. Prosperous storefronts, spacious parks, and manicured front lawns spoke of solid respectability. At the Canton train station, townspeople waved American flags and applauded for the town's most famous resident. Even from inside the train, Caroline heard a brass band playing "Hail to the Chief."

The president helped his wife stand, but before they could exit the car, Nathaniel stopped them.

"I need to meet with local security first," he said.

It seemed a shame to disappoint the crowd who'd been waiting for this moment, but the president nodded. Nathaniel and Sullivan left the train to confer with a uniformed police officer who stood just ahead of the rope line holding back the throngs of people. The policeman gestured to the row of guards who surrounded the depot, and whatever he said must have reassured Nathaniel, because he immediately turned to meet Caroline's gaze through the train window and gave a brusque nod.

"We can go," she said, eager to step into the crisp autumn air.

The crowd cheered as McKinley emerged onto the platform, waving both hands above his head and grinning broadly. The president waded into the crowd, shaking hands and even greeting some of the men by name. This was precisely the sort of thing that ratcheted Nathaniel's paranoia to monstrous proportions. His face was tense, his eyes constantly scanning the crowd, and his hand was on the butt of his exposed pistol.

Mrs. McKinley was eager to get home. As soon as the president freed himself from the throng of well-wishers, they headed toward the carriages that would drive them to the McKinleys' house.

Except Nathaniel wouldn't let them leave the station.

"The police escort I requested hasn't arrived," he said tightly. He and Sullivan herded the entire presidential party into the lobby of the train station, which had been cleared of all civilians. "You'll need to wait here until the local police arrive."

Chanting from the crowd outside could be plainly heard, but all this commotion was stressful for Ida. Caroline held Mrs. McKinley's arm and guided her toward a chair by the window. They managed only two steps before Nathaniel slid in front of them.

"You'll have to sit near the back," he said. "I don't want you being seen through the windows."

"This is utter nonsense," Ida insisted. "Do you think someone is going to shoot me through the window?"

"It would be safer on the far side of the lobby, ma'am," Nathaniel said.

Ida banged her cane on the floor. "I want to see my people. We don't need a police escort. Everyone loves us in Ohio."

"Let the man do his job, Ida," the president said calmly, then returned to conversation with George and Sven.

Caroline scrambled for a topic to distract Ida as they sat near the back wall of the lobby. "What is the first thing you will do once you're back in your own home?"

Ida clasped a hand over her chest. "My own home," she said wistfully, savoring the words. "I can hardly believe I'm finally back. I love every room and window and spigot of that house. I can't wait until the Major and I can return for good."

God willing that won't be for four more years.

"They're here," Nathaniel said tensely as a squad of two dozen mounted police officers finally arrived.

Caroline helped Ida board a carriage, then climbed in too. It was a three-mile ride to the McKinley home, with the police escort riding alongside the carriage and well-wishers lining the streets, waving flags and shouting good cheer.

The McKinleys lived in a two-story frame house with bay windows and an expansive front porch. The house had been draped with patriotic bunting, and a barbershop quartet stood ready to welcome them.

"It's so good to be home," Ida said, her voice trembling with exhaustion as she descended from the carriage. "Do you smell that? Those are my fine Ohio viburnum shrubs. Oh heavens, it's wonderful to finally be home."

Then, unbelievably, Nathaniel had to be a fly in the ointment again.

"Please wait here while I clear the building." He held out an arm to block Ida, then turned to stride up the path and through the front door of the house. Two agents accompanied him, and one skirted the house while the other went inside with Nathaniel to look for anarchists.

"Major!" Ida said. "This is beyond ridiculous. I have been traveling for two days and am not allowed into my own home?"

"It won't be much longer now," the president said.

Caroline leaned over to George. "How long do you think this will take?"

"It looks like they're already done," George said with a nod to Nathaniel, who emerged onto the front porch and gestured for them to come forward.

"That wasn't so bad, was it?" President McKinley chided Ida as they started walking up the front path. Caroline and George walked several paces behind but could still hear Ida fuming.

"I am nearing my limit with that man," she said.

"Now, dear—"

"He's blunt and suspicious and I don't like the way he's always hovering."

George leaned in to speak quietly. "Are you on her side?" he asked casually.

"He's making her needlessly anxious," she whispered back but smiled and nodded to the throngs of people who stood respectfully behind the fence lining the yard. All of them seemed so proud of their local son, but was it possible some disgruntled person had traveled all the way to this idyllic town to cause trouble?

She scanned the faces in the crowd and wondered. The king

of Italy probably hadn't suspected anything when he boarded his carriage with a group of friends.

She shook off the worries. She would not allow Nathaniel's obsessive mistrust of ordinary people to mar her day.

———∾———

Nathaniel tried to let the first lady's belligerent comments roll off his back as he and Sullivan moved from room to room inside the house, but it was getting hard, since Sullivan wouldn't let him forget it.

"She really hates you," Sullivan chided.

"She didn't like me any better the day I got her away from the shooter at the Naval Hospital. We just need to do our job."

He strode toward the dining room at the rear of the house. He needed a complete plan for security in place before tomorrow's election. It was a surprisingly modest house, the ordinary two-story home of a government lawyer, which was how William McKinley once earned his living.

While inspecting the ground floor, Nathaniel overheard Caroline and George planning the election day festivities. Weather permitting, President McKinley would spend most of the day on his front porch welcoming any visitor who wanted to shake his hand. That meant more guards at the base of the walk, because Nathaniel wanted every visitor frisked before approaching the porch.

The hardwood floors creaked beneath his feet as he headed into the office, a hint of cigar smoke and musty books in the air. It was a corner office with a desk, a hand-knitted blanket draped over the chair, and windows on two walls, both screened by overgrown bushes.

"Get those bushes trimmed way back before the gathering tonight," he told Sullivan.

"Absolutely not!" The first lady stood in the doorway, her

face grim. "My father planted those bushes back in 1865, and they are not to be tampered with."

"They're a security hazard."

"My viburnum bushes are nonnegotiable," Mrs. McKinley bit out. "No one in Canton would hurt the Major. He is beloved here."

She limped down the hall, no doubt carrying this latest outrage to her husband. How a man as congenial as William McKinley could tolerate a harridan like that all these years was a mystery.

Nathaniel breathed a sigh of relief once she was gone. The dining room still needed to be inspected, but as he crossed the front hall toward it, a photograph snagged his attention, seizing his heart like a fist.

The girl in the photograph looked like Molly. He didn't even have a picture of his little sister, but the girl in the portrait looked so much like her that it hurt. Brown hair, large eyes, and an impish smile.

He couldn't help himself. He picked up the photograph. If he unfocused his eyes, he could almost imagine it *was* Molly. Would this pain never stop?

"That was our daughter."

It was the president who spoke, standing directly behind him with Mrs. McKinley on his arm. Nathaniel swallowed, embarrassed to be caught handling a personal item, but neither of them seemed affronted. The McKinleys had had two daughters. One died in infancy, but the other lived to be a lively little girl before typhoid took her.

Nathaniel set down the photograph. "She looks like a delightful child."

"She was," President McKinley said. To Nathaniel's horror, the president's lip trembled, and it looked as if he was about to weep. He let out a deep sigh, and his shoulders sagged. "Forgive me," he said in an unsteady voice. "It has been a trying day."

Ida reached up to cup her husband's jaw and turned his to face her. "God knew best, William," she said gently.

The president managed a sad smile as he gazed down at his wife, a look of resignation on his face. The connection between them warmed and strengthened, and as Nathaniel watched, it seemed as if the president drew strength from his wife.

The pair headed upstairs to change into dinner attire, and Nathaniel watched them go. Mrs. McKinley's crippled leg slowed their progress, but even so, it seemed as if the president was still leaning on her. It was the first time he'd ever seen the president turn to his wife for support, and it was a surprise.

After they disappeared into the upstairs bedroom, Nathaniel was alone in the hall. He looked back at the photograph of a girl so like Molly it hurt.

Did God know best? It had been twenty years since Molly had died, but he doubted this choking sense of regret would ever ease. He felt unmoored and exhausted from battling the undertow of regret, made worse by his responsibilities to guard the president. He had only a few more days before he could be free of this assignment and return to life as an ordinary detective.

This feeling of being stretched beyond his limits was becoming more common, and oddly, Caroline Delacroix was the best remedy. The moment she came into view, he felt grounded and energized by a spark of electricity that jolted him back to earth. He both mistrusted and craved the way she made him feel.

Whether McKinley won or lost tomorrow's election, Nathaniel was going to be a free man soon, and then he could figure out what to do with this mass of complicated feelings for Caroline.

Fourteen

It was election night, and Caroline's shoes pinched, her corset was too tight, and her face hurt from smiling, but what a privilege to help host this party tonight. The McKinley house was crammed to the gills, for every local official in northeast Ohio wanted to attend. A team of hired cooks had prepared a steak dinner for those dining inside, while hot chocolate and caramel apples were given to well-wishers who gathered on the front lawn. The mayor, the governor, and the local congressmen were all at the party, but the president insisted that plenty of local townspeople be invited as well. The miracle of modern telegraphy meant that they expected election results sometime around midnight.

It was hard for Caroline to enjoy the cozy warmth and celebration knowing that, at this very moment, Luke was alone in his cell. This election was surely the most consequential one of her life.

Her own anxiety didn't matter. Instead, she circulated among the guests, serving hot buttered rum and witty conversation, and doing her best to keep the mood light as the hour grew late and everyone anticipated the arrival of the telegram.

Throughout the night, she sensed Nathaniel, always in the

background but never far from the president. Her feet ached from wearing heels for the past sixteen hours, but more than anything, she craved a cigarette. Almost every man gathered here tonight held a pipe, a cigar, or a cigarette. The combination of exhaustion, election night jitters, a fine meal, and watching others indulge created a storm of longing. It had been six weeks since she'd had a cigarette, but tonight the craving came roaring back. A few minutes in clean, fresh air would help.

Ida sat enthroned in her chair with both of her nieces beside her. She had a glass of wine and a smile on her face. Caroline crossed to her.

"Is there anything you need from me? I'd like to step outside for some air."

Ida cheerfully waved her away. "Go, go. This place smells like a smokestack."

Never were truer words spoken. Caroline grabbed her cloak and made a beeline for the door to the back garden. It was chilly and dark outside, her breath turning to wisps in the moonlight. Her lungs filled with cold air, the scent of wet peat and old leaves soothing her restless spirit. Part of her still wanted a cigarette, but she took in another deep breath, trying to convince herself the fresh air was better.

"Are you alone out here?"

She whirled to see Nathaniel standing on the back stoop, watching her.

"Must you creep up on me?"

He stepped closer, looking around the darkened garden. "Not creeping, but I saw you leave and you looked upset. I wondered why."

She hugged herself. How could she tell this man that her entire world hinged on what happened in the next few hours? Luke's freedom hung in the balance, and even though it looked as if McKinley would win, she couldn't take it for granted.

"I know you don't like it when I speak of my brother, but a lot is riding on this election for me. At times like these, I could really use a cigarette." She drew a bracing breath of cold air and put on an overly confident demeanor. "But I shall be strong," she tossed off. "A Puritan. I shan't indulge in the dreaded crutch of tobacco. I shan't even take advantage of the moonlit night and fling myself at you again."

Even in the dim light she could see the flush staining his cheeks. "I thought you had forgotten that night."

"A passionate kiss from a handsome man? You must think me far worldlier than I am. You are only the third man I've ever kissed."

He seemed taken aback. "I can't believe that."

"Why not?"

"Well," he stammered. "You're very beautiful. Popular . . ."

"I scare men away."

"That too, surely," he admitted, blushing madly but trying not to laugh, and somehow that made him even more attractive.

"I confess to having a wild streak in my youth, but it mostly amounted to trailing after Luke to carouse at opera houses, boating races, and the like. On our sixteenth birthday, Luke and I placed a bet to see who could get kissed first before the end of the day. I won when I asked the minister at our local church to kiss me, and he did."

"A *minister?*" Nathaniel asked in appalled marvel.

"Indeed! I've always had a thing for serious, sober men. My father found out about it and refused to tolerate a courtship, saying I was too young, and he was right. I still won the bet with Luke, though. Then a few years later, I got into more trouble when I dallied with the assistant secretary to the army. He was thirty-eight and I was nineteen. My father took it badly, and I was banished to a finishing school in Switzerland. I was never half as wild as my reputation. Those were the only two men I've kissed until that night on the staircase."

Nathaniel looked like he wanted to melt into the ground. "I sincerely hope I didn't overstep. . . ."

He looked so mortified, she wanted to comfort him. It *had* hurt a little, the way he froze her out so swiftly after learning about Luke, but it felt like a million years ago now.

"Oh, hush," she teased. "I survived your heave-ho perfectly well. You're not *that* irresistible to the female hearts of the world."

The tension faded from his face, and a hint of the old comradery returned, and she wished they could be like this always. It felt good to have a friend like him, even if she secretly longed for more.

The sound of a galloping horse approached the house. They couldn't see the rider, but the hoofbeats stopped near the front door, and footsteps thudded on the porch steps. Her heart seized, for this was surely the arrival of the telegram.

"I'll bet this is it," she whispered.

"Probably," Nathaniel said. "Are you going to be all right? You look pale."

She'd be all right. No matter what happened, she would figure out a way to get Luke free, but it would help if the president was an ally. She twisted her hands, hearing the front door open and silence descend on the people gathered inside.

Then a cheer. A roar and clapping and foot-stamping came from inside. Champagne corks popped, and people shouted congratulations and huzzahs.

She collapsed onto the stone bench, doubling over and drawing deep breaths of air. Nathaniel dropped to the bench with her. "Are you all right?" he asked. "Caroline?"

She couldn't even speak, just nod, for Luke still had a chance.

Fifteen

The day Nathaniel returned to Washington, the weight of responsibility began to lift. He had designed a plan to secure the White House and keep the president safe while traveling. He could leave the job with a clean conscience. All he needed was Wilkie's signature on his transfer papers, and then he could turn them in to the Secretary of the Treasury and begin his new assignment back in the counterfeit division.

Except Wilkie was being difficult. His wedding anniversary was tomorrow, and he wanted to go shopping for a gift. Nathaniel needed to turn these papers in today, or his transfer couldn't take effect for another month.

Refusing to be put off, he followed Wilkie through half a dozen shops in search of the perfect gift for Mrs. Wilkie. After unsuccessful trips to a jeweler, a silversmith, and a milliner, they were now visiting a perfume store, where Wilkie sampled countless bottles of overpriced imported perfume.

Perfume! This was a man who had once wrestled a bear and waded into a gang of rioting strikers in Chicago. Now he sampled perfume with an embarrassing level of fascination. He spritzed a bit onto a paper card and wafted it before his nose, looking faintly disappointed.

"What do you think of this one?" Wilkie asked, holding the paper toward Nathaniel. They were probably the only two men to ever grace this frilly shop. The walls were covered in lavender fabric, and the glass counters were decorated with floral arrangements.

"I think it's magnificent and your wife will adore it. Now, how about you sign this transfer request?" Nathaniel said, setting the paper on the counter. "I've even brought the pen."

Wilkie ignored the form and slid the bottle back toward the pretty female clerk. "The bottom notes are musky and alluring, but the lilac top notes . . . well, it smells like something my grandmother would have worn. What else have you got? What fragrance sells the moment you offer it? Price is no concern. My wife has endured a year of monstrous neglect from me, and I am of a mind to buy something special."

The clerk shrugged. "Our best-selling perfume comes from Kentucky. A blend of rose and night-blooming jasmine. It's not terribly expensive, but the ladies love it."

Wilkie looked skeptical. "Kentucky?" he muttered. "It's going to be hard to impress Jennette with something from Kentucky, but let's have a whiff."

While the clerk reached for a bottle, Nathaniel slipped the document forward. "If you sign this now, I can still get it submitted ahead of the monthly deadline."

"Not now. I'm shopping."

Nathaniel's head felt ready to explode. "We discussed this. You agreed when I took the job that I could be off the hook after the election. The only way that happens is if I get this form turned in."

The clerk returned with a round bottle, and Wilkie looked skeptical as she lifted the stopper, but his face morphed into pure joy the moment he waved it beneath his nose.

"This is it!" he exclaimed, then leaned in for another sniff, taking a moment to process the scent. "I think I smell a blend of rich tuberose and jasmine . . . but something else to lighten the floral scent. Pears? Or perhaps a citrus base?"

The clerk looked gobsmacked. "I have no idea," she admitted. "All I know is that a lot of people like it."

"Wrap it up. I'll take it."

"Glory hallelujah," Nathaniel muttered. "Would you please sign these forms?"

By now it was doubtful he could get back to the Treasury in time, but maybe if he hired a private carriage instead of relying on a streetcar, he could still pull it off.

"Don't be so hasty," Wilkie said. "I'd prefer not to speak of confidential details in public."

Nathaniel folded his arms across his chest, annoyed as the clerk took forever to wrap the box, but Wilkie finally paid the bill, and they stepped out into the frigid air. The November wind carried a hint of sleet, and Wilkie gestured to a bench beneath a pharmacy awning.

"Could you please tell me what's going on?" Nathaniel asked once they were seated.

Instead of answering, Wilkie took out a slim cheroot and lit it, taking time to slowly draw on it and blow a perfectly round smoke ring that was quickly obliterated by a chilly gust of wind. If Nathaniel didn't know better, he'd suspect Wilkie was nervous.

"Have you been in touch with George Cortelyou about the president's plans for next year?"

"No."

"No? It's very interesting. Apparently President McKinley was dismayed by how popular William Jennings Bryan proved to be in the heartland. He thinks perhaps he's been too closeted in the White House. He plans a transcontinental tour of the country next year. All the way to California and back. A three-month tour."

Three months living on a train would be pure torture, but

since Nathaniel wouldn't be there, it didn't matter. "I wish him joy in it."

"I need you to be on that train."

Nathaniel vaulted off the bench. "Absolutely not! I've drafted a comprehensive plan for securing the White House and the safety of the first family. I did exactly what you asked. Now I'm done."

Wilkie shifted on the bench, his face wincing in discomfort. "You did. But no one understands security on a moving train more than you. That sort of traveling caravan is a dangerous operation, and you're the best we have for the job."

It was true. Once he'd provided security for six months on payroll trains as they traveled to army encampments throughout the United States. He'd planned reconnaissance, surveyed routes, organized transfers, and successfully fought off two attempted train robberies, but he was done. Wilkie couldn't ask this of him. It was true that no one knew more about securing the safety of a target-rich train than he did, but he couldn't go on. Three months of constant vigilance, seven days a week, had taken its toll. Even now it felt like steel bands tightening around his chest.

"John, don't ask this of me."

"I'm asking. I don't want to, but it's the right thing to do, and we both know it."

There was no need for elaboration. If the cross-country tour didn't exist, Wilkie would gladly let Nathaniel go back to investigating counterfeit. That wasn't the case, and there was no need to dwell on impossibilities. Nathaniel stared at a street sweeper in the distance as suffocating walls closed in around him, making it hard to breathe.

"All right. I'll do it," he said.

He was in a foul mood all the way back to the White House. The weather was getting worse, with sleet turning into snow as he approached the iron railing encircling the White House lawn. As he passed through the gates, it felt like walking into a prison.

He choked back his distaste and assumed a mask of calm professionalism. He'd always been able to hide his emotions, locking them down so firmly that no one would ever suspect the cauldron boiling beneath the surface. He nodded to the sentry at the front door and exchanged pleasantries with the cook as he asked her to make a sandwich he could take to his office.

"And a glass of milk, please." It would help with the ulcer starting to burn in the pit of his gut.

The cook beamed as she bought him a glass. "What a fine young man you are! Most men want a beer with their dinner, but I like that you prefer milk. You're the sort who would never drink alcohol in the White House, even after hours."

"True," he conceded, wishing he had the ability to take life a little less seriously. He breathed a sigh of relief as he left the kitchen and headed toward his office. No one downstairs suspected his panic.

He'd just sat down at his desk to eat his sandwich when Caroline appeared in his doorway.

"Good, you're here," she said with a smile. Then it vanished. "What's wrong?"

"Nothing's wrong."

"Yes, it is. You look all stiff and grim. Has something bad happened?"

It was annoying that Caroline could see through him so easily. He had no intention of discussing this weakness with her. "What do you need?"

She smiled prettily. "I'm hoping to use your telephone. There's bad weather coming, and the line to use the one in the basement is atrocious, with people calling to cancel plans. I need to call my older brother. Please?"

He gestured to the telephone and took a bite of his sandwich. Caroline stepped forward and picked up the receiver but made no move to initiate the call.

"It's a private conversation."

At least she had the grace to look embarrassed. He glared while he finished chewing, then drained half the milk and plunked the glass down with a thud. He picked up his sandwich to carry it outside.

"Make it quick," he said as he headed into the hall. Caroline flashed him a grateful smile and closed the door behind him.

He probably ought to leave, but he was in no mood for it, so he quickly set his plate on the floor, then leaned in to eavesdrop. Caroline was lying about her reason for wanting the privacy of his office. He could tell by the way she tried to keep smiling while she talked. A dead giveaway.

The telephone connection was patched through, but it didn't sound like she was talking to her brother. It sounded like . . . *a bill collector?* All his senses went on alert. Tension was coiled in her voice as she asked for more time to come up with the funds. He leaned in closer and held his breath to catch her end of the conversation.

"All I need is two more months," she said. "Repossessing the equipment won't do either of us any good."

Was Caroline in some sort of financial difficulty? He pressed his ear to the door, eyes widening in surprise as details of the debt emerged.

"What are you going to do with thirty used typewriters?" she asked. "I'll pay the interest on the loan, but you'll have to wait for the balance. Give me until February, and I'll pay you in full."

There was another long pause while the bill collector talked, then Caroline answered, her voice quieter this time. It sounded like there was progress on negotiating a payment scheme.

Then the door yanked open, and he reared back a step.

"Eavesdropping!" Caroline gasped.

"You just stepped on my sandwich."

She kicked the plate across the hall, where it cracked against the molding. "How dare you. That was a private conversation."

"That you chose to have in my office when you already know I'm suspicious of you. I wouldn't be doing my job if I ignored it. Who do you owe money to? And why?"

She looked at him with a mutinous expression. "I don't owe money to anyone. But there's a school for immigrant women on the verge of going under, and I'm trying to intervene."

"That's who has the thirty typewriters?"

"And twenty Morse Code sounders, a dozen sewing machines, and two telephone switchboards. The school's owner opted to pay the teachers this month instead of the bill for the equipment."

This must be the school Ludmila was attending in the evenings. The guards had been alerted that she would be returning home after ten o'clock three nights a week because she was learning to use a switchboard. He hadn't realized Caroline was involved.

"Why isn't the school paying its bills?"

"Because when threadbare women eager for classes come to the school, Petra enrolls them regardless of their ability to pay. She is an idealist who knows how to dream but not how to build."

Caroline briefly outlined the problem. Their initial startup money had been spent on renovating a building. Donations helped but weren't enough to pay the bills that came due every month, and they were now eighteen thousand dollars in the hole.

"How are you going to solve it?" he asked.

"I'm going to throw a party," she said. "It's the only thing I know how to do. I'll invite a glittering crowd and hope they'll pay a lot of money to attend. It won't solve the problem, but it will help in the short-term."

It sounded like a foolhardy plan, but it was Caroline's problem, not his. He wished he didn't know this about her. It would be easier to hold her at arm's length if he thought her silly and shallow, but it was becoming hard not to admire her. He bent over to retrieve his sandwich, eager to get back to work.

"In case your brother plans another break-in at the White House, you should know I've ordered six more guards to patrol the residence on November 15th."

He wouldn't be caught off guard again.

Sixteen

Caroline was jumpy all day November 14th. She had no idea what was going to happen but suspected another midnight surprise. More artichokes? A serenade from the navy like Luke once arranged for an admiral's daughter? Most of the staff knew a surprise was coming and had been asking her about it, but Caroline could only reply that she didn't know what to expect.

"I had to order more food to feed those extra guards Mr. Trask hired," the cook said. "He told me they'd be here for three days, so that's a lot of food."

"I hope they stay longer," Betsy the kitchen maid said. "I don't mind having six more handsome young men in the building."

The police officers were different than Nathaniel's men. Less stiff and more fun, they seemed happy to be there. They took turns walking the perimeter of the house, on the lookout for anyone trying to slip inside or leave something on the grounds.

Caroline spent the day answering mail with Mrs. McKinley. Then came a dinner with two dozen Wall Street industrialists, the kind of brash, aggressive men who annoyed Mrs. McKinley, so Caroline attended the dinner to carry on conversation with the men's wives. Waiters circulated around the table, setting bowls of leek soup and pear salad before the guests.

One of the footmen leaned in while filling her water goblet. "No sign of anything yet," he whispered.

She nodded silently, but all night long it felt like she was waiting for Santa Claus or the Tooth Fairy. It was after midnight when she retired to the dormitory. Some of the women slept, but Betsy was awake and helped Caroline out of her gown, bustle, and corset.

"Mr. Trask has been pacing the ground floor all night," Betsy whispered. "Looking behind draperies and inside the potted plants. He's ordered a guard to sit in the kitchen all night long. Two more are circling the grounds. I've been watching them through the window."

Caroline tugged a nightgown over her head. "Show me."

The slope of the top-floor roof meant they only had a low window close to the floor, and she squatted beside Betsy to look through it. Thanks to Nathaniel's new lampposts, the grounds were well-lit, making the uniformed police officers easy to see. One was at the southern post, while the other paced along the perimeter of the fence.

Two more women slipped out of bed to join them at the window. "That one at the fence is from Richmond," Ludmila said. "I've never seen a man fill out a uniform so well."

The four of them watched the guards, speculating on their marital status and wondering what Caroline might expect for a late birthday present. She sincerely hoped it would not involve a navy serenade, for she didn't want anyone getting into trouble over this, and Nathaniel wasn't in a joking mood.

"Maybe whoever's sending the presents already works in the White House," one of the maids suggested. "It could be a secret admirer. Who could it be?"

"Mr. Cortelyou?" Betsy asked.

ELIZABETH CAMDEN

"Yuck," Ludmila whispered. "Can you imagine kissing a man with a mustache like that?"

"Stop." Caroline giggled. "I have to work with him every day. Please don't plant such images in my mind."

"I wouldn't mind working with Mr. Cortelyou," Betsy said. "I like a man with a fine mustache."

That triggered a discussion of whether George was kissable or not. Caroline definitely thought not, but Betsy began pointing out each guard as they crossed the lawn during their rounds, speculating on their eligibility.

"What about the head guard? Mr. Trask?" Ludmila asked. "Would he be good for kissing?"

It was a good thing it was dark so they couldn't see Caroline flush. No one asked her opinion, but all three women agreed Mr. Trask was too straitlaced to kiss.

Caroline secretly disagreed. The kiss they'd shared on the back steps during the state dinner had been the most tenderly romantic moment of her life. She contributed nothing to the speculation, but this midnight huddle by the window was fun. It made her wish she'd had sisters.

It was after one o'clock when exhaustion prompted her to surrender and crawl into bed, for she had a long day tomorrow. If some sort of birthday present was truly coming, it would arrive whether she watched at the window or not.

The next morning she rose at the same time as the kitchen maids, pulling on a dress and finger-combing her hair. She could style it properly later, but for now she needed to know if anything had mysteriously arrived overnight.

Nathaniel sat at the kitchen table, looking tired as he nursed a cup of coffee. She made a quick survey of the room, noting the bowls of eggs and a mound of oranges delivered for this morning's breakfast.

"Well?" she asked a little breathlessly.

"Nothing." He looked half annoyed, as though it was her fault he'd chosen to stay up all night.

A trickle of disappointment tugged, even though the absence of an overnight incursion was surely for the best. She didn't want anyone getting into trouble on her behalf, but a tiny piece of her longed for a hint that Luke's sense of mischief was still alive.

"I'm sorry you went to such trouble for nothing," she said as she poured herself a cup of coffee.

"It wasn't for nothing. I suspect those patrolling guards prevented another infestation of artichokes or whatever your brother had planned. Besides, the 15th has only just begun. I'll have my men patrolling tonight as well."

He didn't sound happy about it, but that was his problem, not hers. Her entire morning was spent with Ida, discussing the food to be served at the inaugural ball. Then she met with the head of the Marine band to discuss music to be played during the parade and festivities. Then an officer from the Department of the Interior wanted to confirm the route of the inaugural parade.

Throughout it all, she wondered if a gift had been delivered, but there was no sign of anything.

At dinner, the staff dining room was crowded due to Nathaniel's additional security guards. To call this space a dining room was a stretch. It was merely an open area on the far side of the kitchen with four tables, each large enough for six people. Staff came down at odd hours to serve themselves from the sideboard filled with food warmers. It was always an odd mix, as upstairs ushers wearing formal suits dined alongside the cleaning staff and gardeners.

The extra policemen took an entire table, while Betsy and Ludmila stole glances from the neighboring table. Such excitement over six young men! Hopefully tomorrow Nathaniel could ease up, and life would return to normal. As it was, he looked tired as he sat beside Sullivan, finalizing the patrol schedule for the evening.

Caroline felt his eyes on her as she walked to the sideboard and filled a plate with green beans and a slice of ham. She scanned the room, looking for a spot to sit. Sullivan noticed and slid over on the bench, leaving her just enough space on the end.

The hallway clock struck six o'clock, and three of the guards vacated their seats as they headed out to patrol. It was a good thing, for George had just arrived. Finally! It was odd to go an entire day without seeing him before dinner.

"Busy day?" she asked as he sat at the neighboring table.

He nodded. "The president and I were over at Treasury. The budget was just delivered, and it's always a monster."

That went without saying. The budget was compiled by the House of Representatives and was responsible for the entirety of federal spending for the coming year, and the president needed to know precisely what he had to work with.

"How many pages this year?" she asked.

"Over a hundred," George grumbled. "Someday the government needs to get organized. The president ought to be able to allocate funding as he sees fit, but just try wresting that power out of Congress. Humph! Instead, we've got dozens of agencies throwing their demands at Congress, where it all gets printed up, and the money is supposed to magically appear on the fifteenth of November. I have no idea how we'll pay for everything."

George continued to grumble, but Caroline looked up to catch Nathaniel's gaze. He was thinking the same thing she was. The budget! All this time they'd been looking for the delivery of a tangible gift, but the budget was the only major item to hit the White House today. Could there be something hidden in it?

"How can I see a copy?" she asked.

George looked taken aback. "They only printed three copies. One has been sent to the Senate, one to the president, and the other is still at the Treasury."

"Who has the president's copy?" Nathaniel asked.

"I do. It's locked in my desk."

Caroline stood, leaving her ham untouched. "George, I need to see it. Now. Tonight."

"I just sat down," he protested.

But Nathaniel and his agents were preparing for another tedious shift walking the grounds overnight, and if the surprise was hidden in the budget, they both wanted to know. It was a ridiculous hope, but she couldn't shake it.

Five minutes later, George was unlocking his desk. The budget was in a large box in his bottom drawer, a hundred loose-leaf papers that had yet to be bound. He handed it to her.

"I'll need it back by eight o'clock tomorrow morning," he said. "Don't let it out of your hands."

"I won't."

Anticipation hummed as she waited for George to leave, then carried the box to her desk. Nathaniel stood beside her as she lifted out the stack of typewritten pages. At least there was a table of contents. She traced her finger down the list of agencies. Agriculture, Army, Bureau of the Engraving, Consular Affairs, Court of Federal Appeals—none of these resonated with her. She didn't even know what she was looking for, but she kept searching the mammoth document. The Census, District of Columbia transportation, Education, Farm Services—

Education?

The budget allotments for education began on page forty, and her fingers shook as she lifted the pages away.

"What are you looking for?" Nathaniel asked.

She dared not answer. It was too farfetched. She didn't want to get her hopes up or look foolish. At last she found the proper page and saw rows of funds allocated for school construction, the printing of textbooks, for training teachers . . .

And for a school in Washington, DC, to train immigrant girls and women.

Her vision blurred. How could this be happening? Her breaths came in shallow spurts, and her heart surged. She clamped a hand over her chest as she blinked, struggling to see.

"Are you crying?" Nathaniel asked in amazement.

"Of course not."

She used her cuff to blot her eyes so she could see again, but yes, on line twenty-four was funding for Petra's school.

She sank into the desk chair. "Line twenty-four," she choked out, and Nathaniel leaned over to read.

Soon the corners of his mouth twitched. "Happy birthday," he said quietly.

She laughed, and he did too. What else was there to do? It was impossible to know how this had happened, but somehow Luke had managed the impossible.

She stood up and clasped Nathaniel's hand as they gazed down at the document, amazement still cycling through her, and she was glad he was there to share this moment. She squeezed his hand, and he squeezed back as electricity flowed between them. If nothing else, line twenty-four was concrete proof that her brother was an amazing man.

The next morning she sought out George for insight the moment he walked into their office.

"How does money get allocated for educational budget requests?" she asked, still a novice where the inner workings of Congress were concerned.

"There's a committee for education, headed by a fellow from Indiana. Check with him."

Preparations for Thanksgiving celebrations meant it took a maddening two days before she was able to find a few hours to escape to the Capitol. She wandered the halls of the grand building in search of Congressman Arthur Blanchard from Evansville, Indiana, the man in charge of the congressional committee for education.

Ordinary congressmen weren't afforded personal offices,

and in the long hours between meetings, they retreated to the congressional retiring rooms draped in velvet, stuffed with comfortable seating, and filled with cigar smoke. It was a masculine retreat into which no lobbyists, visitors, and certainly no women were allowed. Congressman Blanchard was heading down the white marble corridor toward the retiring rooms with a folded newspaper in one hand and an unlit cigar in the other when she found him. She grabbed his arm just before he passed through the door.

"Congressman," she said a little breathlessly, "can you tell me how the school for immigrant girls came to your attention?"

He perused her from the top of her head all the way down to her silk-encased feet. Masculine appreciation was nothing new to her, and if it snagged this man's attention, she didn't mind using it.

"And you are?" he asked.

"Caroline Delacroix, secretary to the first lady."

Recognition dawned. "Oh yes! Your brother Luke tracked me down last summer. He brought the school to my attention. It seems a worthy cause."

Luke had been arrested in June, so it must have been shortly before. It was hard to stand here and discuss her brother with a perfect stranger, but the congressman didn't notice as he launched into a monologue.

"I told him it was a losing proposition, as the federal government rarely tackles one-off schools like this, but he gave me good advice on how to pull a few strings and make it a surefire win. Very clever young man; it worked like a charm. Where is he, by the way? I haven't seen him in ages."

Caroline hesitated. Although Luke's arrest had been leaked to the press almost a month ago, she'd done some fancy footwork, and the newspaper had issued a complete retraction, for the army was still dithering about filing charges. The story never caught traction.

She evaded the question. "Knowing Luke, he's probably off courting some Russian princess or exploring the North Pole."

The congressman laughed. "Ha! Of the two, I'd vote for the North Pole. Everyone always underestimates that young man. Now, I'm off to review these proposals and indulge in a smoke. Best of luck to you with the school."

The school would be Petra's responsibility, and now Caroline could move on to planning the inaugural ball. She was good at being a hostess, but the inauguration would be the largest party in the nation, and it was going to be a daunting challenge.

Seventeen

Winter crashed into Washington with a vengeance. As December morphed into January and then February, it seemed the ice storms would never cease. The ladies' dormitory had no fireplace, and each morning Caroline shivered as she dashed to grab her warmest clothes.

The inauguration would take place on the fourth of March. Mrs. McKinley had no interest in helping plan the day, relying on Caroline and George to design the tightly choreographed schedule. A morning worship service would be followed by a procession to the Capitol for the swearing-in ceremony. While George and Sven polished the president's speech, Caroline took the lead on organizing the luncheon. Special guests would join the president for a sumptuous meal that had to be served on a compressed timetable, for the inaugural parade involving thousands of people could not be postponed for the sake of a delayed soup course.

It was going to be the largest military procession ever assembled for an inauguration, featuring five thousand soldiers. Fifteen separate marching bands and dozens of cavalry units from across the nation would participate. Cadets from the military and naval academies would march, along with regiments from the National Guard.

All of it was a security nightmare, and Nathaniel was a daily presence in their planning sessions. With hands fisted and a clenched jaw, it was obvious he dreaded the day, but never more so than when informed who the president had requested to escort him during the parade.

"Old soldiers?" he asked incredulously, pacing before George's desk.

"There will be eighty Civil War veterans to serve as the president's special escort," George confirmed.

"Eighty old men," Nathaniel said. "We expect forty thousand people crowded along Pennsylvania Avenue, and you want the president to be guarded by old men?"

George shrugged helplessly. "The president specifically asked for 'the old boys' to walk him to the reviewing stand. I have complete confidence in you, Mr. Trask. Find a way."

Find a way had been George's refrain for weeks. Whether it was how Caroline could serve a four-course luncheon in half an hour, find lodging for six hundred visiting diplomats, or stable two thousand horses, the answer was always the same. *Find a way.*

She had. All the government buildings would be closed and filled with pallets on the floors and hallways to serve as temporary barracks for the soldiers. Members of the diplomatic corps from foreign nations expected better, but there weren't enough hotel rooms in the city. Caroline braved freezing winds and ice storms to pound on the doors of private residences, looking for people willing to put up visitors from Europe, Asia, and Latin America. She pled, bargained, and flirted, and after a month, she'd secured decent lodging for six hundred visiting dignitaries.

Her biggest challenge was the inaugural ball, to be held in the Pension Building. Despite its fusty name, it was a majestic space with a three-story Italianate atrium surrounded by towering marble columns and wraparound balconies overlooking the grand hall. That meant Caroline had acres to decorate with thousands of candles, swags of bunting, and towering floral arrangements. Endless rounds of canapés and finger food would be served throughout the ball, all of it accompanied by wines and punch.

Planning the nation's biggest party was a challenge Caroline eagerly embraced, but as the inauguration drew near, her divided loyalties grew. While she planned a party, her brother languished in jail. By making herself indispensable to the president, she hoped to earn Luke a presidential pardon, but what if she didn't?

Sven de Haas was usually on hand. Now that the election was over, the president's chief strategist worried about setting the perfect tone to kick off the second term. She spent an entire afternoon bickering with him about the flags to be displayed at the ball. The president's new agenda would push for an end to American isolation, and Sven wanted as many foreign flags as American. She disagreed, insisting that the evening was an American party and the theme shouldn't be watered down.

She lost that battle, giving her a headache and the need for an hour of peace. She retreated to the White House roof for some privacy and gazed out over the bleak February landscape.

"It's just a party," she whispered. Did the president even realize how hard she'd been working, slogging through ice storms and designing a series of meals, receptions, and the inaugural ball while Ida knitted baby booties in the comfort of her parlor?

She opened the latest letter from Luke, which had arrived in yesterday's post, rereading it yet again. It was typical of all his letters: jokes about the bad food and commentary about the weather. Gray had been sending the guards money to smuggle Luke whatever reading material they could find, but it seemed the guards deliberately taunted Luke by bringing him obscure books in languages he could not read.

But they underestimated her brother, whose hungry mind devoured whatever they brought him. Yesterday's letter was proof of that.

> *The guards provided a copy of the Old Testament in Hebrew, but they failed to notice the transliteration primer for Hebrew, Latin, and Greek in the back. I'm at last putting those tedious Latin classes Dad insisted on to good use! Between the primer and comparing the text with my English Bible, I'm making solid progress on learning Hebrew. Perhaps I shall become a Hebrew scholar while imprisoned.*
>
> *Now, buck up. Even from a thousand miles away, I can feel your worries. Fear not! I am invincible.*

But Luke always said he was invincible whenever he was afraid. It was what he'd said after getting expelled from the Naval Academy, and again after their father died and responsibility for managing the family's fortune landed in his lap while Gray traveled home from across the globe. It didn't surprise her that Luke would try to put a brave face on things, even as the waters were closing over his head and he was drowning.

Most worrisome was his handwriting, for it was sloppy and uneven. His earlier letters hadn't been like that, and it worried her. If his health was beginning to fail, could she really wait for a presidential pardon?

It was time to see her lawyer again and get the process moving.

~~~

Caroline made an appointment with Mr. Alphonse, prepared to pay him a fortune to expedite the request for Luke's presidential pardon. Now that the election was safely behind him, perhaps President McKinley would be quietly willing to help.

Except her lawyer's skepticism about winning a pardon for treasonous activity remained high. He didn't even want to accept an appointment with her, but she insisted.

"Please tell me you're not here hoping to speed up your case for a pardon," he said as he gestured her to a seat across from his desk.

"Indeed I am," she replied crisply. "And I want to move quickly. No more delays."

"You have almost no chance of success," Mr. Alphonse replied. "Why are you dumping a fortune on a hopeless cause?"

She squared her shoulders. If she worried about the magnitude of the problem, she'd have given up long ago, but something about the challenge in Mr. Alphonse's gaze caught her by surprise.

"What are my options?" she asked.

Instead of answering, he went to open his office door, looked both ways, then closed it again. Rather than return to his desk, he drew a chair close beside her and lowered his voice.

"What I'm about to propose is for hypothetical purposes only. I can't suggest anything that might abuse the legal process, but there are ways that aren't entirely aboveboard that have a better shot of getting your brother out of hot water than an unlikely presidential pardon."

"Tell me."

As he outlined the plan, her eyes grew wide. A combination of hope and dread mingled as she considered the suggestion, because it might work. It would break her heart, but it might work. Luke would have to cooperate, and it would be difficult, but it had a good shot at succeeding.

"You didn't hear about this from me," Mr. Alphonse said as he returned to his side of the desk. "I was merely filling you in on how some people might handle a situation like this. Talk it over with your older brother, and if after due consideration you'd still like me to file for a presidential pardon, I shall be happy to assist. Good day to you, Miss Delacroix."

Mr. Alphonse was right. She needed to talk to Gray. She would need a lot of help and money to pull this off, which meant she needed to recruit her older brother to the cause.

~ ❧ ~

Gray had always been more like a father than a brother to her. Her earliest memory was of running across the room to fling herself into his arms when he returned from an overseas voyage. She had idolized him, but Luke's arrest threw a bomb into their relationship, for it was the woman in Gray's life who'd turned Luke in.

Annabelle Larkin was a homespun girl from Kansas who shared Gray's irrational obsession with plants, and they'd quickly fallen in love last spring. It was Annabelle's unusual closeness to Gray that brought her to the attention of the government, for they'd long suspected someone in the Delacroix household of helping the insurgency in Cuba. They pressured Annabelle to spy, and she was the one who'd turned over the evidence that condemned Luke.

Gray forgave Annabelle and married her, an outrage that still incensed Caroline. Then again, Gray believed Luke was guilty, and Caroline knew he wasn't. Gray did his best to mitigate Luke's abominable conditions in the Cuban jail, but he didn't believe in Luke's innocence, and for that she couldn't quite forgive him.

Nevertheless, she needed his help. The plan her lawyer had outlined would require a lot of money and the use of a steamship. Gray had both. She deliberately planned her visit for a time Annabelle would be out of the house.

"Caroline," Gray said warmly as he greeted her in the foyer of his house. "How are plans for the inauguration going?"

"Fine," she said briskly, heading into the parlor. For a man with obscene riches, the family townhouse where Gray lived was a modest affair, close to the harbor and furnished with well-worn antiques suited to his old-world formality.

She immediately noticed the changes that had come with his marriage. A vibrant potted sunflower was positioned on the fireplace hearth, and she scowled at it.

Gray noticed. "Annabelle grows them in the experimental greenhouse at the Department of Agriculture," he said.

Caroline turned her chair to avoid looking at evidence of Annabelle's unwelcome presence. They had business to discuss, and she needed to avoid obsessing over Annabelle's betrayal of Luke.

"My lawyer told me of a way we might be able to spring Luke from jail," she said as she tugged at the fingertips of her gloves to pull them off. "I'll need help."

"I'll give you whatever you need," Gray said instantly, but then again, he didn't know what she was about to propose.

"We need to convince Luke to change his plea," she said. "We get a lawyer in Cuba to file paperwork with the provisional government proclaiming his innocence. He'll have to come up with some sort of explanation for his initial guilty plea, but Luke is good at that. He can run rings around anyone."

Gray shook his head. "I've been begging him to change his plea from the beginning, but he refuses. He's been reading the Bible. He swears he's a new man and won't lie."

"And you believe that?" Luke had never been devout, but a fib like that would get Gray off his back. She and Luke were experts in dodging Gray's nagging, fusty ways.

"I don't know what to believe anymore," Gray said, pacing before the fireplace. "I've been trying ever since Luke was arrested to get him to fight in his defense, and he refuses."

"Maybe I can persuade him."

He cocked a brow at her. "How?"

"I'll go to Cuba and talk to him in person. If anyone can persuade him, I can."

"What then?"

"Then we pay a fortune in bail to get him released until the trial. And then we smuggle him onto the *Pelican* and overseas to freedom."

Gray's breath left him in a rush as he collapsed into a chair. "It will never work. He's guilty as sin, and they'll never grant him bail."

"The Americans won't, but he's in a Cuban jail, and they might. Their island is in tatters. Their roads and bridges and freshwater systems have all been wiped out by the war. You don't think they'd be happy to get their hands on a quick infusion of cash?"

Gray shifted in the chair, his face tense in concentration. "And then Luke makes a run for it?"

"Then Luke makes a run for it," she confirmed.

The family's steamship, a mighty cargo vessel called the *Pelican,* was currently on a run back from Madagascar, loaded down with spices and rare vanilla beans. If Luke got released on bail, he could sail away on the *Pelican*, but it meant he'd never be able to come back to the United States. He'd have to make his home in Europe or Africa or the Far East. Their family would be permanently fractured. Luke would never walk her down the aisle or spoil her children. In saving him, she would lose him forever, but it would be worth it.

"Gray, please. It's our only hope. We can still aim for a presidential pardon, but I don't think Luke can survive another four years in prison. In his last letter, it looked like he could barely hold the pen."

"It's breaking the law," Gray said.

"He's not guilty."

"I think he is."

She straightened. Unless Gray got on board with this plan,

it wouldn't go far. She drew a breath to try again, but a rattle at the front door distracted her as Annabelle stepped inside.

"Gray, you won't believe it," Annabelle said breathlessly, unwinding the world's longest scarf from around her neck. "The department just got a new shipment of cold-tolerant millet from Siberia. We begin testing the strains tomorrow. It's beyond exciting, it's—"

"We have a guest," Gray said, interrupting Annabelle's effusive praise of millet, whatever that was.

Annabelle froze, looking distinctly uncomfortable, but managed a cheery smile anyway. "How nice to see you," she said. "What a splendid gown. You always look so lovely."

"Thank you," Caroline replied stiffly. "It sounds like you are enjoying your work at Agriculture."

Caroline would be polite even if it killed her, although she'd rather bodily fling Annabelle back to Kansas. Gray had once warned Caroline not to make him choose between her and Annabelle, and she didn't want to test his loyalties.

Annabelle took a seat before the fire, and Caroline explained the rest of the plan to them both. Gray could divert the *Pelican* to Cuba and get Luke off the island without anyone being the wiser. From there, Luke could go anywhere in the world, free to make a new life for himself. He could breathe clean air and see the sky and have a real future. He might even be able to work for Gray, managing the family's spice fields in Africa and Asia.

Despite Gray's skepticism, he wanted to know more, but Annabelle's wariness was apparent.

"I want to find a solution for Luke too, but this would put both of you in legal jeopardy, and Luke is guilty. It's not worth it. He *chose* to walk down this path—"

"Bite your tongue," Caroline snapped. Luke couldn't be guilty. She knew it in her bones and would never believe otherwise unless Luke looked her in the eye and swore to it. Even then, she might suspect something, because Luke was crafty and ten steps ahead of them all. For pity's sake, he was managing to get birthday presents to her from jail!

Caroline stared at Gray, praying for his cooperation. He looked torn as he met Annabelle's gaze, some sort of unspoken communication flying between them.

"Annabelle, I need to do this," he finally said. "I'm not ready to divert the *Pelican*, but I need to take another trip to Cuba to see him. At the very least, maybe Caroline can persuade him to fight for his freedom."

Annabelle's shoulders sagged. "Whatever you think is best," she said, but reluctance was heavy in her voice.

Eighteen

Caroline's next step was to get Mrs. McKinley's permission to leave for an entire week. Her intention was to leave for Cuba the day after the inauguration, which would be perfect timing, since Washington would rest in exhaustion following the whirlwind of festivities. She mentally prepared herself as she helped the first lady with the final fitting for her ball gown.

Caroline had expensive tastes, but even she was astounded by the splendor of Ida's inaugural gown. Two seamstresses and Ludmila were on hand to help with alterations and caring for the garment while Caroline watched from the far side of the bedroom. How marvelous the gown looked! Made of cream satin, embroidered with silver thread, and lavishly embellished with crystals and pearls, the gown cost eight thousand dollars, more than most people earned in a year. If the price of that gown ever slipped out to the public, it would trigger a hail of condemnation, but there was no denying that Ida McKinley had good taste. The gown was fit for a queen and tailored to perfection.

"You look amazing," Caroline said.

"You will be the apple of the president's eye," Ludmila added with a wink at Caroline. They still worked on English language quirks, but now that Ludmila was attending night school, her English was even better.

"I suppose it will do," Ida teased in a flash of good humor. Her health was good, her husband had won a second term, and he'd just plunked down a fortune to ensure his wife outshone every other lady in the city.

Caroline only hoped Ida's good mood would last, because getting her permission for the trip to Cuba was going to be a challenge. Caroline had worked seven days a week for the past year, so a single week didn't seem like a lot to ask, but one could never be certain of Ida's mood.

Caroline worked with both seamstresses to carefully lift the dress off the first lady. It was so heavy! Or perhaps she was merely nervous. How odd it felt to be handling thousands of dollars in seed pearls and satin while preoccupied by thoughts of her brother sweltering in a jail cell.

The seamstress helped Caroline hang the dress in the wardrobe while Ludmila filled the satin slippers with wadded tissue paper. How best to raise this delicate topic? Ida was very focused on her own needs, so perhaps that was the best place to start.

"The inauguration is going to be an exhausting day," Caroline said. "I've made certain to keep the following week entirely free of commitments so you can rest."

"Humph," Ida said. "I'll probably need the following *month*. All this inauguration folderol has been exceptionally draining."

It was the perfect opening. "I feel the need for some time as well," she began cautiously. "I'd like a chance to see my brother and will need a week to make that happen."

"But your brother is right here in Washington," Ida said in confusion. "You can see him at any time."

"I was thinking of my other brother."

Ida froze. "The one in Cuba?"

"Yes."

"Absolutely not!" Ida's voice cracked across the room so suddenly that Ludmila dropped a slipper. "It's one thing to have a traitor in the family, but quite another to abandon your post on his behalf."

"As a Christian, I feel compelled to visit the sick and impris—"

"Don't 'as a Christian' me! That man is a traitor and a scoundrel and a turncoat. He deserves everything he gets!" Ida grabbed a slipper and hurled it across the room, narrowly missing one of the seamstresses. "I forbid you to leave your post. Forbid it!"

If Caroline caved before Ida's tantrums, she wouldn't have lasted a week in this job. She raised her chin and prepared to fight for what she needed. "I will fulfill every duty on Inauguration Day and will stay until the last—"

"You certainly shall! It's the very least I can expect."

That from a woman who'd spent the last two months knitting baby booties while Caroline slogged through ice and slush to find housing for six hundred visiting diplomats. Now she wanted seven days off, and she intended to get them.

"You can expect me to deliver a spectacular inauguration ceremony, a luncheon that will come off without a hitch, and an inaugural ball that will echo through the ages. After that, I'm sailing to Cuba for a week."

Ida waved a finger beneath her nose. "You're really pushing it, Miss Delacroix. Really pushing it."

"And I'll keep pushing it until I have my week of leave."

The first lady threw the other slipper, this time knocking over a vase that crashed to the floor, scattering glass shards. A tap on the door interrupted her tirade, and a guard opened it without permission, his hand on the butt of his pistol.

"Is there trouble here?" he asked.

"Oh, don't be ridiculous!" Ida shouted. "I have a bratty and disloyal secretary, but I can handle her."

"Not if you deny me leave to go to Cuba," Caroline said. "I'll quit, and you can find someone else who knows high fashion as well as me. Good luck!"

"I've been dressing myself for fifty-odd years," Mrs. McKinley yelled.

"And you've never looked nicer than since I started shopping with you."

The door to the bedroom still hung open, and three other security guards had gathered to listen.

Mrs. McKinley lowered her head and spoke in a simmering tone like a mother reprimanding a wayward daughter. "Caroline, you're asking for trouble."

"You may be right, ma'am." Her plan in Cuba was plenty of trouble, but it was time to let Ida salvage her dignity in front of the others. "I know I have duties, which is why I feel so terrible about leaving you. Your sister and nieces from Ohio have already agreed to stay on after the inauguration. Everything in the house will operate like clockwork."

Mrs. McKinley opened her mouth to retort, but they both knew it was true, and she stammered in frustration. Instead, she turned to glower at the men in the open doorway. "Oh, be on your way," she ordered.

In the end, Caroline got her permission to go to Cuba, but it was a blow to her relationship with Ida. This sort of dereliction of duty was not something the first lady was going to forget.

Nathaniel began the morning of the inauguration on his knees, praying for a calm head on this most chaotic of days. So far, this country had inaugurated twenty-four presidents without incident, but never on Nathaniel's watch, and his anxiety made sleep the previous evening almost impossible.

By four-thirty he had dressed, eaten, and headed out into the early morning sleet to patrol Pennsylvania Avenue. He walked with a dozen other guards, all looking for potential security flaws along the parade route. Members of the local police had been stationed overnight to be on the lookout for suspicious activity, but they reported no concerns. Nathaniel trusted the police but still walked the entire mile-and-a-half route to be certain all was in order.

He didn't like the president being escorted by elderly Civil War veterans, but there had been no dissuading him. Most of the veterans were in their sixties or older. Some of them walked with canes due to age and some with crutches due to lost limbs. They simply weren't adequate bodyguards, which was why Nathaniel was planting Sullivan among the old veterans, dressed like a Union infantryman and carrying two six-shooter revolvers.

Nathaniel recruited Rembrandt to make Sullivan pass for an old man. Rembrandt was in his element as he swiped talcum powder through Sullivan's chestnut hair.

"And now for a little color beneath the eyes," Rembrandt said, opening the cosmetics palette Caroline had loaned him for the occasion.

"I'm not wearing makeup," Sullivan growled.

"It's not makeup, it's a disguise," Rembrandt replied.

"Fine. I'm not wearing a disguise if it means wearing makeup."

All Rembrandt wanted to do was smudge some bluish-grey shading beneath Sullivan's eyes so he didn't look so baby-faced. They weren't trying to fool the other veterans. They just needed to make Sullivan blend in with them.

"Add some age spots," Nathaniel said, trying to block the laughter from his voice. The pained resignation on Sullivan's face had them all in stiches. Rembrandt outdid himself, tracing tiny age lines at the corners of Sullivan's eyes and adding a hint of fake jowls.

The morning began well. The prayer service ended ahead of

schedule, and the weather for the swearing-in ceremony outside the Capitol was cold but clear. At the White House, Caroline had the salad course already set out on the tables to accommodate the luncheon's compressed timeframe. Nathaniel stood guard outside the dining room but caught glimpses of Caroline as she flitted about directing the waiters, pouring tea, and helping deliver plates during the main course. Rembrandt moved his tripod and camera throughout the room to memorialize the luncheon.

They were two minutes ahead of schedule, but Caroline had one more surprise before the guests left for the parade. She took her position beside the first lady, who nodded permission. The president tapped a fork against a wine glass to get the crowd's attention. Caroline looked like the personification of elegance as she addressed the crowd.

"The first lady has arranged a small gift to thank you for helping make this a special day for her and the president. As you leave, I'll be handing out boxes with two commemorative presidential spoons, each engraved with today's date. She hopes they will help you remember this day for years to come."

Gentle applause met the announcement, and Caroline smiled warmly as she gave each departing guest a small gift-wrapped box.

The parade went off without a hitch. The crowd roared as President McKinley strode down Pennsylvania Avenue, surrounded by soldiers from his old Ohio regiment. Nathaniel watched through binoculars on the White House patio. Even from here, he could see Sullivan marching alongside the president, one hand on the butt of a pistol, but the other waving to the crowd as though he were being celebrated, not the president.

By dinner, it was all over. The crowds dispersed, and cleanup crews moved in to dismantle the viewing stands. Sullivan returned to the White House like a conquering hero, the artfully applied makeup still in place.

"I'm not washing my face for a week," he exclaimed. "I've just had the most memorable hour of my life. I felt like General Grant walking in triumph, waving to the adoring public."

"Wash up, general," Nathaniel said wryly. "The inaugural ball starts at nine o'clock, and the uniform is black tie. No cosmetics necessary."

All the president's guards needed to be as formally attired as the invited guests. Nathaniel had never worn black tie in his life and had to borrow a tailcoat from Wilkie. He wore a starched collar, a scarlet silk vest, and a slim-fitting cutaway jacket. When he examined himself in the mirror, it was impossible to see his shoulder holster and side arm beneath all the finery.

By eight o'clock he was at the Pension Building to await the arrival of the first couple and the vice president. The building was lit up like a Christmas tree, with torches flickering outside and over a thousand electric lightbulbs illuminating the inside. Nathaniel scanned the crowds that had gathered to watch.

The vice president's carriage arrived first, and Theodore Roosevelt looked typically boisterous as he sprang to the ground and then helped his wife from the carriage. Then came McKinley's carriage, and Nathaniel turned his back to it as he scanned the crowds, looking for anyone who didn't belong amidst the well-dressed partygoers.

From the corner of his eye he glimpsed Caroline as she straightened the first lady's train after leaving the carriage. It appeared Caroline's blowup with Ida had been smoothed over. He'd heard about it, of course. Everyone had heard about it, for neither lady bothered to lower her voice as the battle raged. There were no signs of stress today as Caroline and George walked a few steps behind the McKinleys toward the entrance of the building. She wore a gown of sapphire blue with cascades of ivory lace. He wished he had longer to admire her, but he had a job to do.

Music, laughter, and the scent of spiced drinks filled the air inside, but his gaze scanned the room in a pattern—all four corners of the ground floor, the corners of the ceiling, across all three balconies, and down the staircase. His gaze drifted across the guests, the ladies in shimmering fabrics and men in formal blacks.

Hours rolled by, alternating between dancing, a few speeches, and much laughter. Vague hunger pangs began tugging at Nathaniel around midnight. It was time for his twenty-minute break, and he switched positions with Sullivan. He grabbed a wedge of cheese and some grapes before escaping the crowd by heading to the top-floor balcony, where only a few people mingled.

One of them was Caroline. She stood at the railing, gazing at the crowded ballroom below. He gave in to temptation and joined her.

"You look quite dashing in your finery," she said.

The collar was stiff and uncomfortable, but he liked that she noticed. They spent a companionable few minutes in total silence while he ate. Exhaustion was getting to them both, and it was nice to simply enjoy the silent comradery.

But eventually he asked the question that had been burning in his mind. "Are you and the first lady on speaking terms again?"

She grimaced. "We've locked horns before, but yesterday was a little more epic than normal."

"What was it about?"

"She doesn't like that I'm taking a week off to go to Cuba."

He choked on a grape, and it took a moment to recover. "Oh, for pity's sake. I don't like it either."

"Please don't nag me too. I have to go."

"I won't nag, but I don't want you to go. It's not safe." Cuba was a war-torn, dangerous place, and he couldn't go with her to provide protection.

"My older brother is going with me," she assured him as if reading his mind. "I know you don't believe me, but I know

Luke is innocent, and I can't sit up here in the lap of luxury and ignore what's going on down there."

He closed his eyes, wishing he didn't admire her so much. How could he tell her to stop loving someone? This sort of loyalty was in Caroline's blood.

He still didn't want her leaving. For months they had been living under the same roof, and he caught glimpses of her daily. Those moments of connection were important to him. He reached out to cover her hand with his own. They hadn't touched since that night they kissed on the staircase during the state dinner, and a zing of electricity sparked merely from the brief contact of their hands.

"Please come back," he whispered.

She looked puzzled but didn't pull her hand away. "Of course I will. Life in Cuba would be disaster for my hair."

"That's not what I mean. Please come back to the White House." Caroline's presence was what made it worthwhile, a gilded flash of light and joy that made his days bearable.

"Mrs. McKinley is still angry with me, but she hasn't fired me yet. I don't expect that she will."

"Good." He squeezed her hand, then let it go.

He watched as she descended the staircase. He feared she was heading into trouble in Cuba, but was powerless to stop her.

Nineteen

Caroline and Gray boarded a regular passenger ship to Cuba, as the *Pelican* was still traveling back from Madagascar and would only be summoned should Luke agree to their desperate plan to smuggle him off the island.

During their two days at sea, Gray did his best to prepare Caroline for what she would see in Cuba. Luke was going to be gaunt and grubby, the jail dilapidated and cramped, and the climate muggy. They had sent a telegram to Luke, telling him to expect their visit, but didn't know if it got through to him.

Signs of rebuilding were everywhere on the island. Trawling ships dredged the lagoon, cranes lowered boulders to restore the harbor walls, and bridges were under construction. Members from the US Army Corps of Engineers directed the work while hundreds of Cubans carried it out.

Caroline braced herself as their carriage arrived at the jail. Gray clasped her hand, a reassuring lifeline as they headed toward the building, her heeled shoes wobbling over the scrabbly courtyard. The jail was a squat, one-story building with narrow slits for windows. A couple guards played dice beneath the shade trees, and Gray nodded to them as he passed. He'd

161

been to Cuba several times to see Luke and knew how to navigate this world.

The doorway of the jail was open, and the warden sat at a desk in the front hall. Caroline's eyes traveled the interior while Gray haggled with the warden for permission to bring in a bag of food and books for Luke. The warden pretended great reluctance, but this was another ritual Gray had told her about. The warden inspected the contents of the bag, sorting through the beef jerky, a few chocolate bars, and several canisters of peanuts. He fanned the pages of the novels but refused to let them bring in the bottle of pills. Gray always added one or two items he knew the warden would confiscate. The face-saving gesture meant that the food and books usually got through.

"Don't get too upset," Gray cautioned her for the millionth time as a guard began leading them down a narrow corridor, a set of keys jangling. "He's going to look very different, but it's nothing that a few months of decent food and sunshine can't cure."

The guard banged on the door to Luke's cell and spoke in Spanish while turning the key in the rusty lock. It clanked as he pulled it open and held it for Caroline. It was dim inside the cell, but Luke stood on the other side with a wide smile.

Oh, good heavens. He looked like a pirate, with a dark beard and surprisingly long hair tied behind his head. She rushed into his arms, ignoring the smell, and tried not to cry.

A few minutes later Gray passed the bag to Luke, who grinned while pawing through it, tearing off a strip of beef jerky before he'd even finished taking inventory of its contents.

"Caroline? You want some?"

"It's all yours," she said with a shake of her head.

He continued making short work of the beef jerky while she scanned the cell. A cot and an upended crate used as a table were the only furnishings. Luke insisted she and Gray sit on the cot while he sat on the floor.

"Did you like the artichokes?" Luke asked as he settled against the wall, resting an arm over his bent knee. His amusement felt as natural as if they were loitering in the garden of their townhouse.

"I did indeed," she replied. "How on earth did you smuggle them into the White House? The head of security is still annoyed about it."

"Who said I had anything to do with it?"

"Because Gray didn't do it, and neither did Philip the Meek nor anyone else we know in Washington."

"Maybe some things should simply remain a mystery," Luke said with a maddening grin. "Enough about artichokes. Tell me everything that's going on at home."

He listened eagerly as she recounted her work for the first lady and the recent inauguration. Gray spoke about the *Pelican's* overseas adventures in Madagascar and Ceylon, and to her amazement, he even described his wedding to Annabelle. It was a dangerous topic, for this entire mess was Annabelle's fault. Caroline watched Luke while Gray spoke, searching for a scintilla of resentment, but there was none. Gray swore that Luke harbored no animosity toward Annabelle, but she couldn't quite believe it, even as Luke nodded and teased while listening to details of the wedding.

"You weren't kidding about the Hebrew," she said with a nod to the book with foreign lettering on its spine. It sat alongside a Bible, some novels by Mark Twain, and books in languages she couldn't begin to understand.

Luke noticed and tugged the top book off the stack. "This one is in Arawak. It's one of the native languages in the Caribbean. The guards give me stuff like this because they think it annoys me." He smiled. "It doesn't. I like trying to sound out the words. It's a challenge and a glimpse into a part of the world I knew nothing about. Plus, it has pictures. Look at these." He flipped through the pages until he landed on an old Spanish woodcut depicting Indians harvesting tobacco.

It might not annoy Luke, but it annoyed her. Gray sent good money to bribe the guards into supplying Luke with something to read, and *this* was what they brought?

Luke showed her some of the other books. He seemed especially pleased with the Hebrew Bible and even took a stab at reading aloud to them. She couldn't help giggling, for the exotic words and cadence sounded impressive.

"I've read the Bible cover to cover every month since I've been here," he said. "Now I'm going line by line with it against the Hebrew version. I'm fumbling in the dark, and my biggest regret is not having a rabbi here to help me with it, but I like the challenge. Say, could you send me an English–Hebrew dictionary? It would be easier than using the Hebrew–Latin primer in the back of the book."

"I'll send one as soon as possible," Gray said.

They only had an hour left, and it was time to broach the subject. She looked through the narrow slit in the door and didn't see a guard, but that didn't mean one couldn't be lurking nearby, listening to every word.

She turned back to Luke and spoke quietly. "I've been working with a lawyer back home who has a suggestion for how to get you out of here."

Luke stilled, fully alert as he locked gazes with her. "How?" A world of hope was contained in that single syllable.

She began carefully, for he wasn't going to like her answer. She outlined how easy it would be to hire a Cuban lawyer to change his plea. The only tricky part would be getting the Cuban authorities to grant bail, but in this Gray could help. He had powerful connections throughout the Cuban planting class.

Given the way Luke crossed his arms over his chest, he didn't like the idea. "The problem is that I'm guilty," he said. "I did everything they accused me of, so what good would getting me bail do?"

"We could smuggle you onto the *Pelican* and send you overseas," Gray said quietly.

Luke stood and began pacing the tight confines of the cell. "Absolutely not. Don't you dare ask me to participate in something like this."

"It's the only surefire way to get you out," Gray said.

Luke whirled to face him as he pointed at her. "You're going to drag Caroline into this mess as well?"

"I'm here of my own accord," she defended. "I'm willing to run the risk."

"I'm not." Luke's voice was definitive. In a swift move, he flung his Bible, and it smacked her in the chest. "Maybe you scoff at that, but I don't. Honor and dignity mean something to me, and I'm not going to swear to the conditions of bail if my next move will be sneaking onto a ship and out of the country."

"What honor is there in rotting in a jail cell?" Gray demanded.

Luke opened and closed his mouth several times. It looked like an explanation was trying to claw its way out of him, but he clamped his mouth shut and went back to pacing. Two steps, pivot, then two steps back. Was this the limit of his ability to move for the past seven months? Anguish welled up, threatening to swamp her.

"Luke, please . . . I can't bear the thought of you in this cell forever. It's such a pointless waste when we can get you out."

He leaned against the cell door, arms crossed. "Don't cry over me, Caroline. I've had a lot of time to read and think while I've been locked up. There can be honor and dignity here. Paul the Apostle was imprisoned, and he found dignity in it."

"You're comparing yourself to Paul the Apostle?" Gray asked in disbelief.

Luke's face darkened. "Use your head, Gray! I'm trying to save her from getting implicated in a felony. You shouldn't have even brought her here."

"If you hadn't gotten yourself arrested for treason, I wouldn't have had to!"

Caroline flinched. This cell was too small for the anger roiling between her brothers. "Stop it, both of you. Luke, we can get you out, but only if you cooperate. Will you let us help you?" She held her breath, barely able to hold on to her composure. It was made worse by the misery in Luke's eyes.

"I'm sorry to let you down," he said. "A thousand times, I'm sorry, but this is where I deserve to be. I won't sneak away."

"At least let us try to get you into an American prison. Conditions will be—"

He cut her off, grabbing both her shoulders and looking her directly in the eyes. "I need you to *listen to me*," he said, giving her shoulders a shake, his voice uncharacteristically stern. "I am exactly where I need to be, and you need to leave this alone. Do you hear what I'm saying?"

"I hear you. I don't agree."

"Leave it alone, Caroline," he warned again, his face hard. "I don't want a transfer to an American prison." He dropped his hands and looked away. When he turned to her again, his eyes were sad, but he summoned a smile. "I don't want to drag you down with me," he said. "Go back to Washington and set the city on fire. Do something amazing. Sail alongside the eagles and never look back. And, Caroline, as much as I appreciate your visit, please don't come back. I don't want you remembering me like this."

~ ⌒ ~

Caroline stood on the deck of the steamship, hands clasping the railing as the vessel plowed through the sea toward home. Gray stood beside her, silently looking into the horizon, his thoughts surely as dark as her own. Wind buffeted them with its salty tang and stinging mist.

"I'm not giving up," she said firmly, but her voice was carried off by the wind.

"There may come a time when you'll need to become resigned to it," Gray said gently.

The words stung because they were true.

Twenty

Nathaniel ordered the officer at the guardhouse to inform him the moment Caroline returned to the White House. It was nearing midnight, and he should have left his office hours ago, but knowing Caroline's return from Cuba was imminent made sleep impossible. Besides, he still had plenty of work planning the cross-country trip the president insisted upon. They would stop at sixty-eight locations, and he needed to contact the local police at each stop. He dialed up the kerosene in the desk lantern and focused on the harbor of Natchez, where the president and his wife would enjoy a brief riverboat excursion.

Caroline would probably look delightful on the riverboat. She'd probably wear summer whites and one of those broad-brimmed, daringly feminine hats. He threw his pencil down in frustration. He couldn't explain this overwhelming urgency to see her again, but during the days she'd been gone, he'd thought of her constantly.

What kind of harebrained woman walked into a war-torn environment where the local population lacked food and basic resources? Knowing Caroline, she'd shown up in a silk gown and satin pumps, with perfectly styled hair and one of those wasp-waisted getups, all of which would make her a prime kidnapping target.

Plus, her trip was doomed to failure. He'd had John Wilkie pull whatever was known about Luke's case, and it stank to high heaven. Caroline didn't deserve this. Her ship was supposed to have docked hours ago, so why wasn't she back yet?

There could have been trouble in Cuba. Transportation breakdowns or brigands, and Caroline didn't speak Spanish. He should have figured out some way to stop her from leaving.

The telephone rang, and he snatched up the receiver. "Trask here."

"The lady you asked about is heading toward the staff entrance."

His shoulders sagged in relief. "Does she look okay?"

There was a moment of confusion on the other end of the connection. "I guess so," the guard said. "Was I supposed to be looking for something?"

"No, that's fine. Thank you." He replaced the receiver on the hook, willing his heart to resume its normal rate. He wasn't responsible for Caroline's safety, and besides, she'd obviously come through the trip just fine. A couple hours late, but more or less on time.

He pulled on a suit jacket and headed downstairs to intercept her. He needed to see for himself how she'd fared, but by the time he got to the far side of the house, he only caught a flash of a sapphire blue skirt as she disappeared up the stairwell to the staff quarters. He vaulted after her.

"Caroline?" His voice echoed up the stairwell. The clicking of her heels paused, but she didn't say anything, and that wasn't like her. He vaulted up the stairs, catching sight of her on the flight just outside the third floor.

She looked terrible. Flawlessly dressed, as usual, but drained and despondent. He ached for her.

"How can I help?" he asked.

For once, she seemed to be at a loss for words as she glanced around the interior of the stairwell, the single lightbulb casting a garish light that made her face look ashen. Finally, she simply shrugged.

"I don't know," she said, lowering herself to plop onto the top step. "Maybe by not saying 'I told you so.'"

He sat on a step a few treads below hers to avoid touching her skirt. He listened as her story came out in fits and starts, detailing the heat and the stench of the prison, the dilapidated conditions, and the cramped cell. Most of all he felt the despair pouring off her in waves, so different from the normally radiant Caroline. She hung her head, palms to her forehead as though it was too much effort to hold it up.

"I need you to tell me not to have a cigarette," she said, her voice muffled.

His heart turned over. "You can have one if it will help. You've been through a lot in the past few weeks."

The toe of her red leather boot peeped out from beneath her skirt to tap his shoulder. "You're not helping."

Then he would divert her attention. "Did he tell how he got the artichokes into the kitchen?"

She laughed a little. "I asked. He wouldn't tell."

"But he's behind it?"

"There's no doubt in my mind." Exhaustion made her voice faint, but even so, he could hear the affection. "I wish I could convince you he is innocent."

He clasped the toe of her boot with his hand, giving her foot a quick squeeze. "I know *you* believe his innocence, and I also know you're a loyal American. No one could work so hard in such a thankless task unless they were."

"Well, that's something, I suppose." She sighed and looked away. "Someone like you probably can't understand why I'm so irrational about this. Unless you have a brother or a sister, it's hard to describe the bond. It's more than a friendship. We share the same blood, the same history. Even the same heart."

"I had a sister once." The words inadvertently popped out, surprising him as much as her.

"You did? I thought you said you had no family."

"That's true too. My mother left when I was young, and my dad died when I was fourteen. Molly was still a little kid, and I was the only one left to look out for her."

Caroline leaned in closer, her face intrigued. If sharing his own loss would help her deal with this separation from her brother, he would do so. He told her about living in Chicago and working as a photoengraver during the overnight shift at the newspaper. He spoke of how he came home to wake Molly each morning, help her dress, and walk her to school.

Their walk ran alongside one of the logging runs on the river. Chicago was the largest lumber market in the nation, with schooners coming in from the Great Lakes and the Canadian timberlands. During logging season, Molly was fascinated by the thousands of logs that cascaded downstream until they arrived at the mills, where burly lumber-shovers guided the logs onto chutes and into the mills.

But logging season didn't last forever, and during the down times, Molly begged Nathaniel for the chance to swim in the river, especially during the sweltering days of August. Their tenement bordered the river, and leaving Molly alone and unsupervised for so many hours in the day was a recipe for disaster, so he taught her to swim. She was a natural, and he called her his little water sprite, which she loved. He took her to the public park to swim in the lake at least once a week during the summer.

But the river beckoned. They could see it from their fourth-floor apartment, and Molly pestered incessantly, especially when she saw the Italians who lived on the opposite bank wading in the river. What eleven-year-old child had the wisdom to see the danger? It was late summer, and the logging season was tapering to an end. Days could go by without a schooner, and the heat sometimes drove people to take a quick dip in the river.

"I was always so tired during those years," he said. "I worked the overnight shift at the newspaper and only had a few hours to sleep each morning. Then I went to class, came home and fed Molly, and then it was time to go to work again. One day I fell asleep after class. I had an hour before I needed to make dinner, and I fell asleep. When I woke up, Molly was gone."

He immediately suspected where she'd gone and darted to the window to see if she was wading in the river. There was no sign of her, but what he saw chilled his blood. Hundreds of logs barreling downstream. A schooner had arrived and unloaded its haul. If Molly had been in the river . . .

He hadn't even put on his shoes. He merely vaulted down the stairs and tore across the yard to the riverbank. There was trouble downstream. A group of Italians clustered on the bank, standing over something.

"It was Molly," he said blankly. "She was still wearing her school clothes, but her feet were bare. She'd hiked up her skirt to wade in the river, but the current could be so strong. And then the logs came, and she didn't have a chance."

Caroline's face was horrified. "I'm so sorry," she whispered.

Molly would be thirty-one if she had lived, probably married with a bunch of kids. Now she would always be eleven years old, a beautiful water sprite who would forever be his greatest failing.

"After Molly died, I felt like a weight settled on top of me, sucking me down. It comes back sometimes. It's a sense of failure, drowning out whatever good is in my life. I've lived that day over a million times. What if I'd had just one more cup of coffee? What if I'd been firmer with Molly about enforcing the rules?"

Her smile was sad but knowing. "Gray always wanted me and Luke to walk the straight and narrow. It wasn't his fault when we didn't. What happened to Molly wasn't your fault either. God has created a huge, complex tapestry with our lives. It's got shadows and darkness shot through with highlights of gold. We can never go back and undo those threads and weave them into something else. I wish we could."

She laid her hand on his shoulder, and her compassion flowed into him like a balm. What he wouldn't do to have a woman like this in his life. He laid his palm over her hand, gently squeezing.

"I'm glad you're home," he said.

"I am too."

Disappointment from failing in Cuba was heavy in her voice. Her brother was a traitor and the first lady was a harridan, but she'd been working with those dark threads from the day he met her. She managed to live a luminous life of joy and hope despite the darkness dogging her heels, and there was much to admire in that.

He only feared her optimism might someday be crushed by the slow wheels of justice.

Twenty-One

Nathaniel braced himself for the nationwide presidential tour. The three-month trip was going to be the longest time any president had been away from the White House, involving a journey from coast to coast, and from the Great Lakes all the way down to the port of New Orleans. As spring morphed into summer, the tour took shape as more stops were added to the itinerary and details were finalized.

All along the way, there would be parades, speeches, dinners with local officials, and a nonstop stream of well-wishers. Thousands of people were expected at each stop. Most cities on the route wanted to treat the president to a parade with an open-air carriage ride for the first couple to see the town at its best. Nathaniel made a trip to John Wilkie's office in an attempt to veto all open carriage rides.

"The parades are an unacceptable security risk," he said. "You should see the letters the president has been receiving lately."

Wilkie propped his feet on his desk, slowly puffing on a cigar. "What kind of letters?"

"Mostly from crackpots," Nathaniel admitted. "An astrologer claims the stars are aligned for the president to die on the

174

next full moon, and a woman from Nebraska has foreseen the president's death by falling off a grain elevator. Fortunately, there are no trips to grain elevators on the tour."

"So what's the problem?"

"I can't guarantee the president's security," Nathaniel said tightly. "Not with only four men."

"There will be dozens of local police officers at each stop," Wilkie said mildly.

"Who I'll need to train in scarcely ten minutes before the president's wife starts banging her cane to disembark. I know this woman, and the president can't stand up to her."

Thank heavens Caroline would be along on the trip. She was a godsend for keeping Mrs. McKinley pacified, even though it was getting harder for Nathaniel to maintain a professional distance from her. With such thin security on the train, he couldn't be distracted by a pretty girl.

But he cared for her. A great deal. Their forced proximity during the journey would be sweet torture, for he could only admire her from afar. That would have to be enough.

"I have complete faith in you," Wilkie said. "You will have the support of local police at every stop along the way. Everything will be fine."

Nathaniel wished he shared Wilkie's confidence.

Caroline's days were busier than ever in the weeks leading up to the train tour, so she welcomed her rare evening free from duties. Mrs. McKinley had retired to bed early, meaning Caroline could do the same. She curled up atop her bedding, still wearing a skirt and blouse. Ida often changed her mind and decided she needed Caroline after all, but Caroline could shed her vest, unpin her collar, and kick off her shoes. It was time to finally begin a reread of *Northanger Abbey*, a silly novel she secretly adored. In deference to the kitchen staff who were already abed, she read by the light of a single kerosene lantern turned low.

She hadn't even finished the first chapter when a gentle tapping on the door disrupted the silence. "Man on the floor," a soft voice called from the opposite side.

Caroline sighed but hurried to answer the door. The rest of the staff shouldn't be disturbed because of Ida's demands.

Sullivan was in the hallway. "There's a man here to see you," he said quietly. "He says he's your brother Gray. He looks upset. He wants to see you right away."

Her heart seized. It was nine o'clock, and Gray wasn't the sort to make unexpected calls unless something was seriously wrong. She didn't even bother to put her shoes back on, just hiked up her skirt and followed Sullivan to the main floor, where Gray paced in a small meeting room.

He looked terrible. His collar was askew and hair tousled, as though he'd been dragging his hands through it. She closed the door, and he grasped her by the forearms to lead her to a chair.

"What's wrong," she demanded. She knew it was about Luke, and it was surely bad.

"Luke is in trouble. He's got pneumonia and is going downhill fast. The Cubans transferred him to the American hospital at the military base in Havana."

She clasped a hand over her throat. She ought to have known that dank cell would be the death of him, and now he was battling for his life. "How bad is it?"

"Bad enough that the Cubans are afraid he might die. An army doctor has seen him, and he's getting the best care possible, but they don't know if he's going to make it."

"I'll go to him." Luke wouldn't die alone. If she left now, she could be there within two days, but Gray kept talking.

"Things are going from bad to worse," he said. "His guilty plea has been recognized, and now that he's back in American custody, a date has been set for his trial. If he survives the illness, he'll go on trial with no more delays, and we both know he intends to plead guilty. He's charged with a hanging offense."

"What are we going to do?" she asked, her voice shaking.

"What about Philip Ransom? Does he have any pull at all that might help?" For once, Gray looked panicked and uncertain, and it rattled her. Gray was supposed to be the strong one who always knew what to do, but Philip the Meek wasn't the right person to depend on in an emergency.

She shook her head. "Philip can't even maneuver himself out of a clerical job in the basement. He can't possibly pull strings overseas."

"Then we need to get Luke transferred to the mainland," Gray said. "I don't trust a trial in Cuba. They could slam him through an impromptu trial without any press or publicity. The outcome won't be good."

He outlined the only plan that made any sense. He would sail to Cuba immediately and provide whatever aid he could for Luke, while Caroline leaned on her connections here to get Luke transferred to the mainland.

It felt right to take action. No more waiting. It was time to pay another call on Captain Holland.

Caroline brought her attorney for her confrontation with Captain Holland. She hadn't been much of a match against the captain during their last meeting, but Mr. Alphonse was the best criminal attorney in Washington. He had a firm grasp of criminal and constitutional law and a nodding acquaintance with military law.

"Let me take the lead," Mr. Alphonse whispered just before they entered Captain Holland's office, and she gratefully agreed.

This time there was no cordial banter. Mr. Alphonse got directly to the business at hand the moment he and Caroline were seated across from Captain Holland's wide mahogany desk. Her attorney and Captain Holland unleashed a torrent of legal terms like *amicus curiae, convening authority, bifurcation, comity*. . . . Her head whirled at the verbal jousting she had difficulty following.

All she cared about was getting Luke transferred to the mainland. She'd worry about proving his innocence later, but for now she wanted him out of that hot, tropical climate. When she said as much, Captain Holland interrupted her.

"He's already been transferred to the American military hospital in Havana. He's getting exceptional care."

"We want him transferred to the United States for trial," her attorney said. "We want him to regain his health so he can fully participate in his defense, and I want regular contact with my client."

"If you want to see him, go to Cuba," Captain Holland said. "My guess is that he'll fire you, just like he's fired every other attorney he's had. This entire case is bad for troop morale and our efforts to appease the Cuban opposition. It was better when he was being held by the Cubans."

That comment took her aback. "Why?" she asked.

"Now that he's back in American custody, we are forced to proceed to a trial," Captain Holland said. "The Cubans were probably hoping the pneumonia would finish him off and resolve the political embarrassment."

She flinched at his callous tone, but something he'd just said didn't ring true. "But they transferred him to you when he got sick. The Cubans *don't* want him to die."

He slanted her a look as though disappointed at her naiveté. "That's what they want you to think. They'll do anything to keep the Americans happy until their island is rebuilt. Then they'll happily kick us out."

"What are his odds in a trial?" she asked.

"Not good. Trust me, Miss Delacroix, we loathe the prospect

of a trial because it has the potential to stoke the rebellion. Nevertheless, we can't afford to be lenient in such cases, and a death penalty is almost a certainty. This is a headache I don't need, but the latest report I've had from Cuba is that your brother's health is not improving. Nature may take its course and spare us all from the indignity of a trial."

It was a slap in the face, but she couldn't afford to let it show. If officers in the navy were secretly praying for a convenient death, she had no doubt they'd eventually succeed.

She stood. Mr. Alphonse tried to tug her back down, but she shook him off and braced her hands on Captain Holland's desk to lean over him.

"Please understand that if 'nature takes its course' and my brother suffers a miserable death in a prison hospital, I will raise a firestorm unlike anything you've ever seen. I want Luke to have three solid meals a day. Daily visits from a doctor. Clean drinking water and no dank cells. The president told me I could trust you to make this happen, and I'll be watching."

The meeting ended shortly after that, and Mr. Alphonse privately advised that she accept the likelihood of a trial in Cuba. Tears clouded her vision as she bid him farewell, but she couldn't be rational at a time like this.

She almost stepped in front of a streetcar as she darted across the road and toward a church, for the only thing she could do was pray to God for mercy.

The church was empty and quiet as she fell to her knees. Luke was a good man despite his irreverence. He'd been studying the Bible. He'd engineered funding for Petra's school for poor women. While it was possible he'd committed a terrible crime, there was no sin that couldn't be forgiven. Jesus had promised them that.

And wasn't Luke's salvation what she should care about the most? He could find peace in the hereafter, if not on earth. God had never promised them a long life, and she might need to become reconciled to the fact that Luke would not have one.

Her knees ached by the time she rose, but her heart was still heavy as she walked back to the White House.

"Where have you been?" the housekeeper asked when Caroline entered the kitchen. "Mrs. McKinley has been banging her cane, shouting down the house in search of you."

"What now?"

The housekeeper rolled her eyes. "She's in a mood because the blueberry muffins were burned this morning. We still haven't heard the end of it."

Caroline drew a fortifying breath, bracing herself for a difficult day, but there was a limit to her patience, and she feared she was about to reach it.

Twenty-Two

Nathaniel had spent an hour inspecting the exterior security measures when he got wind of Mrs. McKinley's latest tantrum, for apparently, she'd had a rich one with Caroline that afternoon. Sullivan told him the news when he stopped by the north yard sentry box.

"It was all about some burned blueberry muffins," Sullivan said in a low voice. "She ordered Caroline to get the housekeeper to make another batch, but there were no more blueberries. Didn't matter. She wanted Caroline to go out and find some, and Caroline refused. That caused another ruckus, and Caroline threatened not to go on the train trip, and Mrs. McKinley shouted 'Good riddance' and kicked her out of her suite. Everyone is hoping this blows over, because *nobody* wants to be trapped on that train for three months if Caroline isn't there to tame the dragon."

Nathaniel ought to reprimand Sullivan for speaking disrespectfully of the first lady, but everyone knew it was true, and they had complete privacy at the sentry box. He'd have to see what he could do about getting Caroline back on board.

Even though it would be easier on him if she stayed home. They worked so closely together, and yet she was untouchable.

She was an itch he couldn't scratch. Securing the president's safety required his full attention, and he couldn't afford to indulge this inconvenient infatuation.

She'd been out of sorts for the past few days, ever since Gray Delacroix visited late at night, and he suspected it had something to do with her brother in Cuba.

It wasn't hard to guess where Caroline had gone after getting banished from the first lady's presence. Taking the stairs two at a time, he made his way to the White House roof and quickly spotted her staring out over the back lawn. Several cigarette butts lay near her feet, and she puffed on another. She must have heard him approach, for she swiveled and shot him a glare.

"Don't you dare give me any grief about smoking," she warned.

He held up both hands in surrender. "I wasn't planning on it. It sounds like you've had quite a day."

He joined her at the rail. She was on the verge of cracking. The signs were all there. The trembling of her hands, the stiff spine, the look of vulnerability swirling amidst anger and exhaustion.

"What's wrong?" he said softly. "This is about more than blueberry muffins."

The hand holding the cigarette trembled harder. "My brother has pneumonia. He might die. Even if he recovers, the army is going to keep giving him shoddy treatment until he really does die, because then they won't have to deal with the scandal of a trial."

"Where did you hear about this?"

She told him how a navy lawyer filled her in on the legal proceedings. President McKinley had given her a glimmer of hope for a pardon in four years, but she didn't think Luke would last that long. In the meantime, she was frantically trying to lean on her connections to get him transferred to the mainland and decent legal help.

"And now he has pneumonia," she said. "I can't bear thinking of him struggling for every breath of air just to stay alive. And then Ida has conniptions over burned muffins."

She dropped the cigarette, and he covered it with his boot to crush it out. She braced her hands on the railing, her head sagging. Her voice became so faint, it was a struggle to hear her.

"I don't know how much longer I can keep doing this," she whispered. "I can barely string a sentence together, and she orders me to turn the city upside down in search of blueberries."

He laid an arm across her shoulders, wishing he could provide better comfort. She didn't deserve this. It hurt to see her so despondent, for Caroline was usually a Valkyrie, ready to stride forth into glorious battle. Not today.

"I can't get on that train," she continued, still staring at the yard below. "If word comes that Luke has taken a turn for the worse, I need to be able to go to him. I can't be in Kansas or California or hunting down blueberries."

The train left tomorrow, and she needed to be on board. Not for his sanity, but for the good of her brother. He used a calm voice to cut through her misery.

"If Luke's health begins to fail, trust that your older brother will be at his side," he said. "For now, you need to preserve your link to the McKinleys. If you quit now, you're losing your best chance for a pardon." He squeezed her shoulders. "After coming so far with Mrs. McKinley, you're not going to be defeated by a request for blueberries. When times get tough, you get tougher."

It looked like she tried to smile but failed. "Not this time. I'm done. I can't do this anymore. I'll move to the Florida Keys and wait for word in case Luke needs me. I can hire a boat and be there in a few hours."

"To sit by his deathbed? Or are you going to get on that train and fight for him? And I'm not talking about a pardon, I'm talking about solidifying your position with the McKinleys.

Get your photograph taken with them at every public event and send copies to the officers at the military prison. Let them know who they're dealing with. They won't dare let him die if they know how powerfully connected his family is. It's not going to be easy, but it's your best shot, and you've got to depend on your older brother to fight the battle on the other front."

"Why are you talking like this? Building me up when I know you think Luke is guilty?"

He looked away, afraid that if he met her eyes, she'd see how much she meant to him. "I'm building you up because I know what it is to be torn down. And I don't want that happening to you."

He faced her, drinking in the sight that had held him captivated from the moment he set eyes on her. "You are in the early stages of a battle. There are almost four years until the president's term is over. Don't burn yourself out too quickly. Learn to see the joy in each day. Even if it means finding a basket of blueberries or calming an anxious woman who has been overwhelmed from the moment her husband was elected to the presidency. There's valor in that, Caroline."

She stepped closer to him, her dress brushing up against his legs. He could smell the lemony soap in her hair.

"I feel stronger just being with you," she whispered.

He embraced her, holding her close. The current of electricity, never far below the surface when she was near, flared to life. "You drive me to distraction," he admitted, "and that's dangerous. At the same time, I crave it more than my next breath of air."

She pulled back to look at him, and her tear-stained face was radiant, more luminous than if a Renaissance master had tried to capture her spirit. They both knew pain, fear, and the gnawing sense of helplessness. They both struggled to find the resilience to stand up and fight another day. He leaned down to touch his forehead to hers, wanting to be her companion, her hero, her everything.

"I'll be with you," he said, his voice rough with emotion. "I'll guard your back and clear a path before you. When fear threatens to drown you, I'll be there to haul you out. You can count on me."

She held him tight as the sun sank beneath the horizon. Tonight there was no more reserve, no more barriers. Tomorrow they'd go back to their formal roles, but for now they clung to each other, knowing the months ahead would be a long and trying journey. At this perfect moment of calm, they grew stronger together.

Twenty-Three

Nathaniel made a final inspection of the train a few hours before their departure. With eight cars in the presidential entourage, the train was fitted out with everything the president would need to conduct business for the next twelve weeks. The dining car had been furnished to seat thirty people, for they'd frequently be joined by congressmen and prominent guests for segments of the trip. The parlor car featured enlarged windows for an expansive view as they traversed the nation. The president had his own sleeping car, while the staff had a male sleeping car and another for the cooks, the wives of congressmen, and of course, Caroline.

Most impressive was the system set up for communication. The traveling presidency would have a stenographer, two telegraph operators, a cable technician, and an officer from the railroad to handle any difficulties along the way. Rembrandt and members of the press would accompany them, and an entire railway car was set up for communication purposes.

Alfred Medina was the technician who would keep the system operating. A wiry man with thick glasses and a surplus of nervous energy, he was part electrician and part telephone operator, and nervous about working for the president. He blotted the perspiration from his bald head as he showed Nathaniel how the system worked.

"While the train is moving, we'll be out of telegraph contact, but once we pull into a station, I can patch us into their wire and telephone systems in short order."

Alfred gestured to the other side of the car, where a countertop bolted to the wall held four typewriters. "This is where the journalists can type up their reports. I'll have a telegraph line open for the president at all times." He tugged at his collar and mopped his brow again.

"Relax," Nathaniel said. "You'll find President McKinley an easygoing man." He silently hoped Alfred would never need to cope with Ida McKinley, for the first lady could frighten a man like this into leaping off a moving train.

At least Caroline had consented to come on the journey. Their encounter on the roof still burned in his memory. They were becoming dangerously close, and this attraction couldn't continue during the tour. Each day they would be in new towns and unfamiliar venues with thousands of people turning out to see the president. Nathaniel would honor his word to support her should the situation with her brother turn dark, but the rest of the time, he needed to keep her at arm's length.

He gestured to a strange box that looked something like a telephone. "What's this?"

"It's the intercommunication box," Alfred said. "If an announcement needs to be made to the other cars, that will do the trick."

That caught Nathaniel's attention. "Can I hear what's going on in other cars?" If so, it could be a security lifeline, but Alfred shook his head.

"It only communicates one way, but it's a better system than bells," he said.

Internal bells were how the staff communicated inside the White House. This new system might be worth looking into, but that would have to wait. The train was about to depart, and somehow Nathaniel suspected that the next few months would be among the most memorable of his life.

~⁂~

Excitement hummed in the air as Caroline found her seat for the first evening's dinner aboard the train. Each table was covered with fine linen and set with china, crystal, and a menu card. Tea candles adorned each table, and the shaded electric sconces on the wall had been dimmed for evening dining. Silver clinked against china as twenty-eight people gathered in the presidential dining car. Most worked for the president, but two journalists and three congressmen had been invited for the first part of the journey. The congressmen's wives had been invited too, making for a lively gathering. Rembrandt set up his camera and took a few photographs to commemorate their first night's journey.

It was a lovely dinner, with fresh lobster baked in a delicate wine sauce. Caroline ought to be embarrassed by her niggling sense of annoyance, but Nathaniel had been ignoring her from the moment they set off from Washington earlier that afternoon. He deliberately looked past her as people selected their seats, choosing to sit with Rembrandt and Alfred Medina, the communications officer with the nervous tic. Even though Nathaniel was avoiding her, she still sensed him stealing glances at her, but each time she tried to catch him in the act, his gaze immediately slid away.

Caroline dined with the three congressmen's wives. Emmaline Foster's husband was likely to become the next Speaker of the House, so the McKinleys were catering to him by inviting him to share their small table, but his wife had to sit at the ladies' table. Mrs. Foster had a headful of tightly pinned steel-gray curls and a smile of barbed wire.

"Please stop daydreaming," Mrs. Foster snapped at Caroline. "For the third time, I am telling you that I insist on sharing a carriage with the first couple on our visit to Monticello tomorrow, and yet you stare into space and ignore my request."

Caroline maintained a pleasant expression even though Mrs. Foster was treating her like a peasant. "The carriage assignments are already in place," she said. The train would pull into Charlottesville in the morning, and after a quick tour of the University of Virginia, the presidential party would ride in a string of carriages to Thomas Jefferson's historic home. "The security team made the arrangements for seating. I don't know if there is any leeway."

"Then please inquire," Mrs. Foster said. "My husband and I have only a limited time to travel with the president, and I didn't expect to spend it foisted off on the help."

Caroline seized the opportunity. "Let me go ask for you," she said, leaving her seat and heading to Nathaniel's table on the far side of the car. "Might I speak with you alone for a moment?" she said to him.

He shifted uneasily and didn't meet her gaze. "I'm in the middle of the lobster," he said. "It's likely the last time we'll be served seafood on the train."

"I have a question about security during tomorrow's trip to Monticello."

He didn't look happy, but he couldn't shirk his duties either. He dabbed his mouth with a napkin, pushed away from the lobster feast, and gestured her toward the corridor connecting to the next car.

The communications car was empty but already a sloppy mess, and they weren't even six hours into the journey. The journalists had left papers and reference manuals stacked up beside a jumble of wires and telegraph machines. It looked like organized chaos, but at least the car was private.

Nathaniel pulled the door shut but didn't face her.

"How long are you going to keep ignoring me?" she asked the moment the door was secure.

His shoulders tensed, and he took a deep breath. "Caroline, let's not do this," he said, still not turning around.

"Are we really going to pretend that nothing happened last night? Because I can't live beside you every day and act like we're strangers. I can't."

At last he turned. "You're the toughest woman I know. Of course you can."

She didn't feel tough. She'd come on this trip because Nathaniel promised she could lean on him. Every mile they traveled from Washington increased the vague sense of panic that kept her on edge. Luke's pneumonia could take a turn for the worse and kill him within hours, and she wouldn't even know until they pulled into their next stop.

"There was an extra space at my table tonight. You could have joined me."

"I don't think that's a good idea."

She stiffened. "You said that when I was nervous or afraid, you would be there for me. That you'd clear a path for me and guard my back. Mrs. Foster has been throwing darts at me for hours, and you can't take your attention off your precious lobster."

"You're being irrational," he said, clipped formality woven through every speck of his posture, voice, and expression. "I'll be there for you when times get tough, but for the day to day, I need to keep my distance."

A knock on the door interrupted them, but it was only Mr. Medina peeking through the window, so she gestured for him to leave and turned her attention back to Nathaniel.

"Can't you at least look at me? Smile at me like a normal human who has blood in his veins and an actual beating heart?"

"I take my duties seriously."

"To the president. To the train porters. To fake Vermeers and rigid schedules and the lobster dinner."

"It was fresh lobster," he defended.

"I should matter to you more than lobster!" she shouted.

The door handle wiggled and the pounding continued, but she didn't care.

"You need to restrain yourself," he said. "I can't do my duty when you're flinging yourself at me."

"You didn't mind last night," she said. The memory of the blazing sunset while they clung together on the roof still made her heart pound.

The banging on the door became incessant, and Nathaniel used it as an excuse to leave her and yank it open.

"What?" he demanded.

Mr. Medina twisted his cap in his hands. "The intercom line is open. Everyone in the dining car can hear what you're saying."

Caroline gasped. She'd been pouring her heart out in front of the McKinleys and the staff and that horrible congressman's wife?

Nathaniel went stock still, and the color drained from his face, the pallor in sharp contrast with his puritanical dark suit. He shook himself and crossed to the open communication line, leaning down to speak directly into it. "You all can go back to your dinner now," he choked out. "Show's over."

He tugged on some levers to close the connection, and a dull roar of applause sounded from the neighboring car. This was embarrassing, but there was only one thing to do.

Caroline squared her shoulders and smoothed the tension from her face. "Shall we rejoin them?" she said, striving to project the epitome of unruffled poise.

Nathaniel looked ready to combust. "We've just made fools of ourselves."

"No, we showed ourselves to be normal people with beating hearts and human emotions. I know sometimes you'd prefer if we were boring, cold-blooded husks, but I'm afraid we have both been exposed."

And frankly, she wasn't sorry. Life was short, and she didn't want to go through it half-alive by denying her feelings. She headed toward the dining car without looking back.

~ ⁒ ~

Nathaniel straightened his collar as he watched Caroline sashay through the connecting corridor with the poise of a queen. A smattering of laughter greeted her arrival. She smiled and performed a little curtsy before gliding back to her seat. He couldn't mimic her aplomb. He'd worked hard for his reputation of unfailing restraint, and the last five minutes had blown it to smithereens. He tightened the knot of his tie and adjusted his jacket before following Caroline into the dining car.

More clapping sounded as he stepped inside. Caroline took her seat beside the congressmen's wives, who looked at him with appalled curiosity.

Rembrandt stood to whisper in his ear. "You're an idiot. A stick-in-the-mud shouldn't toss a catch like Caroline Delacroix back in the sea."

Nathaniel would like to toss her a lot farther than that. They were going to be trapped with most of these people for months, and now they all knew his private business. The ribbing continued as he took his seat, but Sullivan regarded him with new respect. True, Caroline was a looker, but this sort of public exposure was nothing to be proud about, and his mortification lasted all through the rest of the meal.

Things got worse in the smoking car after dinner. The president was relaxing with George Cortelyou and the visiting congressmen but flagged Nathaniel down as he tried to pass through to the men's sleeper car.

"A word, Mr. Trask," the president said, rising from his velvet chair. Nathaniel braced himself, having a pretty good suspicion what was on Mr. McKinley's mind. He followed the president

to a tall potted palm at the back of the car and forced himself
to meet the president's gaze like a man.

President McKinley used his cigar to emphasize his demand.
"I'd like your assurance that there will be no attempt to take
advantage of Miss Delacroix's affection for you."

Nathaniel cleared his throat. "Of course not, sir."

"Mrs. McKinley considers the young lady tantamount to
a daughter. As such, we have a paternal interest in her well-
being."

"Of course, sir." To brave the wrath of any father figure
was bad enough, but to have it come from the president of the
United States was an altogether different magnitude of mortification.

President McKinley smiled and clapped him on the shoulder.
"Good! I trust we won't need to have this discussion again."

Nathaniel didn't breathe easy until he was in the sleeper car.
He climbed the ladder to his upper berth and slid inside. It was
a narrow mattress with only a cubby at the foot of the bed for
his belongings. He lay sleepless for almost an hour before Sullivan arrived and tugged the curtain aside.

"What did the president say?" he whispered.

"To keep my hands off Caroline."

"Ouch," Sullivan said. "I guess you'd better do it, then. Orders are orders."

Nathaniel nodded and jerked the curtain closed. It was going
to be a long twelve weeks.

Twenty-Four

Caroline ought to have enjoyed the tour, for each day brought outings to colorful local attractions, the chance to mingle with enthusiastic crowds, and a rollicking crew of lively companions aboard the train. She stayed constantly by Mrs. McKinley's side at each stop, helping carry the conversation when Ida could think of nothing to say and making their excuses when Ida wanted to return to the train early.

But Luke was always hovering in her thoughts. A letter from Gray reported that Luke had recovered from his battle with pneumonia but was still housed in the military hospital as a precaution. At their stop in Richmond, she gave thanks at the cathedral, falling to her knees in silent prayer, then impulsively deposited both her sapphire earrings into the collection box for the poor.

She also made certain that a copy of the photograph Rembrandt took of her standing on the steps of Monticello alongside the McKinleys was sent to Luke at the army hospital. Military personnel screened all the prisoners' letters, but that was exactly how she wanted it. She wanted them to know Luke had powerful connections.

In her letter, she even included the fatherly warning President

McKinley had given to Nathaniel when their flirtation was exposed. Gossip about the president's warning had spread like wildfire through their party. It was an embarrassing way to start the tour, but perfect for letting the people guarding Luke know of her close ties to the president. If it bought an iota more care for Luke, it was worth it.

At each stop, the communication car hooked into the local telegraph wires to receive incoming cables. Caroline always awaited word from Gray, hoping for news of Luke. At their last stop, he'd wired to say that he'd had a letter from Luke and would forward it to the post office in Charleston for her to pick up.

This morning they were touring the Charleston Naval Shipyard, where Mrs. McKinley would christen an ironclad battleship before a cheering crowd. Caroline helped Ida down from the carriage and admired the harbor, where dozens of American flags snapped in the wind and a brass band played in the distance. Sunlight glinted on choppy waves, and she shielded her eyes to admire the steel-hulled battleship they were about to christen.

Nathaniel awaited them at the dock, along with a dozen members of the local police. She couldn't help admiring his austere form as he stood at attention, awaiting the arrival of the presidential party. It had been five days since *l'affaire de lobster*, as the disaster had been dubbed, and Ida had been teasing her ever since.

"Your young man looks in fine form this morning," Ida said.

"He's always in fine form."

Ida let out a bark of laughter. "You'd best do something to hold on to him. The Major warned him away, but you don't want to be an old maid. You need to keep that young man interested."

I intend to, she silently vowed.

The ceremony rolled out according to plan. The mayor of

Charleston gave some opening remarks, then the president delivered his five-minute speech. After that, a navy admiral accompanied Mrs. McKinley into position to smash the bottle against the hull of the ship.

The crowd cheered, and the band began a rousing tune by John Philip Sousa. Mrs. Foster hovered in the background, waiting for her opportunity to pounce and share the McKinleys' carriage back to the train depot, and Caroline was more than happy to surrender her seat to her.

Caroline thrust Mrs. Foster toward Ida. "You can help her back to the train," she said. "I've heard wonderful things about the historic Charleston Post Office. I'm off for a quick peek."

A local police officer had already told her where to catch a trolley that took her straight to the famous post office. It was a magnificent three-story building of white granite in the classic Renaissance Revival style. Inane wishes that Nathaniel could see it tugged at the corner of her mind, for he appreciated fine architecture.

Inside, it was even more impressive, with opulent red marble and mahogany floors. Her footsteps echoed off the vaulted ceiling as she approached the front counter.

"I've been told a letter is waiting for me," she said. After receiving her name, the clerk disappeared into a back room and soon returned with an envelope addressed in Gray's bold handwriting. Its thickness indicated several pages inside. She caught the returning trolley and waited until she was safely aboard to tear open the letter, setting Luke's aside to read Gray's letter first.

It wasn't good. Gray wrote that although the worst of Luke's pneumonia was gone, he wasn't rallying as expected. He remained in the American hospital, manacled to the bed and wasting away. The doctors were at a loss as to how to proceed.

The envelope containing Luke's letter rested in her palm. She laid her hand over it and sent up a single word of prayer. *Please.*

She'd braced herself for bad news, but what she read was worse than she could have imagined. His penmanship was spindly and lopsided, but more concerning was that only a few sentences were lucid. After asking after her health, his words were confusing and nonsensical.

> *You can't trust the Dutch. Their ships are lousy, as the legend of the Flying Dutchman attests. That ship carried treasures beyond imagining, but it has corrupted the captain.*
>
> *The crew from the north has vanished, and the road to a city of columns is in danger. The trouble comes from the westernmost key.*
>
> *Please remember, you can always trust a good dancer and the second in command.*
>
> *You know what to do.*

At the bottom of the letter were several lines written in Hebrew that she couldn't begin to decipher.

"Oh, Luke," she whispered, for this letter was tangible proof he was breaking down. He'd been imprisoned for more than a year, and his mind was no longer functioning properly. The Flying Dutchman? She vaguely remembered the legend of the ghostly ship doomed to forever sail on the high seas. Laden with silks and spices plundered from the Far East, it was ruined by the greed of the captain, and the ghost ship was condemned to endlessly drift upon the ocean.

She stared at the letter, baffled by the incoherent rambling, but perhaps Luke was trying to tell her something. Trust a good dancer? She and Luke both loved to dance and were good at it. Gray had two left feet and would rather have a tooth pulled than get on a dance floor. Was Luke trying to tell her to trust himself rather than Gray? Was he implying that he was second in command to Gray's senior position in the family?

She sighed as the trolley drew near the train depot. The letter raised uncomfortable questions, and she feared Luke would not last much longer.

~~~

The following week they traveled through the Blue Ridge Mountains and crossed into the splendor of Tennessee. From the train's oversized windows, Caroline watched as they sped past fields of cotton, rye, and tobacco. Lumbering cattle grazed in pastures, followed by endless stretches of lush forest. The president spoke at the state capitol, and they were all guests of honor at a Scottish festival featuring bagpipes, traditional games, and highland dancing.

Mrs. Foster took the opportunity to sneak in a dig at Caroline. "If you can't land Agent Trask, perhaps you can settle for one of those men in kilts," she said.

For some reason, Mrs. Foster delighted in Caroline's unrequited crush on Nathaniel and called attention to it at every opportunity. In Nashville, they threw pennies into a wishing well, but Mrs. Foster threw a quarter. "I'm throwing an extra big coin in hopes you can land Agent Trask," she giggled.

When they boarded carriages to return to the train, Mrs. Foster noticed an empty spot beside Nathaniel and flagged Caroline down. "Yoo-hoo, Caroline!" she called out with a broad wave to attract the attention of the entire party. "Look! There's an empty seat beside your young man."

Caroline ignored the invitation, sending Mrs. Foster a sidelong smile as she joined the McKinleys in the president's carriage. She tried not to let Mrs. Foster get under her skin, but it was hard, and they were only a week into the tour.

When their itinerary turned south, they visited a felting mill and toured Fort McPherson, where they dined with the troops. Then they headed toward Atlanta, where the president met with leaders of the burgeoning textile industry, then toured a Jewish synagogue.

It was at the synagogue that Caroline hoped to find someone who could help her make sense of the final passages of Luke's letter.

Both McKinleys were fascinated by the synagogue, admiring the ornate cabinet that held the Torah scrolls. In honor of their visit, the candles in all the chandeliers had been lit. With great care, the rabbi opened the gold-embossed ark to lift out the Torah and carry it to the dais. The scrolls were unwrapped and unrolled. To Caroline's delight, the rabbi read in Hebrew, his rich voice speaking the ancient language in a manner that filled the air. Then he sang the passages, the words lifting and falling in a delightful cadence.

She must get this man alone! It was impossible to know what Luke had written in the Hebrew passage, but her deepest fear was that he might be guilty and was using Hebrew to confess something shameful. She didn't want anyone else to witness what the rabbi had to say.

Her opportunity came earlier than expected, for the rabbi's wife had prepared traditional Jewish pastries to share with the party. Although they'd been dining like royalty on the train, the chance to sample the pastries sent everyone eagerly following the rabbi's wife.

Caroline hurried to the rabbi's side, Luke's letter clutched in her hands. "Sir? May I have a moment?" she asked, her voice uncomfortably loud in the cavernous chamber.

Perhaps he was used to people seeking a private moment, for he did not seem surprised as he gestured her toward a pew. Members of her party were still funneling out the door, and she prayed they'd leave quickly so she could speak in confidence.

Only Nathaniel lingered. "Caroline?" his gentle voice echoed in the nearly empty hall. "Are you all right?"

She nodded. "I want to speak with Rabbi Ginsburg for a moment."

Their eyes met across the distance, but he nodded and followed the others to the reception area.

Caroline braced herself as she passed the letter to the rabbi. "My brother sent me this letter from prison." She pointed to the Hebrew passage. "I hope you might tell me what he wrote at the bottom."

The rabbi adjusted his spectacles and lifted the letter closer to his face. "Your brother has poor grammar."

"To be expected," she said. "He's been teaching himself."

Rabbi Ginsburg took only a moment more to finish reading. "In the first line, he says he is very ill. He says he may die."

Her gasp echoed in the chamber, and she clapped a hand over her mouth, her worst fears coming to life.

"Then he goes on to quote Ecclesiastes," the rabbi continued. "Here his grammar is perfect. I am guessing he has a Hebrew Bible?"

"He does."

The rabbi nodded. "He has picked and omitted various pieces, but here is what he wrote:

> To every thing there is a season. . . . A time to be born, and a time to die; a time to plant and a time to pluck up that which is planted;
> A time to kill, and a time to heal; a time to break down, and a time to build up;
> A time to weep, and a time to laugh; a time to mourn, and a time to dance.

"That is the last of the quoted passage," the rabbi said. "Then he goes back to writing in his own broken Hebrew. The grammar is bad, but he writes that it is nearing his time to break down and die. He prays that for his sister, it is your time to laugh and dance."

He handed back the letter.

My God, he is saying good-bye to me.

She wasn't going to collapse or give up. She was going to figure out a way to save Luke before it was too late.

If Caroline was going to make any sense of this letter, she needed another pair of eyes to help. Maybe she was too close and emotional to interpret whatever Luke was trying to say to her.

That meant she needed Nathaniel. He was a detective. He had an eye for detail and might be able to spot something she'd overlooked.

Except that ever since *l'affaire de lobster*, he had been assiduously avoiding her. He was scrupulously polite and professional, but it was clear he intended to honor the president's request and keep his distance.

At dinner that night, he dined with Sven de Haas, Alfred Medina, and a pair of AP reporters. Dessert was an amaretto cake, but the real treat was a gourmet selection of cheeses paired with wines. Nathaniel rarely drank, and she pounced on her opportunity to get him alone.

"Can I ask you to come to the parlor car?" she asked.

He immediately went on alert. "Why?"

"I need your professional opinion on something." It was impossible to ignore the knowing glances flying among the men, and she met them head on. Turning to the maddening Sven, she kept her voice loud enough for everyone in the dining car to hear. "I shall naturally be on good behavior and keep my hands to myself, so Mr. Trask's spotless reputation will remain unsullied."

Mercifully, Nathaniel rose without qualm and followed her through to the parlor car. It was dim, and he immediately turned the dial on the gas lamp to glow brighter.

His face was drawn with concern as he turned to her. "How's your brother?"

It felt entirely natural. They knew each other so well that he didn't even need to ask what her worries were.

"Not good," she said, handing him the letter. "His last letter is nonsensical, and Gray thinks he's losing his hold on the world around him. I'm not so sure. I wonder if he's trying to communicate something, but I can make no sense of it. I need a fresh pair of eyes."

Nathaniel sat on one of the padded benches to read, and she watched as his eyes traveled over the puzzling text. She didn't even need to explain her concerns to Nathaniel, as he immediately began breaking down the passages.

"The city of columns is Havana," he said.

"How do you know that?"

"Havana has always been known as the city of columns because of all the Spanish architecture."

She looked at the passage Luke had written. *The crew from the north has vanished, and the road to a city of columns is in danger.*

"Havana is in danger?" she asked.

"No, the *road* to Havana is in danger, and the trouble is coming from 'the westernmost key.' Does Luke have any connections in Key West?"

"Not that I know of."

"Who is the good dancer?" Nathaniel asked.

"I am, but he is too."

Nathaniel read the relevant line aloud. "'Please remember, you can always trust a good dancer and the second in command.'" He set the paper down and looked her in the eye. "It sounds like he is telling you to trust your own judgment rather than your older brother's. Do you have any reason to doubt Gray?"

The thought was appalling. "Gray has always been like a

father to us. He's also been a lifeline to Luke, so I don't understand the reference to trusting the second in command, or who that could even be. Gray has been to Key West, but I never have. I have no idea what Luke can be saying about trouble flowing from Key West."

Nathaniel turned the page over to where she'd written the translation of the Hebrew text. More than anything, she hoped Nathaniel could give her an alternate interpretation of the passages from Ecclesiastes other than Luke telling her he was about to die and not to mourn him.

Nathaniel sighed deeply. "I don't like the sound of this."

"I don't either."

"'A time to mourn and a time to dance,'" he read, "then he flat out tells you to dance. I think you must be the good dancer he speaks of in the first part."

"Unless, of course . . ."

"Unless we're reading too much into this, and it is the ramblings of a confused and delirious man."

She'd rather believe Luke was somehow up to his old tricks, like finagling a way to send a basket of artichokes or a dozen cadets to cheer a lonely girl on her birthday. Instead she was left with the uncomfortable conclusion that he was indeed losing hold of his sanity.

Nathaniel continued studying the letter. "He writes, 'You know what to do,' but you *don't*. The good news is that the army is allowing his letters to get through, so wait for more information. I know this is frustrating. Remember, this is a battle that might take months or years. When you have more details, you'll be able to draw a better conclusion."

Unless the army ordered a quick trial and execution. She closed her eyes and prayed. *Dear Lord, what do you want me to do?*

"Your brother quotes Ecclesiastes," Nathaniel said. "It's always been my favorite book in the Bible."

She turned to him, question in her eyes, and he responded.

"In the dark time after Molly died I hated myself. I was strangled by grief and regret, but when I read Ecclesiastes, it brought comfort. We can't control the seasons in our lives, only how we respond to them. God planted eternity in our hearts, a longing to find meaning in the world. I still haven't found meaning in Molly's death. I don't know that I ever will. But Ecclesiastes teaches that such questioning is normal, and that brings me great comfort."

Peace settled on her shoulders at his words, and she slipped her hand into his. He returned her squeeze, but she wouldn't put him in an awkward situation, so she withdrew quickly.

"Thank you," she said quietly, wishing for more but grateful for the fleeting moment of compassion he provided.

Twenty-Five

Contrary to his initial fears, Nathaniel was enjoying the cross-country tour with the McKinleys. After leaving Atlanta, the presidential party moved on to Alabama and Mississippi, stopping several times a day for visits at various locales. At each stop, Nathaniel and Sullivan were always first off the train, meeting with members of the local police to confirm security for the visit. By the time the entourage arrived at the venue, he was usually able to watch some of the ongoing festivities. He had accompanied the president to inspect army bases, lay memorial wreaths, and tour factories. He'd been to county fairs and watched hog racing. He escorted Mrs. McKinley to tour rose gardens and visit orphanages.

Caroline was breathing easier, having gotten a telegram from Gray reporting that Luke was well enough to be discharged from the hospital and was now confined to a private cell at the military base in Havana. Nathaniel still worried about her, though.

Today his challenge was to keep the president safe during a paddlewheel steamboat ride on the Mississippi River. He and Sullivan arrived an hour ahead of the president to secure the venue. A crowd had already begun gathering behind a barricade set up by the police, and Nathaniel scanned the faces, noting the excited families with young children in tow, vendors hawking pastries, and the ever-present journalists with their notebooks. A weathered man with no shirt but a huge pair of angel wings anchored to his back held up a Bible and preached doom.

"Keep an eye on that one," he said to the local police chief.

"We've already got him covered, but you don't need to worry. Old Jake has been pacing the wharf for years and never done any harm."

Old Jake might be a harmless loon, but Nathaniel still didn't like it. He asked a local officer to continue scanning the crowd as he and Sullivan boarded the steamer for an inspection. As steamboats went, this was a compact one, with only three levels: the main deck, the boiler deck, and the hurricane deck on top, where the McKinleys would ride for the best view of the passing countryside.

Nathaniel searched each storage room and closet to ensure no stowaways had slipped aboard. He headed up to the top level, where a spacious sun deck surrounded the pilothouse. A high tea would be served on the deck in the middle of the four-hour tour, and a canvas pavilion had been erected to shield the first lady from the sun.

"It all checks out," Sullivan confirmed, and Nathaniel agreed. He remained on the top deck to watch as the line of carriages carrying the president's party approached the wharf. Mounted police officers rode ahead, alongside, and behind the carriages, and as instructed, there were no identifying decorations on the McKinley carriage.

By the time the president arrived, at least a thousand people had gathered to hear a brief speech. Cheers broke out as McKinley approached the podium, and a local band played "Hail to the Chief," a song engraved on Nathaniel's brain. When he was an old man, that tune would no doubt summon memories of this once-in-a-lifetime summer.

He scanned the crowd through his binoculars, searching for anyone who didn't belong. All sorts had turned out today. Well-dressed men and ladies in their finest rubbed shoulders with longshoremen and street vendors. A little girl carried a lollipop almost as big as her head, and the child's anxious mother tried to stop her from rubbing it in her hair.

The cheering went on for a full minute after McKinley mounted the podium. Caroline stood near the podium with the congressmen's wives, smiling and clapping in the morning breeze. By heaven, she was lovely, and he stole a few seconds to indulge in the simple pleasure of admiring her.

A part of him wished they both lived in Chicago, where he could lead an uncomplicated life as an artist, and she could be a secretary for some local official. There wouldn't be much money, but they could live simply. During the day he'd make engravings, and in the evenings they would go out to one of the many beer gardens, where they'd laugh and dance and sing long into the night.

"Get your head out of the clouds," Sullivan said. "The speech is almost over, and we need to report to the main deck."

"Of course," Nathaniel said, pulling away from the railing. He shouldn't be mooning over Caroline anyway.

Twenty minutes later, the presidential party was aboard, the gangway lifted, and the entrance secured. As the steamboat pulled away from shore, his tension began melting away. They were on a secure boat, and he could enjoy the ride like all the others onboard.

Everyone headed to the top deck, where the mayor of Natchez pointed out sights of interest to the president and congressmen. It didn't take long to sail past the city, and then the slow-moving steamboat carried them into the marshlands, where cypress and tupelo trees draped with Spanish moss grew along the banks. Egrets picked through the cane grass while gulls swooped overhead.

All the while Nathaniel was intensely aware of Caroline. First she helped Mrs. McKinley to the main table, then she fetched a pitcher of iced tea and a plate of lemon cookies for the ladies. Twice she caught him admiring her, but maybe there was something about the languid weather that made it easy to let his guard down, and he didn't look away like he normally would. It was a perfect day, and the natural beauty of the river made him long for an easel, his sketchpad, and a whole box of pastels. All around him, the sounds of the party unfolded, but he didn't mind being alone. The beauty of the countryside and Caroline Delacroix was enough to keep him entranced for hours.

After a while, Caroline approached him at the railing. She wore summer whites with a shawl of ivory silk so delicate that it was nearly translucent as it draped across her shoulders. She stood a little closer than was proper and met his gaze.

"The other guards are all at the front tables, gorging on shrimp and crawfish," she said. "No one will blame you if you join them."

"I'm happy here," he said.

Oh, she was in a mood. He could tell by the gleam warming her eyes as she twitched her shoulder, letting the shawl slip lower. The expanse of bare flesh she'd just exposed was unbelievably tempting.

"Please pull your shawl back up," he said, fighting the smile that threatened.

"But I'm not cold."

"I'll have to leave unless you do."

She put the shawl into place. "Better?"

Not really, but they were in full view of the president and the rest of the entourage who knew about his shocking weakness where Caroline was concerned, and it was for the best.

"Better," he confirmed. They both turned to face the river, a full six inches between them, and yet their connection flared to life. He was aware of every square inch of her as they sailed farther upstream.

"Are you really going to ignore me the rest of the trip? All the way to California and back?"

"I've never ignored you," he said. She was constantly in his thoughts, and he liked having her there, even if she was a distraction.

"President McKinley isn't my father. He has no right to dictate who I court. You know what I'm asking."

He did. Every impulse longed to close the distance between them, for he'd never been so drawn to a woman before. They were attuned to each other. They couldn't be more different in background or comportment, but they saw the world through the same eyes. They shared the same values, the same passion for art and beauty. He wanted her, and she wanted him. They weren't yet free but would be soon.

"I've always loved counterfeit detection," he said. "The challenge of it, the pursuit of it. Counterfeiters think like me. They are detail-oriented and patient. I love matching my wits against theirs."

"Yes?" she asked, clearly wondering where this was leading.

"On September 15th, Wilkie has promised to transfer me back to the counterfeit division. I'll be out of the White House."

She turned to face him, sheltering her eyes from the sun with her hand. "And where will you be on September 16th?"

"Courting you."

If possible, the gleam in her eyes intensified, and it took every bit of self-control to resist hauling her into his arms.

"I shall look forward to it," she said, then returned her gaze to the marshland alongside the river.

The next two hours were possibly the most delightful of his life as they shared the afternoon, but all too soon, it was over.

The steamboat neared the port, and the familiar tension returned. He stayed on the top deck while sailors tossed ropes toward men on shore to secure the ship. The crowd was thinner now, but a few hundred were still here. Old Jake with his angel wings still paced the wharf, shouting doom and proclaiming the end of days.

Then someone else snagged Nathaniel's attention. A man who didn't look like he belonged. He carried a satchel and a plaid coat draped over his arm. He looked annoyed. None of that fit.

Worse, Nathaniel had seen him before. He raised his binoculars, focusing them on the scowling man. A receding hairline and saggy jawline, but most of all Nathaniel recognized the anger in the man's eyes.

"Don't lower the gangway," he hollered below, then raced down the stairs, taking them three at a time until he reached the main deck. The McKinleys were at the front of the line to leave the ship, but he put an arm out to block them.

"Sullivan, take them to the kitchen. Lock the door. There's a threat on the landing."

Sullivan didn't argue and neither did the McKinleys as they hurried down the passageway toward the kitchen. With its lack of windows and interior location, it was the most secure room on the ship.

The scowling man had been following them, for Nathaniel remembered seeing him at a speech in Pensacola. That was six days and three hundred miles ago, but he remembered the plaid coat and the man's dark expression. Whatever was driving this man to follow the president was a powerful force, and it needed to be stopped.

Nathaniel gathered members of the local police and the ship's crew and described the man who worried him. "He's around five foot ten and between sixty and seventy years old, carrying a canvas satchel and a plaid coat. He's white, with a receding hairline and a stocky build." He surveyed the four crew members who'd gathered to help. The oldest and least intimidating of the lot was an elderly man wearing a steamboat uniform and a nametag identifying him as Josiah Wilbert. "I want to detain him, and I want you to do it, Mr. Wilbert."

"Me?" the old sailor asked in surprise.

Nathaniel nodded. "You're in a uniform for the steamboat, so you won't alarm him like a police officer might. Tell him he has been selected for a special meeting, and there's a free meal for him at the embarkation port. I don't care how you persuade him to come, but I need him back there, and I don't want him to be alarmed. Can you do it?"

"Yes, sir."

"Be respectful. He hasn't done anything wrong yet, but I need to know why he's following us."

Nathaniel and Sullivan quickly put a plan together, and then he spun the cylinder on his pistol to confirm it was fully loaded and holstered the weapon. The McKinleys were in a secure location, and he gave permission to lower the gangway.

Mr. Wilbert was the first one out, with Nathaniel following a few steps behind. The scowling man was at the front of the crowd, and Mr. Wilbert headed toward him, Nathaniel loitering behind.

"Good afternoon, sir," Mr. Wilbert said.

The scowling man said nothing, just gave a brief nod of acknowledgment.

"A handful of guests have been selected to be treated to a meal in the canteen, and you're on the list. Would you care to follow me?"

The scowl vanished, replaced with a look of hopeful optimism. "Did the president ask to meet me?"

"I'm not sure how you got selected," Mr. Wilbert hedged. "Please follow me."

The scowling man followed Wilbert toward the canteen, and Nathaniel arrived a few minutes later. It was cooler inside the open-air restaurant, with fans overhead to keep the air moving.

A slight breeze came in from the river running alongside the canteen. Most of the tables were already occupied, but Mr. Wilbert found an open table for the scowling man.

Nathaniel gestured for Mr. Wilbert to leave with a quick flick of this head. He counted a dozen heartbeats, then approached the man's table. "It looks as if we'll be sharing this table," he said companionably as he took a seat across from the stranger. "I'm Nathaniel Trask. And you are?"

Nathaniel offered his hand, and it was a moment before the scowling man gave him a brief handshake. "Horatio Jankowski. Look, I'm sorry if this is your table. A man from the steamboat company told me I was picked for something."

He stood, but Nathaniel gestured him down. "Sit, sit. There's no mistake. I actually wanted the chance to speak with you. I remember seeing you at the president's speech earlier today."

A look of anger flashed, but it was quickly masked. "That's right."

"What did you think of it?"

Jankowski shrugged.

"I only ask because I'm curious. Have you ever heard the president speak before?"

Again, Jankowski shrugged, but his lips thinned and his brow lowered. It was the start of a fighting stance. Nathaniel countered with a deliberately calming expression.

"My job is to keep an eye on events as the president travels," he said. "What is it you do for a living?"

"Machinist," Jankowski said tersely. "I keep the spinning frames operating at a cotton mill up in Jersey City."

"You must have seen a world of change in the past few years," Nathaniel said in a sympathetic tone. "How did you learn that trade?"

Up close, Jankowski was older than Nathaniel originally assumed. He had to be at least seventy, and that was good. Violence rarely simmered in a man this old.

Mr. Jankowski pulled his bag onto the table, pointing to the closing mechanism. "See that clasp? I made it myself. I've always had a knack for metalwork. It's good work, and it has value. I don't care what those people at the mill say."

"I can see that," Nathaniel said, pretending to admire the clasp but noting the size and heft of the bag. It could hold a pistol, but not a rifle. He catalogued every detail of Jankowski's appearance, noting the worn heels on his boots and the clean fingernails. It had been a while since this man had his hands on mechanical equipment. There was something off about Mr. Jankowski, and Nathaniel needed to keep asking open-ended questions.

"What was your business in Pensacola?" he asked in his most casual voice.

It didn't work. Jankowski's jaw tensed, and his hands fisted around the handle of his bag. "I came to hear that boy speak," he said angrily.

"What boy?"

"The president," Jankowski said. "He may be calling himself William McKinley, but that's not his real name. No, sir."

Nathaniel stilled, noting beads of perspiration on Mr. Jankowski's forehead. It wasn't hot in here, but Jankowski was getting agitated.

"What's his real name?" Nathaniel asked calmly.

Instead of answering, Jankowski unlocked the clasp on his bag. A moment later he held a small folding case, which he opened to reveal a daguerreotype of a young man in a soldier's uniform. The image was old and faded, the once finely embossed leather worn smooth from wear.

"That's my son," Jankowski said in a shaking voice. "Edgar Jankowski. *My son.* Killed at the Battle of Chickamauga. That's what my wife and I were told, but the moment I saw a photograph of McKinley, I knew it wasn't true. I have no explanation for why Edgar would do this to us, but the president is my son, and a great lie has been perpetrated."

Jankowski's hand shook as he blotted his forehead, and his breathing was ragged.

"You believe that William McKinley is actually your son?" Nathaniel asked, his voice carefully respectful.

"I *know* he's my son," Jankowski said. The anger was back. "I knew Edgar would figure a way to survive the war, and I've always been on the lookout for him. I'm fairly sure he used to send us messages through the electrical machinery installed at the mill, but I couldn't interpret them. It wasn't until I saw William McKinley's photograph on a campaign poster that I had solid proof he's alive. Now all I have to do is get my hands on the boy and force him to admit it."

Nathaniel nodded toward the daguerreotype. "May I see the picture?"

Jankowski pushed it across the table. The resemblance was indeed startling. The young man had a similar hairline and deep-set eyes with straight black brows and even features. Edgar Jankowski wore a soldier's uniform and held a rifle proudly before him. He looked directly at the camera, a tiny hint of a smile on his face. A young man of promise and idealism who never came home, forever immortalized in this faded image.

It was hard to look at. The war had ended decades ago, but the pain of this young man's passing was alive and real for the man sitting across from Nathaniel. This had to be handled carefully.

"I can see the resemblance," Nathaniel said, rubbing his jaw as though in deep concentration. He pretended to gaze into space but was actually noting the location of all the police officers in the canteen. Two were in uniform, but Sullivan and two others were not. All were surreptitiously watching him.

He set the daguerreotype on the table with care. Jankowski had to be neutralized for the safety of the president, but Nathaniel wished he had the miraculous words that could soothe the anguish of the man across from him.

"Have you asked other people about the resemblance between your son and the president?"

Jankowski snorted. "Plenty. My wife thinks I'm insane, but I've always known that Edgar was out there somewhere."

"Where is your wife?"

"In heaven since last February, God rest her soul. She'd been suffering from consumption for years, but now she's in God's hands, and I can finally track Edgar down. I don't think I'll ever forgive him for letting his mother go to her grave believing him dead." Jankowski folded his arms and leaned back in his seat, watching Nathaniel through speculative eyes. "What did you say your role on this train was?"

"I help organize the speaking events," he said vaguely.

"Have you met him?"

"I have."

At last he had Mr. Jankowski's complete attention. The older man's face transformed with heartbreaking anticipation. "Can you get me through to him? Please. I've been waiting thirty years . . . *more* than thirty years. I must see him."

Nathaniel would never let this man within view of the president, but he needed some things put in place before he said so.

"Wait here. Let me see if it would be possible." Nathaniel left the table and spoke to one of the plainclothes officers. "Head back to the ship. There's a photographer on board named Rembrandt. Tell him to get here immediately and bring his equipment. I want to get a photograph of this guy."

"Yes, sir."

On his way back to the table, Nathaniel brought Sullivan along. "This is a friend of mine," he told Jankowski genially. "Can you tell him your story? It's fascinating."

Mr. Jankowski needed no further urging. He eagerly explained that the president was actually his long-lost son, providing additional details about the messages he'd received from various pieces of machinery over the years.

Rembrandt soon arrived at the canteen, lugging his equipment. They would need Jankowski's cooperation to hold still for a photograph that would be distributed to every town and train station along the path the president would travel.

Nathaniel stood. "Let's see if we can persuade that photographer to take our picture. I've enjoyed our conversation and would like to remember this meeting."

Mr. Jankowski's brows lowered. "I don't have a lot of spare coin for that sort of thing."

"My treat," Nathaniel said. "If you give me your home address, I'll even send you a copy."

As Mr. Jankowski stood for the photograph, Nathaniel quietly gave instructions to Sullivan, who stepped away to carry them out.

After the photograph had been taken, Nathaniel slid a piece of paper before Mr. Jankowski. "I'd like you to write a short letter to the president, and I promise to deliver it," he said. "I want you to include your name and address as well."

Jankowski seemed eager for the chance to make his case and began writing. Behind him, Nathaniel watched as Sullivan led the McKinleys off the steamboat and into a waiting carriage.

There could be no reasoning with a man who thought electrical machines were sending him messages. While a piece of Nathaniel sympathized with Jankowski's pain, it was time to be blunt, forceful, and intimidating. He waited until the president's carriage was gone, then took the letter from Jankowski.

"I am going to deliver this letter to the president. If you hear nothing from him, it is because he wishes no contact with you. He is the most powerful man in the nation, and if he wishes to pursue a relationship with you, he will. You will not attempt to contact—"

Mr. Jankowski shot to his feet. "Unacceptable!"

Nathaniel stood. "I repeat. You will not contact the president. Any further communication will be considered a threat.

These four officers are going to sit with you for a while. I will arrange for dinner to be sent over, and tomorrow you will board a train back to New Jersey."

Jankowski shook his head in disbelief. "That's not going to do it, boy. I won't give up."

Possibly, but the police departments along their upcoming route would be blanketed with Jankowski's photograph, and the police in Jersey City would be instructed to keep an eye on him.

And Nathaniel would be on the lookout. As he headed back to the train, the gnawing anxiety never far beneath the surface roared to life.

~ ❀ ~

The mood in the dining car that evening was unexpectedly boisterous, exacerbating Nathaniel's headache. Only three hours had elapsed from the moment he had recognized Mr. Jankowski in the crowd, but he was exhausted as he took a seat at dinner. Most of the others in the dining car had mugs of beer or glasses of wine, but Nathaniel was in no mood to celebrate.

The president made a point of stopping at Nathaniel's table. "Well done, Mr. Trask," he said formally, offering a quick handshake.

Nathaniel stood. "Thank you, sir."

The interaction took only a few seconds, then McKinley was on his way toward his own table.

Sullivan tried to push a beer on Nathaniel. "Relax!" he said. "We have no duties until we pull into New Orleans. You spotted the bad guy. Neutralized him. We should be celebrating."

Nathaniel wasn't entitled to celebrate. A dangerously unstable man had gotten within shooting distance of the president several times over the space of a week before Nathaniel had spotted him.

After dinner he retreated to the privacy of the sleeping car, where he could think. He brought his logbook and sat at the only table to record the day's events. What could he learn from this breach that could be used to tighten security in the future? According to Mr. Jankowski, his wife and others in their town knew of his delusions about the president. As soon as Rembrandt developed the photograph, Nathaniel would distribute it and hopefully keep Jankowski neutralized, but how many other delusional men were out there?

It was impossible to sleep that night, for it might only be a matter of time before a crack in his security split wide open, and there'd be nothing he could do.

Twenty-Six

The following weeks would forever be crystallized in Caroline's mind as an enchanted interlude, so different than anything she'd ever experienced in her life. In San Antonio they visited the Alamo and were serenaded by a mariachi band. In El Paso they were greeted with armfuls of roses, and President McKinley walked right up to the border, where he shook hands with the Mexican president.

Their traveling caravan moved through endless western vistas dotted with buffalo and wheat and an immense sky. They visited army outposts, ranches, and even an ostrich farm, where the hatching of two huge eggs was so fascinating that they delayed their departure to stay and watch. The beaming farmer named the newly hatched birds Mr. and Mrs. McKinley. They went through the desert southwest, where she had her photograph made while standing beside a cactus that towered more than twice her height.

In California they walked through fragrant orange groves and tasted pineapple freshly cut from the stalk. Ida's sister, Pina, and her niece Mary joined them in California for the last few weeks of the journey, which meant Caroline had more free time.

More than anything, Caroline looked forward to seeing the

Pacific Ocean for the first time. In San Luis Obispo, they were scheduled to tour an old Spanish mission, but all Caroline could dream of was a chance to see the ocean only ten miles away. Ida was well cared for by her sister, and Caroline nagged Nathaniel to take her to the coast.

"Sullivan and the local sheriff can guard the president, and we're so close I can smell the salt in the air. Please?"

Her cause was helped by Rembrandt and George, who both wanted to see the Pacific as well. She could see the longing just beneath Nathaniel's austere expression and decided to tease him into temptation.

"George will assure we will be well chaperoned, so you need not fear I shall compromise your famed modesty."

He cracked, giving her one of those closed-mouth smiles she adored, and agreed to rent a carriage to take them to the coast. It was a dusty ride as the carriage lurched over bumpy paths, but at last they arrived, and Caroline hiked up her skirts to climb the scrub-covered ridge, for the roar of the ocean could be heard on the other side.

"Oh my word," she whispered upon seeing it. How different it was from the ocean in Virginia, where the harbors were heavily developed and protected by breakwaters. Here she stood on a rugged cliff, buffeted by the wind as she gazed at the splendor below. George scrambled down the cliffside toward the beach, but Rembrandt had lugged his equipment to the top of the ridge.

She reached for Nathaniel's hand and smiled at Rembrandt. "Will you take our photograph?" she asked. This was a magical day, and she wanted to remember it forever.

"Certainly," Rembrandt agreed, and began prowling for a level spot on which to place his tripod.

Nathaniel kept gazing out at the ocean with a quiet expression of awe. "It makes a person feel small, doesn't it?"

Small but filled with immensity. "Yes," she whispered. They

had traveled from coast to coast, and soon they would turn around to head home, where Nathaniel would finally be free.

"September 15th is less than a month away," she said.

"Twenty-six days."

She smiled, glad he knew the exact number. "You must be looking forward to getting back to counterfeit."

"Among other things."

She *loved* his dry sense of humor, for his eyes gleamed as he sent her a look of pure admiration. If Rembrandt weren't five yards away, she'd give in to temptation and steal a kiss.

"What could be more exciting than counterfeit?" she teased.

Again, that closed-mouth smile as he shrugged. "Sometimes I investigate fraudulent documents. Occasionally issues of banking records. All of it is very interesting." He turned and gazed out over the sea with an expression of aching wistfulness. "But no matter what I do or where I am assigned, my heart will be with you."

She leaned into the wind, savoring the sun on her face and the clean scent of the air. Whatever the future held, they would be together soon.

⁂

Nathaniel counted the days until he'd be free of the White House job, but as his day of liberation drew near, it seemed time slowed. He was constantly within yards of Caroline but couldn't touch her. He dined with her, conferred with her to ensure the first lady's comfort, and they even went sight-seeing together. They stole glances when no one was looking, and sometimes he secretly slipped a note beneath her dinner plate to tell her something silly or sweet.

He wouldn't break his word to President McKinley by making advances toward Caroline until he was no longer working in the White House, but she was making it hard. In Los Angeles she bought a Spanish flamenco dress and modeled it for everyone in the dinner car, swaying to make the tiers of black and scarlet lace flare. A moonlight serenade had been planned in San Francisco, and Caroline managed to pawn the first lady off on Pina, allowing her to join the table where he sat with Rembrandt and the reporters. The way the candlelight illuminated her profile ought to have been captured by an artist.

They had a three-day stop in San Francisco, where he accompanied the president on the famed cable cars to visit the Japanese Tea Garden. Caroline was yards away the entire time, keeping them all amused with witty observations and flirtatious chatter.

One morning the McKinleys were invited to a luncheon at the Presidio, and Sullivan was the only guard needed, for the first couple would be well protected on the military base. Mrs. McKinley's sister accompanied them, which meant Caroline was free as well.

"There is a museum worth seeing," she said as she sat next to him in the parlor car after breakfast. The toe of her slipper peeked out from beneath her hem and tickled his ankle.

"I am impervious to temptation," he said, wishing a frisson of electricity hadn't just shot through him, but he didn't move his leg.

"They have a Vermeer on display."

That was all he needed to hear. "Let's go."

Most of their group had already departed for the Presidio, so he and Caroline went to the museum alone. The Vermeer was near the back in a position of honor. It was *The Milkmaid*, another of Vermeer's famously quiet scenes of domestic tranquility. A sturdily built woman poured milk into an earthenware bowl, shades of ochre and umber giving the picture a somber tone. The kitchen scene was dim, but pale light from the window above lent quiet dignity to the maid's chore.

"It reminds me of the Vermeer in the Corcoran, the dreary one of the lady reading the letter," Caroline said. "This one is dull too, but beautiful. It makes me want to step inside the painting for an hour or two."

"Yes," he agreed, for the painting quietly paid tribute to the dignity God imbued into seemingly mundane acts of daily service.

A family of tourists came lumbering toward the Vermeer. "Why did the artist bother painting such a homely woman?" the father asked as he drew alongside them.

"She's not homely, she's flat-out ugly," a boy said.

"She's not too ugly," the mother defended. "I'll bet she's making a bread pudding, and this picture is making me hungry. When can we go to lunch?"

"Come on, two more rooms," the father said. "We paid to see everything, so let's get moving. This is great art we've paid to see."

"I still say that woman is too ugly to be in a painting," the boy said as the trio moved into the next room.

Nathaniel tried not to smile as he stared at the Vermeer, but he was dying to know Caroline's opinion.

"What do you think?" he asked when they were alone again. "Is she too ugly to be in a painting?"

Caroline took a moment before responding. "She has a dignity and strength that shines through even three hundred years after Vermeer painted her. I can tell by the way she handles that pitcher that she knows what she's doing, and she makes me embarrassed that I can't cook."

He laughed. "Me too."

"I agree that it's a lackluster painting," she added. "But I like it better than the one in the Corcoran, for nothing could be as frightfully dreary as that *hausfrau* reading a letter."

"You still prefer the fake Vermeer of the girl with the rabbit?" he challenged.

She flashed him a delightfully flirtatious glance. "Why would I confess to such a thing when you will use it as ammunition against me? In your eyes, it will be proof that I value the silly and sentimental over the ponderous lady with the letter."

That was *exactly* what he was about to do, for she loved that rabbit painting even though it was a complete and total fraud.

"You can't imagine how much I'm looking forward to September 15th," he said, watching her carefully. A tiny tilt of one side of her mouth was the only indication she understood his meaning.

"We are of like mind," she responded.

It was time to rejoin the others, and they turned to leave the museum, walking with a respectable eighteen inches between them. He'd never felt closer to her.

~ ❦ ~

Caroline found the trip back east less eventful than the first half. There were fewer stops as they traveled through the plains of Wyoming and Nebraska, and by the time they reached the Midwest, Ida's energy was flagging. The president still made the scheduled stops at stockyards and factories in Illinois, but Ida decided not to leave the train. That meant Caroline needed to remain on the train as well.

It was embarrassing how often she stationed herself by the wide portrait window as the presidential party departed. She always watched Nathaniel, so tall and formal, conferring with local police at each stop. She loved his sober comportment and calm diligence. Other people in the crowd might have open collars and sleeves rolled up due to the heat, but never Nathaniel. He wore his black vest and suitcoat everywhere. Was it to hide his shoulder holster or in simple deference to the president? Either way, she liked his formality. She liked everything about him, including the restraint he showed in keeping his distance from her, even though he chafed against it as much as she did.

They made more stops in densely populated Ohio and Pennsylvania, but Caroline breathed a sigh of relief as they reached New York, for a special visit had been planned to see Niagara Falls. It was not an official event, rather a private excursion requested by the president. He and Ida had vacationed at Niagara Falls as newlyweds, and he wished to relive the memory.

While a trip to view Niagara Falls was easy for a young army major and his bride, it was quite another to arrange such a trip for the president of the United States and his invalid wife. It required dozens of police officers to clear the woods and secure a section of the park for the private visit. The McKinleys took only Nathaniel and Sullivan with them as they went off to enjoy an afternoon in the woodland along the falls.

Caroline's only responsibility today was to ensure the three AP journalists did not leave the train. The McKinleys had been adamant about their privacy and had asked Caroline to remain with the journalists in the parlor car to ensure none of them wandered off in hope of scoring an exclusive story. She had to crack open the windows, because the journalists all smoked like fiends as they played cards at a nearby table. At least she no longer felt compelled to join them, for she had at last conquered her cigarette cravings. Perhaps she was finally growing up after all.

She took the gift of a few hours to ponder Luke's latest letter. Once again he'd included Hebrew passages at the end, but in the English portion he wrote more about Key West.

> *The Flying Dutchman is using a link in the western key. Find the link and cut it. Trouble is still brewing there.*

In his earlier letter Luke had implied trouble came from Key West. Now he told her to cut the link in Key West. What link? And how was she supposed to cut it?

It was almost time for dinner before the McKinleys returned, both in good cheer. Oddly, Nathaniel and Sullivan looked furious when they boarded the train. Caroline didn't have time to ask why as she followed Ida into her private car to help her dress for dinner.

The frost between Nathaniel and Sullivan stretched throughout dinner. As usual, they dined with Rembrandt, but Nathaniel remained stonily silent, even during the dessert course of deep-dish apple pie, which was his favorite. The moment Rembrandt left for the smoking car, Caroline occupied his vacated seat beside Nathaniel.

"How was the visit to the Falls?" she asked.

Nathaniel's mouth thinned, and it looked like he didn't want to talk, but Sullivan was bursting at the seams.

"The president ordered us to hang back the moment we were in the woods," Sullivan said. "It was against every basic tenet of security, but what were we supposed to do? It was a direct order from the president."

"Sometimes you don't follow orders," Nathaniel said tightly.

"I hate to inform you, but Mr. McKinley outranks us both," Sullivan said, annoyance darkening his normally cheerful blue eyes. "If the president orders me to go stand on my head and sing 'Mary Had a Little Lamb,' I will do so."

"Did you follow orders?" she asked Nathaniel, who seemed irritated she should even ask.

"I'm not going to let the President of the United States wander off alone into the woods with an invalid woman. *Of course* I trailed them. They had no idea I was there."

"You can't know that," Sullivan challenged. "I don't want to get in trouble over this, and they might have known you were following them."

"They didn't know," Nathaniel bit out.

"How can you be so sure?" Caroline asked.

"Because I got an eyeful," he snapped.

Understanding dawned, and she tried not to laugh. "An eyeful of what?" she asked innocently. She'd been around the

McKinleys long enough to know they could be embarrassingly affectionate, but it was new and unwelcome to Nathaniel.

She was still thinking about it later that night as she settled into the parlor car with all the others after dinner. She tried to concentrate on the evening's newspaper, but her thoughts kept straying to Nathaniel and the dwindling days until they could be together. It was September 4th, and they had two more days in Buffalo while the president visited the World's Fair, but then they would be heading home to Washington.

What would it be like when Nathaniel no longer had this job to distract him? She watched as he bent over tomorrow's security schedule at the neighboring table. He never did anything halfway. Would he truly begin a whole-hearted courtship, or would he find some other excuse to keep her at arm's length?

She sighed and turned to the next page in the newspaper. The word *Cuba* leapt out from one of the headlines. It seemed the rebellion was heating up again. There had been a bombing north of Havana, and a newly reconstructed road and a bridge to the city had been destroyed.

The road to a city of columns is in danger.

The breath left her in a rush. Luke had known this attack was coming. He'd tried to warn her.

Then a worse thought descended. Did he have a hand in this? If so, why would he have told her? A chill descended, and her hands shook. What was she supposed to do now?

It was impossible to know what to think anymore, but one thing was certain. Luke's latest letter had another passage in Hebrew, and she needed to find someone to translate it for her as soon as possible.

Twenty-Seven

The World's Fair had been open all summer, but this was the first time the president had been able to visit, and Nathaniel dreaded the security nightmare it represented. The fairgrounds consisted of 350 acres of open parks and towering buildings. A man-made lake and waterways that simulated the canals of Venice meandered through the grounds, making a quick exit a challenge.

Nathaniel gaped at the crowd filling the Esplanade in the center of the fairgrounds. As far as his eyes could see, there were people everywhere. Ticket receipts indicated that 116,000 people had arrived in the park today, and the local police chief estimated that more than half had come to the Esplanade for the president's speech. *Sixty thousand people.* How to manage them? It boggled his mind, and he could only pray to God as the president stepped up to the podium.

Please, he silently implored. *Please be with us today and let this be safe.*

American flags framed the podium. Behind the stage were bleachers filled with invited guests wearing formal clothes despite the heat. Four tables at the base of the stage held the journalists, busily scribbling on their pads.

How to scan a crowd of sixty thousand? The people at the back looked as tiny as ants. Nathaniel tried to comfort himself with the thought that to those distant throngs of people, the president looked just as tiny. No sharpshooter, no matter how skilled, could accurately shoot that far. He kept his eyes trained on those closer to the stage. Almost everyone looked hot but excited as the president began his speech.

"Expositions are the timekeepers of progress," the president declared. "They record the world's advancements. They stimulate the energy, enterprise, and intellect of the people, and quicken human genius."

Nathaniel loved that phrase, *quicken human genius,* for it was exactly how he felt. He felt on the cusp, as though his life was destined to morph into something new and exhilarating soon. Was it because this assignment would be over in nine more days? He was so eager to begin the rest of his life. He wanted to be free again.

He continued scanning the crowd with hope filling his spirit. A new day was coming, and evidence of the future was all around him. The fair was filled with inventions, blazing light, and promise for the days ahead. This afternoon he would stand guard over the president at a reception, but tonight he would watch the fireworks alongside Caroline.

And in nine days it would be September 15th, when his future could truly begin.

Ida's sister, Pina, rejoined the presidential party in Buffalo, giving Caroline the opportunity for a free day at the World's Fair. While most of the fairgoers crowded the Esplanade to hear the president speak, Caroline was on a desperate quest to find someone who could translate the single Hebrew line from Luke's latest missive. These letters were far more important than she'd realized. Luke *knew* about the bombing of the road to Havana, and she hadn't spotted his warning in time. She would do better in the future. His latest letter told her to cut the link to the *Flying Dutchman* in Key West. But what did that mean?

The fairgrounds were huge, with ninety buildings and half a dozen parks. There was a Machinery & Transportation Building, the Electricity Showcase, and a Temple of Music. Caroline was most eager to see the Liberal Arts Building, for the program noted that it included an exhibit on the Wonders of the Ancient World. It was the most likely place to find someone who could read Hebrew.

Thankfully the president's speech meant crowds were thin, letting her scurry down the center aisle of the Liberal Arts Building, scanning both sides in search of the Wonders of the Ancient World. She passed exhibits on Shakespeare, a display of Renaissance tapestries, and one on advances in modern cookery. She finally spotted two massive reproductions of Egyptian columns framing the ancient-world exhibit. A tweedy-looking man with bushy sideburns looked eager for someone to talk to.

"Are you here to see the mummy?" he asked. "We open the sarcophagus twice a day, and the next opening will be as soon as the president's speech is over."

"No, thank you," Caroline said. "Do you perhaps read Hebrew?"

The question took the tweedy man aback, but he gamely introduced himself as Professor Mayfield and offered to help her find someone who could. "I only have middling abilities in Hebrew," he said. "My colleague from Princeton is completely fluent and will be manning the exhibit tomorrow, if you'd like to return."

The president's train returned to Washington tomorrow, and besides, the unsettling need to know what Luke had written clawed at her. She presented the letter to the professor.

"You can see there is only a single line at the bottom," she said. "Can you make any sense of it? Please?"

Professor Mayfield took the note from her, frowning as his eyes scanned the text for several moments.

"This is very odd," he finally said. "It must be my poor understanding of Hebrew, because this line doesn't make sense."

"What does it say?" Caroline asked, her mouth suddenly dry and heart thumping.

"It says, 'Stop talking to Holland. He is dangerous.'" Professor Mayfield handed her the letter. "But that doesn't make any sense. Holland is a country, not a person, but the writer calls it a 'he.'"

Caroline's blood ran cold. Captain Holland. Luke had somehow figured out she had been talking to Captain Holland, and she shouldn't have been. Realizations came cascading in. Luke had told her to beware of the Dutch. He warned her of the Flying Dutchman and its corrupt captain. All of it was veiled warnings about Captain Holland, but she'd been too blind to see it.

She still didn't know how to cut the link in Key West, but perhaps Nathaniel or Gray could help.

"I have to run," she gasped, snatching the letter back.

"You don't want to wait for the opening of the sarcophagus? It won't be long now."

She shook her head and ran, bumping into tourists wandering the exhibits. She would send a telegram to Gray immediately, for he knew Captain Holland too and might know what to make of this odd message.

***

Nathaniel stood with other members of the president's party backstage at the Temple of Music. Soon McKinley would deliver a brief farewell address, then shake some hands. It was their final event before they boarded the train back to Washington.

The president insisted on attending this farewell reception even though the first lady was too tired to join him. All Nathaniel had to do was survive the next hour, and they could return to the controlled safety of the train.

"Ice!" Sullivan crowed as he carried a pitcher and glasses on a tray to where they waited backstage behind the curtain.

"Bless you," President McKinley said, still hot from the outdoor speech. "Perhaps after the reception we'll all have something a little stronger."

Sullivan grinned. "I saw the train's cook wheeling in a huge crate of fruit, red wine, and brandy."

"It sounds like fresh sangria," the president said with a hearty smile. "We shall have a fine time tonight!"

The local police lieutenant popped his head behind the curtain. "The squad is here and in place," he said.

Nathaniel glanced at the president. "Ready?"

"I need two minutes." President McKinley shrugged first into his vest and then into his formal coat. It was hot for such attire, but the president never made public appearances without being formally dressed. It was only going to get warmer as thousands of excited people funneled through the auditorium for a chance to shake his hand.

President McKinley wiggled a red carnation into his lapel and gave a nod of acknowledgment to the master of ceremonies, who stepped around the curtain to provide an introduction. Applause filled the auditorium as the curtains pulled back, and Mr. McKinley gave a broad smile to the crowd, waving and nodding to those lined up near the front.

Nathaniel moved into position directly behind the president's right shoulder, while Sullivan stood on the other side. The president spoke for only two minutes, commenting on the weather, praising the fair, and thanking the crowd for attending.

Then they stepped down from the stage to stand at the front of the auditorium's center aisle for the hand-shaking. Two officers began walking down the aisle, inspecting people as they funneled closer to the president.

The line moved quickly, with dozens having passed in the first five minutes. Nathaniel scanned for anomalies, but mostly he saw overly hot, excited people. An immensely fat, grandmotherly woman leaned on a cane as she trudged forward, two ordinary-looking men behind her.

Then came an insipid man, indistinguishable except for his hand and arm swaddled in bandages, but behind him was the tallest man Nathaniel had ever seen. He was a black man, at least six and a half feet tall, and his hands were in his pockets. He wore the uniform of a Pullman porter.

"Hands out of your pockets," Nathaniel called to him, and the porter obeyed.

Then two gunshots cracked through the air, and chaos broke loose.

The next few seconds lasted for an eternity.

Nathaniel leapt in front of the president, but McKinley was already falling to the ground. Sullivan lunged toward a cluster of men struggling over a gun. A fight broke out. The black man tackled the shooter and struggled for the gun as a third shot rang out. Nathaniel straddled the president's body, bracing for the impact of another bullet, but none came. He gaped at the thrashing men only a few feet away.

The man with the bandaged hand—the bandages had been hiding a gun. The porter wrenched the pistol away, and Sullivan dove in and punched the gunman in the face, blood flying. Police swarmed, grabbing the gunman's hands and pinning him to the ground as the pummeling continued.

Blood was spreading over McKinley's chest and abdomen. "Get a doctor," Nathaniel shouted to one of the officers.

Despite his injuries, the president was still conscious. "Go easy on him, boys," he gasped to the men beating the shooter.

The following minutes were a haze of confusion. People screaming. Bodies pushing and shoving as the gunman continued to thrash while shouting obscenities. Then a policeman punched him so hard that he stopped talking.

Two men arrived carrying a stretcher they set down beside the president. "Sir, we're going to move you to the medical building," the orderly said.

McKinley nodded. "All right. Do it."

Nathaniel squatted alongside the orderlies. The color drained from McKinley's face and he groaned in agony as they heaved him onto the stretcher. That groan ripped through Nathaniel's heart, but he had to stay calm. As soon as the police cleared a path for the makeshift stretcher, they were on their way.

The hospital was only a few acres ahead. Heat and sunlight pounded down, and appalled onlookers watched as they carried the president, covered in blood but still conscious. Some of the onlookers wept, some crossed themselves.

It was cool inside the modest hospital as orderlies scrambled to prepare the operating room. Nathaniel walked alongside the president the whole way. They set him on the operating table, and McKinley gestured for Nathaniel. He looked awful, his face pasty white and covered in perspiration.

"Be careful how you tell her," he whispered. "Be very careful."

Nathaniel's heart lurched. He had failed everyone. His president. Mrs. McKinley. This good man lay gasping for air, all because Nathaniel hadn't noticed that bandaged hand in time.

"We'll be very careful, sir."

Twenty-Eight

It took Caroline forever to find the communications tent where she could send a telegram to Gray about the shocking warning in Luke's letter. Did Captain Holland have something to do with bombing the road to Havana? She could only pray that Gray might be able to make sense of these confused ramblings.

There were three people ahead of her in the line to send telegrams, and she'd never been so tempted to cut to the front. Especially because the woman at the counter was taking so long parsing her words to save a few pennies.

"She's been haggling over those words for the past five minutes," the stocky businessman ahead of Caroline groused. "I'm tempted to pay the fee myself just to move her along."

A commotion in the distance snagged Caroline's attention. Odd. Some people were running toward the fairground's exit, while others were rushing the other way.

"Do you know what's going on?" the man in front of her asked.

"I have no idea," she replied, but the commotion continued.

The businessman stepped out of line to approach a cluster of people standing beneath a nearby lamppost. He leaned in as the crowd began speaking and gesticulating wildly. She wanted to join them but wouldn't surrender her place in line. Thankfully, the businessman soon returned, his face grim.

"They say the president has been shot."

"No!"

It couldn't be. She had been in a carriage with him only a few hours ago, and everything had been normal. The last event for the day was a simple indoor reception in a controlled setting with plenty of security.

"It was at the Temple of Music," the businessman said. "An anarchist. He got off three shots before the cops got him."

"What about the president? Is he dead?"

The businessman shook his head. "They've taken him to the fairground's hospital. He's in surgery now, God save his soul."

Caroline ran, heading toward the hospital. The crowds got thicker, people standing before the building in stunned disbelief.

Had Ida been told yet? It would be dreadful. Ida was going to be destroyed, but someone needed to tell her. Caroline bumped past a burly man and through a group of gawking young boys, shoving forward through endless crowds. She finally reached a line of police officers standing shoulder to shoulder and blocking access to the hospital. She approached the one with the most brass on his uniform.

"I need to get inside," she said. "I'm with the president's party."

"No one's getting inside, ma'am."

"Please!"

Why at this most important moment in her life couldn't she think of a way to be more persuasive? The policeman's face was implacable; she had no chance of swaying him. A group of grim-faced men clustered on the hospital porch, and she recognized one of them.

"George!" she shouted, and thankfully she got his attention.

He broke away from the group and strode down the hospital path toward her. The police parted to let him through, and he tugged on her elbow to pull her from the crowd and toward an empty spot beneath the hospital awning.

"How is he?" she asked through chattering teeth.

"Alive. He kept saying he isn't seriously hurt, but there's no such thing as a shot to the abdomen that isn't serious. One bullet struck his vest button and is only a flesh wound, but the other went into his gut. A third bullet went wild. They're operating now."

"Has the first lady been told?"

He nodded. "A messenger was immediately dispatched. You should go to her."

"Of course. Is there anything else you need me to do?"

"Pray," he said.

~∞~

News of the shooting flew through the telegraph wires all over the nation, and reporters were congregating outside the hotel that had been quickly identified as housing the presidential party. Police guarded the doors, but Sven was there and let Caroline through. Inside, she found other members of their party assembled in the dining room, which had been closed to the public.

Army reinforcements had already arrived to help with security, for angry crowds were swarming the police headquarters where the gunman was held. He had been identified as Leon Czolgosz, the son of Polish immigrants and a fervent anarchist.

Caroline didn't care about the shooter. All she cared about was Ida. A doctor had already gently informed Mrs. McKinley of what had happened and offered her a tonic to soothe her nerves.

"Is it working?" Caroline asked the doctor.

"She's stable," he replied. "The hospital is telephoning regular updates to us, and there's been no change. The hospital director suggested the first lady remain here, as there's already enough chaos at the hospital. Everything will be touch and go for the next few hours."

Caroline nodded and headed upstairs. She placed her hand on the cold brass doorknob and bowed her head, praying for wisdom. Enough people were sending up prayers for the president, but she prayed for Ida.

Dear Lord, please give me the wisdom to comfort her. She's already lost both her daughters. Please don't take her husband.

She drew a steadying breath and entered the room.

Ida sat in her wheelchair, staring out the hotel window. Her face looked carved in stone, but she was sitting upright and wasn't in hysterics. A nurse and Pina sat nearby, looking frightened.

"There's been no change," Caroline said as she moved to Ida's side, keeping her voice calm and soothing. "Is there anything I can do for you?"

"You can find a pistol, then go out and shoot that man," Ida replied, her steely tone a clear indication that she was nowhere close to collapsing in a puddle of grief.

"Anything legal?"

"Sadly, no." Ida stared straight ahead with her fists clenched. "I feel so helpless."

"We all do," Caroline said.

She didn't know what else to say, and silence lengthened in the room, becoming unbearable. Pina wrung her hands while the nurse fidgeted in discomfort. Ida kept staring out the window.

Unbidden, one of Caroline's earliest memories came to the surface. She must have been less than four years old, for her mother was still alive. Caroline had been sobbing over some long-forgotten incident, but Mama's voice had soothed her, coaxing her to sit in a chair while her mother undid her braids to comb her hair. How lovely it had felt to relax under her mother's soothing ministrations.

"Would you like me to comb your hair?" Caroline asked Ida. "It's mussed in the back."

Ida immediately straightened, her spine rigid as a bayonet. "I can't have mussed hair. If I am called to visit the Major, I must look presentable."

Caroline reached for a hairbrush. A Bible lay on the bedside table, and she passed it to Pina. "Perhaps you can read some psalms while we all wait," she suggested. "It's going to be a long night."

Pina looked grateful as she opened the book, landing quickly on Psalm 23, the eternal words a soothing comfort while the president's life hung in the balance. Ida sat calmly as Caroline unpinned her hair, spreading its length down her back. In truth, it wasn't terribly mussed, but perhaps the gentle act of having her hair combed might bring a smidgeon of comfort on this most horrible of days.

Pina read psalm after psalm, and Caroline ought to be concentrating her prayers on the president, but all she could think of was Nathaniel. Where was he? Was he all right? This was going to hit him hard, and Caroline feared he might be headed for a very dark place.

~ ⁊ ~

Caroline did not sleep, but by morning the world looked brighter. The president had made it through surgery and survived the night. The fairground's temporary hospital was unsuitable for his recovery, and he had been transferred to the Milburn home, a stately house less than a mile away that belonged to a personal friend of the president.

George Cortelyou arrived at the hotel before sunrise to confer with Caroline privately, reporting that the president was alert and coherent.

"He even wanted to know how his speech has been received in the papers," George said. "I didn't have the heart to tell him that all papers are only reporting news of his shooting, but he's already strategizing how to make hay of things. He's asked all available cabinet members to come to Buffalo immediately. He wants them to keep pushing on his legislation."

George reported that the surgeon thought a visit with Ida might be too stressful for the president. What an irony that cabinet members were being summoned to discuss politics, while a visit with the notoriously unstable Ida was thought to be a health risk.

"Personally, I think a visit from his wife might be helpful," George said. "He keeps asking after her. Do you think she can compose herself for a visit?"

"I do," Caroline affirmed. Then she asked the question that had been nagging her from the moment she'd heard about the shooting. "Where is Nathaniel?"

The corners of George's mouth turned down. "Nathaniel is obsessed with sniffing out additional assassins. He thinks there are more in the shadows. John Wilkie arrived late last night, and they've been holed up at the police station ever since."

Caroline watched George's face carefully, bothered by the hint of disapproval just beneath the surface, but she needed to get Ida ready for a visit to the president. During times of crisis, the first lady leaned heavily on her husband, as though the simplest decision was beyond her. In such times the president had always firmly instructed Ida on how to behave, and this morning Caroline would do the same.

"You are not to cry," she ordered once she helped Ida rise from bed. "You must appear calm and in good spirits. He worries about you, and the best tonic for him will be to see you sailing through this crisis like a champion. You are a woman of strength and valor, like Deborah from the Bible, defending her people. Today you will be just as strong, fighting to prop up your man."

Ida stared straight ahead but paid fierce attention to every word. "Keep talking," she said.

Caroline complied. "Bring your Bible with you. Be prepared to read his favorite psalms. Look him in the eyes. Smile. Hold his hands and let your strength flow from you and into him. I know you can do this."

"I can do this," Ida repeated, straightening her shoulders and composing her features.

Caroline kept up the stream of orders mingled with compassion as the carriage drove them to the Milburn house. To her surprise, Ida did not even request her wheelchair but walked into the home leaning only on her cane, her chin high and shoulders back.

Mrs. Milburn welcomed them inside. She was surprisingly young, with kind eyes and dark hair swept into a modest bun. "He is awake," she said, ushering them toward the dining room that had been converted into a convalescent room.

Caroline paused outside the room. "Would you like me to go in with you?"

Ida hesitated only a moment, then squeezed Caroline's hand. "Nonsense. I will be the soul of valor. An Old Testament heroine. Deborah. Esther. Ruth."

She took a deep breath, then walked through the arched opening and sat beside the president's bed. Caroline cringed at how pale and slack he looked, but he turned his head and managed a smile for his wife.

"Don't you look lovely," he murmured.

Ida clasped his hand. "We must get you better, my beloved. People back home are missing you."

Her voice was gently teasing, and Caroline sagged with relief. Ida McKinley had risen to the occasion.

She backed away to give them privacy and headed to the kitchen, where a beleaguered cook kept a percolator filled with coffee.

"May I borrow a sheet of paper?" she asked.

The cook nodded, and a few moments later, Caroline found a

private space to write out the telegram to send Gray. Despite the tragedy of McKinley's shooting, the rest of the world carried on, and it was time to heed Luke's warning about the danger of Captain Holland before it was too late.

Twenty-Nine

Nathaniel sat at the table in a room in the police station, a pad of paper on his lap as he watched John Wilkie calmly interrogate the shooter. The only other person in the room was a government stenographer who sat at the far end of the table. It was the stenographer's job to capture every word the would-be assassin spoke, but Nathaniel looked for more: a change in inflection, a nervous tic. Anything that revealed the anarchist's true thoughts. Surely a man this dull-witted couldn't be working alone. Nathaniel would parse every word, looking for clues to an accomplice.

Leon Czolgosz was an unemployed millworker from Ohio with no formal education and limited vocabulary. He was only twenty-eight, with ordinary features, light brown hair, and large eyes. He might even be considered handsome, but Nathaniel's flesh crawled even being in the same room with him. It was an effort to sit passively and watch for any hint of deception.

"Where did you get the gun?" Wilkie asked casually, and Czolgosz obligingly gave the name of the hardware store in Cleveland. So far Czolgosz had consistently answered all questions put to him with simple, direct language.

"Was anyone with you when you bought the gun?" Wilkie asked.

"No. I done it alone."

"What about after you arrived in Buffalo? Have you any associates in the city?"

There was a pause, a look of confusion, and Wilkie rephrased the question using simpler words.

"Do you have any friends in Buffalo?"

"No. I done everything alone."

Wilkie proceeded to ask the same question from a number of different angles, all designed to trip Czolgosz up if he wasn't telling the truth. He asked how the gunman selected his boardinghouse and how he paid the bill, because it was too expensive for an unemployed millworker.

"Are you sorry you did it?" Wilkie asked, and Czolgosz snorted.

"I'm not sorry," he said. "I'd do it again if I could. But do it better. Get the job done."

"Really?" Wilkie asked. "How will your parents react when they learn what you've done?"

Shame flashed across the younger man's face, but it was gone quickly, replaced by disdain. Czolgosz raised his chin and spoke clearly. "The history of progress is written in the blood of men and women who have dared to espouse an unpopular cause."

Wilkie leaned forward. "Keep talking."

"People only have as much liberty as they have the intelligence to want and the courage to take."

Wilkie nodded as though intrigued, which inspired Czolgosz to keep spouting off anarchist doctrine. He was mouthing someone else's philosophy, and Nathaniel was certain he knew who it was.

He adjusted the knot on his tie, a signal to Wilkie that he needed to communicate something. Two minutes later they left the room, leaving Czolgosz still manacled to his chair.

"What is it?" Wilkie asked once they'd stepped into the hall-way.

"Ask him about Emma Goldman. She runs an anarchist newspaper in Chicago, and he's repeating direct quotes from her press. Find out if they know each other or if he's ever worked for her newspaper. I think we can make a connection."

Wilkie nodded, and they returned to the interrogation room. This time Wilkie unlocked one of Czolgosz's hands so he could smoke a cigarette. The delicate dance to implicate Emma Gold-man hit pay dirt soon after.

"Oh, I know her all right," Czolgosz bragged. "She was glad to meet me and said I could be a soldier in her army."

"Tell me more," Wilkie said, and Czolgosz continued to boast about each encounter he'd had with the famed anarchist and professional rabble-rouser. It sounded as if he'd trailed her across the country to political speeches and rallies, tracking her down after each speech for another chance to bask in her fame.

Shame washed through Nathaniel, making it hard to hold his head up. This failure was going to haunt him for the rest of his life, but at least he could be sure everyone involved in this plot was captured. If Emma Goldman had inspired Leon Czolgosz to take three shots at the President of the United States, she must be made to answer for it.

⁓

Wilkie disagreed. "We can't arrest her just because she's met the gunman," he growled.

They were walking back to the hotel after twelve hours of interrogation. It was dark and the streets were empty, but Na-thaniel felt compelled to act. Guilt made him short-tempered and unable to think of anything beyond identifying everyone who'd played a role in the president's shooting. Emma Gold-man wasn't the only anarchist Czolgosz had implicated. He'd referenced almost a dozen people he'd been consorting with, and most were well-known anarchists committed to the violent overthrow of the government.

Czolgosz was too simple to have carried this out on his own. It was possible that Goldman and her compatriots had already boarded a ship to flee the country, escaping responsibility for the violence they'd unleashed. Nathaniel wouldn't let that happen.

"We need to round them all up," he said. "I can't turn the clock back and step in front of the bullets, but I can arrest the people who inspired that fool. I'll present their heads on a platter to Mrs. McKinley."

"And won't that be a treat for her," Wilkie said flatly.

"Shut up, Wilkie. I've studied anarchism, and I know how these people think. They represent chaos and violence. They have nothing to offer the world other than tearing down the accomplishments of decent, hardworking people."

A part of him knew he sounded irrational, but he had to stay hard. He was hanging on to his sanity by a thread, and if he softened, he would break.

~ ❧ ~

Caroline found the church service on Sunday morning a blessed oasis of peace after the chaos of the past two days. The pastor began with a prayer of thanksgiving for the president's continuing recovery, and the mood inside the church was a combination of relief, hopeful expectation, and comradery.

Caroline knelt, sending up prayerful thanks as earnestly as she could. The president was on the mend, and Ida was weathering the storm better than expected. What an astounding blessing on both counts.

And yet, on the other side of the aisle, Nathaniel sat staring stonily ahead. This was the first time she'd seen him since the shooting, and something seemed off. He'd always been stern, but this was different. A layer of anger smoldered just beneath the surface, and it was worrisome. She stared at his flinty profile for an unseemly length of time, hoping to catch his attention, but it didn't work.

After the service, people lingered in the foyer and filled the churchyard. Many wanted to recount where they had been when it happened, while others sought a chance to rub shoulders with the dozens of high-ranking Washington officials who'd flocked to town. Vice President Roosevelt had arrived in Buffalo the day of the shooting, but now that the president was on the mend, George thought Mr. Roosevelt's presence conveyed a morbid implication to the public. On George's recommendation, the Roosevelts left the city to continue their vacation in upstate New York.

Meanwhile, the secretaries of Agriculture, the Treasury, and the War Department had all gathered and would soon begin paying calls on the president, who intended to carry out his duties from his sickbed. Newspapermen jostled for position, and photographers took pictures, but the only person Caroline wanted to see was Nathaniel.

She scanned the throngs of churchgoers so intently that she almost missed him, for he'd already escaped the crowd and was a block away, striding down the tree-lined street in haste.

"Nathaniel, wait!" she called, lifting her skirt to hurry down the sidewalk. There was no break in his stride as he kept walking, but she was at last able to close the distance between them.

"Wait," she panted when she was only a few paces behind. She tugged at his elbow and forced him to slow down. "How are you doing?" she asked as she drew alongside him.

"Busy," he replied. "I meet with a lawyer at noon to draft the federal arrest warrants. We'll start rounding people up soon."

"That's not what I meant."

There was no change in his expression as he kept striding ahead, talking without looking at her. "Wilkie is being difficult, but all I need is one judge. Just *one judge* willing to sign those warrants. I'll arrest them all—the anarchists, the publishers of the radical press, even the people who organized that rally in Cleveland. They've all got blood on their hands."

This harsh, angry side of Nathaniel was alarming. She slid her hand down his arm and wrapped her fingers around his palm.

"But how are *you* doing?" she pressed.

"I'm fine. I'll be better when Emma Goldman and the rest of her ilk are in jail."

She stopped, still grasping his hand and making him stop as well. He kept staring straight ahead, so she positioned herself to look squarely into his face. They were alone, and no one could hear them.

"Nathaniel, look at me. Tell me what you're feeling."

He turned his face away to stare somewhere across the street. A gust of wind buffeted some fallen autumn leaves, and he waited until they fell to the cobblestones before he finally spoke, his voice so soft that she could barely hear it.

"I can't bear to see her."

"Mrs. McKinley?" Maybe this was why he'd made himself scarce. Except for the few hours she'd been allowed to visit the president, Ida had been constantly in Caroline's presence.

He gave the barest of nods. "For as long as I live, I'll never be able to look her in the face again."

"She doesn't blame you."

His gaze turned cynical. He didn't need to speak, for the agony in his eyes made it apparent he blamed himself and always would. Caroline opened her mouth to speak but couldn't find the words to ease his pain.

"I need to go meet with that judge," he said, pulling away and stepping around her to continue his journey.

She watched his back as he walked away, fearing this tragedy had broken him in a way she could not fix.

A flurry of activity descended on the Milburn house as members of the cabinet began assembling in Buffalo. Caroline made arrangements at local homes for their accommodation and hired carriage drivers to transport the men to and from the president's sickbed each day. George was a constant presence, carefully monitoring the president's energy and allowing a few visitors, but most of the work went on in the parlor. Cabinet members advanced plans, and clerks drafted articles to be released to the press.

Ida had been relocated to the Milburn house, and Caroline's time was split between sitting with Ida in an upstairs bedroom and attending George's business meetings in the downstairs parlor. It had been five days since the president was shot, surely the oddest five days of her life. While the mood upstairs with Ida was tense and teetered on the edge of a nervous collapse, downstairs was different. Caroline had a front-row seat as George cleared the way for a vote on the president's proposal to end American isolationism. Sven was there as well. He met with cabinet officials and congressional leaders, searching for pockets of resistance to the president's agenda and devising plans to counter it.

The Secretary of the Treasury wanted to move quickly. "No one can sell this proposal better than the president himself," he said. "Get him to Washington now, while sympathy is still high."

"Not until he is ready to travel," George said.

"But you said he is on the mend," the secretary blustered.

George remained implacable. "He is, but sticking him on a train for two days could jeopardize that."

The bickering continued, and Caroline lost interest in the quagmire of congressional maneuvering, reconciliation bills, and procedural motions. She hadn't taken this job out of political motivation. She'd stupidly accepted the job because she thought it would be *fun*.

Her gaze strayed out the window, where a delivery boy rode past on his bicycle, tossing several copies of this afternoon's newspaper toward the house. Normally he would have ridden up to the front porch, but the soldiers standing guard in the front yard made it impossible for anyone to get close.

She excused herself from the discussion of international tariffs and went to collect the newspapers. She was only yards away from the president's sickroom, but she was entirely dependent on the newspaper to track the ongoing investigation into the shooting.

She nodded to the pair of army guards sitting on the front porch. One of them had already snatched a copy of the paper and had opened it wide, his nose buried deeply in the interior. It was a little disconcerting. Shouldn't he be guarding the house rather than engrossed in the newspaper?

"Any news?" she asked.

He startled and closed the paper. "Just checking up on the world, ma'am."

She took an educated guess. "And what vital events have occurred in the world of baseball?"

The guilty flush on his face indicated she'd guessed correctly. He sent her a bashful smile. "The Brewers beat the White Stockings, five to one. Life is good."

She ought to be annoyed, but oddly it was exactly what she needed to hear. Inside the house, it was tense with anxiety and political rumblings, but in the rest of the world, life went on. Baseball games were played, the apple harvest was in full swing, and college classes were in session. While her corner of the world was shrouded in darkness, she needed to remember that somewhere the sun was shining.

"Did the Washington Senators play?" she asked.

The soldier looked momentarily surprised but cracked the paper open again in search of an answer. "They beat Boston, five to three."

"Good," she said softly, then leaned down to pick up the rest of the newspapers. She'd leave a few for the men in the parlor, but first she needed to scan every page before delivering a copy to Ida. If there was one negative word about the president, that page would be "lost" before it was delivered to her. Caroline carried the newspaper to a wicker chair at the far end of the porch. It would be easier to read out here amid the rustling of autumn leaves instead of the political haggling inside.

The front page was a shock. Emma Goldman had been arrested in Chicago and would soon be transferred to stand trial in Buffalo. A ghoulish political cartoon labeled her "the high priestess of anarchy." Ten others had been arrested on the strength of their participation in various anarchist groups and publications. A sick feeling took root as she continued reading, for the news got worse. Members of Emma Goldman's family had been arrested to pressure her into turning herself in. The adolescent children of Abe Isaak, another anarchist, had also been arrested, one girl only fifteen years old.

"This isn't America," she whispered. "This isn't America."

But it was, and Nathaniel had his hand in it.

~

After exchanging a dozen frustrating telegrams, Caroline finally tracked Gray down in Kansas, where he'd gone to help with the sale of the farm belonging to Annabelle's family. The farm had no electricity or access to a telephone, so it had taken some doing for them to arrange a time and place where he could accept a long-distance telephone call from her.

She stood in the hallway off the hotel kitchen where a telephone was anchored to the wall. It wasn't private, but she would finally have a chance to talk to Gray about Luke's cryptic message regarding Captain Holland. She had made no headway in what Luke was trying to say about Key West, but perhaps Gray could make sense of it.

It had been a long day, and her shoes pinched while listening to a series of operators patch her call through the switchboards in Pittsburg, Columbus, Indianapolis, Springfield, Topeka, and finally to the pharmacy in Junction City, Kansas, where Gray was awaiting her call.

"Caroline?" his voice finally came over the line. "How are you doing? How's the president?"

All over the nation, it was the only thing people were talking about, and she answered as best she could. President McKinley had been doing well but seemed weaker today. Perhaps setbacks were to be expected during the long recovery process. Then she got down to the matter at hand.

"The Hebrew portion of Luke's last message said to stop talking to Captain Holland. That he is dangerous."

"But I thought you trusted Captain Holland," Gray said.

"I did, but Luke clearly doesn't. As soon as I'm back in Washington—"

A telephone operator's voice interrupted them. "Breaking in with an emergency message from Milburn house," she said. "Doctor Winston needs to speak with George Cortelyou immediately."

Caroline's heart seized. "Gray, I need to go."

"Go," he ordered, and Caroline dropped the earpiece, running to the dining room where the air was thick with cigar smoke and political gamesmanship.

"George, you're needed on the telephone."

He must have noticed her stricken expression, for he sobered as he stood. "What's wrong?"

"I don't know. Dr. Winston is asking for you."

George followed her back to the telephone, holding the earpiece so they could both listen as Dr. Winston's tinny voice came across the wire.

"Gangrene has taken root in the president's wound," he said. "It's spreading quickly, and his temperature has soared. There is no hope. I don't expect him to survive the day."

Caroline sagged against the wall. Infection was everyone's greatest fear, but he'd survived a full week and had been getting better. She stared at George, irrationally hoping he'd say something to mitigate the doctor's terrible message, but he looked as stunned as she felt.

"The president has asked for a pastor," the doctor continued. "He knows he's dying."

George thanked the doctor and hung up the earpiece.

What are we going to do? What are we going to do?

She didn't realize she'd been speaking aloud until George answered her.

"We send for the vice president."

Thirty

William McKinley died at two o'clock in the morning, eight days after being shot. Theodore Roosevelt arrived later that day to a city in shock. There would be no formal inauguration, only a grim swearing-in ceremony that would occur in a few hours.

Caroline tried to blank out the noise from downstairs while sitting at Ida's bedside. A doctor provided heavy sedation for Ida, who had reached her limit. Downstairs, hammers banged as black crepe was nailed over the windows. Doors and footsteps thudded with the constant coming and going of government personnel. Ida didn't even flinch as another needle was inserted into her arm to administer more sedative.

"The Major will want to go back to Ohio," she said, staring out the window. "It's where our daughters are buried."

"I shall arrange it," Caroline said. It would have to be after the official state funeral in Washington, but Ida had the right to determine where her husband would be laid to rest.

Ida turned her head to look at an enormous wreath of white lilies that had been delivered earlier. "I'd like to take the lilies," she said. "The Major loves the scent of lilies, and he will enjoy having them on the train."

Caroline glanced at the doctor, who also noticed that Ida continued to speak of her husband in the present tense. Perhaps it was just the shock. She sat by the first lady's bedside until the additional sedation took effect, but wasted no time in drafting a schedule for someone to be by Ida's side for the next several days. She couldn't be left alone, but Caroline had other duties in urgent need of attention.

Mercifully, Ida's sister was ready to fill the void. "This looks fine," Pina said after reviewing the schedule. "You look exhausted. I'll take over."

Caroline squeezed Pina's hands, then headed downstairs, where plans for swearing in a new president were underway.

George didn't want the ceremony in the same house where President McKinley's body still lay, so a home a few blocks down the street was chosen. Members of the cabinet, a judge, and two newspaper reporters would be the only witnesses.

Caroline was grateful she would not need to attend, for the train carrying the president's body would leave for Washington within a few hours. What a terrible few days lay before them. Had it only been nine months ago when she and George were planning the grand inaugural festivities?

Now they would plan the president's funeral.

Nathaniel sat at a small table in the kitchen of the Milburn house. Staff took their breakfast here, but he was unable to eat. He just stared, knowing there was something he should be doing but unable to remember what.

Caroline approached. She hunkered down on the kitchen floor, her hand on his knee, and she was saying something, but she spoke too quickly for him to understand.

"What?" he finally asked.

"The security schedule. President Roosevelt's train leaves for Washington at six o'clock this evening. You've got plenty of soldiers from the army who will be aboard, but they need assignments."

She shoved a paper into his hands. The security form. He needed to fill it out, but hearing Mr. Roosevelt being called president had thrown him.

Because President McKinley was dead, and it was his fault. Now he needed to guard a new president. He set the form on the table, staring at the blank lines needing to be filled in with security personnel. Caroline stood over him, as though she expected him to do it immediately.

"I'll do this soon," he said, pushing the form a few inches away. He couldn't look at it yet and took a long sip of coffee instead. Maybe it would help beat back this avalanche of exhaustion clobbering him. He doubted he could rise from this chair if his life depended on it.

Caroline looked at her watch. "I'll be back in ten minutes. Please have it ready."

The acid of the coffee ate at his stomach. The thought of being responsible for another president's life was . . . well, he couldn't do it. Not now, anyway. Normally he could fill out this form blindfolded, but not now.

Maybe later. Maybe soon he'd have the strength to stand up and help with the flurry of activities going on around him, but right now it would be far too much effort. He stared at the cup of coffee growing cold before his eyes, wondering what he should do.

⁓

Caroline and George juggled telegrams, made lists, and took turns using the Milburn house telephone. They needed to transfer the president's body, arrange for the lying-in-state at the Capitol, and summon thousands of troops to march in the funeral procession. She wanted church bells to toll along the route as the funeral train made its journey to Washington, and wrote out a list of towns to contact for local arrangements. There would be two memorial services, one in Washington with thousands of dignitaries, and another private ceremony in Ohio. She would make the arrangements for both.

All of it needed to be scheduled within the next twenty-four hours, but the most urgent matter of business was coordinating President Roosevelt's security on the train to Washington. That duty fell to Nathaniel, but a glance down the hallway showed him still staring blankly at the form. It had been twenty minutes, and he hadn't made a single mark on it.

George interrupted her thoughts. "Caroline, the hearse to carry President McKinley to the depot is here. Have the flowers arrived yet?"

She glanced at her list of tasks. "I sent a pair of army privates to collect them from the florist. They should be here shortly."

The president's hearse would be draped with an American flag and a mourning bouquet of white lilies, but she also wanted red carnations. Mr. McKinley was famous for wearing a red carnation pinned to his lapel each day, and she ordered boutonnieres of red carnations for the men who would accompany his body home.

"And Mrs. McKinley? Will she be able to travel on the president's train?" George asked.

"Pina says she will. She will be sedated, but I've arranged for a private nurse to accompany her. George, I think I need to contact Wilkie."

"Why?"

She glanced down the hallway toward Nathaniel sitting at the kitchen table. "There's something wrong with him. He can't function. We need to assign someone else to oversee security for President Roosevelt's trip to Washington."

"Are you sure? I haven't been paying him any mind."

She had. Nathaniel had been completely detached ever since McKinley's death ten hours ago. She scrambled for the most delicate way to phrase the problem.

"He's taking it badly. He blames himself, and he's exhausted. We cannot ask this of him."

George nodded. "Can you handle the telephone call to Wilkie? I just got word that I've been asked to witness the swearing-in ceremony. It's in twenty minutes."

"I'll take care of it."

It would break her heart to convey this news to Nathaniel's friend and supervisor, but she couldn't ignore the problem, and there was no time for delay.

⸻

Six hours later Nathaniel stared out the window of the presidential train as it sped through the countryside, a notebook on his lap with a list of the towns they would pass on the way to Washington. His only official duty was to place a little checkmark beside each church that tolled their bell as the train passed. Caroline planned to send a note of thanks to each of them after the funeral.

Rain droplets rolled across the window and obscured much of the view, but he spotted the steeple of a white clapboard church rising above the trees in the tiny village of Osterburg, Pennsylvania, straight ahead. As the train drew closer, the faint tolling of church bells could be heard, and he made a check beside the town's name.

All around him, the other passengers spoke in muted tones. This was the railway car holding the dozens of journalists who'd flooded into Buffalo to cover the president's shooting. Sullivan and a pair of army officers rode in the car with President McKinley's casket. Wilkie and half a dozen other agents rode in President Roosevelt's car, but Nathaniel was relegated to ride with the journalists.

It was just as well. He'd rather be back here, noting the tolling of the bells.

"Complete disaster," he heard one of the journalists on the

bench ahead of him say. "Why wasn't everyone frisked before entering the building?"

The other journalist shook his head. "It was obviously a total breakdown of security. Pathetic."

Nathaniel turned to stare at the sodden fields of ryegrass passing outside the window. He'd overheard similar comments the entire journey. He didn't defend himself, because they were right. He kept staring at Caroline's list of churches, carefully noting each one that had gotten her message to ring their bells.

One of the journalists stood to call out to someone near the front of the car. "Hey, Robertson, what date was President Garfield assassinated?"

Robertson stood to reply. "September 19th, 1881. Here we are, exactly twenty years later, and we've got another president shot to death. When are we going to figure out how to handle presidential security?"

There was some general nodding and murmuring, but two rows ahead, Rembrandt got out of his seat and headed down the aisle toward Nathaniel. There was pity on the photographer's face as he took the vacant seat beside him.

"Pay them no mind," Rembrandt said quietly. "They don't know you like I do."

"They're not saying anything I don't already know." Nathaniel didn't have the energy to feel angry or defensive. Part of him wished he could ignore what was being said, but he needed to listen for the tolling of the bells. There were over a hundred churches on the route, and he wanted to turn in an accurate list to Caroline. That meant he had to listen.

Earlier, one of the journalists had reported that Emma Goldman had been released from jail. In cities all over the nation, people had been agitating for revenge, and the police, lawyers, and politicians all did their best to pin the crime on prominent anarchists.

Others disagreed. A handful of lawyers came forth to claim

that the First Amendment granted anarchists the right to speak their minds freely, and Goldman had been released.

Another weight settled on Nathaniel's chest. It probably wasn't Emma Goldman's fault, anyway. It was his fault. Rembrandt and the others had been saying all sorts of kind things to soften his role in this tragedy, but he knew the truth.

"How about you and I go out for a decent meal once we're back home?" Rembrandt suggested. "We can go out for a nice plate of Chesapeake blue crabs."

Rembrandt was trying to be nice, but the next town on Caroline's list was coming up, and Nathaniel had a duty to perform. He gave Rembrandt an apologetic look.

"Forgive me, but I need to be sure this list is accurate."

Mercifully, Rembrandt understood. He clapped a reassuring hand on Nathaniel's shoulder, then returned to his own seat a few rows ahead.

It was pitiful, but this mindless checklist was the only thing holding his sanity together right now, and he wasn't going to let Caroline down.

On Tuesday, September 17th, Nathaniel put on his best suit to stand alongside thousands of others lining Pennsylvania Avenue to watch the president's funeral procession. Wilkie had suggested he leave White House duties entirely, but that was unthinkable. He couldn't leave in the middle of a national emergency. It would be the ultimate failure.

Nevertheless, his demotion was obvious to all. Sullivan was now in charge of presidential security, and Nathaniel was one of hundreds of men stationed every ten yards along the funeral route. A light drizzle started to fall as the procession began, dribbling down the side of his face, but he refused to move. He needed to stand at attention and bear witness as his last official duty to a good and decent man.

First came a drum corps, playing a somber muffled drum beat, followed immediately by a hearse bearing the president's flower-draped casket. After that came President Roosevelt in an open carriage drawn by four black horses, followed by the Supreme Court justices wearing their robes of office, then officers from the army and navy in full military regalia.

Signs of Caroline's hand in the dignified ceremony were everywhere, from the red carnations worn by the presidential guard, the brigade of old Civil War soldiers, and the selection of a lone silvery bugle's soaring requiem as the procession passed. It was very Caroline. Perfect, always.

Not like him. He stood in the rain, the wet wool of his suit itching and the sense of failure nearly strangling him, but he owed it to his president to stand at complete attention. When he had the energy he would plant red carnations in a park down by the river. Mr. McKinley used to walk there in the evenings, and those carnations would be a quiet memorial to one of the best men Nathaniel had ever known.

A man he had failed.

Thirty-One

Out with the old and in with the new.

That was the mantra Caroline repeated to herself in the days after the president's funeral. She managed the thousands of condolence messages while George masterfully juggled the new president's schedule. Pina shouldered the primary duty of comforting Ida, leaving Caroline to help steer the White House toward welcoming in a new administration. She handled tasks both high and low. She ensured protocol was met for visiting dignitaries and served coffee to the journalists who camped outside the White House. She decided menus, handled correspondence, and planned the Ohio funeral.

The Roosevelts gave Mrs. McKinley as much time as she needed to vacate the White House, but already architects and planners had begun discreetly measuring the building for a substantial renovation. The Roosevelts had six children, ranging from four to seventeen in age. The modest family quarters were inadequate, and the new president took the bull by the horns to begin the long-delayed expansion Ida had refused to allow. The greenhouses would be torn down to build a west wing where the administration's daily business would occur, leaving more room for the president's family in the residence.

Boxes of condolence letters had accumulated, and Caroline took them to her office to identify those from heads of state that required an immediate reply, then packed the others away to be addressed in the coming months. Her concentration was broken by a cascade of childish laughter echoing down the hall. The Roosevelts had yet to move in, but they visited almost every day to begin planning their move and the renovation.

The children's laughter intensified, followed by clattering and a strange squeal. Could that possibly be the nickering of a horse?

Dropping a stack of letters, Caroline ran into the hall, gasping at the sight of a pony prancing nervously in the marble corridor just inside the north entrance.

"Get that animal out of here!" she shrieked.

A young boy giggled and reached for the pony's bridle as a mortified White House usher rushed inside.

"I'm sorry, ma'am," the usher gasped. "One of the older boys distracted me while this one snuck it in."

Behind him, a cluster of boys looked delighted as the usher led the pony outside. Caroline followed to be certain the pony was well away from the house, then glared at the boys, uncertain if she had the authority to reprimand the Roosevelt children. The only adult was a languid young lady watching the entire incident from the far side of the portico as she smoked a cigarette.

"Oops," the young lady said with deliberate indifference.

This was surely Alice Roosevelt, the oldest of the Roosevelt children, who was already in the process of scandalizing Washington society. As much as Caroline wanted to smack her, she recognized a bit of herself in Alice's wildcatting ways. Still, she wouldn't let Alice disrespect the White House.

She strode forward, plucked the cigarette from Alice's hands, and ground it out on the pavers. "If you must smoke, I'll show you a spot on the roof where you can get away with it. Don't embarrass your father by doing it where reporters can see you."

She paused to scan Alice from head to toe. "Stop slouching, because even now people are watching you. You're going to have a lot of eyes on you in the years ahead, so start off on the right foot."

She got no reaction from Alice, but she didn't expect one, nor did she care. At least the pony had been led safely away from the White House, but the children shrieked as they began batting a cricket ball across the lawn.

She needed to go back inside and check on Nathaniel. The job of overseeing White House security had been transferred to Sullivan, but Wilkie gave Nathaniel another assignment inside the house. If Nathaniel ended his days in the White House with the horrific catastrophe of the assassination, he might never recover.

She headed downstairs to the communications room, where Nathaniel had been assigned to scan telegrams and monitor telephone calls. Amidst the flood of condolence messages, there were matters of business that needed to be flagged. It wasn't difficult, but it served as a way to salvage Nathaniel's pride.

It was crowded in the communications room, and activity was in full swing as the telegraph machine clicked and messages were decoded. Nathaniel sat in a rolling chair that could slide from station to station.

She smiled as she approached him. "I came to coax you to lunch. The cook made corned beef on rye." It was Nathaniel's favorite sandwich, but he didn't show much interest.

"I've been skipping lunch these days," he said.

She knew, which was why she'd asked the cook to make corned beef sandwiches.

"You might be able to go without lunch, but I can't. And I hate eating alone. Join me?" Anything to get him moving and interacting with people.

To her relief, he stood and followed her to the kitchen, where all the cooks were busy. The new president would be hosting a farewell dinner tonight for the two dozen state governors who'd come to Washington for the funeral. Pots of water boiled, loaves of bread cooled, and pans clattered. Caroline grabbed two plates, plopped a sandwich onto each, and carried them to the staff tables, where Nathaniel sat with a listless stare.

"Go ahead and eat," she prodded. "Don't worry. The telegrams will wait until you get back."

He pulled the plate toward himself but didn't touch the sandwich. "I know. It's a pointless job." He traced the edge of the plate with his finger. "Thank you for suggesting it to Wilkie, though. It's obvious I shouldn't be in charge upstairs."

She stilled, watching him carefully. "You aren't offended?"

"I don't have the energy to be offended."

With a slow push of a finger, he rotated the sandwich plate, staring at it with no interest. The spark of professional absorption she'd always found so attractive was gone. It was as if a candle had been snuffed out, leaving him a lethargic shell of a man. She scrambled to think of something that might spark his curiosity back to life.

"I wonder if Wilkie might put you on the track of that fake Vermeer in the Corcoran," she said impulsively. "The charming one of the girl holding the rabbit."

He lifted his eyes to look at her. "Why would he do that?"

"Because it's a form of counterfeit, and if the Secret Service won't do anything about it, who will?"

He shrugged and continued rotating the plate with a single finger. His numbness frightened her, and she scrambled for a way to cut through his despondency.

She grabbed his hand and squeezed. "It wasn't your fault," she said quietly.

He pulled his hand away. "I was two yards away when Czolgosz fired that gun. Of course it's my fault."

There was no heat in his words, only blankness. Everyone in this city was grieving, but only Nathaniel blamed himself.

It was as if the weight of the nation sat on his chest, making it impossible to breathe.

"Sullivan was even closer, but it wasn't his fault either. There were two dozen police officers in the building that day. You don't need to shoulder all the blame, Nathaniel."

This had to be handled carefully. She couldn't minimize what had happened, or he would reject her outright.

"You mustn't let your failures define you," she said gently.

He gave her a sad smile. "But I do."

"What do you suppose God thinks of you right now?"

That took him aback. For a moment he looked bewildered, but it was quickly replaced by shame. "I can't imagine it's anything good."

"Wrong," she said. "You are unconditionally loved. Unconditionally forgiven. You are a child of God, deserving of more credit than you're giving yourself. None of us are perfect. We will stumble and fall and make mistakes time and again, but we can't wallow in our failure. Someday we have to accept God's grace to stand up and try again. Nathaniel, you are *forgiven*."

He said nothing and went back to rotating the plate, and she mustered her forces to try again.

"God knew exactly what Czolgosz was going to do that day, and He let it happen. I don't know why, and I wish you hadn't been chosen for such a pivotal role in it, but you mustn't blame yourself."

He still wouldn't look at her, but the finger rotating the plate slowed. Then stopped. At least he was thinking about what she'd said.

"Would you please eat a little of that sandwich?"

He shrugged.

"What about the fake Vermeer? I'd like to ask Wilkie to assign you to investigate the fraud. Would that interest you?"

He shrugged again. She wanted to scream, not from annoyance but from anguish. Nathaniel was supposed to be the strong one, the person who didn't falter or panic and who never surrendered. Now he didn't even have the energy to lift a bite of food to his mouth. She picked up the plate and set it on the sideboard, then returned to him.

"I'll ask the cook to leave that there for you. It will be waiting for you when you're ready."

As will I, she silently thought as she returned to work.

Caroline stood beside Ida's wheelchair as Dr. Tisdale administered another injection of sedative. Since the president's death, Ida had become overly reliant on this nerve medication, and it didn't seem to be helping much anymore. While sometimes the injections calmed her, at others the exact same medication caused her to become angry and paranoid.

Dr. Tisdale noticed the same thing as Caroline escorted him down the staff staircase. "If she shows no sign of improvement by tomorrow, I shall adjust the amount of bromide in the dosage," he said.

Dr. Tisdale had treated all of Ida's many nervous conditions over the years. He surely had more experience with disorders of the mind than anyone she knew. They were alone in the stairwell, and she needed his insight, even if she felt awkward asking for it.

"Some of the people on the president's staff are taking his death badly," she began.

"To be expected," the doctor replied as he adjusted the sit of his eyeglasses. "Is there anyone in particular you are concerned about?"

It felt terribly intrusive to go behind Nathaniel's back, but he wasn't going to reach out for help on his own.

"Nathaniel Trask," she said quietly. "He is completely despondent. Not angry or despairing, just . . . blank."

"It sounds like a nervous breakdown, a form of neurasthenia. An overstimulation of the nervous system leads to a breakdown of the mental systems. Just like a machine can break down from overwork, so can a man."

"Is there anything that can be done?" she asked.

"Keep him busy, engaged in the world. If that is too much for him, institutionalization can be an effective—"

"Short of institutionalization," she said.

Dr. Tisdale lifted his medical bag. "I can inject him with the same sedatives I use with Mrs. McKinley. It will only dull the effects, but it won't cure him."

She blanched at the suggestion that the doctor would resort to the same medications that now held Ida captive to his treatments.

"Nathaniel would never permit it," she said.

"Well, then." Dr. Tisdale took a heavy breath and looked her straight in the eyes. "I suspect you will like my final suggestion even less."

None of his other ideas sounded palatable, but she was at her wits' end. "Let's hear it."

"I think he needs to get back up on the same horse that threw him. Agent Trask is a man, and he needs to do something to regain his pride. He needs to *earn* it back."

Dr. Tisdale was right; she didn't like it. Every instinct urged her to protect Nathaniel, not throw him back to the wolves.

But the doctor was correct. Nathaniel was a man of extraordinary diligence and aptitude. He needed to use those God-given tools to do something to redeem himself. The face-saving job in the basement wasn't likely to make him feel like a hero. He needed to solve a crime or rescue a damsel in distress—do something to shake him out of his lethargy. He needed his soul called back into service, but she didn't know how to do it.

Caroline met the White House butler in the dining room to review arrangements for that evening's dinner for the governors.

"Let's use the Wedgwood china and the ordinary silverware," she suggested. "Nothing too fancy yet."

"Yes, ma'am," the butler said. "And do you have a recommendation for the floral decorations?"

"No more red carnations. It's time to welcome a new administration, so let's have simple arrangements of roses with greenery." *Out with the old and in with the new.*

A crash sounded from outside, and a glance out the window showed one of the Roosevelt boys wading in a fountain, kicking water at his siblings. Caroline sighed. Ida was heavily medicated and unlikely to hear anything, but it would be better if the children weren't so noisy.

"Let's head downstairs to discuss the wine list," she said.

Before they got far, a tall, strong-jawed woman intercepted Caroline in the staff hallway. She wore plain but flawless attire and carried a notebook propped in her arm.

"Miss Delacroix?" the woman asked.

"Yes. Can I help you?"

The woman offered her hand with a sad smile. "I am Isabella Hagner. Mrs. Roosevelt's secretary."

"Oh." It felt like a punch in the chest. How intensely awkward. "My goodness. Well! What a surprise."

Out with the old and in with the new. It applied to her now.

Caroline took a fortifying breath and returned Miss Hagner's handshake. "Allow me to introduce you to James Macklin, the head butler. You will find him to be a godsend in your work here."

The two exchanged nods of greeting, then Mr. Macklin made a discreet exit. Caroline escorted Miss Hagner to the crowded office she would need to vacate. Both Roosevelts would be bringing their own secretaries, which meant George would be out of a job soon too.

"Hopefully you will have a more spacious office once the west wing addition is complete."

"I appreciate everything you've done to steer the commemorations over the past weeks," Miss Hagner said. "No one envied you that task, and it has all been beautifully tasteful."

"Thank you," Caroline said, wondering at the odd lump in her throat as her gaze wandered the shabby, crowded office. The arrival of her replacement shouldn't be a surprise, but it was. She had loved it here and hadn't expected this meeting so soon. It was time to say something gracious. Something that wouldn't hint that her heart was splitting at its seams. "I hope you will be as happy in this job as I was," she finally said, embarrassed at the prickling of tears.

Miss Hagner nodded. "Is there anything I can do for you?"

Caroline was about to demur, but the faint sounds of children playing outside filtered through the walls. They were normal, happy children. They shouldn't be resented because they were too young to appreciate the tragedy the nation had been through.

She chose her words carefully. "I'm sure the Roosevelt children are delightful, but Mrs. McKinley's nerves are sensitive. Would it be possible—"

"Say no more," Miss Hagner said gently. "I shall take care of it."

And she did. Within a few minutes, the noise of the children subsided, then vanished altogether.

Caroline continued sorting through the condolence letters, unexpectedly dispirited by her replacement's arrival. She'd been so busy over the past two weeks that there'd been no time to think about her own future, but it was coming fast. Never had the prospect of change been so frightening.

Thirty-Two

Caroline spent all day Friday helping Ida pack for her return to Ohio. It was unexpectedly painful, for the first lady's spectacular wardrobe contained a treasure trove of memories. With each gown she packed, Caroline remembered a state dinner, a reception, or a visit to a local attraction. Pina and Ludmila helped strategize how to pack the gowns into a dozen trunks for transportation back to Canton while Ida directed operations from her wheelchair in the corner.

"What will happen to this one?" Pina asked as she reverently laid out Ida's inaugural gown. The satin dress literally crackled with a thousand seed pearls and crystals.

Ida's voice was imperious. "I think it belongs in a museum, but for now it will go to Ohio."

Ida was scheduled to depart in two days. Caroline had the niggling fear that Ida expected her to continue her secretarial duties in Ohio, which was unthinkable. She would wilt in Canton, especially knowing that Luke and Nathaniel needed her in Washington. Any hope of a presidential pardon for Luke had vanished, but she still had access to powerful friends in Washington.

Her chest felt heavy as she opened another trunk. The hope

271

of a presidential pardon was a talisman she'd clung to during the long months of Luke's imprisonment, but now it was gone forever. Since Luke intended to plead guilty, the best she could hope for was a life sentence to be served somewhere in the continental United States. She would have to draw on all her connections to make it happen, which meant she needed to remain in Washington.

She opened the top bureau drawer to begin packing the accessories. Her heart squeezed as she lifted the crystal-studded hair snood Ida had loaned her the night of the state dinner, when she'd huddled with Nathaniel on the back staircase. She placed the snood on a layer of tissue paper, carefully folding it into place. What a wonderful time these eighteen months in the White House had been. Difficult, challenging, and sometimes painful, but overall a time of gilded memories she would forever cherish.

"Ida McKinley!" Pina gasped as she spotted the hidden trove of cosmetics in Ida's top drawer. "Have you been using face paint?"

"Nonsense," Ida retorted. "Those belong to Caroline."

All eyes in the room turned to Caroline, who would gladly shoulder the blame. "Yes. I purchased every item in that drawer." It was a true statement, as Caroline had a better eye for selecting the perfect natural shade of cosmetics, but she and Ida both indulged in wearing makeup.

"Then we ought to leave these with her," Pina said, holding the box of cosmetics away from her body as though handling explosives.

"No, no, Caroline is coming with me," Ida insisted. "So are the cosmetics. Pack them in the toiletry case."

Caroline froze, knowing it was time to clarify her intentions. She reached for some handkerchiefs to fold—anything to avoid looking Ida in the face while delivering the painful news.

"Actually, I intend to stay in Washington," she said. "But you should still take the cosmetics with you. I have my own."

"What's this nonsense?" Ida said. "You agreed you would serve through the Major's second term." Her iron tone did not bode well, and Caroline chose her words carefully.

"Of course, but that was when we believed it would be in Washington. I have obligations here—"

"What obligations?" Ida demanded. "You were certainly willing to traipse all over the country on the train tour. I need you in Ohio. You have a duty."

Caroline set the handkerchiefs inside a trunk. "I'll gladly keep in touch to provide advice to Pina or anyone else who helps with the secretarial duties, but my family is here, and I need to stay."

Ida banged her cane on the floor. "Your family is with me," she insisted. "You're going to Ohio."

"No, I'm not," Caroline said, trying to keep her voice calm. "I belong in Washington and can't leave."

Ida's temper snapped. "What kind of ingratitude is this? I have done *everything* for you! I treated you like a daughter. I opened doors for you and gave you a world of opportunities."

The words stung because they were true. Since the day she walked into the White House, Caroline had been showered with experiences beyond her wildest imagination.

"I'm truly sorry—"

"No, you're not. You're a selfish and ungrateful brat, and I want you out of here." Ida pushed on the wheels of her chair to cross the room, where she tugged the rope-pull to summon a servant.

Pina and Ludmila froze, watching in wide-eyed dismay as Ida's temper spiraled higher. An usher tapped on the door, and Ida commanded him to enter.

"Get the head of security," she barked. "I want this woman out of my house." She turned her hurt, furious gaze to Caroline. Her voice began to crack as she yelled in anguish and outrage. "You're an ungrateful brat! I did *everything* for you! Do you hear me? Everything! And now in my hour of need—"

"Ida, perhaps you shouldn't be so hasty," Pina offered timidly. "Caroline has her own life—"

"Yes, a good life with me. Or at least she *had* a good one. That's all over now."

Sullivan arrived, looking bewildered by this awful turn of events. How humiliating to have him witness this spectacle, but Ida was adamant.

"I want this woman out of my house," she ordered. "Take her straight downstairs and out the back door. I'll have a servant collect her belongings, but I can't stand to look at her a moment longer."

Caroline picked up her reticule. There would be no convincing Ida to back down, not after such a public declaration. The other women looked frozen, like they'd shatter if they moved a muscle. She hated to abandon them while Ida was in such a fury, but if she tried to mitigate the damage, she'd only stoke Ida's temper hotter.

She nodded to Pina and Ludmila. "I'm sorry," she murmured, then risked a glance at Ida. "I'm truly sorry, ma'am."

Sullivan looked mortified as he escorted her down the hallway, waiting until they were several yards away before speaking. "What was that all about?"

How could she explain it? In the space of one minute, a relationship that she'd come to treasure had completely imploded. Perhaps it was only Ida's grief lashing out, but it still hurt.

In a moment Caroline would walk out of the White House for the last time, but she couldn't leave without saying goodbye to Nathaniel. He was wounded and adrift and didn't fully understand what he meant to her. She wouldn't simply disappear from him because Ida's temper had snapped.

"I need to go downstairs and tell Nathaniel what happened," she explained to Sullivan as their footsteps clattered down the empty staff stairwell. "It will only take a moment."

Sullivan put a hand on her arm, regret on his face. "I'm afraid I can't allow that."

"Don't be ridiculous. It's only me."

"Mrs. McKinley is still in charge. I follow her orders."

Caroline stood in drop-jawed disbelief, but he was serious. Sullivan was now in charge of security, and he'd be putting his job at risk if he deviated from a direct order. Ida was mad enough to collect more heads, and Sullivan was always a rule-follower.

"Very well," she said calmly, heading toward the staff door at the back of the house. Butlers and wait staff were busy preparing the dining room for dinner, but none of them knew she'd been fired. She didn't meet anyone's eyes as she passed through the butler's pantry, the china room, and toward the staff door, where she paused and turned to Sullivan. He offered a handshake, but she brushed it away and pulled him into a hug, standing on tiptoe to whisper in his ear.

"Look after him," she said. She pushed him back but kept a hand braced on each shoulder, forcing him to look at her. "You and I have walked through fire together," she said, surprising both of them with this earnest rush of emotion. "I will never forget you, and I don't blame you for following Ida's orders, but now I'm relying on you to look after Nathaniel until he's on an even keel again. Try to make him sleep. Make him eat. Order it if you have to. Don't you dare let me down."

"I hear you," Sullivan said, looking sick at heart for throwing her out. "Do you have enough money to get home?"

She nodded. Fortunately, she'd had her reticule when Ida's tantrum descended or else she'd be forced to borrow streetcar fare. "Good luck, Sullivan," she said before heading out the door.

Then she paused and turned back to him. "I have another request," she impulsively said.

"Name it."

"Make sure Nathaniel stays at his post for the next hour. Have him monitoring the telephone calls."

He nodded. "I can do that."

Caroline left the White House without a backward glance, for she needed to find somewhere to place a very important call.

⁓ ℘ ⁓

Nathaniel sat in a rolling chair, sliding down the line of telephone operators as various calls came in. He supposed he could walk instead of using the chair, but it would take too much effort.

The communications room in the White House basement was now the busiest room in the building as messages of condolence flooded the lines. Those calls were dwarfed by new government business, for President Roosevelt had already initiated massive changes that demanded attention.

It was hard to care. He didn't have the energy. Maybe because he no longer really slept. He never left his post before midnight, and he returned promptly at six o'clock the following morning. Sleep during those few hours was scanty, for he was intensely aware of any noise in the building and the sound of streetcars outside. Even the pacing of the night guards woke him. In the morning he awoke exhausted but managed to shave, pull on a suit, then head downstairs to his post. He had no appetite and no ambition beyond going through the daily motions of life. Nothing penetrated this oppressive fog of lethargy.

Clicking and rattling poured from the telegraph machines, but a new telephone call arrived, and he rolled his chair a few feet to listen in.

A woman's voice came over the line, and he straightened, recognizing Caroline's voice.

"Margaret?" Caroline asked the operator. "Don't patch me through to anyone yet. Just hold the line open."

Margaret met his eyes. "It's open, ma'am."

"Security can hear me?"

"He can," Margaret said, still looking confused. He was confused too. He rolled his chair closer, scanning the switchboard to figure out where she was calling from, for it was an outside line.

"I need to talk to Sullivan. He should be in his office. Patch me through, please, but hold the line open."

Now Nathaniel was deeply concerned. Margaret looked to him for permission, and he nodded. This was out of character, which meant something was going on. Margaret patched the call through to his old office. Why did Caroline want him to eavesdrop on this call? It made no sense unless she was leading Sullivan into a trap. His stomach turned at the thought, but he leaned in closer, monitoring Sullivan's voice as he answered the line.

"I'm sorry about what happened this afternoon," Caroline said, her voice aching with sadness.

"I am too," Sullivan replied.

"I wish I'd had a chance to say good-bye to the rest of the staff. I understand you needed to follow Mrs. McKinley's orders—"

"Caroline, I'm so sorry," Sullivan said.

They continued talking, and Nathaniel was soon able to put the pieces together. *Caroline had been fired!* He clenched his fists, fighting the urge to vault out of his chair and find her. She didn't deserve this, and it cut through the veil of his despondency like a bolt of lightning.

He forced the anger down to focus on what she was saying. Something about the other women in her dormitory. She asked that the work schedule permit Ludmila to keep attending classes and that Mrs. Fitzpatrick get a raise for all the extra work she'd been doing.

"And tell Nathaniel that I'm thinking of him," she said. "I'll think of him every hour of every day, even though I'm not in the White House anymore. Walls and guards and circumstances

277

can't separate us. Tell him I'll wait for him, no matter how long it takes."

Now other operators in the room were cocking their heads to listen. Caroline continued peeling back the layers of her soul.

"Tell him that I finally understand what he was trying to say about the boring Vermeer in the Corcoran," she said, and he lifted his head, all senses on alert. "The woman holding the letter isn't boring, she is the personification of *loyalty*." Her voice was rough with emotion. "She is missing her man and will wait faithfully for him, no matter how long it takes. Even though the picture is mostly darkened with gloom, Vermeer captured tenderness and love in the way she holds that letter. She will never give up on the man who wrote that letter, even in the bleak, dark world Vermeer painted for her. The light coming through the window is hope, and no matter how grim, I will always cling to that hope and use it to light my days. That portrait in the Corcoran may be the most beautiful painting on this earth. Tell Nathaniel that."

"I hear you," Sullivan said. "He does too."

"Good."

The line disconnected.

Nathaniel sat motionless as Caroline's words sank in. They were an avalanche of love and acceptance despite the dark shadows of his world. Caroline knew all his failings and shame, but she was standing by him and had just announced it in front of a dozen White House employees.

And she was right. Walls and guards and circumstances wouldn't separate them. For a while he had let his grief do so, but now it was Caroline who was hurting and needed someone to stand by her, and he would do so.

Thirty-Three

Caroline's heart was still thudding as she paid the pharmacy owner for use of his telephone. The pharmacist and probably every operator in the White House had just heard her declaration of undying love, but she didn't care. Nathaniel had heard it, and that was the only thing that mattered. He needed to know he wasn't alone and that she would wait for him no matter how long it took for him to emerge from this debilitating melancholy.

It was dark by the time she stepped off the streetcar in her Alexandria neighborhood. It had been eighteen months since she'd slept in her own bed. She was eager to get home, but guilt ate at her over the way things had ended with Ida and how she'd been forced to walk out on Nathaniel.

She'd have the townhouse to herself, since Gray and Annabelle were still in Kansas. They'd given Mr. and Mrs. Holder, the two live-in servants, leave to visit their grown children in Baltimore. Caroline probably ought to stop for something to eat, for the house had been vacant all week and probably lacked food, but she had no appetite.

The streetlamps were on, but her spirit still felt gloomy as she turned the corner onto her street. At the end of the block she could finally see the stately, three-story townhouse where she'd grown up, and she quickened her steps, eager to get home.

Except there was a light on in the house. It was in the back near the kitchen. Could the Holders have accidentally left a lightbulb burning before they went to Baltimore? If so, Gray would have a fit. He mistrusted electricity, thinking it a fire hazard and an expensive one, at that.

A hint of misgiving rose within her. It wasn't like the Holders to leave lights burning, and something didn't feel safe.

Then she chided herself. It had been a long day and her feet hurt, and she wasn't going to wander in search of a hotel because the Holders had left a light on. For all she knew, the Holders had already returned from their trip.

She mounted the steps, inserted her key in the knob, and twisted it open.

"Mr. Holder?" she asked as she stepped inside. The front rooms were dark, but the skinny hallway running to the back of the house was dimly illuminated by the kitchen light.

She froze. A man's heavy coat was draped over the parlor sofa. It didn't belong to Gray or Mr. Holder, for it was tattered and filthy.

Footsteps sounded from the kitchen, and a man's silhouette was framed in the hallway.

"Caroline?"

The voice was familiar, but it couldn't be. He was so gaunt, like a skeleton. He moved farther down the hall, the light from the streetlamp finally shining on his face.

"Luke?" But it couldn't be. He looked so different. "Luke!"

He said nothing but smiled and held his arms open wide. She wanted to race into them, but she couldn't move. She could only stare. The room swayed, and she started to topple just as Luke's arms clamped around her.

"Whoa, there. Have a seat," he said, guiding her into a chair, which was good, because for the life of her she wouldn't have been able to keep standing.

She landed on the chair with a thump, keeping both hands braced on his shoulders. How bony he felt, his shoulder blades prominent beneath her palms. It was Luke, but he was pale and gaunt. She tried to stammer out a question but was breathing too fast to form anything but gulping noises of disbelief.

"Are you laughing or crying?" he asked.

"I don't know!" she managed to say. Despite looking ghastly, humor glinted in his eyes. His black hair was so long that it was tied in a ponytail, but his beard was gone. Probably recently, given the nicks along his jaw. "I can't believe you're really here."

"I just got in an hour ago. I was eating the remnants of a loaf of bread when I heard you coming home."

"I think you need more than plain bread. Like an entire chicken and a chocolate cake. Maybe a side of steer."

He laughed. "All in good time. I can't keep much food down yet and have to go easy on it. Plain bread works."

If Luke had somehow escaped the Cuban prison, she needed to get him out of here immediately, for this was the first place the military would look for him. Part of her wanted to send for a doctor, but the other part wanted to smuggle him into a wagon and out of town.

"How did you get out?" she asked.

"Orders of the president," he answered.

Her eyes grew wide. President McKinley had been firm when he said he couldn't help, but had he changed his mind? Had he put something in place to go into effect posthumously? "Did he . . . did President McKinley . . . ."

Luke shook his head. "No. It was the other guy. Mr. Roosevelt."

"No!"

His eyes brightened with ironic amusement. "I was working for him all along. I think he felt pretty guilty about what happened."

"Roosevelt?" she gasped. "What on earth were you doing for President Roosevelt?"

She listened in amazement as Luke recounted how closely Roosevelt had tracked developments in Cuba after leaving the island as a war hero three years earlier. Roosevelt suspected corruption had taken root among the occupying American forces and wanted an undercover man on the ground to look for it.

"You don't send someone in the military to investigate the military," Luke said. "That's why they sent me. I always knew that if I was arrested I'd have to keep my silence. The vice president had no authorization to poke around, so it was a completely clandestine project, and he was running a big risk doing it. If I admitted I was in the middle of an undercover operation, it would endanger the whole plan, and there are lives on the line."

He went on to say that he'd infiltrated the group of Cuban rebels, who were being paid by someone in the American military to keep the rebellion alive. Luke pretended to be sympathetic to their cause in an effort to learn who was funding them from Washington. That was why he'd had the names and contact information of the rebels in his possession when he was arrested.

Luke suspected Captain Holland in the procurement office was at the root of the problem, but it was hard for Caroline to concentrate on the political scheme he outlined. So many questions remained unanswered, but at the moment all she cared about was that he was out of jail and his name had been cleared.

"Did you give my letters to Philip?" he asked.

"Philip the Meek? Why would I do that?"

Luke vaulted off the sofa, knocking over the parlor table as he stood to full height. "You didn't turn over my letters?" he asked, his eyes wide in horror.

She stood too. "You never told me to give them to Philip."

"I told you in every letter!" he shouted in exasperation. "I told you to trust a good dancer. To tell the good dancer everything."

"Is Philip a good dancer?"

Luke looked ready to implode. "Philip won statewide waltzing contests for three straight years!" he roared. "You were in the front row of the audience our sophomore year when he won first place! Why do you think everyone at the Naval Academy called him Twinkle Toes?"

"I thought they were teasing him for being a lightweight."

"Philip isn't a lightweight," Luke snapped. "He's the biggest spy in the American government. That's why Roosevelt put him on the job."

She gaped at him, unable to get her mind around it. "But he's so bashful and timid!"

"He's very good at letting you think that. Meanwhile he's got spies all over the globe who send him information in that seedy little basement office, and he's running rings around everyone."

"And the second in command? Who did you mean by that?"

"The vice president, obviously!"

Caroline threw up her hands in frustration. "Why didn't you just write directly to Philip or Roosevelt in the first place?"

"Because everything I wrote was read by the military before getting sent, and I couldn't risk exposing them as part of an undercover surveillance mission. That's why I had to write in riddles and Hebrew. Honestly, I think you should go confess to Philip you are a complete and total nitwit for thinking him a mild-mannered clerk all these years."

Caroline sat back down, sagging as relief washed through her. Luke was back. She still didn't understand the plot he was in the middle of foiling, but she didn't need to. Fifteen months of tension lifted from her shoulders, and she still didn't know if she wanted to laugh or cry.

For the first time in his life, Nathaniel walked off his job in the middle of a shift. The assignment monitoring incoming messages was nothing but a face-saving task, and Caroline was hurting too badly for him to ignore. She'd been valiant in her telephone call, but he'd caught the edge of desperation in her voice. She was near the breaking point. They were all exhausted from the past few weeks, and it was time for him to pick up and start carrying his share of the burden.

Caroline was right about the Vermeer portrait. It was about loyalty, and he would prove his loyalty by being at her side. Tonight could be the start of something new and wonderful. They were both free. Nothing but his demons stood in their way, and he'd slay them eventually.

Hope motivated his steps as the streetcar delivered him to Caroline's neighborhood. He strode down the sidewalk, faster and faster as he neared her address. The house was lit up. Good!

He knocked, his heart still thudding from the run and every nerve ending tingling in anticipation. He smiled as he heard her footsteps approach. The door opened, and there she was, looking flushed and beautiful. She was the most radiant woman he'd ever seen in his life, especially when her eyes widened in delight and a smile illuminated her face with pure joy.

He tugged her into his arms and kissed her deeply. She returned it, twining her arms around his neck. He lifted her from the ground, kissing her with everything he had in him. For once, everything was right, and he'd never felt so certain about a woman in his life.

"I'd prefer it if you unhanded my sister," a wry voice said from the room behind her.

Nathaniel jerked back, spotting a mangy-looking man with long hair lounging on a sofa.

Caroline looked only mildly embarrassed as she performed the introductions.

"Nathaniel, this is my brother Luke, fresh from a Cuban jail. Luke, Nathaniel."

He stared incredulously at the gaunt man on the sofa. It was hard to believe. Caroline had been out of her mind for over a year, and Luke's last chance for salvation had died in Buffalo along with the president. It was simply too much to take in.

"Are you sure?" he asked her.

Caroline burst out laughing and kissed him on the cheek. "I'm sure," she said. She led him to a chair, where he listened in disbelief as Caroline said something about Luke being released on orders from President Roosevelt, and that he was "completely harmless." Not guilty at all! Nathaniel could barely get his mind around the whirlwind of news, but one question leapt to the forefront.

"How did you get the artichokes into the White House?"

"Artichokes?" Luke asked. "What artichokes?"

Caroline raced to sit beside Luke on the sofa. "Tell us," she coaxed. "I've been dying to know too."

Luke shrugged. "I can't do that without exposing my partner in crime."

"Twinkle Toes?" Caroline asked.

The term made no sense to Nathaniel but seemed to annoy Luke, who sent his sister a tight smile.

"Darling, you know I adore you, but I'd rather that highly confidential information not be shared with your rule-following Romeo."

"We can trust him," she said. "He works for the Secret Service, which answers to the Treasury. It's completely independent of the military."

The sarcasm vanished from Luke's face, replaced by a look of speculation. "How much do you trust him?" he asked Caroline.

"With my life," she said promptly.

Her unflinching endorsement cut through Nathaniel's annoyance. He grasped the arms of the chair to stop from bolting across the room to continue their kiss where he'd left off.

Luke closed his eyes, then leaned over to brace his forearms on his thighs. All teasing was gone as he rubbed his jaw and stared at the floor.

"Sorry, Caroline, but I can't trust him. The last fifteen months have been too rough for me to risk it all on Romeo."

Something was going on. Why had Caroline drawn the distinction between the Secret Service and the military? Who had Luke been working for? Nothing was clear to him, and his investigative instincts kicked into gear. He wanted to pull on this thread and see where it led, but Luke wasn't going to allow it.

Caroline's eyes were apologetic as they met his. "Thank you for coming over tonight," she said. "I'm sorry I can't ask you to stay. . . ."

She looked exquisitely uncomfortable as the sentence dangled, and he stood. He wouldn't make this any more difficult than necessary, but he wouldn't leave without saying good-bye either. He closed the distance between them and cupped a hand beneath her chin, tilting it up as he leaned down and kissed her, long and deep.

"Meet me outside in an hour," he whispered into her ear. He had to see her alone. The past weeks had been brutally hard, but the first ray of light had pierced the darkness.

He gave her a quick, final hug, then slipped away.

Nathaniel waited on a bench across the street from the Delacroix townhouse, still astounded over the events of the past hour. He was happy for Caroline. Having her brother back home was her dearest wish in the world . . . but it was worrisome too.

Relief for Caroline mingled with his strangling sense of guilt. Over the past weeks he'd completely abdicated his professional duties. Worse, his despondency had been a needless distraction for people shouldering immense duties during the crisis of the assassination and the presidential transition.

It was time to drag himself upright and assume his duties again, because tonight he had spotted something that couldn't be ignored. Despite Caroline's radiant assertion that Luke was entirely innocent and had been acting only for the good, it wasn't true. He had no doubt Luke Delacroix's shrewd nature might sweep the entire matter under the rug unless Nathaniel acted. Caroline's first loyalty was going to be to her brother, but Nathaniel would act in the best interests of the nation. This needed to be handled delicately.

A little over an hour later he spotted Caroline slipping outside, sparking a quick flash of well-being at the sight of her. How he adored her! He stood, raising a hand to catch her attention on the dimly lit street. Even from here, he could see her smiling as she darted toward him, hands outstretched.

"How are you feeling?" she asked as she grasped both his hands, springing up to give him a kiss on the cheek. She smelled like lemon soap and happiness.

"Better." It was the only word he could think of to describe the strange whirlwind of emotions that had careened from despondency to joy and then anger at the way Mrs. McKinley had treated Caroline. Everything about tonight had been overwhelming.

"Luke has gone to bed for the night," Caroline said. "Let's walk along the harbor where we can be alone."

She took his arm and led him a few blocks down the street to a wooden boardwalk stretching along the harbor wall. Moonlight glinted on the water, and the gentle slosh of the incoming tide sounded against the old rocks. She turned to step into his arms, and for a few moments they simply held each other. It felt like they were the only two people in the world.

"It's after September 15th," she said against his shoulder.

"We can start living our lives like normal people. No more working around the clock or sleeping in dormitories with half a dozen others. No more prohibitions against seeing each other. We can behave and court like ordinary people."

He stepped back to get a better view of her, loving the way the moonlight illuminated her face. "And how should an ordinary man court the most charming woman in the city?" he asked, a smile beginning to tug at his mouth.

"Little presents. I love little presents."

He nodded sagely. "I can do little presents. What else?"

"You could give me a kiss now and—"

He cut her off with a deep kiss. He could feel her smiling against his mouth, and eventually he had to pull back because he started smiling too.

"Keep going," he coaxed. "I'm learning, and I want to do this right."

"You could take me on outings." She shivered a little while looking up at him.

He rubbed his hands up and down her arms, partly to warm her, partly because he simply wanted to. "Don't forget who you're talking to. I've lived like a monk, so you'll have to suggest examples of these 'outings' I should take you on."

"How about the new exhibit at the Smithsonian?" she suggested. "There's a reception for a medieval manuscript exhibit next week. It was postponed due to the president's funeral, but events are starting again. It will be a modest occasion with some refreshments and the chance to wander a new exhibit before it opens to the public. I know I can get us in. Will you accompany me?"

"Of course." Her mention of the president's funeral cast a pall over him, but he tried not to let it show. He kept stroking her arms, trying to think of something cheerful to say and shake off the gloom.

Impulsively, he unfastened his kestrel tie clip and reached

out to grasp the edge of her shawl, pinning it on her. "Here," he said. "My first little gift."

"Are you sure?" She touched her fingers to the silver pin. "I know how much it means to you."

"That's why I want you to have it." Actually, he simply wanted to give her something, and the tie clip was the only thing he had on hand. "I'm glad about Luke," he finally said. "You deserve to be happy."

"So do you," she instantly replied.

He wasn't quite convinced of that yet. Not after the burden he'd been. The only way he could salvage his pride was to stand up and resume his responsibilities. That meant he couldn't ignore what he'd seen tonight.

He withdrew a few inches to study her expression carefully. "Who is your brother working for?" he asked softly.

A little shiver ran through her. "The very best people," she finally said with one of her typically charming smiles, which was a dead giveaway that the question made her uneasy.

When he'd first arrived at her house, during that initial rush of elation, she'd said Luke had been released on President Roosevelt's orders, but when Nathaniel tried to learn more, Luke silenced her. Something was going on, and it seemed underhanded. When he said as much to Caroline, she got defensive.

"There is corruption in the military," she said. "They sent Luke to investigate."

"Who is 'they'?"

She folded her arms across her chest and refused to answer.

"I don't want to argue about this, but there are rules," he said. "Lines of authority and reporting. The government can't operate if the left hand doesn't know what the right hand is doing. I have to report all this to Wilkie."

"Do what you think best," she replied lightly.

She was always so poised. So perfect and ladylike, even in the most trying of times. Another weight settled on his chest. He'd run across town to provide comfort but ended up badgering her over Luke instead.

"I'm sorry about Mrs. McKinley," he said, reaching out to tuck a strand of hair behind her ear. "It goes without saying, but you didn't deserve what happened."

She turned her face into his palm, pressing a kiss to it. "I'll survive."

Of that he had no doubt.

They held each other as the moon rose high. In a way, they had never been more free to be together, but in the past they had always been on the same side, united in their mission to keep the president and the White House in order.

Now he feared they might be heading in opposite directions.

***

It was after midnight before he returned to the men's dormitory in the White House. He was the only one still awake as he lay flat in bed, staring at the exposed beams of the ceiling. Sleeplessness was nothing new to him. He hadn't slept more than a few hours since McKinley was shot, but tonight was especially challenging as waves of euphoria battled old demons and worries about the future. He was honor-bound to report what he'd learned, for rogue investigations and spy rings couldn't be allowed to take root within the government.

Nathaniel placed a telephone call to Wilkie first thing in the morning and was ordered to report to the director's office at nine o'clock. He was still planning how best to reveal what he knew without placing Caroline's brother in jeopardy as he entered Wilkie's office.

Instead of questioning him about Luke Delacroix's unexpected arrival, Wilkie crossed the room with an expression of rapt anticipation on his face. "What do you make of *that*?" he asked, holding a five-dollar bill inches from Nathaniel's face.

Nathaniel scrutinized the bill, noting the quality of the engraving, the shade of ink, the tiny cotton and linen threads in the paper. He held it up to the light, and his mouth went dry, his heart started pounding. A surge of excitement flared to life, for he'd just spotted his old nemesis. The bill was a brilliant forgery, but he'd know the work of the Kestrel Gang anywhere.

"They're back in action," he said.

Wilkie nodded. "And I want you to find them. That bill turned up in Milwaukee last week. I'm moving you back onto the case. I want you to nail them to the wall this time."

Nathaniel nodded. It was what he wanted too, but he was torn in too many directions. Caroline. Milwaukee. The simmering problem with Luke. The burning desire to shake free of the strangling lassitude that had been choking him. It was time to strike out and conquer once again, to test his skill against a worthy opponent and win. He would relay what he knew about Luke and turn it over to Wilkie . . . but his hand curled around the five-dollar bill in anticipation. It was only a tiny slip of paper, but hunting down its source could be the key to his healing.

"What do you need me to do?" he asked.

Thirty-Four

For a fleeting moment when Caroline awoke the next morning, she feared the past twelve hours had been a dream. But she lay in her childhood bedroom instead of the White House dormitory. She heard Luke humming down the hall, and Nathaniel's kestrel tie clip was on her bedside table, so it was all true.

She closed her eyes to murmur a prayer of thanks. As said in Proverbs, she must learn to trust in the Lord rather than her own understanding. Life was unfolding according to plan, and gratitude filled her heart.

Luke was down the hall, and she tugged on a robe to seek him out. The humming came from the room shared by their butler and his wife. The door was open, and she peeked inside, wincing at the sight of Luke's ghastly bare back. His ribs, spine, and shoulder blades were all prominent beneath his skin.

"What are you doing in here?" she asked as he rummaged through the closet.

"Looking for something to wear," he replied. "None of my clothes fit anymore, but Mr. Holder is a lot smaller than me."

Or at least, he had been. The butler's shirt hung on Luke's bony frame, and the pants needed a pair of suspenders to hold them up. It would have to do, for they were both eager to get to Philip's office to start planning their next steps.

"I need to warn you that Nathaniel plans to tell John Wilkie about your return," she said as she clipped the suspenders to the back of his trousers. "He seemed a little miffed that unauthorized investigations were being carried out and the Secret Service didn't know about them."

"Rule-follower," Luke grumbled.

"He's very straitlaced," she defended. "I rather like that about him."

Nathaniel's famously upright comportment might not mesh well with her daredevil brother, but she couldn't worry about that today. Luke was champing at the bit to get to Philip's office.

"I can't believe Philip is at the center of this whole mess," she said as she helped Luke into a jacket. "For the past year I've sat in his office to cry and bemoan your fate, and he never breathed a word."

"That's because he's a spy, and a good one, at that."

"I wish you'd quit defending him. I'd like to hog-tie him for all the grief he's caused me."

"How about we hog-tie Captain Holland instead? He's the one who caused all the trouble."

Never had truer words been spoken. This entire experience had been a lesson in humility. While she imagined herself a sophisticated woman with exceptional insight and access throughout Washington, she'd been duped not only by Captain Holland but by Philip the Meek as well.

"Hello, Philip," she said with a tight smile as she waltzed into his cramped office an hour later.

He had the grace to look abashed, but only for a moment before greeting Luke with a back-pounding hug.

"Be careful not to break his ribs," she pointed out. "He's frail as a toothpick, thanks to you."

Philip ignored her as he cleared a stack of books from a

chair and gestured for Luke to sit. "Tell me what you know," he prompted, his genial face settling into a mask of concentration.

"Captain Holland is at the bottom of everything," Luke said. "The main rebel leader in Cuba is a man named Mateo Ferraz. He thought I was just a rich American coming down to dabble in a little smuggling and revolutionary mischief. I smuggled his rum and cigars but never made much progress in winning his trust. Anyway, when I was arrested, Mateo's name was among the rebels in my list of contacts, so he was rounded up too. We were all housed in the same Cuban jail."

Understanding began to dawn, and Luke met her gaze with a nod. "*That* was why I didn't want to be transferred to an American prison. By staying close to Mateo, I knew I could eventually win his trust and figure out who was funding the insurgency from Washington. It took a while."

It turned out that some of Mateo's cousins had moved to America decades earlier, and one of them married into Captain Holland's family. Mateo first met Captain Holland during a family holiday in Puerto Rico.

"They go fishing together every December," Luke continued. "I guess it was enough for Holland to have a sense of Mateo's political leanings. When Holland needed a man to keep the insurgency alive, he turned to Mateo."

Caroline still didn't understand. "Why would prolonging the war benefit Captain Holland?"

Luke was ready with an answer. "Holland signs off on the contracts for armaments and warfare, but not reconstruction. My guess is that he's been skimming from that budget for a long time, and when the military budget skyrocketed, he was like a pig at the trough. He didn't want it to end. When peace had been achieved, money for the war evaporated. He wanted to keep it stoked."

It made Caroline feel nauseated. Captain Holland lived his

cozy life in Washington while ordinary soldiers bled and died in Cuba.

"Mateo and I were in separate cells, but we were let out in the yard for around an hour each day," Luke continued. "He saw me sweating and suffering along with all the other rebels who'd been arrested, and that's what eventually won his trust. He told me of his connection to a high-ranking American officer and wondered if it could help us get out of jail. I said it might, but only if he gave me the name. He eventually told me it was Captain Holland. He eventually told me *a lot* of things, which is how I knew about plans to blow up that road to Havana. Now we can arrest Holland and haul him into a court of law for sabotaging the war effort. He's been funding the rebels with money and ammunition for two solid years."

Philip shook his head. "Everything you've told me is hearsay, not even enough to get a search warrant. Captain Holland is one of the navy's highest officers. He's got powerful friends, and he outranks me."

"He doesn't outrank President Roosevelt," Caroline said.

"We're leaving the president out of this," Philip said. "It doesn't look good for him to have been dabbling in this, and we can do it without him. All we need to do is trick Holland into action, and it shouldn't be hard."

The plan Philip outlined was breathtakingly simple. They could manufacture a fraudulent telegram from Mateo to Captain Holland, claiming Mateo had escaped from prison, along with an offer to continue the rebellion. To raise the stakes, the telegram would report that Luke Delacroix was an American spy investigating military embezzlement, and he'd escaped the prison on the same night. It would force Holland into action. All they had to do was carefully monitor Captain Holland after receiving that telegram to see what he would do.

Luke's smile was devilish. "I want to be in on the stakeout. Nothing would give me greater pleasure than hauling that man's carcass into court."

"Whoever is involved in the stakeout needs to blend in," Philip said. "That means your hair has got to go."

An expression of amused dismay crossed Luke's face. "I like looking like a reprobate."

"You don't look like a reprobate, you look like a skeleton with hair," Philip said. "Eat a decent meal, sit in the sun, and get a haircut. Then I'd be prepared to send you on—"

A knock on the door cut off their conversation. Luke shot out of his chair and pressed his back against the wall beside the door. No one knew he'd returned to Washington, and it was best to keep it that way. Philip crossed to the door and opened it. Caroline recognized Freddie Alden, one of the Secret Service agents who guarded the White House.

"You have been summoned to the Treasury Department," Freddie said to Philip. Then he moved farther into the room and closed the door, revealing Luke hiding behind it. "You too."

Luke gave his Cheshire cat's smile. "Who wants to see us at Treasury?"

"John Wilkie. Chief of the Secret Service. He's long suspected someone was running their own investigations out of this office."

Luke swiveled an accusatory glance at her. "Is this Romeo's doing?"

"I told you he planned to tell Wilkie. And I'm afraid he operates very much by the book. The only details I gave him were that you suspected corruption in the military and were working for the very best of people. And, Philip, I was being generous by characterizing you that way."

Philip looked annoyed. "I've always suspected the Secret Service was spying on me."

Caroline shifted in her seat. Over the past year, while she had been praying for Luke, she'd never thought any further than getting him safely back home. Now she was forced to confront the uncomfortable prospect that her daredevil brother and the straitlaced Nathaniel might have difficulty seeing eye to eye.

She was about to find out.

∽∘∼

Caroline entered Wilkie's office with Luke and Philip twenty minutes later. Nathaniel stood in the corner, dressed in one of his plain black suits. His expression was all business, but when he saw her, he gave her one of those closed-mouthed smiles that always made her weak in the knees, especially since this time it reached all the way to his eyes.

"Have a seat," Wilkie said as he gestured to a cluster of chairs facing his desk. They all sat except for Nathaniel, who remained watching from his position leaning against the far wall.

"I'd like to hear about this investigation into military corruption," Wilkie began in a silky voice.

Philip fidgeted in his chair, reverting to his Philip the Meek persona. "I don't know what you're talking about or why I'm here. My old college roommate is back in town, and we were just touching base."

Nathaniel wasn't buying it. "You're engaged in undercover operations at the behest of the vice president, who had no authority to authorize such actions. It's a travesty, and probably illegal."

Philip immediately shifted tacks. He'd been caught and flashed a roguish smile. "It actually wasn't technically illegal," he said. "There is no law against asking an old friend to go to Cuba to sniff out suspected criminal activity."

Luke gave an angelic smile. "And as a private citizen, I was happy to do my civic duty."

"It sounds like the two of you ran off to start your own private crusade," Wilkie said dryly. "We can save the legal niceties for later, but I need to know what you suspect about the military. I've got teams of investigators who can carry this out with both secrecy and benefit of the law."

Mercifully, it looked as if Philip and Luke were willing to cooperate. The Secret Service was nowhere within the military chain of command, meaning they could be a neutral party to carry out the investigation. Caroline held her breath as Luke relayed what he'd learned while imprisoned alongside Mateo. He laid out the facts with confidence, but a hint of teasing mockery lay beneath the surface the entire time, keeping her on edge. Luke loved needling authority.

When he outlined the plan to use a fake telegram from Mateo to dupe Holland into action, Nathaniel flatly rejected it.

"That's entrapment," he said. "I won't condone an investigation based on a lie."

Luke rolled his eyes. "I forgot my smelling salts, so go stand in the hall if this is making you feel faint. I say we cut straight to the chase. It's Saturday. Holland's office at the War Department is empty. We can break in and have a look around."

Again, Nathaniel shook his head. "If you want inside his office, you need a search warrant and probable cause. We need to do everything aboveboard."

"And how does one do an undercover operation in an aboveboard manner?" Luke asked tightly.

Caroline bit her lip as all her misgivings started playing out before her. Nathaniel had gone back to his rigid formality, while Luke was hurling darts at the man she loved.

Even with all their bickering, within an hour, Wilkie and Philip devised a plan that was both legal and clever enough to provoke a guilty man into revealing his hand. Despite Nathaniel's earlier rejection, Wilkie affirmed that using a fake telegram from Mateo was perfectly lawful. If Holland took the bait and sprang into action, the government would have probable cause for a search warrant.

"There's another man we need to catch," Luke said. "Holland never personally delivered the funds to Mateo. There's a go-between in Key West, and I don't know the identity of that man. All I know is that Holland wires money to Key West, then the go-between sails it to Cuba. We need to figure out who that man is."

"Once we arrest Holland, we'll be able to search his house and find the third man," Wilkie said. "First we arrest the mastermind, then we go after his minions. It will take some time for me to arrange the fake telegram originating from Cuba, so let's do the stakeout of Holland's house tomorrow."

Philip nodded. "The moment he is arrested, we'll need to start tracking down that unknown link in Key West. If news of Holland's arrest makes the newspapers, that third man is likely to make a run for it. I want this entire operation wrapped up in a week."

It made sense to Caroline, but a hint of tension passed between Nathaniel and Wilkie. There was a time when she wouldn't have even noticed it, but she'd become highly attuned to Nathaniel's emotions and noticed his slight stiffening as he sent a tiny shake of his head to Wilkie.

Wilkie nodded in return, then shifted his attention back to Philip. "I'll be assigning another agent to assist with the case. Agent Trask is needed elsewhere."

"Who?" Philip demanded. "And why? I don't want news of this operation going any further than the people in this room."

"I'm sending Trask to Milwaukee on assignment. He leaves by the end of the week."

"What?" Caroline shrieked. She stood, gaping at Nathaniel in dismay. This felt like a slap in the face.

Nathaniel held up his hands to pacify her. "Caroline, I didn't want to tell you this way."

The strength drained from her, and she sank onto her chair, staring at Nathaniel in confusion. "Tell me what?" she said weakly.

"The Kestrel Gang is back in action. Their counterfeit bills have been spotted in Milwaukee, and I need to get up there quickly to track them down."

Her mind did the calculations. It would take a few days to get to Milwaukee, and then a couple weeks to investigate. He could be back before Thanksgiving. That wouldn't be too horrible, would it? But it still hurt that he would leave Washington after everything they'd been through together. After all they had before them.

"We'll miss the reception at the Smithsonian," she said inanely.

"Yes."

Couldn't he at least sound a little regretful? He had no obligation to seek her permission to go on an assignment, but she wished he had found a way to tell her.

Nathaniel must have sensed her pique, for he continued to justify his need to leave. "The Kestrel Gang is the most damaging group of counterfeiters in the past decade. They've brought chaos to the money supply and show no sign of slowing down. I spent eleven months in St. Louis tracking them down and was so close to cracking the case. No one knows their patterns as well as me. I've got to go."

He kept talking, but all she heard was "eleven months." *Eleven months.* That meant he could spend almost an entire year in Milwaukee! But why should that surprise her? When she met him he had just come off a five-month assignment in Boston working on the counterfeit stamp operation. The nature of his job would always keep him on the move, for counterfeiters could spring up anywhere in the nation. How foolish she had been to believe she and Nathaniel could court like ordinary people.

She beat back the impending panic and forced a dignified expression onto her face. "Is this going to be an eleven-month assignment like you had in St. Louis? Or will you be back next weekend to escort me to the Smithsonian, like you promised?"

At least he had the grace to look sorry. "I don't know the answer to that," he said. "Tracking down counterfeiters is a complicated operation. It usually takes weeks or months. But, Caroline, this is too important for me to ignore."

Something inside her snapped. "You will *always* have duties too important to ignore! Your entire life has been dedicated to serving other people, and you ought to get a medal for it." She turned her ire on Wilkie. "Give this man a medal. He's moved all over the country at your behest and has nothing to show for it. No wife, no home, certainly not a day free of responsibilities or a shred of fun. He ought to at least get a medal."

Luke clamped a hand on her arm, then leaned over to whisper in her ear. "Stop it. Don't lose your temper in public, and don't say anything you might regret later." He released her arm and slid back into his seat.

It was good advice. Luke smoothly covered her loss of composure by returning to their discussion about the plan to take down Captain Holland. Philip was insistent that no other agents be brought into the case. If Nathaniel couldn't help, Philip wanted to work alone with Luke.

"That won't work," Wilkie said. "We need men monitoring Holland's home, his office in the War Department, and the local telegraph office. You need to become accustomed to the idea that you can't continue to run that little spy operation out of a basement map library."

"There's nothing 'little' about my spy operation," Philip said. "I earned the trust of Theodore Roosevelt and have been doing good work on his behalf for years."

"That's all over now," Nathaniel said. "Roosevelt is president, and he doesn't get his own private army or investigative service."

Caroline's gaze trailed out the window as the men argued about legalities and lines of reporting. She ought to care, but she didn't, for her heart felt crushed. Nathaniel had already reverted to his law-and-order demeanor by spotting flaws, pouncing on technicalities, and strategizing solutions.

At least he wasn't staring vacantly into space anymore. He was coming back. The man she loved was emerging from the shell of despondency and engaging in the world again. He'd fallen off a horse and gotten kicked in the face, but he was saddling up again, and it ought to be a relief.

It *was* a relief. This was the man she'd fallen in love with! How could she resent the fact that he was back, even if it meant that, on his list of priorities, she would fall somewhere below the Milwaukee assignment and the Holland takedown and possibly even a fine lobster dinner. Her mouth twitched at the memory. How long ago that first night on the train seemed.

Some things would never change. There would always be crime and corruption in the world, and Nathaniel would always put it first. He wasn't wrong to do so, but it still hurt. How foolish she had been to think that her life would magically be different after September 15th. It wasn't Nathaniel who was going to change. It would have to be her.

Could she do it? Could she tolerate life with a man who never knew where he would be assigned next month or next year? It would take a special kind of person to thrive in that sort of life, and in truth, she didn't know if that person was her.

Thirty-Five

Nathaniel began the next morning in the attic of the Treasury Department, gathering up his old files documenting the Kestrel Gang and preparing them for shipment to Milwaukee. He wanted it done this morning, because this afternoon he had been assigned to surveil Captain Holland's house with Luke Delacroix. He wouldn't leave for Milwaukee until the end of the week, so he'd been assigned to the Holland investigation for these final few days.

Dust prickled his nose as he pushed another trunk aside. He had to crouch low to avoid the sloping roof as he hunted through decades of old files and discarded furniture. He finally located the last of the trunks from his eleven-month stint in St. Louis and opened it, taking the inventory page from the top and tilting it to catch the dim light from the attic window. A smile tugged as he scanned the list he'd personally compiled four years earlier. He had been *so close* to catching these guys.

Footsteps sounded as a departmental clerk knocked on the open attic door. "Found what you were looking for, sir?"

"I have," he said. "These two trunks need to be brought downstairs and earmarked for shipment to Milwaukee."

He couldn't save President McKinley, but he could save the

central banking system of the United States if he could stop the Kestrel Gang from flooding the market with fake currency. He was good at this. It was what he'd trained for all his life. He felt like a bloodhound on the trail of a fresh scent, and every instinct clawed at him to chase them down.

But being away from Caroline would hurt. They'd spent the past eighteen months together, living under the same roof, working side by side every day of the week. They'd been through fire and rain together. She knew all his failings and secrets. He would never turn his back on her, but could she endure the inevitable separations that his job required?

She would understand. She knew how much he needed this.

Even so, he worried about her as he rode to meet her brother for the afternoon stakeout.

Tension made his muscles ache, but he ignored the sensation. He needed to succeed in this. First he would help round up Holland, then he'd shift gears toward Milwaukee and his chance at unraveling another criminal scheme. He *needed* this.

"Ready for fun and games?" Luke asked as they met at the small park across from Captain Holland's house.

"You didn't cut your hair," Nathaniel said as he dismounted.

Luke merely shrugged. "I don't recall ever meeting Captain Holland, but he still might recognize me. The hair is a good distraction."

Probably true. People tended to focus on oddities, and a man wearing a ponytail was certainly odd.

Nathaniel tied his horse to a hitching post by a cluster of trees. The fake telegram was due to be delivered soon, and the park across from Holland's house had plenty of tables perfect for setting up a chess match. A drawn-out game of chess would allow them to linger for hours without drawing suspicion, except that Luke kept whistling the world's most grating tune as they set up the chessboard. It was going to be a long day.

Wilkie's investigation showed that there was no telephone

in the Holland household, so Holland would need to leave the house to send a return message to Mateo. Secret Service agents had been posted at the three nearest Western Union stations to intercept any telegram he tried to send. As an extra precaution, Nathaniel would tail Holland in case he made some other move, while Luke would get to the nearest telephone to warn Wilkie their target was on the move.

Nathaniel could only pray Captain Holland would act soon, for Caroline's brother was annoying. Within seconds of setting up the chessboard, Luke took a flask from his coat pocket and unscrewed the cap.

"It's two o'clock in the afternoon," Nathaniel said tersely. "We aren't drinking."

Luke took a swig from the flask. "Maybe you won't, but I will."

"I don't work with drunk men."

"If you think a sip of Madeira is going to knock me under the table, your education in the normal pleasures of life is sadly lacking."

Nathaniel ignored the comment as he lined up the chess pieces. He needed patience. This man had just endured more than a year of captivity on behalf of the nation and was due a modicum of respect.

"I'll take the white, you can take black," he said once the chess pieces were in place.

"Entirely fitting," Luke replied.

Nathaniel studied the board for a full minute before making his initial move. Luke moved a knight before Nathaniel's hand was even off the pawn.

"You need to wait until I release the chess piece," Nathaniel said. "I still had the option to change my mind."

"Fine, but speed it up."

There was no need for speed. The telegram hadn't been delivered, and they might be here for hours. They each moved three more times, and Nathaniel wondered if Luke was deliberately goading him by carelessly moving his black piece only a second after each of Nathaniel's carefully analyzed moves.

"Check," Luke said after moving a knight into position.

Nathaniel captured the knight with a pawn. "That was a stupid move. You weren't even looking at the board."

"That's because I'm looking at Captain Holland's house and don't need to win a chess game to prove my manhood. How about I circle around to the back of the house and peek in the windows?"

"To what end?"

"To see if I can find out who's home and who he consorts with. It's called being decisive."

"It's called an illegal search and can invalidate any evidence we find. Your move."

Luke casually shifted another pawn, once again acting without even studying the board. "What I'd like to know is if you're going to capitulate and take Caroline to the Smithsonian. You can still take her to the reception if you delay your trip to Milwaukee by a day."

Nathaniel wasn't about to discuss his near-sacred feelings for Caroline with her irreverent brother. Besides, Luke had just dangerously exposed the black queen. He could capture it, but it would come at the cost of his own bishop. He analyzed the board, projecting several moves ahead to see if he could get the queen at a lower cost.

"I think you ought to take her," Luke continued. "She pretends to be invincible, but if you prick her feelings, she'll never forget."

Nathaniel grunted in reply, anything to get Luke to shut up. He slid his bishop, pausing to analyze the downstream implications of—

"Once again!" he said in annoyance. "You need to wait until my hand is off the piece before moving."

"Such a rule-follower," Luke sighed as he returned his pawn to its original square. "Really. Take my advice. You need to escort Caroline to the Smithsonian, or she'll—"

"I want to be in Milwaukee by the end of the week." Even adding these extra few days in Washington were costly to his mission.

"You know what the Bible says about men who need to take it easy. You are supposed to lie down in green pastures. Enjoy the still waters, restoreth your soul. There is a time to work and a time to play. A time to go to the Smithsonian and a time to be an idiot."

"That's not in the Bible."

"The principle is. Did Caroline ever tell you how our mother died?"

Nathaniel looked up, taken off guard by the topic change. "No."

"We were four years old. It was a perfectly ordinary day, and we were waiting in the foyer for Mother to take us outside to admire the tulips just coming into bloom. Mother was at the top of the staircase. When she saw us waiting for her, she laughed and said she had better hurry. A moment later she tripped and tumbled down the stairs. She broke her neck. I think she was dead before she even hit at the bottom."

Luke casually moved a pawn and kept talking. "After that, Caroline became terrified of everything. Stairs, loud noises, going outside. It was months before she was willing to use the staircase again, and Gray had to hold her hand the entire time. I suppose all those fears were normal, but she also withdrew from people. She wouldn't make friends or take care of the puppy our father bought to cheer us up. My father thought something was wrong with her and brought in a minister. He said she was stricken with 'a terror of abandonment,' whatever that means. Now you've managed to awaken all those feelings by being an ardent Romeo one day and a block of ice the next."

Getting lectured by the most irresponsible man on the planet wasn't something Nathaniel could take lying down. "*You* abandoned her by going to Cuba."

"That's right, I did," Luke said, a flash of temper in his eyes. "And it chafed at me every day while I was imprisoned. The difference is that I'm her blood and she won't ever abandon me. But you? She'll drop you like last year's fashions if you hurt her."

Nathaniel mulled over the words but couldn't accept them. "Caroline understands," he said shortly, hoping it was true. She certainly knew what a wreck he'd been since McKinley was shot and how returning to work had helped beat back the savage waves of despondency. She knew how much he needed this.

Across from him, Luke stilled. "Here comes the telegram," he whispered.

A rider carrying a Western Union satchel dismounted before the Holland house and headed up the front path. Captain Holland himself answered the door. He accepted the telegram, reading it while the messenger waited. Holland stared at the card for an entire minute, then glanced up, tipped the messenger, and closed the door.

"No return message," Luke said.

"It might still be coming." The message would be a shock to Holland, and he might take plenty of time to analyze the implications.

Nathaniel strolled over to his horse, methodically checking its saddle to be sure it was ready to follow Holland if he left the house.

"He's leaving," Luke whispered, and sure enough, Holland had donned a light jacket.

But instead of leaving by horseback, he was cutting across his lawn to a neighboring house, walking up the path and knocking on the front door. To his dismay, Nathaniel noticed the telephone wire leading from the neighbor's house to the street.

"That house has a telephone," he warned. This was a development they hadn't foreseen. If Holland started the wheels in motion via that neighbor's telephone, they would have no way of tracking it.

"I'm going in," Luke said, taking a step toward the house, but Nathaniel dragged him back.

"Don't be insane," he whispered sternly, but Luke still stared across the street where Holland had already been invited inside the neighbor's house.

"I'll get in through a basement window, and you're not going to stop me." Luke jerked his arm away, loping toward the house in long strides.

"Get back here," Nathaniel said in a furious whisper, but Luke ignored him, jogging toward one of the basement windows. A quick glance up and down the street showed no passersby, and Luke was now crouched in the window well. What was Nathaniel supposed to do? The fool was going to be caught, but trying to haul him out of there would only call more attention to him.

He plopped back down onto the park bench, staring at the house in helpless frustration. Sunlight glinted on the glass of the window as Luke pried it open. Nathaniel's stomach turned as Luke wiggled through the window, compromising their entire investigation.

Minutes passed, and a bead of sweat trickled down Nathaniel's neck as he waited, counting his heartbeats. He glanced at his watch. Five minutes had passed. Then ten. When the tension became unbearable, he moved behind a screen of trees to pace, but he still kept an eye on the house. How much was this rash move going to cost them? It was hard to believe this scoundrel was actually Caroline's brother, for although she could be impulsive and frivolous, she was sensible. She could be reasoned with, not like this—

The front door opened and Luke shuffled out, a middle-aged

man and woman standing on the front stoop to watch him go. Luke's head hung low as he lumbered down the path, looking like a beaten dog. He carried a loaf of bread beneath his arm.

The man and woman still watched, and Nathaniel took cover behind the wide trunk of an ancient oak tree. The homeowners eventually retreated inside, but Luke continued his shambling, unsteady gait as he crossed the street and into the park. He was a mess. His clothing was disheveled and his hair had come free to hang over his shoulders.

Finally, Luke drew alongside Nathaniel with a grim expression as he tossed him the loaf of bread. Nathaniel caught it.

"They mistook me for a vagrant breaking into their house for food," Luke said. "They felt sorry for me." He gestured Nathaniel in closer and continued speaking. "Holland was already on the telephone when I got inside, but I overheard plenty before they caught me. He was talking to someone from a bank, who was annoyed to be called at home, but Holland said it couldn't wait until Monday. He wanted the guy to open the bank right now so he could get his money. It sounds like he's getting ready to run. He clammed up when the maid started screaming her head off at the sight of me hiding on the basement stairs."

He went on to report that the telephone was in the kitchen, and when the homeowners brought him in for a hot meal, Captain Holland had hung up and didn't say another word.

"Did he recognize you?"

"I don't think so," Luke said. "I kept my hair hanging in my face, and I got out as soon as I could. Holland is ten steps ahead of us, with a plan already in place to flee the country. He's got money, papers, everything lined up." He trembled so badly that his voice shook. "I feel like everything I've worked for is slipping away, and I don't know how to stop it."

"I do," Nathaniel said quietly. If Holland had papers, they'd been forged. Tracking down financial crimes was his specialty, and he was ready to pull out the big guns.

Nathaniel and Luke spent the rest of the day in Wilkie's office, untangling the Holland conspiracy. Luke shared more details of what he'd overheard while eavesdropping from the neighbor's basement. Holland had been angry as he shouted over the line, claiming the only reason he worked with Foster's bank was because they were big and ought to have plenty of ready cash on hand. The Foster bank was the largest on the East Coast, and Nathaniel had gotten to know Congressman Foster and his wife during the long presidential train trip.

Nathaniel quickly rattled through what he remembered about the Fosters. Mrs. Foster was a preening, social-climbing busybody who had done her best to make Caroline miserable. She couldn't possibly keep a secret, but her husband could. A proper investigation of Foster and his bank would require the cooperation of a judge and banking experts. Going through the proper legal steps would slow them down. By then, Captain Holland could have fled the country, and they still hadn't discovered his accomplice in Key West.

Wilkie met his eyes across the desk. "Do you think the Fosters could be in on this?"

"I don't know," he admitted.

"What about Caroline Delacroix?" Wilkie suddenly asked.

"What about her?" Nathaniel asked. Bringing Caroline into this conversation was a needlessly painful distraction. Guilt had been gnawing at him since the moment the word *Milwaukee* had been uttered in her presence. She deserved more than he'd given her, but the Kestrel Gang needed to be stopped. The economic integrity of the nation's currency depended on it.

"We can use Caroline to get through to Mrs. Foster," Wilkie said. "They're friends. It won't raise any alarm bells, and perhaps she can sniff out if there is any unseemly association between Mrs. Foster's husband and Captain Holland."

"Caroline is *not* friends with Mrs. Foster," Nathaniel said, possibly the understatement of the century. "She'd rather eat nails than spend time with Emmaline Foster."

"Caroline is a patriot," Luke said. "If she can help bring Captain Holland down, she'll pounce on the opportunity."

It was true, and Nathaniel knew they didn't have much time to get her on board.

Thirty-Six

Nathaniel's immediate reversion back to his old ways hurt more than Caroline could admit. While she was grateful he was emerging from the despondency that had crippled him, it was as if he immediately reached for his blinders to focus on the next duty at hand. Even now, he was spending the day holed up with Wilkie and Luke while she twiddled her thumbs at home.

No more! It was time to regain a sense of normalcy after the chaos of the past few weeks, and she knew exactly where to begin. Shopping had always been a guilty pleasure, and today she had the perfect excuse to indulge, for Luke desperately needed clothes that fit. She ventured in and out of men's haberdasheries, trying to enjoy herself as she wandered among the bolts of fine wool fabrics and shelves brimming with silk ties, vests, and cuff links. She'd love to see Nathaniel in one of these suits. The only time she'd seen him in anything but his sober black suit was the night of the inaugural ball, when he'd looked so handsome in the cutaway tails and high-starched collar that it nearly took her breath away.

Well! Nathaniel would shudder if she tried to deck him out in this finery, so she picked out a suit for Luke, three broadcloth shirts, and a spectacular fuchsia silk tie. It was time to inject a flash of color back into their lives, even if her spirit wasn't quite there yet. For a while she'd thought she was on the verge of joining her life to a man who was a dear friend but also took her breath away.

He was still those things, but it would be hard to build a life with him if he was in Milwaukee. Or Boston. Or wherever else Wilkie chose to send him.

She paid for Luke's new clothes and arranged to have them delivered to the townhouse, for she'd planned an epic day of shopping and couldn't be weighed down with packages. If she returned to the emptiness of their home, she'd start moping over Nathaniel's abandonment again.

Or Ida's rejection. Ida had been the closest thing to a mother she could remember, and the way things had ended hurt. Working for Ida had mostly been a thrill and a joy, but how quickly and tragically it all came crashing down.

Outside the shop, a gust of wind sent some fallen leaves scuttling down the street, their brilliant orange shade beginning to brown at the edges. She felt like those leaves, discarded and fading. She wandered down the street, gazing into bow-fronted windows to admire the antiques and bric-a-brac, but it didn't really help.

She turned to continue walking and almost bumped into George Cortelyou.

"Hello, Caroline," he said warmly.

"George!" How wonderful to see his familiar face. She hadn't had a chance to say good-bye after her expulsion from the White House. He looked hale and hearty, even though with the president's death, he was out of a job too.

"I'm sorry about how things ended," George said kindly, for he was quite possibly the only person on earth who truly understood what Caroline was up against with the first lady. "You didn't deserve what happened."

"How is Mrs. McKinley?" she asked, determined not to let regrets mire her down.

"She and her sister left for Ohio yesterday. She's doing as well as can be expected."

"Good," Caroline said honestly, for she truly wished only the best for Ida. "And you? What's next for you?"

"I've been keeping busy," George replied. "President Roosevelt is creating a new department to govern the nation's business and trade. It's going to be called the Department of Commerce, and I shall be secretary there."

"Wonderful! And who shall you be secretary for?"

"You misunderstand," he said with a kind smile. "I'm going to be the Secretary of Commerce. My first job is to manage the department's creation."

She gasped in astonishment. "Oh, George!" She impulsively rushed into his arms for a hearty embrace. "No one deserves it more than you." Her voice choked up, and tears clouded her vision. Her emotions had been careening wildly ever since Buffalo, but this was such good news. George had always been a rock for her, and the new president couldn't have chosen a better man.

She disentangled herself, tamped down the swell of emotion, and chatted for a few minutes about his new position, but George had a full schedule.

"I need to consult with Treasury about financing the new department. I can only hope it doesn't ruffle too many feathers."

"It surely will, but no one in the city can handle ruffled feathers as well as you," she said honestly.

Memories crowded as she watched him walk away. They had been living in a gilded age but hadn't realized it until it was over. Now they were both headed toward a new and uncertain future, but she would be forever grateful for those eighteen months in the White House. She was a better person for it. She had entered the White House as a girl who loved to throw parties, but she'd left as a woman. Wiser, sadder, but more confident of her true value in the world. Her heart was full to the breaking point, for echoes of that gilded age would live with her forever.

∼ᦐ∽

The bittersweet memories still swirled as she returned home, and she was surprised to see Luke sitting with Nathaniel and Wilkie in the parlor. All three men were huddled around the table, papers spread out before them, expressions earnest.

"Where have you been?" Nathaniel asked as he got to his feet.

"Shopping," she replied archly. "Where else would I be on a Monday afternoon?"

"Come sit down," he said. "We need your help."

A flush stained the top of his cheekbones, and his eyes were alive with anticipation. This was the man she loved, always so engaged with keen, professional absorption. She sat, wishing she could inspire a similar level of devotion.

"Captain Holland has funneled his ill-gotten gains into the Fosters' bank," Nathaniel explained. "We don't think the Fosters are part of the scheme, but we need to start investigating without triggering anyone's suspicion. We need you to call on Mrs. Foster. Get inside her house, break the ice, and see if you can recruit her to our side."

"You want me to cozy up to Emmaline Foster?" she asked in disbelief. "That woman made snide comments to me all the way from Virginia to Louisiana. She barely tolerated me when I was Ida's secretary, but now she has no use for me at all."

"She will if it means saving face for her husband's bank," Nathaniel said. "This has the makings of an ugly scandal, and the Fosters will need to salvage their reputations."

"Maybe I could ask Mrs. Foster to accompany me to the reception at the Smithsonian. Or would that be too humdrum?"

The barb found its mark, and Nathaniel flinched. Then the air went out of him, and he braced his elbows on his knees. Her remark about the Smithsonian was meant to be a flippant jibe, but it had hurt more than she intended. When he spoke, his voice was so soft that she could barely hear him.

"Caroline, I need this," he said, still staring at the floor.

She met Luke's gaze. For once there was no laughter or mockery in her brother's face, just a sad understanding. She wanted to help Nathaniel, but it seemed that in restoring his pride, she would be setting him on a course that would take him far away from her.

But wasn't that what she'd sworn to do that night she called him at the White House? She'd spoken of how she would faithfully wait for him, no matter how long it took. She vowed that walls or distance could not separate them. She had not foreseen the Milwaukee assignment, but she would need to find a way to deal with the distance. Nathaniel needed to strike out on a new adventure, and she would remain loyal while he did so.

She pulled her chair closer to the group and set her misgivings aside. If this was what Nathaniel needed, she would support him.

~ ❧ ~

Caroline approached the Fosters' house, armed with the mortifying ruse Nathaniel had designed. Implementing it would be humiliating and embarrassing, but she would do it.

Luke drove her to the elegant Foster townhouse in Georgetown. He'd finally cut his hair and looked sharp in his natty new clothes as he drew the horses to a halt outside the residence.

"Good luck," he said with a wink, knowing how much she loathed this mission. After all, Mrs. Foster had delighted in goading Caroline for her crush on Nathaniel, and this afternoon would stir all those painful memories. She squared her shoulders and prepared to do battle.

The Fosters lived in an ornate French-style chalet, and a maid answered the door. Caroline had to loiter in the parlor for an unseemly amount of time while the maid went to see if Mrs.

Foster was "at home." The interior of the house was a gold and ivory display of ostentation, and the delicate gilt chairs looked like works of art rather than something to sit on. Nevertheless, Mrs. Foster eventually appeared and invited Caroline to tea.

"How are things progressing with Agent Trask?" Mrs. Foster asked once they were settled at the tea table. "Is there new hope on that front?"

It wasn't hard to let the hurt show on her face. "I'm afraid not," she said. "It's terribly disappointing. He's been reassigned, and since I'm no longer at the White House, well, there's no longer any reason for our paths to cross."

Mrs. Foster's face was all sympathy as she tutted, but Caroline spotted the secret delight in the older woman's eyes. She put on a brave face and set down her teacup. It was time to get to business, and she would follow Nathaniel's instructions to the letter, for everything was designed to either flatter Mrs. Foster or throw her off balance.

"Are you acquainted with Captain Holland of the navy?" she asked.

The blunt question took Mrs. Foster aback. "I'm acquainted, but I don't know him well."

"Does your husband?"

Mrs. Foster smiled tightly. "The Hollands are not our sort of people."

Once Caroline would have interpreted that comment as simple snobbery, but perhaps Mrs. Foster knew something unsavory.

"Can you tell me more? I'd very much like to know everything I can about the Hollands."

The corners of Mrs. Foster's mouth turned down, and she shifted in her chair, glancing at the door in a silent message that Caroline should feel free to leave at any moment. "I can't imagine where this line of questioning is going."

Everything about her comportment indicated she was distinctly uncomfortable. It was time to shift tactics and let her feel superior.

"My heart is a little battered after being rejected by Mr. Trask," Caroline said. "It was mortifying, but it's time for me to move on. I understand Captain Holland has a son who is an eligible bachelor. Robert Holland? I saw him from afar and found him quite appealing. I would very much like to meet him, and anything you could do to help would be grand. You're so connected. Perhaps Robert Holland will be my answer."

Mrs. Foster nodded sagely. "Now I understand, my dear. I've heard some rumors about young Robert Holland. An unfortunate reliance on drink, I believe. That's long in the past, but I'd still caution you against getting too close to that family."

"Why?" Caroline asked. "I can't afford to have my heart broken all over again. Not at my age—I'm almost thirty years old! I'm considering pursuing Robert Holland, but I don't know who to turn to for insight. If there is a blemish on his family's reputation . . ."

She let the sentence dangle, hoping it would prompt Mrs. Foster's voracious appetite for gossip to burst through its dams.

It worked, and Mrs. Foster leaned forward, no longer able to contain herself. "More than a blemish," she whispered.

Caroline waited, but no more information was forthcoming. "And is the blemish on Robert? Or his parents? Please, it would so help if I knew what sort of people they are."

"Well, Captain Holland is in a position of great power in the navy," Mrs. Foster said. "He set up a charity for widows and orphans of the navy, which is all very admirable, but he rarely distributes any of the funds. And when he *does* withdraw some of the money, I've noticed that he always enjoys a new carriage or a fine gold watch. Not that I begrudge him drawing a salary. Charities require experienced men at the helm, but I never see more than a few dollars going to the widows. Just new horses, carriages, jewels, and gaming."

Raising money for charity was hard work. She and Petra had learned that the hard way, but this was the first she'd ever heard of a widows and orphans fund for the navy. "You know that I help with a school for immigrant woman, but I know little about raising money or proper accounting. Might I see Captain Holland's account for the widows and orphans fund so I could use it as a model for my own charity?"

Mrs. Foster was aghast. "There are rules, my dear. Confidentiality! Our clients are entitled to their privacy."

Perhaps. And the people of America were entitled to know how government officials spent their money. Luke believed that Captain Holland was skimming from the military budget, and she suspected he was using the widows and orphans fund as a front to cover his embezzlement.

"If money from the charity is being used less than honestly, it could be a problem for your husband," Caroline said.

"Are you insinuating something?" Mrs. Foster demanded. "I will not allow the reputation of my husband's bank to be sullied."

Caroline dropped her innocent expression and straightened her spine. For the first time since meeting Mrs. Foster, she looked at her with complete candor and respect. "I don't want your bank to become a casualty of Captain Holland's greed."

Mrs. Foster's eyes glinted. "Spit it out, Caroline. What are you implying?"

She told her. Captain Holland had been amassing a slush fund by skimming from the War Department. The widows and orphans fund was only a façade. With no oversight, it was his personal nest egg that had grown fat over the years, and he'd used the Fosters' bank to carry it out.

Caroline watched as Mrs. Foster's expression morphed from anger, to fear, to outrage, and knew that they'd found an ally.

Thirty-Seven

Nathaniel had never seen a Secret Service operation swing into high gear so quickly, which was good because he was leaving for Milwaukee by the end of the week. Caroline's insight into a sketchy widows and orphans fund was enough to get a search warrant, for there was no record of this charity anywhere within the government. The Fosters were desperate to keep the investigation quiet and willingly opened their bank to the Secret Service. They'd rather be thought dupes in the eyes of a few government agents than considered complicit in what was sure to be a national scandal.

"Anything I can do, don't hesitate to ask," Mr. Foster had said earlier in the day when Nathaniel presented him with a search warrant. Mr. Foster helped them pull all of Captain Holland's personal accounts as well as the paperwork for the charity. He even let them use the bank manager's office to plow through the records.

Luke waited for the office door to close before causing trouble. "Why are we even here?" he demanded. "You should have gotten that warrant to search Holland's house, not the bank. Who cares about the money? I want the name of Holland's accomplice in the Florida Keys."

It was hard to concentrate with Luke's fireworks going off beside him, but Nathaniel kept his voice calm. "The moment Holland knows we are on to him, that evidence is going to disappear."

"Exactly! So why aren't we searching his house right now?"

Wilkie pulled another chair up to the banker's desk, flipping through the paperwork used to establish the widows and orphans file. "Relax. I have two men surveilling the Holland house, and two more at the War Department. Nothing is going to happen without us knowing it."

Luke let out a string of curses as he paced the tight confines of the office. It was like being trapped in a box with an angry bumblebee, but Nathaniel screened it out as he scrutinized the documents Captain Holland had used to initiate the scheme.

There was a letter of authorization from the War Department to set up the charity, and another from the War Department's chief of finance that authorized .001% of all money spent on military armaments to be diverted to the widows and orphans fund.

Both documents were forgeries. Good ones, printed on government stationery with official watermarks, but the letterhead had a tiny flaw. Real documents used hot metal typesetting, while the forged ones had been engraved. Captain Holland probably stole blank pages from the Government Printing Office and took them to a private printing agency to forge the letterhead. All it took was those two documents for the Fosters' bank to divert a tiny fraction of income from a massive fund into his fraudulent charity.

Luke's smile was tight. "Now you can track your precious money. Can I go hunt down the third spy? He's still out there."

The telephone on the desk rang. All conversation stopped while Wilkie listened to someone speaking quickly on the other end. Wilkie stood as he hung up the receiver.

"Holland is on the move," he said tersely. "Our man watching the house says Holland is loading trunks into a carriage."

Luke shot out the door, and Nathaniel followed.

~~~

Horseback was the fastest way to get to Holland's house, and Nathaniel followed Luke as he cut through backyards and forded streams. Cold water splashed his trousers, but he ignored it, for every second mattered. If Holland got out of the country, they might never learn the identity of his accomplice in Key West.

Nathaniel blanched in horror at the column of black smoke pouring from the back of the Holland house. "He's burning everything."

Luke vaulted off his horse and ran behind the house. Nathaniel followed. For a small fire, the mound of burning papers created plenty of smoke. Holland stood near the flame, a rake in one hand while he sloshed liquid from a tin of kerosene over the papers.

"No!" Luke roared as he ran forward, kicking at the flames, scattering papers and embers across the lawn.

Holland panicked. He dropped the rake and heaved another stack of papers onto the flames. Luke dove after them, reaching into the fire even as Captain Holland sloshed more kerosene onto the blaze. Nathaniel kicked the tin away, and Holland turned on him, punching him in the jaw.

Nathaniel's teeth cracked and pain made him see sparks, but he didn't resist. Striking a federal agent was a crime and could be used as an excuse to arrest Holland. Behind him, Luke flung pages out of the fire, but all were burning, their edges curling and turning black.

Nathaniel stamped on them, hoping to salvage them, but Holland attacked again, landing two more punches to his face. The salty tang of blood leaked into his mouth, and it was hard to keep standing, but the unprovoked attack would be enough to get Holland locked up. Nathaniel pulled his gun from its holster and pointed it at Holland.

"That's enough," he said. "Captain Holland, you're under arrest for embezzlement from the US War Department."

"It ought to be treason," Luke snarled, still trying to save the documents.

Nathaniel kept his gun trained on Holland but spoke to Luke. "Don't kill yourself. I'll find all the evidence we need even without those papers."

"Evidence of what?" Holland asked, his hands in the air but outrage on his face. "I'm burning old paperwork in the privacy of my own home. This is an outrage."

"Fueling a foreign war is an outrage," Nathaniel said, satisfaction filling him as he watched understanding dawn on Holland's panicked face, but behind him, Luke continued his frenzied quest to salvage the papers. Nathaniel couldn't ignore it any longer, and he hauled Luke back from the flames.

"Stop! Luke, you've got to stop."

The burns on Luke's hands were evident. The cuffs of his sleeves were blackened and smoking, but his hands were worse. None of the papers looked salvageable.

Luke dropped to his knees, sagging as he stared at the smoldering embers. "We were too late," he whispered.

"It's not too late." Nathaniel had grounds for an arrest, and the entire ugly scandal was about to be blown wide open.

~ ❧ ~

Caroline felt sick as she paced outside the hospital's examination room, too tense to sit on the hard bench in the hallway. Luke's hands had been burned, but the doctor hadn't finished his work, and it was too early to know the severity of her brother's injuries.

Nathaniel sat on a bench, holding a chunk of ice wrapped in a towel to his swollen lip. They were the only ones in the hallway, for Wilkie and the other agents were all at Holland's house, scouring for more evidence, but almost everything had been burned.

Luke was right. They *should* have moved faster. She'd gotten a glimpse of his face as they carried him in on a stretcher. He looked destroyed, his face a mask of anguish. To have sacrificed so much for this cause only to lose the evidence in a bonfire was heartbreaking. She had begged to be let inside the room as the doctors began the painful task of treating the burns, but they'd warned her away.

So did Luke. "I don't want anyone seeing me like this," he had told her, his voice heavy with despair.

It wasn't fair. Luke deserved a medal, not this.

Nathaniel was far more levelheaded than she was, calmly sitting on the bench and telling her for the third time not to worry. "Holland is in jail. Wilkie will have the time and freedom to launch a proper investigation. It will all be aboveboard."

Normally Nathaniel's unshakeable demeanor appealed to her, but did he always have to be so logical? She wanted to scream or throw something, not be calm and rational.

"Sit down," he urged. "It seems like forever since we've had a chance to talk. Tell me what's next for you now that the new team is on board at the White House."

She kept pacing. "I have no idea."

And it bothered her. Except for that single trip to see Luke in Cuba, she had worked every day for the past eighteen months. Now she had the freedom to do something else, but she didn't know what. It was like being adrift at sea without any wind in her sails and no harbor in sight.

"What about that school?" Nathaniel asked. "I'm sure Ludmila would love to see you there."

Caroline sighed but didn't slow her pacing. "I care about the school, but I'm not a teacher. I care about Ida, but I can't move to Ohio, if she'd even take me."

"You have to do something."

"Why?" she demanded. "I have worked around the clock for eighteen months, and I'm tired. Maybe I want to take a week and do nothing more stressful than order from a restaurant menu. Or visit friends. Or the Smithsonian," she couldn't resist adding.

"Not the Smithsonian again."

His tone rubbed her the wrong way. "Yes, the Smithsonian! Must you always work? Must I?"

The nurse behind the desk sent them both a warning glance. "Shhh."

Caroline turned away, hurt by Nathaniel's refusal to answer. There would always be something to keep him chained to work. While she admired his dedication, a small, selfish part wondered if she could live with it, because she didn't think he'd ever change.

She took the seat beside him. "I hope you won't go to Milwaukee."

"I know," he said quietly.

She held her breath, waiting for him to continue, but silence stretched between them. The ticking of the clock on the wall behind her was the only sound, and she supposed that was her answer. He would leave.

What should a good and loyal woman do? The logical part of her mind said a woman should do everything possible to support her man. Dr. Tisdale had even suggested how important it was for Nathaniel to get back up on the horse that threw him. He had failed in an epic manner before the entire nation. While no one knew his name, plenty of newspapers had lambasted the Secret Service for their failure to protect the president.

Being a detective was something Nathaniel excelled at. Ever since the challenge of tracking the Kestrel Gang rose before him, his spark of life was back. He needed the sense of accomplishment he could find in this work, and she ought to be the sort of woman who would support whatever he needed.

Should she help him pack his bags for Milwaukee? Or should she draw a line in the sand and order him to stay? She didn't want to, because she was afraid of his answer.

As if confirming her suspicions, he stood. "Look, I've lingered too long already. I need to get back to the Holland house and help with the investigation. I just wanted to be certain you were all right."

Did she look all right? Her heart was breaking, but she lifted her chin and affected a nonchalant air. "By all means, go. I'll be fine. I always am."

He nodded, pressed a kiss to her forehead, and left. As she watched his tall, dark form walk away, she wished he hadn't believed her so readily.

A few minutes later the doctor emerged from Luke's room. "He's got second-degree burns on both hands," he reported. "He's already blistering, and the wounds are seeping. The biggest problem was removing the bits of paper and dirt from the damaged skin. It was a painful process, but I gave him a dose of morphine to make the procedure bearable. I've covered the wounds with a salve and bandaged them. Now the best cure is time."

"Can I see him?" she asked.

The doctor nodded. "He's in decent spirits, considering. He had Nurse Rumstead laughing, and it takes a lot to crack that old battle-axe."

That had to be good! Luke's moods could always turn on a dime, and she prayed he would weather this latest disappointment.

He was sitting up in bed, wearing an awful white smock, with both hands heavily bandaged. Two nurses, a young redhead and an older woman, tidied the room to remove bandage clippings and bottles of antiseptic. Even weak, underweight, and suffering wicked second-degree burns, Luke was flirting with both nurses.

"Look at you," she said, feigning good cheer. "You've got two women dancing attendance. I don't even know why I'm here."

"Nellie is only here because she pities me. Isn't that right, Nellie?"

The younger nurse blushed furiously, while Nurse Rumstead tried to look stern, but her eyes still twinkled in amusement. "I want you to call me when the morphine begins wearing off, do you hear me, young man? No heroics."

There was a bit more banter as the nurses cleared out, and Caroline lowered herself into a chair at his side, watching his mood carefully.

"How are you feeling?"

"Pretty miserable," he said, but he still sounded cheerful as he glanced at his hands. "The morphine helps, but it still hurts. The doctor calls them second-degree burns, but I call them first-degree torture."

It looked like it took all his effort to turn his head on the pillow and manage a weak smile, but it reached all the way to his eyes, and he seemed at peace.

Perhaps it was the medication that had caused his mood change, and she still needed to put his mind at ease. "Nathaniel says he can build a case against Holland even without the papers."

Luke gave a resigned nod. "I did the best I could. For the past year I've prayed, and tried, and prayed some more. It's been a lesson in patience and humility. It's in God's hands now."

That caught her by surprise. Luke had gone through the motions of being devout while imprisoned, but she had expected it to fade quickly now that he was out. He had always been an irreverent rascal, but he wasn't pulling her leg. He seemed completely genuine.

"That's a change in attitude. It looked like you wanted to

rip Nathaniel's head from his shoulders when they carted you in here."

"Oh, I did!" he said, his irreverent grin back. "Then I had a few minutes to walk back from the ledge, pray, and see things in a bigger perspective. I was able to cut the head off the beast. Nathaniel and the others at the Secret Service can take over to track down the third man. Maybe they'll get him, maybe not, but I can honestly say I did my best."

She nodded, relieved that Luke seemed genuinely at peace with what had happened. "I need to wire Gray about everything. I wired him the day after you returned home but never got a response. I should send another. What shall I tell him?"

"Tell him to get that farm sold and get back to Washington. I miss him."

She nodded and couldn't help marveling that in the past year, her brothers had finally learned to accept each other despite their stark differences in personality, and despite the ignominy of Luke's arrest.

Or maybe because of it. She wouldn't want to relive the horror of this past year for anything in the world. Last month a few strands of gray hair had appeared at her temple. She'd yanked them out, but she knew who had caused them, and her name was Annabelle Larkin.

Or Annabelle Delacroix, now that Gray had married her. Whatever her name, it was Annabelle who had betrayed them all when she turned Luke in last summer.

Now that Luke was out, they would have to figure out how to cope with what had happened, for Caroline couldn't imagine they could all share the townhouse, not with this much animosity between them.

"Gray is quite taken with Annabelle," she began hesitantly.

"I should hope so, she being his wife and all."

"We're going to have to find a way to deal with her. If you'd prefer not to live under the same roof—"

"Stop right there," Luke said, a spark of energy returning. "I don't resent Annabelle. She's a loyal American. She thought I was a spy and followed her conscience. How can I resent her for that?"

"Fifteen months in a Cuban jail didn't teach you that?"

Luke managed a weak shrug. "I wasn't making much progress before my arrest. I didn't gain Mateo's trust until we were locked up together. If not for Annabelle's actions, I'd probably still be floundering. Those months in jail did me good, and I'm not just talking about figuring out Holland's identity. I'm talking about the isolation and forced self-examination. I found pieces of my soul I didn't know existed. I see God's hand in that, and I'm grateful for it. I'll never resent Annabelle for what she did."

Caroline straightened her spine. "Perhaps you can forgive her, but I never will."

"You don't need to sound so proud about that," Luke said, mild disapproval in his tone. It took her aback. In all their years, Luke had never scolded her, and it hurt.

"What do you see in her?" she burst out in frustration. "We have nothing in common with her. All she's done is bring chaos into our lives."

Luke glanced away, his eyes pensive and a little sorrowful. When he finally answered, his voice was low and sad. "I like the way she looks at Gray. It's obvious how much she adores him, and not because he's rich or powerful. She loves him for who he is. She is utterly pure and good. I'd give anything to have a woman like Annabelle look at me like that."

Luke's blatant admiration for her despised sister-in-law was troubling. Luke was supposed to be on *her* side, not Annabelle's.

The door opened, and the pretty redheaded nurse came inside, blushing gorgeously as she set a pitcher of water at Luke's bedside.

"Is there anything else I can bring you? Just name it, and I'll find it."

"Thanks, Nellie," Luke said. "I'll be fine."

The nurse hesitated. "If you're sure, then. . . ." The sentence dangled while Nellie looked at Luke with her heart in her pretty blue eyes. When Luke shook his head, she left the room, disappointment on her face.

Caroline lifted a brow at him. "You're an emaciated wreck and can still charm any woman within ten yards of you. Don't go getting mopey because no woman will want you. Did you see how that nurse looked at you?"

Luke's eyes gleamed. "I saw her, but she didn't see me. Not really. I can flirt and tease and flatter. No matter how good I try to be—and trust me, in the past year I have tried extraordinarily hard to be good—at my core, I'm still a lousy rat. Nellie didn't see that part."

If he wasn't a gaunt skeleton wrapped in bandages, she'd want to smack him. Yes, Luke had always been the naughty one, but he was also charming and generous. She knew him better than anyone, but a part of what he said was true. He had demons inside, and it was anyone's guess if he'd be strong enough to conquer them now that he had a new lease on life.

※

Caroline pulled her cloak tighter as she stepped outside the hospital. The blustery wind was chilly, or perhaps she was simply more fragile than usual. Exhaustion tugged at her as she wondered if she should buy a new cloak. She fiddled with the tie. The cord seemed to have frayed since last autumn.

Distracted, she almost bumped into a man coming up the hospital steps.

"Gray!" she gasped. "Where have you been? You didn't respond to my telegram!"

Gray swept her into a hug. "We came back the moment we

heard Luke was home. Now he's landed himself in the hospital?"

Caroline glanced over his shoulder. Annabelle stood a few feet away, looking cold and out of place.

"Annabelle," she said with a frosty nod, and Annabelle returned it with a hesitant smile.

Caroline had nothing else to say to Annabelle and turned her attention back to Gray, filling him in on how Luke's hands got burned in a foolishly heroic attempt to salvage papers from a fire.

"He's awake if you want to go in and see him," she offered.

"No, I need to know how *you're* doing," Gray said, both hands on her shoulders as he peered into her face, his eyes crinkled in concern. "I'm sorry about President McKinley. I know how much you admired him."

A sheen of tears prickled. She nodded, for speaking right now would be difficult. Buffalo seemed like another lifetime, but the president had died only three weeks ago. Since then she had planned his funeral, welcomed a new administration into the White House, and helped Luke take down Captain Holland. Gray knew none of those things. He'd been completely cut off out in Kansas and could have no concept of the bone-numbing ordeal she'd been wading through.

"I'm doing okay," she managed to say without meeting his eyes.

"I have a carriage. Can I arrange for it to take you back to the White House?"

The question took her aback. Gray didn't even know about what had happened.

"No," she said, her lip beginning to wobble.

Gray looked closer. "What's wrong?" he demanded. "Caroline, tell me."

"Ida fired me," she choked out. "I don't work there anymore."

Her face crumpled and two fat tears spilled over, and then a terrible, keening wail came out of her throat. Was that noise really from her? Gray pulled her into his arms, rocking her like a baby, and the last thread broke. She bawled like an infant.

"I'm so sorry, baby girl," he murmured, his voice rough with sympathy.

It made her cry harder. Why was she breaking down like this? She hadn't shed a single tear after the president died. It had been a week since Ida threw her out of the house, but the pain of rejection hadn't lessened. How mortifying to collapse in front of Annabelle, but Caroline cried so hard she couldn't even breathe. The exhaustion, the grief. It was all too much. If Nathaniel was here, she wouldn't feel so fragile.

As if he could read her mind, Gray said the least helpful thing possible. "Where's Nathaniel?"

She pulled back to wipe her face. "Off doing whatever it is that's so important." Like catching Captain Holland's associates, but she wished to the bottom of her heart he'd stayed with her this afternoon.

"Go on inside," she said, blotting her tears. "Luke is anxious to see you." Then she looked at Annabelle. It was time to act like a good Christian, even if she didn't feel like one. "You too," she said to Annabelle. "Luke specifically said he's looking forward to seeing you again. He bears no grudge."

Gray's face lit up. Her tiny show of concession seemed to mean the world to him. "Come with us," he urged.

She scrambled for an excuse but could find none and led the way back inside. She stood near the back of the room to watch the reunion from afar. Moving his arms caused Luke's burned hands excruciating pain, which made any sort of embrace impossible, but his smile was wide as Gray pulled up a chair beside the bed. After a few greetings, Gray dove right in with the hard questions.

"Did you have to lie to me every time I visited you in Cuba?"

"Do we have to start this off with a reprimand?" Luke asked, and the wind immediately went out of Gray. He winced and turned away but regained his composure quickly.

"You're right. I'm sorry . . . you're entirely right."

Now it was Luke who looked guilty. "Don't apologize. I've caused everyone a lot of grief, and I'm sorry about it." The conversation faltered to an awkward stop. Luke glanced over at Annabelle, who looked exquisitely uncomfortable. "Is that a new dress?" he asked politely.

Annabelle glanced down and fingered the maroon cotton frock. "No, it was my mother's. We remade it in the nineties to fit me. Of course, now it's almost 1902, so it probably needs updating again."

Gray reached for her hand. "Or we can go shopping and buy something new. I know that strikes terror into your thrifty soul, but we can afford some new gowns."

"Or maybe Caroline can take her shopping," Luke said, his eyes calculating.

Caroline shifted in discomfort. "I'm very busy these days," she dissembled. The last thing on earth she wanted was to be cloistered with Annabelle. Bitter feelings of resentment still lingered, and the petty side of her wanted to keep them stoked.

The silence became awkward, and Annabelle finally spoke. "Caroline and I have very different styles," she said with an apologetic smile.

Annabelle had been nothing but conciliatory from the moment their world imploded. If their family was ever to mend, Caroline had to participate. She didn't want to, but Gray desperately wanted a truce, and she needed to grow up and quit priding herself for holding on to a grudge. If a woman as fresh and cheerful as Annabelle could adore her boring older brother, she couldn't be all bad.

"I have better taste than you," she said to Annabelle, her

voice deliberately casual. "I'd love to take you shopping. We shall wreak terrible havoc on Gray's bank account."

The relief on Gray's face was palpable. Patching their family back together might still have its rocky times. It was going to take effort and humility, but it was time for her to move beyond the trauma of the past year and into a season of peace and renewal.

A genuine smile began to tug, for she would *love* to see Annabelle decked out in some pretty new clothes.

Thirty-Eight

It didn't take Nathaniel long to learn the name of the third man in Key West. Ever since Captain Holland's arrest, he had been singing like a bird, hoping to fall on the mercy of the court by revealing everything. He confessed to setting up the fraudulent account early in the Spanish-American War. When the war ended after only a few months, it was in his interest to keep money flowing into the armaments account, which was why he stoked the fire of the Cuban rebellion by funneling money to the rebels. Captain Holland wired funds from Foster's bank to an accomplice in Key West, who then brought the funds to Mateo in Cuba.

That intermediary was Daniel Perez, a shrimp boat owner living in Key West. Records subpoenaed from the Western Union Telegraph station confirmed a lively correspondence between Holland and Daniel Perez for years.

"I want you to come with me to Key West to question Perez," Wilkie said. "I need your eye for detail and familiarity with the case."

They were in Wilkie's office, the records from Western Union spread out on the worktable. Altogether there were over forty messages between the two men, along with eighteen bank transfers shifting thousands of dollars to Key West. It was the smoking gun Nathaniel needed, but there were other criminals out there.

"What about Milwaukee?" he asked. "Going to Key West will set my trip back a few days." If he had to be delayed, he'd much rather spend that time with Caroline instead of sweltering in Florida.

"Key West first, then Milwaukee," Wilkie said. "It will be like old times!"

But Caroline deserved more than Nathaniel had been able to give her lately. A great deal more. He needed to go after the Kestrel Gang, but he needed Caroline too.

"What if I was married?" he asked. "Could I bring a wife with me to Milwaukee?"

"Miss Delacroix?" Wilkie asked in surprise.

"That's the one."

Wilkie shook his head. "She would destroy your cover. You have a way of blending in no matter where you go. She doesn't."

That was true. And dragging her all over the country wouldn't be fair to her. While Caroline had been happy living in a sleeping berth on the presidential train for months on end, he couldn't see her adjusting to a tiny apartment in some Milwaukee neighborhood with nothing to occupy her time. She deserved better than following him around the country.

A piece of him had always doubted he was good enough for her, but since that afternoon in Buffalo, he *knew* he wasn't. Tackling crime and solving problems was the only way he knew how to put a bandage over the gaping wound in his soul.

"Quit looking so glum," Wilkie said, cutting into his thoughts. "We leave for Key West tonight. I've already wired to the sheriff to expect us."

"I'll be ready," Nathaniel said, and he could only pray that by the time he returned, he would have figured a way to be worthy of Caroline.

⁓

It was October, but it was still stinking hot in the sleepy island town of Key West. After disembarking from the steamer, Nathaniel and Wilkie headed straight to the small clapboard building that served as both the sheriff's office and the jail. It wasn't hard to find, for it was located on the town's main street beneath coconut palms and bougainvillea vines. The explosion of fuchsia blossoms made Nathaniel's fingers itch for some pastels to sketch them, but business came first.

"Bad news," Sheriff Jackson said as the leathery-skinned man strode forward to greet them. He wore a uniform, but the collar and top few buttons were open, the cuffs were rolled up, and hair that was far too long brushed his collar. Quite a difference from the spit and polish of Washington. "The man you're looking for cut himself hauling an anchor aboard his boat last week. No one thought anything of it, but an infection took root. He's in bad shape. The doctor doesn't expect him to make it."

Nathaniel sagged. They'd come a long way to interrogate Daniel Perez, and the timing seemed suspicious. "Could he have gotten wind of the investigation? Could he be faking?"

The sheriff shook his head. "No way. His fiancée has been bawling her eyes out for days, and her little kid is just as bad off. Perez might have been a scoundrel, but he loved that woman and her boy and would never do this to them. Just lousy luck all the way around."

"Can we talk to him?" Nathaniel asked. It was essential to get verification of Holland's story. There might be more conspirators in Cuba of whom Captain Holland knew nothing.

"You can try," the sheriff said, already heading outside. "Mourners have already started gathering. Daniel Perez was a well-liked man."

The sheriff accompanied them down a street and across two

alleys to a small one-story shack with a sloping roof and a large front porch. Half a dozen men loitered on the porch, drinking beer and playing cards, but no one looked happy. Sheriff Jackson casually shook hands with a few of the men, then asked to be let inside.

"You'll have to pry Marta from his side," one of them said.

During the walk, the sheriff had told them about Marta, a young widow with a six-year-old son. Marta had been wanting to get married for years, but Perez insisted he would only marry when he had a house worthy of such a princess. Years had gone by, and she became a laughingstock on the island, but she steadfastly vowed she would someday be Mrs. Daniel Perez.

Their footsteps thudded on the dry plank boards of the porch, and the door squeaked as they stepped inside the dim interior. Every window in the house was open wide, but a foul stench hung in the air. The bedroom lay through an arched opening. A woman knelt by the bed, a rosary dangling in her hands. Two older women and a priest were there as well.

Daniel Perez lay on the bed, watching them approach through glassy eyes. This man was not faking. His bandaged hand lay on a pillow, swollen to twice its size, with angry red streaks leading all the way up his arm. Perspiration soaked the sheets as he lay weakly on the bed.

Sheriff Jackson wandered to the bedside. "These two men are from Washington," he said gently. "They'd like to talk to you. It would probably be best to send Marta and her aunts out of the room for a spell."

Perez's eyes met Nathaniel's. "Are you from Captain Holland?"

"Captain Holland is in jail," Nathaniel said gently, watching Perez closely.

Understanding, but no fear, dawned on Perez's face. He closed his eyes and spoke quietly in Spanish. A moment later Marta rose from her knees and gestured for the two older women to follow her out of the room, closing the door behind her. The priest remained.

"I have already confessed everything to Father Thomas," Daniel said. His eyes roamed across the shabby room, with its scuffed furniture and thin cotton drapes framing the windows. "I knew it was wrong, but how could I bring Marta to a house like this? I wanted a palace for her. I worked so hard. In three more months I would have had enough for a new house, with space for her boy, with everything she ever dreamed. Now I have nothing to give but thirty pieces of silver."

Nathaniel sat in one of the chairs vacated by an aunt. "Do you have the strength to talk to us? It will help us understand."

Daniel nodded and reported that he made runs to Cuba whenever a shipment of money came from Captain Holland. His mind kept wandering, jumping from topic to topic, jumbling names together, timeline confused. Over and over he spoke of Marta and her boy, Julian. He spoke of how he went out of his way to dive for conch since the boy loved them. Marta nagged him to come home, but how could he disappoint the boy?

"I thought we would have forever," he said, staring out the window. "Forever is now only today. I don't think I will live through the night."

Forever is now only today. The phrase was a kick in Nathaniel's teeth. How often had he told Caroline they could be together some vague day in the future? He had always put duty first. He'd always thought duty was a man's highest calling, but what Daniel Perez had done to Marta was a shame. Had Nathaniel been any better with Caroline? He was on the verge of heading out to Milwaukee. He wouldn't even take her down the street to the Smithsonian.

Wilkie grew impatient with the long pause and moved in closer to Daniel's bedside. "Can you tell us who you stayed with in Cuba? I need the names and addresses."

Nathaniel held up his hand. "You don't need to answer that," he said to Daniel. At Wilkie's confused look, Nathaniel stood. "This man's forever ends today. Let him spend it with Marta."

⁓

Hundreds of thoughts battled for Nathaniel's attention on the train ride back to Washington. He didn't know why God had put him in a position to have his greatest fear in the world come to life, but it had happened, and there was no undoing it.

One thing was certain. God didn't inflict this so Nathaniel could retreat into a shell and become a soulless workhorse for the rest of his life. Caroline's words came back to his mind. *"You are unconditionally loved. Unconditionally forgiven. You are a child of God, deserving of more credit than you're giving yourself."*

The McKinley assignment hadn't gone well, but it was time to accept that he had failed. Failure was a normal part of being human, not a permanent condition. He had been kicked in the teeth, knocked down, and failed.

But he had the strength to get back up and be the kind of man Caroline Delacroix deserved. In the past few weeks, he had taken her for granted. It was time to do better.

They were still on the train when he told Wilkie he wasn't going to Milwaukee.

"But you're the best man for the job!" Wilkie said, looking at him with disapproval.

"I'll help you train someone else who would be better. If I go to Milwaukee, half my mind and all my heart will be left in Washington. I'll be no good to you."

Wilkie grumbled but accepted it.

His excitement mounted as the train drew closer to home. As soon as he arrived at the platform in Washington, a part of him wanted to dash across town, pound on Caroline's door, and sweep her into his arms to begin showering her with affection and adoration.

The other part urged restraint. He would lavish as much care and planning into winning her back as he'd briefly devoted to a mission in Milwaukee. Her birthday was coming up, and Caroline liked presents. Big or small, it didn't matter to her, and he had an idea for a perfect one.

But he couldn't do it alone, and her brother Gray was the logical person to help.

He took a streetcar to the spice factory where Gray worked. He'd never had much contact with Caroline's older brother, but he knew that she idolized him and Gray would probably be willing to help.

The Delacroix Global Spice factory was a cavernous warehouse containing dozens of stainless-steel spice mills that each stood ten feet tall. Workers fed seeds, leaves, and dried berries into grinders, filling the air with the pungent scent of spice. He asked to see Gray Delacroix and was led to a hallway where ordinary business offices were mercifully segregated from the noise of the factory.

Through the window in an office door, he spotted Gray where he sat at a desk, poring over paperwork. With his serious demeanor and threads of silver in his dark hair, Gray couldn't be more different from Caroline's bright radiance.

He looked up in surprise at Nathaniel's knock. "Agent Trask, isn't it?" he asked after opening the door.

Nathaniel nodded and offered his hand. "You should probably call me Nathaniel," he said, hoping this was the beginning of a long friendship.

If all went well, they would soon be brothers.

Thirty-Nine

Caroline clutched a letter from George as she made her way to the temporary quarters for the Department of Commerce. Someday, she was sure, the Department of Commerce would be one of the largest departments in the government, but for now it occupied two rented floors in an office building on Fourteenth Street. The rooms were eerily vacant as she walked down a hallway, searching for George, since there were no clerks to ask.

The empty rooms would soon be filled, as his letter indicated. He needed to hire dozens of secretaries and clerks to get the department up and running and had offered Caroline her choice of several positions.

She found him at the end of the hallway, arguing about lighthouses with a balding man as he paced the floor in frustration. "If we are to oversee coastal ports, it makes sense for us to handle lighthouse oversight as well," George said.

"Lighthouses are the purview of the Corps of Engineers," the bald man replied. "I see no cause for them to be transferred to Commerce."

George finally noticed her standing in the open doorway. "Caroline! Come inside and tell me if you think the Department of Commerce should add lighthouses to our list of responsibilities. The president has already charged us with the inspection of coastal ports. I think lighthouse oversight is a logical extension. What do you think?"

"Is this a test?"

"Yes. Of your political acumen. Are lighthouses a good match for us?"

"My political instincts tell me to side with the man on top rather than the man taking notes."

"Excellent answer!" George said. "All right, Mr. Soames, step outside for a few minutes while I interview Miss Delacroix. If we can hire her, she will brighten each day at Commerce."

She waited until the older man left. She still held George's letter, not wanting a job for herself but rather for the first set of young women graduating from Petra's school. Ludmila and fourteen other women were now trained in typing and clerical skills. When she explained this to George, his brows lowered.

"I won't be hiring frontline staff for months. I need high-level operation management. That's why I want you. Your political instincts are as good as anyone I've met. I'd like you to manage my office."

Merely looking at the files stacked on George's desk made Caroline tired. She had loved her work at the White House, but the prospect of leaping back into the governmental whirlwind as a new department took shape was exhausting.

"Come, Caroline," George gently scolded, "I've always known you could do more than host tea parties or manage Ida's volatile moods."

"I *like* planning tea parties. And it turns out I couldn't quite manage Ida's volatile moods, as we all know." It hurt even to broach the subject, and George's eyes softened in sympathy.

"Perhaps if you write to her?"

She shook her head. "Any letter I send will be returned unopened. I'll never stop hoping for a reconciliation with Ida, but it's best done in person. I'll go to Ohio someday soon."

Her voice trailed off. She couldn't go to Ohio until after Nathanial returned from the Florida Keys. He wouldn't be in town long before he'd be rushing off to Milwaukee, and she didn't want to miss him. It was foolish to schedule her life around a man always so willing to dash off on missions, but she couldn't help it. She thought of him every hour of each day.

"As soon as the Holland investigation is complete, I'll be able to think about going to Ohio," she said. "Once Nathaniel is back in town, I'll know when I can leave."

"But he returned two days ago. Didn't you hear?"

She blanched. Nathaniel hadn't raced to her side the moment he was back? "Where did you hear that?"

"He's been holed up with John Wilkie, working on something. I stopped by to discuss tax revenue, but he was in a meeting with Nathaniel and a few other men I didn't know. He told me he couldn't meet until the Milwaukee project was launched."

The word *Milwaukee* struck fear into her. If Nathaniel had already been back in town for a while, he might leave at any moment. It was mortifying to be left dangling by a man who couldn't even be bothered to come see her after returning from Florida.

She stood. "If you'll excuse me, I think I need to go see John Wilkie."

Caroline mounted the steps at the Treasury Department and headed straight to Wilkie's office. This building contained over two hundred rooms and a dozen different agencies. She had no idea where Nathaniel was stationed, so she marched straight to Wilkie's office to find out.

"Nathaniel is very busy," Wilkie said, glancing up from the papers on his desk.

"He's *always* busy. I'd like to see him before he becomes busy in Milwaukee."

Wilkie took off his eyeglasses and sighed in exasperation. "Don't bother him, Caroline. He's doing very important work. Leave him alone."

She narrowed her eyes. "Tell me where I can find him, or I'm delivering a basket of artichokes to the White House kitchen overnight, and you know I can do it."

"Room 207," Wilkie promptly said.

She headed off toward the stairwell. Her threat about the artichokes was serious, for Luke had finally confided how they had been smuggled into the White House. Partially finished ventilation tunnels in the basement had been abandoned when Ida ordered the White House renovations to stop. The tunnels were covered over but not fully sealed, and Philip took advantage of it. Now that plans for the west wing were back on, that gap would be closed, but Wilkie didn't know that, and another delivery of artichokes would be a huge embarrassment to the Secret Service.

She walked up to the second floor and down an acre of marble corridors until she arrived at a small office with its door open. It was a tiny room, crowded with crates, file cabinets, and a small desk where Nathaniel sat engrossed in some paperwork. A brass plate on the door read Bureau of Counterfeit Detection.

"Back to your one true love, I see," she said.

His head shot up, and he stood. "Caroline!" He glanced around nervously, shoving papers into files and tossing a piece of canvas over a crate. Heavens, such secrecy. "What do you mean?" he asked. "You're my one true love."

She sent a pointed look at the brass plate. "Are you sure? It seems you've always loved counterfeit best."

"You first, counterfeit second," he said. "Come in. We've been discussing you."

Caroline stepped into the office and only then noticed her older brother sitting in an alcove chair just behind the door.

"Gray!" she said in surprise. "What are you doing here?"

He looked completely relaxed as he lounged in the chair, coat off and shirtsleeves rolled up. Rather than answer, he looked at Nathaniel. "Should we tell her?"

Nathaniel looked hesitant. "Her birthday isn't for two more days."

Caroline's heart was already pumping faster. "Oh, don't be such a stickler for details. Tell me now."

Gray stood and reached for his suitcoat. "Go ahead and give it to her now. She'll nag you incessantly if you make her wait. And I should be on my way. This office suddenly feels very crowded."

She didn't want to be rude by turning her brother out, but she lived under the same roof as Gray and saw him every day. Nathaniel was about to leave for Milwaukee, and there were so many things they needed to discuss before he vanished from her life for an unknown length of time.

Gray shrugged into his coat, kissed her on the forehead, and made his departure.

"What was that all about?" she asked as soon as they were alone again. Nathaniel barely knew Gray, but they'd seemed very cozy together just now.

Nathaniel pulled the recently vacated chair a little closer to his desk. It was the only visitor chair in the crowded office. "Please, have a seat."

She preferred to remain standing in the open doorway, pretending to survey the office, because it hurt too much to look at his handsome face, carved with a combination of awkwardness and pleasure.

"Rumor has it you've been back in the city for two days. Couldn't you spare ten minutes for me?"

"I spared you a lot more than that. Gray and I have been working on a birthday present for you. I also had some counterfeit work to handle here at the Treasury Department."

"Preparing for Milwaukee?" Even saying the word made her feel queasy.

Nathaniel's face gentled, and he moved to stand before her, taking her hands in his own. "I'm not going to Milwaukee."

Her heart skipped a beat. The affection blazing in his eyes triggered a whirlwind inside, but she was too afraid to hope. She squeezed his hands and tried to keep her voice steady. "No?"

"No. I'd rather stay here." He said it openly, with no conflicted feelings and only a wonderful tenderness in his face that made her want to gaze at him forever.

"Why?" she managed to ask, still not daring to hope. She knew how much tackling the Kestrel Gang meant to him. If he was willing to walk away from them, *that* would be the best possible birthday present.

"I find there's a girl in Washington I care too much about to leave. I decided to stick around and pursue her."

A whole new world of possibility was beginning to open up for her. She squeezed his hands tighter, still keeping her gaze locked with his but her voice carefully nonchalant. "My goodness. She must be something special to tempt you away from the lure of Milwaukee."

A corner of his mouth twitched. "I thought about her all the way to Key West and back."

"What sort of thoughts?"

"I thought about how lucky I was to have found her. She's as elegant and pretty as a rose, but she's got a spine of pure steel. She's loyal. And patient. She knows how to weather a storm without ever losing a bit of class. Mostly I thought about how grateful I am that she's stuck with me through some of my own storms. Thank you for that, Caroline. I'll never be able to express how much that meant to me."

He gave her one of those famous closed-mouth smiles that always made her heart pound. But she still wasn't ready to declare all forgiven.

"Why didn't you come see me right away?"

"I needed to square things with Wilkie. Get my replacements trained and on their way to Milwaukee. And I didn't want to come back to you empty-handed. Gray and I have been working on obtaining the perfect birthday gift, and it took a little more effort than expected. I hope I wasn't too forward in buying it. I don't know if you'll like it or—"

"I'll like it," she interrupted. Maybe it was foolish, but receiving gifts always thrilled her, no matter how big or small, and the fact that Nathaniel was willing to walk away from Milwaukee still had her over the moon. He could buy her a stick of gum and she'd love it.

"Your brother helped pay for it, so he deserves a lot of the credit," Nathaniel said. "It's over there." He nodded to the boxy object he'd tossed the piece of canvas over when she arrived.

"Can I open it now?"

He nodded, his trepidation growing ever more apparent. She stood and walked to the canvas, lifting it away, and almost fainted when she recognized what it hid.

"Where did you get this?" she gasped.

"From the Corcoran."

It was Vermeer's painting of the lady reading a letter. The breath left her in a rush. Her heart felt full to overflowing, and she was speechless.

Nathaniel closed the distance between them and took her hand. "I'll never forget what you said about this painting. How it's about loyalty and the importance of hope, even in a sometimes bleak and dark world. Your brother is a brilliant negotiator. It took some haggling to convince the director to sell it to us, but we got there in the end."

Before she could say anything, Nathaniel lifted away more of the canvas, revealing the painting of the girl with the rabbit behind the Vermeer.

"This one is a fake," he said. "I was finally able to prove it to the director of the museum, and he wanted it off his walls."

"I love it," she said. "I love them both and I love you. I'll never forget that day in the museum. It was when I first glimpsed that soul of an artist you've got hidden deep inside. It was when I started falling in love with you."

Her knees were losing strength. She felt overwhelmed and plopped down into the only available chair, hand clutched over her heart as she gazed at the Vermeer, awed that he'd gotten it for her.

And the fake one of the girl with the rabbit. She couldn't help but smile as she looked at it, for it was charming and silly and she loved it, even if it was a fake.

She nodded to it. "Are you going to track down the artist who made that counterfeit Vermeer?"

"Only if you want me to."

She looked at him in surprise. "You're willing to let him get away?"

The corners of his eyes crinkled as he sent her a gentle smile. "I can't solve all the crimes in the world. I used to think my highest calling was to put duty before all else. I've learned a few things over the past month. Life is short. We can't know what it holds in store for us, but I won't ever take you for granted again. I asked to be demoted back down to this office because it means I'll be able to put you first. I'll be able to stay in Washington. I love you too much to risk letting a job stand in the way of making you happy."

Her breathing became ragged again. "Don't make me cry," she sniffled. "I've cried far too much in the past few weeks."

He rushed to kneel at her side. "When have you cried?"

His voice was achingly soft as he cradled her in his arms. Too many memories flashed through her mind to form them into a sentence. The president's death. The fallout with Ida. Luke. All of it had been such a chaotic whirlwind of emotion, but the strangest thing was, when she looked at Nathaniel and he touched the side of her face, it was as if they communicated without words. He'd been at her side for all of it. He knew. He understood.

"I know everyone hates Ida," she whispered, "but she adored the president, and they had a wonderful marriage. How quickly it all ended for them. Any day could be our last, but God never promised us more. Only a time to weep and a time to laugh. A time to mourn and a time to dance. I can accept that. I just don't want to do it alone."

He squeezed her hands and touched his forehead to hers. "Then why don't you marry me, and we can do all those things together?"

She laughed. It was a gulpy, tearful laugh, but a real one. Nathaniel would never rival the great romantics of the age, but that was part of the reason she loved him.

"Yes, I'll marry you," she said with a joyful heart.

She was ready to emerge from their season of tearing down, weeping, and mourning, and step into a time to build, to laugh, and to dance.

Historical Note

Ida McKinley's legacy in the historical record has been mixed. She was widely disliked by the president's staff due to her obsessive dependence on her husband and reluctance to participate in traditional hostess duties. Her epileptic seizures were treated with anticonvulsive potassium bromide, a treatment that became less effective over time, leading to ever-increasing dosages. Contemporary historians believe these massive doses may have resulted in bromism, a neurological disorder that can cause anxiety, irritability, and aggression.

The few times Ida asserted herself as first lady, her actions tended to be out of step with the era. She was a supporter of female suffrage and higher education for women. As the temperance movement gathered momentum, she openly served wine and spirits in the White House. She became reclusive and spent her time knitting more than three thousand baby booties, which were donated to various charity auctions. In particular, she was interested in supporting homeless shelters for destitute women and the nascent American Red Cross.

The coast-to-coast train tour Ida took with President McKinley made her the most widely traveled first lady of her era. She also became the first presidential spouse to visit a foreign country while in office when she crossed the border into Juarez for a breakfast reception.

Following her husband's death, Ida returned to Canton, Ohio, where she visited her husband's grave nearly every day. She died in 1907, never having fully recovered from the depression she suffered following her husband's death.

President McKinley's assassination sparked wholesale changes in the system of protection surrounding the president. There were more than a hundred police officers and Secret Service agents on duty when President McKinley was shot at the Temple of Music. James Parker was the African-American Pullman porter who tackled the gunman and is credited with making the third shot miss the president.

Leon Czolgosz immediately confessed to the shooting and claimed to have worked alone. Over a dozen well-known anarchists were arrested in the days following the shooting, but they were ultimately released due to insufficient evidence of collusion. Czolgosz was convicted in a two-day trial, sentenced to death, and executed by electrocution a mere forty-five days following McKinley's death.

George Cortelyou served as personal secretary to three presidents: Grover Cleveland, William McKinley, and briefly for Theodore Roosevelt. He later served as the Secretary of Commerce and Labor, US Postmaster General, and Secretary of the Treasury.

John Wilkie was a journalist who became the unconventional choice to head the Secret Service from 1898–1911. Following McKinley's assassination, Wilkie and George Cortelyou worked to revamp presidential security, including protection for the president's family, which until McKinley's assassination was not authorized. The Secret Service's budget, staffing, and procedures were increased, and they kept the president safe until the assassination of John F. Kennedy sixty-two years later.

Questions for Discussion

1. Caroline is repeatedly frustrated by Nathaniel's duty-bound behavior, which is the same thing that drew her to him to begin with. How common is it for people to be attracted to a quality that later becomes an irritant?

2. If you were Caroline, could you forgive Annabelle? Was there anything to forgive?

3. Caroline resolves to support Nathaniel's assignment in Milwaukee, even though she doesn't want to. All over the nation, families are separated by military service or other professional duties. Is there a point at which this becomes untenable?

4. Caroline believed Luke was merely going through the motions of being devout while imprisoned, and she expected it to fade quickly after he was out. How common is it for people to become devout during a crisis? How can one sustain faith after the crisis is over?

5. Ida McKinley was overwhelmed and poorly equipped to be the first lady. Many of her problems stemmed from

ill health and drugs that affected her mood. Does understanding the root cause of her struggles help you see her in a more sympathetic light? Do you know anyone whose difficult demeanor may be rooted in similar issues?

6. When Caroline forces herself to make peace with Annabelle, she tells herself that "it is time to start acting like a good Christian, even if she didn't feel like one." Do you believe this sentiment, or is there an element of dishonesty in it?

7. Near the end of the novel, Caroline encounters George Cortelyou during her shopping trip, and they talk about their final days in the White House. Caroline reflects "they had been living in a gilded age but hadn't realized it until it was over." How common is this? Have you ever experienced a challenging era of life that took on added luster in hindsight?

8. Caroline is strong throughout most of the novel but almost breaks down over a fight about blueberry muffins with Ida. Why do you think this incident almost made her crack?

9. At one point during Nathaniel's depression, Caroline suggests, "You mustn't let your failures define you." What did she mean by this?

In 2021, look for Luke Delacroix's story in

The Prince of Spies

Book Three of the HOPE AND GLORY series

Luke Delacroix appears to be a charming but harmless man-about-town in gilded-age Washington, DC. In reality, he is a spy secretly moving chess pieces in the halls of Congress to carry out an ambitious agenda. His current mission is to scuttle the reelection of Congressman Clyde Magruder, the only real enemy Luke has in the world.

Trouble begins when Luke meets Marianne Magruder, the congressman's daughter, whose job as a government photographer gives her unprecedented access throughout the city. Luke is captivated by Marianne's quick wit and alluring charm, leading them both into a dangerous gamble to reconcile their growing love with Luke's need to clear the way for vital reforms in Congress.

Three generations of antagonism divide Luke's and Marianne's warring families, but they will risk everything to forge a truce. Can their newly found love survive a political firestorm, or will decades of family rivalry drive them apart forever?

Elizabeth Camden is best known for her historical novels set in Gilded Age America, featuring clever heroines and richly layered storylines. Before she was a writer, she was an academic librarian at some of the largest and smallest libraries in America, but her favorite is the continually growing library in her own home. Her novels have won the RITA and Christy Awards and have appeared on the CBA bestsellers list. She lives in Orlando, Florida, with her husband, who graciously tolerates her intimidating stockpile of books. Learn more at www.elizabethcamden.com.

Sign Up for Elizabeth's Newsletter!

Keep up to date with Elizabeth's news on book releases and events by signing up for her email list at elizabethcamden.com.

More from Elizabeth Camden

Regency England, late 1800s New York, and 1920s Maine come alive in this romantic and inspiring novella collection from three acclaimed, award-winning Christian historical fiction authors! Includes Kristi Ann Hunter's "A Search for Refuge," Elizabeth Camden's "Summer of Dreams," and Amanda Dykes's "Up from the Sea."

Love at Last by Kristi Ann Hunter, Elizabeth Camden, and Amanda Dykes
kristiannhunter.com; elizabethcamden.com; amandadykes.com

◊ BETHANYHOUSE

You May Also Like . . .

Ex-cavalry officer Matthew Hanger leads a band of mercenaries who defend the innocent, but when a rustler's bullet leaves one of them at death's door, they seek out help from Dr. Josephine Burkett. When Josephine's brother is abducted and she is caught in the crossfire, Matthew may have to sacrifice everything—even his team—to save her.

At Love's Command by Karen Witemeyer
HANGER'S HORSEMEN #1
karenwitemeyer.com

Determined to uphold her father's legacy, newly graduated Nora Shipley joins an entomology research expedition to India to prove herself in the field. In this spellbinding new land, Nora is faced with impossible choices—between saving a young Indian girl and saving her career, and between what she's always thought she wanted and the man she's come to love.

A Mosaic of Wings by Kimberly Duffy
kimberlyduffy.com

As Chicago's Great Fire destroys their bookshop, Meg and Sylvie Townsend make a harrowing escape from the flames with the help of reporter Nate Pierce. But the trouble doesn't end there—their father is committed to an asylum after being accused of murder, and they must prove his innocence before the asylum truly drives him mad.

Veiled in Smoke by Jocelyn Green
THE WINDY CITY SAGA #1
jocelyngreen.com

BETHANYHOUSE

More from Bethany House

In this sweeping companion to the Hallmark TV series *When Hope Calls*, Lillian Walsh rushes to a reunion after discovering the sister she believed dead is likely alive. But Grace has big dreams beyond anything Lillian is prepared for. Can Lillian set aside her own plans and join her sister in an adventure that will surely change them both?

Unyielding Hope by Janette Oke and Laurel Oke Logan
WHEN HOPE CALLS #1

When Beatrix Waterbury's train is disrupted by a heist, scientist Norman Nesbit comes to her aid. After another encounter, he is swept up in the havoc she always seems to attract—including the attention of the men trying to steal his research—and they'll soon discover the curious way feelings can grow between two very different people in the midst of chaos.

Storing Up Trouble by Jen Turano
AMERICAN HEIRESSES #3
jenturano.com

Determined to keep his family together, Quinten travels to Canada to find his siblings and track down his employer's niece, who ran off with a Canadian soldier. When Quinten rescues her from a bad situation, Julia is compelled to repay him by helping him find his sister—but soon after, she receives devastating news that changes everything.

The Brightest of Dreams by Susan Anne Mason
CANADIAN CROSSINGS #3
susanannemason.net

◊ BETHANYHOUSE